PURE FLAME

His lips were warm and firm as they covered her mouth, then moved along her throat. As he turned his head to kiss her shoulder, she bit his ear sharply. He let go of her for an instant, cursing.

Cathryn flung herself away from him and ran, trying to hold her full skirts up and out of the way.

"This will be easier if you don't fight me, Catriona," Revan stated and made a sudden lunge at her.

He caught one arm and whirled her back against his bare chest, holding her tightly with an arm around her waist.

Her chemise was loosely laced at the top and her breasts strained against the fabric as if aching to be free. He put her other arm behind her back and held it there, firmly. Then, with a look that touched her like pure flame, he bent close to her and, taking the ribbon on her chemise into his strong, white teeth, he gently pulled it loose . . .

DEFIANT BRIDE

SCOTNEY ST. JAMES

ZEBRA BOOKS
KENSINGTON PUBLISHING CORP.

ZEBRA BOOKS

are published by

Kensington Publishing Corp.
475 Park Avenue South
New York, NY 10016

First printing: April 1987

Printed in the United States of America

This book is dedicated to a sister and friend, Joy Howrey, in appreciation of her assistance, encouragement, and unfailing humor, and to my family for their patience and support.

A special thanks to Sandy Kennedy for her help and enthusiasm.

Prologue

Legend has it that the last wolf in Scotland was killed in the 1740s. Time had run out for these proud, savage hunters and, in the name of civilized progress, they were routed from their native highland hills and slaughtered ruthlessly.

Like the Scottish wolf, the Highlander himself became the victim of that same civilization. He, too, was wrested from his home to be destroyed. His way of life was ended, his country undergoing tremendous change.

Many who fought this tide of progress perished; others were driven away to foreign lands, never to see their beloved home again. Only a few — the stubborn, the bold, the reckless — remained to attempt to delay the time of change.

To survive, they fled to remote areas and there, in secret, memory-haunted glens, kept the old ways. Like the wolves, they hid in their dens and stayed with their own kind. Through the years, some of them were forced into the open and destroyed, but the ancient rites never entirely died.

The fugitive wolf and the fugitive Highlander were much the same, each fighting a losing battle, hoping only to gain a little more time.

And, despite the legends, who can say for certain that, somewhere in the uncharted wilds of Scotland, a few fierce survivors may not yet live?

Chapter One

The lone horseman was back. Silhouetted against the gray Scottish sky, he sat high on the craggy hillside overlooking the glen below.

Cathryn knew he was watching her and felt again the strange sense of unease she had experienced the first time she had seen him there.

Quickly she looked about and decided he must have come alone this time, for there was no sign of any other living being to disturb the hazy serenity of the Highland afternoon.

The day he had first appeared remained vivid in her memory. She had been there in the high pasture where the livestock belonging to her father was brought for the summer shieling.

Each April the clan herdsmen moved the cattle and sheep to the upper parts of the glen to allow them to spend the summer months growing fat on tender meadow grasses before being driven to the Lowland markets in the autumn. Sometimes the herdsmen brought their wives and children to live with them in the crude stone cottages scattered here and there throughout the hillsides. The children played all day and through the long evenings that remained light until nearly midnight. Sometimes at night there would be singing and dancing.

Despite the holiday flavor that clung to the shieling, the women spent a good many of their waking hours working at such tasks as weaving, butter churning, or candlemaking.

Cathryn had long loved the summer pasturing, but in the last few years she had come to it as a woman and not a child. Each August her father, one of the lesser clan chieftains, sent her up to Elspeth, the tiny, leathery-faced wife of his herdsman, Gregor. Under Elspeth's expert supervision, Cathryn was learning the essentials of housewifery. In the one-roomed hut with its peat fire in the center of the floor, she had learned to bake bread, to weave, and to churn.

Elspeth was a good teacher, patient and kind-hearted, and Cathryn had warmed to her from the first. This year it seemed Elspeth had gone out of her way to make the chores easier than ever before, and each day, in the early afternoon, Cathryn found herself shooed outdoors to stay until the evening meal.

"Och, lass, these chores can wait. Awa' with ye oot into the sunshine whilst ye have the chance. Soon ye'll be a grand lady with a husband and no time for traipsin' oot across the moor."

Elspeth's smile was gently sympathetic and Cathryn tried not to show how unsettled she felt every time she saw the old woman gazing at her, muttering "Puir child," under her breath.

Once out of Elspeth's sight and into the clear bracing air, she felt as though a great burden had been lifted from her young shoulders. She was happy to spend hours tramping through the newly bloomed heather, searching out the nests of red grouse or fields of wild thistles. She was equally content to find a sun-warmed rock where she could sit staring dreamily down over the shaggy backs of the grazing animals. She loved the misted outline of distant mountains before her and the brisk wind at her back.

On that day when she first saw the rider, she had struggled through a long morning at the loom. It seemed everything she touched went wrong. After a hasty meal at midday she was anxious to escape into the sunshine.

Leaving the dim, smoky hut behind, she made her way up the hillside to a low granite boulder where she sat watching the sheep. Drawing up her knees, and wrapping her arms about them, she soon grew drowsy and dropped her head in

10

utter exhaustion. She had never realized learning to be a housewife would be such a dreary task. She always thought that when she married she would come to her duties with eagerness and a light heart. However, now that her wedding date was at hand, she found her heart to be neither eager nor light.

Sighing, she raised her head and in that instant, first saw the mounted figure, off to the right and high above her. Almost before she could realize apprehension at his sudden appearance, her view of him was cut off by the approach of nearer, far more threatening horsemen.

Cathryn scrambled down off the rock and was immediately surrounded by eight or nine men sitting astride horses. One of them, a broad-shouldered giant with curling red hair, threw back his head and laughed a great shouting laugh.

"By God, men, look what we've found!"

"Aye, she's as comely a lass as you'll ever lay eyes on, Owen."

Cathryn's gaze swept the circle of men and her heart sank at the crude look of them. They had the appearance of outlaws, and beneath the leering grins on their faces, she sensed a desperate ruthlessness.

"Who are you?" she demanded. "What are you doing on this land?"

The man's bold gaze traveled swiftly down the length of her figure. "You might say we're a lonely wolfpack out looking for little lost sheep."

His words brought forth a chorus of coarse guffaws. Cathryn pretended she did not grasp his meaning.

"There are no lost sheep here," she retorted. "Now stand aside and let me pass!"

The big redhead rubbed his chin thoughtfully. "No timid little lamb, this one."

"A bit too sassy for her own good," said an older, even rougher-looking man. "She should be taught respect."

"What would *you* know about respect?" Cathryn asked. "A gang of reivers like you!"

"Now, don't worry your wee pretty head about it, my girl," spoke up another man behind her. She whirled to see who

11

had spoken and felt chilled to the bone when she met his cold blue eyes. "You living here amongst the high and mighty Campbells are under the king's protection, and he can tell you there haven't been reivers in the Lowlands for fifty years." He turned slightly and spat into the wind, as if to show his opinion of the king.

His action and the soft, burred sound of his voice brought new suspicion to her mind.

"Highlanders!" she hissed.

"That's right, lass," said the man they called Owen. "At your service."

Cathryn turned back to face him. His wide smile seemed more lecherous than before.

"The only service you can do me is to leave me alone!"

"What? Alone on this hillside? Why, you'd be at the mercy of any band of marauders that might happen by!"

This display of droll wit obviously pleased his comrades for they laughed and nodded with approval.

"And just what do you consider yourselves?" Cathryn snapped.

"Highland gentlemen seeking hospitality."

"The sort of hospitality you deserve is a noose around your neck!"

" 'Tis not what we had in mind." The redhead looked menacing as he swung down from his horse. "We'd hoped for a bit of sport."

"You're mad!" she flung at him. "All I have to do is scream and help will be here at once. The herdsmen are just beyond that hillock there."

His laugh was unpleasant. "We may be mad, but not mad enough to believe that. We know very well where each and every one of Campbell's men is at this moment. We wouldn't have stopped if there had been any danger. Right, men?"

A round of affirmative answers rose, and Cathryn began to know real fear.

As the man started toward her, he stumbled and lurched forward. Cathryn curled her lip in disgust.

"You're drunk!" she exclaimed. "You reek of whiskey!"

She backed away from him a few steps and felt the horse

belonging to the blue-eyed man at her back, blocking her way. She was trapped and she knew it.

Panic-stricken, she looked frantically about for a weapon. Swiftly, she grasped a stone lying on the ground at her feet and drew back her arm.

"Get back! If you touch me, I swear I'll smash your ugly face!"

"I like a lass with fire and spirit," Owen roared, lunging at her.

Cathryn gasped and ducked sideways to avoid his groping hands. His fingers caught in the neck of her dress and with one downward pull, he had half-torn it from her body.

Still clutching the stone, she swung blindly and was pleased to hear his cry of pain.

"Why, you damned vixen!" The redhead sank to the ground, holding his bleeding head.

Deep laughter rang out and Cathryn raised angry eyes to see the circle of horsemen part around the figure of the man she had seen high on the hill. He gently urged his horse forward.

Standing her ground, Cathryn was unaware how wild and defiant she looked, her long bronzed hair tangling in the wind that whipped about her, great silver-green eyes blazing with fury. She stood straight and tall, her fingers still curled menacingly around the rock.

Under his bold, amused gaze she remembered her torn dress and realized she was half-naked. She blushed deeply but, clutching the remnants of her gown to her breasts, met his look defiantly.

After a time, he leisurely unfastened the cloak he wore and, slipping it from his broad shoulders, tossed it to her.

"Cover yourself."

She accepted it gratefully until she noticed his gaze never left her bared flesh. Angry again, she turned her back and clumsily wrapped the cloak about herself.

The stranger then turned his attention to the big man sitting on the ground.

"Well, Owen, I thought the lass in need of rescuing, but it appears I was wrong. Let's pray that clout on the head jarred

13

your brains back into place."

Cathryn was amazed at the humbling effect the sarcastic words had upon the big man.

Staggering to his feet, he stood in front of the stranger, head bowed and eyes upon the ground.

"Sorry, lad. I must have been daft."

"Perhaps you were just bewitched by the young maiden here." His eyes, gleaming with devilish delight, met Cathryn's again. A smile hovered at the corners of his straight, firm mouth. "No doubt you thought you had come across a sweet young blossom ripe for the picking. Instead, you found a Scottish thistle — pleasing to the eye, but prickly to touch."

"Aye, she's a thorny one," Owen agreed, shaking his shaggy head ruefully.

"We'll soon be home again and I'm sure you'll find our Highland roses more accommodating. But for now I think you'd best get back to the business at hand."

A meaningful look passed between the two men, and finally the stranger shook his head. "No, let's ride north. We'll leave this for another time."

"Right, lad." Without another word, Owen turned his horse and rode away, followed by the rest of the men.

The man on the horse turned his attention back to Cathryn. "Now, lass, are you all right?"

Cathryn's eyes sparked an angry green. "Your belated concern is very touching!"

Ignoring her furious outburst, the man went on. "I could take you home if you like. Is it far?"

"No, only over that hill there. I am perfectly capable of getting there by myself."

"Very well, then. I'll be on my way. When next I pass by, I hope I shall find you in a better temper."

His grin was insolent as he wheeled his stallion and rode away.

Cathryn stamped her foot in frustrated anger. Gathering his cloak more tightly about her, she stalked all the way back to the shieling hut and flung herself through the doorway.

She was relieved to find Elspeth was not in the cottage.

She hurriedly changed into a different dress, hiding the torn one and the cloak beneath the straw pallet upon which she slept.

Later that night, as she lay on that same pallet trying to fall asleep, she was still stirred to anger by the memory of the stranger's mocking smile.

And now he was back. Forcing her mind away from those memories and back to the present time, she glanced again at the hillside. The stranger was no longer silhouetted against the stormy sky, but moving down the rocky path toward her, his horse carefully picking its way among the stones.

Cathryn looked about her, trying to decide what she should do. She glanced back at the man and saw he was now so close she had little choice but to stand her ground.

As he stopped his horse beside her, she lifted her chin haughtily and waited for him to speak first. He looked at her for a long moment, then broke the uneasy silence by saying, "You look like some fierce ancient goddess standing there, lass. I had thought you only a simple shepherdess."

The amusement in his soft Highland voice irritated her, and she was instantly on the defensive. Therefore, it was a bit disconcerting when she found she had to take a step backward to enable herself to look all the way up into his darkly tanned face.

He was dressed entirely in black, from a rough cape thrown over his broad shoulders to the toes of his high scuffed boots. Even his hair was black, untidily pulled back and tied with a thin leather strap. His eyes were so dark beneath their slanted brows she could distinguish no color in their depths. His face was lean, the cheekbones high and sharply defined. As her gaze moved to his mouth, she was aware once again of his insolent smile, the white teeth gleaming against the background of shaggy black beard.

"Do I pass your inspection?" he asked softly.

Cathryn felt a blush slowly rising to her face, and she dropped her eyes quickly.

"I imagine you came for your cloak, sir," she murmured.

15

"I'll get it for you."

She turned to go inside the cottage, but his next words stopped her.

"It's not the cloak I came for."

"Then . . . what?"

His smile broadened as he replied, "Why, I've come back for you, love."

"What are you talking about?"

Against her will, she backed away from him, eyes widening in sudden fear.

"Just that. You see, I'm a healthy young fellow who has need of a wife." He studied her with an amused expression. "After a bit of thought, I've decided you shall be my choice."

Cathryn gasped in shock at his audacity. "You must be as drunk as your men were the day they accosted me. For, if you are not drunk, you must be insane!"

He threw back his head and laughed loudly.

"You are still as prickly as the thistle, I see. But if you will take me in to speak with your father, you will soon see just how serious I really am."

She began to splutter in anger, but he cut right through her intended reply. "And, my dear, one of the first things you will have to learn is that a Highlander never gets drunk. He drinks whiskey from the cradle and never knows an ill effect from it."

"Perhaps not, but you will remember that I almost felt the ill results of your men's whiskey!"

"I've always heard redheads have vile tempers, but I have never had dealings with one quite so temperamental as you. Those glints of light in your hair and the bad temper you own—both are like the flames of Hades."

"Oh . . ." Frustrated rage boiled up within her, and she cried, "Speaking of the flames of hell . . . may I wish you there!"

Before another word could be spoken, he had thrown one long, lean leg over the horse's neck and was standing on the ground close in front of her. She could not prevent a small gasp as she quickly leaped away from him.

"Is that any way to speak to an admirer?" Though his tone

was deadly, she sensed his mirth at her fright.

"How can you be an admirer? In fact, how can you be anything other than what you appear—a dangerous Highland outlaw?"

Her scathing words were lost on him, however, for he was busy with a close scrutiny of her person. He walked slowly around her, bold eyes raking her figure from head to feet.

She became aware of the thinness of her dress and the way the gusting wind was molding it to her body. His eyes missed nothing of the rounded fullness of her breasts or the line of her long and slender legs. Her back stiffened under his stare and she felt the touch of his eyes upon her hips as surely as if he had laid his hand there. By the time he had finished his unhurried inspection and was facing her again, she was blushing angrily, feeling at a distinct disadvantage.

"You are beautiful . . . what *is* your name?"

"Cathryn," she answered automatically.

"You are beautiful, Cathryn . . . no, I think the Gaelic suits you better . . . Catriona." His voice was warmly caressing as he repeated it to himself. "Catriona."

"You are very daring, sir, to use Gaelic in a district where it has been outlawed by the king."

"Indeed, you are right. From now on, I must take care to use it only in our private bedchamber."

"You are crazy! Mad!"

"You are very fierce for a woman, aren't you?" He shrugged. "Oh well, passion is a quality I shall welcome in my wife."

His words seemed to echo inside her head. "Wife! I have never heard of anything more idiotic."

"What is idiotic about it? I merely thought our children might prefer it if we were married."

"Our children?" she shrieked. "Of all the incredible gall!"

"Aren't you pleased I want to marry you? In the old days I would simply have carried you away to some cave in the mountains."

She decided his grin was positively lewd, and it sent tiny prickles of fear along her scalp.

"How could you possibly want to marry me when you

didn't even know I existed a few days ago?"

"I think I knew it the moment I first saw you, looking so proud and defiant. And since that day, I must confess, I have thought of little else but you. I have been haunted by the memory of your eyes, all silvery-green like the leaves of the thistle . . ."

He closed the distance between them with two quick steps and reached out a hand to lift a strand of hair from her shoulder. She flinched at his touch.

"Don't be frightened, lass. For all your display of fire and fury, you really are rather a timid little thing, I think."

Again, his mockery stirred her anger. "Timid? If I had a dagger in my hand at this moment, I would show you just how timid I can be! You will find my fire and fury are quite real."

"And very dangerous, no doubt." He chuckled softly. "Ah, sweetheart, we are going to have a very . . . interesting marriage."

Blindly, she struck out at him, but he caught her flailing hand and imprisoned it tightly within one of his own. With the other hand he cupped her chin and lifted her face to his.

"You must learn not to fight me, love." His lips were unexpectedly soft and warm as they closed over her own. His hand held her chin firmly and she could not move away. The kiss was long and slow, a deliberate display of his easy mastery over her. Inwardly, she felt a hot fury spreading throughout her body and her whole being sang out for revenge.

When he raised his head, he spoke with a huskier tone to his voice. His Scottish burr was even more pronounced. "The moment I saw you, I knew you were the one I wanted."

She began to struggle again.

"Nay, don't fight me any more. You will soon learn I always get what I want. Now take me to your father so I can ask for your hand properly."

"My father isn't here! He's . . . well, it doesn't matter. He's just not here now."

" 'Tis a shame, for I had hoped to settle the matter today. Will he be here in a week's time?"

"I . . . oh, why don't you leave me alone?"

He grasped her arms as she tried to turn away, and when she began to protest and struggle, he tightened his grip. He stilled the torrent of angry words with another kiss.

"I am sorry I haven't the time to woo you in a more fitting manner, Catriona. I will simply have to court you after we are wed."

She was speechless in the face of his calm assumption she would be willing, even glad, to marry him. He stared into her stunned face for another moment, then returned to his stallion and threw himself onto its back with ease.

"I would like to take you with me now, were it not for the necessity of speaking with your father. Besides, I have business that needs finishing before I can turn my mind to more pleasant matters. So I will give you one more week and then I will come back to get you, love."

Speech returned to her with sudden intensity. "You don't need to ever come back! I won't marry you — nothing in this world would make me marry you."

He guided the huge horse to the spot where she stood and, leaning down, put an arm around her waist and lifted her to his own level. His arm felt like a band of steel cutting into her body and she was choked with terror. She thought he would kill her.

Instead, he said in a gentle voice, "Did you know there are twenty ways to say 'I love you' in Gaelic without using the same words twice? We must try them all."

This time his kiss was a demanding, even cruel, one, at odds with the tender words he had spoken. She was shocked to see the unrestrained passion in his eyes. She tried to push away from him and he lowered her until her feet again touched the ground.

Looking down at her, he grinned arrogantly and said, "You are going to make a lovely bride, lass."

Before she could think of a stinging retort, he had turned and was galloping away, his cloak flying out behind him.

Cathryn stood where he had left her, her mind in a turmoil. This man was the single most threatening element ever to enter her life. Fortunately, she would be saved from

19

him by two things: tomorrow she was to leave the mountain pastures and go back to her father's house, and, by the time he returned at the end of a week, even if he found her, she would already be married to Basil Calderwood.

Revan MacLinn rode silently at the head of his men, his shoulders hunched against the chill rain that had begun to fall late in the afternoon. It was a long and wearying ride to Wolfcrag Castle, hidden away in the Highlands, and they had to move slowly due to the flock of milling sheep they were driving before them. With nothing else to occupy his mind, Revan let his thoughts drift back to the girl.

Never before had he been so deeply aroused by a woman. He had been obsessed with thoughts of her rebellious beauty since first he had seen her, so angrily defending herself against his men. He shuddered to think what might have happened to her had he not been there to call them off.

The Wolfpack is an apt name for them, he thought grimly, a wry smile pulling at his mouth. They were certainly snapping and snarling over her!

Sometimes Revan was almost in despair over their actions, for they could be a crude and savage lot, but they had been loyal to him, and he knew them for the good and true men they actually were. No wonder they grew a bit uncouth, living in the back regions of the hills, venturing out only to make a raid against some unsuspecting Lowland farmer or herdsman. Not exactly training for polite society.

Still, Revan mused, they can't go around accosting stray girls whenever they meet them. Though, in truth, they'd almost found their match in that one!

His mind's eye recalled her wild beauty, her slender, erect figure. She had been like a wildcat backed into a corner by howling wolves. Spitting and fighting, but all for a lost cause. Lost, that is, until he had taken a hand in the proceedings. And she hadn't even thanked him!

Something about the girl's innate dignity brought his mother to mind, but there his pleasant thoughts ended abruptly.

His mother—how he hated the way life had treated her. It was maddening to see her wander through the chill rooms at the castle, listless, disinterested in everything. There was a time when she had been a vital and energetic woman actively engaged in carrying out the many duties of the wife of a clan chieftain. But that, like so many other good things in life, had been before Culloden.

Culloden. Even now, over ten years later, the effects of Culloden were still being felt in the Highlands.

The MacLinns were Jacobites and had been, down through all the generations since King James VII had been forced from his throne by his unscrupulous and scheming son-in-law, William of Orange. They had raised their voices in protest, like many others in the Highlands, for they much preferred their rightful king to the self-serving Dutchman, a foreigner who couldn't even speak their language.

Government troops were channeled into the hills to quiet the clansmen, but after one major victory against the English at Killiecrankie, the Jacobite rebellion disintegrated and came to nothing. Highlanders faded back into the mountains and glens, leaving the way open for the Usurper's soldiers. Forts were built and manned, and the clans were forced to sign an oath of loyalty to the king.

From his exile in France, James sent word for the Highlanders to obey the king and sign the oath, and many of them did. The MacLinns did not. They were too stubborn to knuckle under, and the secluded isolation of their castle made them nearly immune to governmental retributions. They were ignored by the king, for they were only a small branch of the MacQueen clan, and hidden away as they were, really not all that influential.

After the death of William, he was succeeded by his sister-in-law, Anne, who had no children or legal heirs. The Jacobites felt this would be their chance to regain lost power, and they began to look forward to the day when the rightful Stuart king would again take the throne. At the death of James VII, they transferred their hopes to his son and heir, James VIII.

In 1701 the English Parliament passed an Act of Settlement, designed to assure that when Anne died, she would be followed to the English throne by the Electress Sophia of Hanover, the granddaughter of James I. Four years later, the Treaty of Union was pushed through, and Scotland no longer existed as a free and separate country. No one fought the merger with England harder than the Jacobites, and it was a gloomy day indeed when the Scottish Crown, Sword and Sceptre were wrapped in linen and put into storage in Edinburgh Castle.

The hopes of the Jacobites were dashed again, also, for by this time, Anne had died and was succeeded by George of Hanover, son of the Electress Sophia. As far as they were concerned, foreigners still ruled their nation while the legal king was in exile.

The clans rose up in arms for James VIII, and though the rising was successful for a time, it, too, eventually failed, probably as much from lack of aggressive leadership on James's part as anything else. But the Highlanders were becoming a thorn in the side of the English government, and it was clear they would have to be quelled once and for all.

That time came with Bonnie Prince Charlie, James's oldest son. He was a young man with magnetism, courage, and more than a little daring, and when he laid claim to the English crown, the clans took up arms to defend his right.

At first, all went well with the Prince's campaign. There were minor skirmishes and victories, and it wasn't long before he and his followers danced in Edinburgh. Had he marched on for London then, it might have ended differently, but his advisors were of different opinions as to how to proceed, and those who favored a retreat for the winter won out. That was a mistake impossible to rectify. The Jacobite army had been at its peak, but waiting passively for spring, it began its decline.

Many of the men who eventually went into final battle against the English troops did so with very little hope of a victory. They were risking everything for an ideal and for their beloved prince. The brave battle that began on the empty, windswept moors that April day in 1746 ended in bitter and bloody defeat, a slaughter that would never be

22

forgotten.

Revan stirred, old emotions crowding in on him. He had lost a father and two brothers at Culloden, but like every other Highlander, he had lost much more. Their way of life was gone; their homes were destroyed, their traditions outlawed, their survivors transported away to other countries. Punishment was to be swift and effective.

The MacLinns, despite the loss of their chieftain and most of their young men, had to consider themselves among the fortunate. The ancestral home of the clan was so hidden away it was nearly impossible to locate. Instead of obeying the new laws, they had simply withdrawn into their secret glen, and in defiance of the king, they vowed to keep their Jacobite customs until the last man of them was dead.

One of his clansmen shouted, rousing Revan MacLinn from his bitter reverie. He straightened his lean frame in the saddle and shook off the ghosts of the past. He had been burdened by it for too long now. He let his thoughts wander back to the girl, Catriona—perhaps, he told himself, a smile playing about his mouth, the future is suddenly going to be something worthy of consideration, and I can let go of the past.

Parson Buchanan shut his prayer book with a snap and droned out the words, "You are now man and wife."

Cathryn lifted her eyes to her new husband's face and gasped in shock. The tall man standing beside her was not Basil Calderwood. Instead, he had the dark and mocking face of the stranger she had met on the moors.

A loud rapping at the door jolted her out of her dream, and for a moment she lay still, letting her eyes roam over the familiar surroundings of her bedroom. It was a relief to find she was in her own four postered bed, safe from that bold, disturbing gaze.

The knocking at the door sounded again, more impatiently.

"Come in," called out Cathryn, but even as she spoke the door burst open and Mary, the young girl who served as her personal maid, flew into the room in her usual hurry. Pulling aside the draperies to let in the gray half-light of morning, she faced Cathryn with a cheerful grin.

"Your father says you're to get up now. Mr. Calderwood is downstairs in the library and he's been askin' about you."

"Basil? Here?"

"Aye, he came to see your father about some business matters, but he'd like a word with you before he leaves."

Cathryn threw back the bedcovers, reluctantly stepping out into the chill room. She quickly washed her face and hands then slipped into the gown Mary was holding for her.

As she brushed her hair, she asked, "Do you know what kind of business he's seeing Father about?"

" 'Tis something about his sheep, miss. He seems proper upset." Then she giggled and added impudently, "Old Horse-face sure has the wind up his drawers this time!"

"Mary!" Cathryn was shocked at her maid's impertinence. "Don't be brazen. I would appreciate it if you would show a little more respect for Mr. Calderwood."

"Yes'm," Mary murmured, but her round face was still alight with unchecked insolence.

Cathryn sighed to herself as she hurried down the stairs. Something had to be done about the girl's cheekiness — she knew she shouldn't condone such brash behavior.

As she opened the library door, she heard Basil's voice raised in anger. "We must find a way to outsmart the Highland raiders. I propose we band together and send an envoy to London to demand more protection from the king. Why, during this past week alone I've lost fifty more sheep from my flocks, and it seems the outlaws have gotten away with ease."

"Yes, and where were the king's soldiers?" muttered Hugh Campbell, Cathryn's father. "Sitting in some dark tavern swigging ale, no doubt, allowing these rebels to roam freely."

"That's exactly why I think we should send someone to speak for us. What's the use of having these English forts in our district if the soldiers do nothing to defend us against thieves and raiders?" raged Basil, as he paced back and forth in front of Campbell's desk.

The two men were almost direct opposites in appearance, the younger one being tall and thin, with sharp jutting facial features, and the older one of a more solid, stocky build.

Campbell stroked his short gray beard thoughtfully before replying, "Maybe a word or two in the right direction might do some good. It won't hurt to try. Why don't I speak to some of our other neighbors and see if we can't elect a man to send to London?"

Just then he caught sight of Cathryn standing in the doorway. "Ah, daughter, come in. As you've no doubt heard, Basil and I have just been discussing the problem of outlaws. We've both lost more sheep at their hands."

"Does anyone know who these thieves are?" Cathryn questioned, stepping into the room and closing the door behind her.

Unexpectedly, a picture of the men she had met up in the summer pastures flashed into her mind. It seemed likely they could be responsible for the raiding, and though she wondered if she should mention her encounter, the remembered humiliation of her treatment at their hands kept her silent.

"I've spoken with General Whitton and he seems to think it is the work of one small group of men," said Basil. "They're led by a dangerous fellow whom they call 'The Wolf.' He's been seen in the area recently and it can hardly be a coincidence that wherever he goes, livestock disappears."

"The Wolf, eh? A fitting name," sneered Hugh Campbell, "for a cunning rogue who leads his pack against decent citizens. As for myself, I think he has snapped at the heels of the English for too long."

"They need to track down the cur," agreed Basil. "He's preyed on innocent people long enough."

The Wolf—once again Cathryn's thoughts flashed to the mocking stranger with the dark golden eyes. Hadn't his men referred to themselves as the wolfpack? Still, she couldn't believe a real outlaw would have been quite as daring as he had been.

Her father was rising to his feet. "Enough of this talk about thieves and stolen sheep. You two have other things to

25

discuss, so I'll leave you now."

When he had left the room, Cathryn turned to Basil and asked, "Why did you wish to speak with me, sir?"

Flicking an imaginary speck of dust from the sleeve of his elegant waistcoat, Basil replied, "I thought I should inform you I have taken the liberty of accepting an invitation to dine with General Whitton at the fort."

"Oh?"

"Yes, it will be our first social outing as man and wife. The general requests our presence the evening after our wedding."

"But . . . what about the trip we'd planned to Edinburgh?" Cathryn asked.

"I'm sorry, my dear, but we'll just have to postpone it for a while. Actually, this dinner party is a bit more than just a social occasion. I need to discuss this problem of the raiders with Whitton, and I can't think of a better opportunity. Besides, I've always believed one should attend to business before indulging in idle pleasures."

"I see. Well, of course, you must do what you think is right."

Cathryn struggled against her strong feeling of disappointment. She had so looked forward to seeing Edinburgh!

"I certainly believe in keeping on the right side of the English," Basil stated. "I'm in need of more than one favor from them."

"Yes, I understand." Cathryn forced a smile. "We can always take our trip later in the year."

"I knew you would agree with my decision. The security of my property is far more important than a holiday." He strolled to the window and stood looking out, his back to her. Then, casually, he said, "By the way, I spoke to Mistress Thomas, the seamstress, and told her to send her girl over with several dresses from which you are to choose your wedding gown."

"But I intended to wear the dress my mother wore at her wedding," Cathryn protested. "You recall that I showed it to you."

"Yes, of course. But I thought perhaps you might prefer

something a little more in fashion."

"Fashion really hadn't entered into it," she replied. "As you know, my mother died when I was quite young, and wearing her gown was a sentimental gesture on my part."

Basil turned to face her. "Should you let sentiment guide you, Cathryn? You must realize our wedding is to be attended by a great many people and it is rather important you look your best."

"I understand that."

"I know your mother's dress was probably very lovely once, but you've got to admit the lace is a bit yellowed and its general appearance is rather . . . well, rather shabby. Do you see my point?"

Cathryn sighed. "I suppose so." The words came slowly. "It probably wouldn't look as nice as one of Mistress Thomas' new gowns."

"Then you'll choose one from her selection?"

There was a momentary silence before she sighed again and nodded.

"Yes, I'll choose a new one."

"I'm pleased you've decided to be so reasonable about this, Cathryn. Recently I have thought there was a slight touch of stubbornness in your attitude, but perhaps I have been mistaken. And, naturally, I will stand the cost of the wedding dress. Choose whatever you like."

She merely inclined her head, but it seemed to satisfy Basil.

"Well, my dear, I've got to be on my way now. There are several more matters I have to look into this morning. Tell your father I shall call upon him again later in the week."

When Basil had gone, Cathryn gave vent to her ire by flinging herself into a chair. She was angry at Basil for not understanding and honoring her wish to wear her mother's wedding gown, and she was angry at herself for giving in to his demands so easily. Most of all, she was angry with her father because he was to blame for the position in which she now found herself.

Although Basil Calderwood was considerably older than Cathryn, when he had come to ask her father's permission to marry her, Hugh Campbell had readily agreed because he needed the money and support an alliance with the Calderwoods would bring. Long known as an irresponsible spendthrift, Campbell had for some time been in embarrassed circumstances, reduced to dependence on patrons and kinsfolk. Marrying his only daughter to a wealthy man would be very much to his advantage.

More to his advantage than mine, thought Cathryn rebelliously. Quickly she stifled the ungrateful thought, for she knew her father felt he was doing the best thing for her, as well as for himself, and he would expect her to appreciate his efforts. She realized he would be upset and probably quite furious if he knew her true feelings.

"Be glad I have made such an arrangement for you, Cathryn," he'd said. "Any girl would be proud to be Mrs. Basil Calderwood."

Still, Cathryn wondered at her feelings for Basil. Although he was a gentleman and treated her kindly, she felt something was lacking in their relationship. She had always expected to be more excited at the prospect of being a bride, and somehow, the very austerity of her bridegroom filled her with unease.

She often tried to envision what life would be like in the staid Calderwood household and wondered if she would ever be other than tongue-tied and inefficient under the sardonic gaze of Mistress Mettleton, Basil's housekeeper. The very thought of trying to hold some authority over that woman filled her with dread.

Well, someday when she was older and a little more certain of herself, she would rid herself of Mistress Mettleton and hire a more amiable housekeeper, she decided.

She let her mind drift ahead to a time when she would be the self-assured lady of the house, able to handle her domestic servants with ease. Perhaps by that time she would be the mother of a brood of laughing children, and she imagined them gathered around her as she read to them from their favorite storybook. Her face was instantly aflame, for she realized the children she pictured in her mind had black, unruly hair and not the ginger red of the Calderwoods.

Jumping to her feet, she fled up the stairs to the sanctuary of her bedroom, intent on busying her mind with the last-minute details of her trousseau.

Chapter Two

At last the wedding ceremonies were over, and all that was left for Cathryn to endure was the traditional bedding of the bride. A group of laughing matrons led her through the narrow cobblestone streets of the village from her father's house, where boisterous guests continued to feast and toast the newly married couple, to the grim stone house where she and Basil would live.

Mrs. Mettleton met them at the front door with lighted candles and a slightly disapproving look on her face. The women were too engrossed in their hilarious, ribald mood to pay her any heed, but her very presence cast a pall of gloom over Cathryn.

The ladies led the way upstairs to the master bedchamber, and Cathryn had her first look at the room where she was to truly become Basil's wife. She couldn't suppress a shiver, for the room was as bleak and homely as the man himself. There were no frills, no embellishments. The plain oak bed had dreary dark blue velvet hangings, and the only furniture was plain and serviceable. Her mind was already busy with the changes she would like to make here. Perhaps a new coverlet and curtains for the bed, some bright cushions—

"Now stop that daydreaming and let us help you out of your wedding gown," said one of the older women kindly. "It won't be long before your bridegroom will be knocking on the door!"

This was met with loud coarse laughter, but Cathryn knew they meant no harm. It had long been a tradition at Scottish weddings for the older women in the clan to dress the bride for her wedding night.

Carefully they removed the elegant silk and lace dress she had worn, and one of the women laid it gently across the only chair in the room.

"My, you were a bonny bride, Cathryn! I don't think I recall ever seeing a bonnier one."

"Seems a shame . . ." began another, but she was abruptly hushed by Cathryn's aunt, Janet.

"Mind your tongue, Elizabeth. We've little enough time here without having to stop to listen to your chatter. Get the nightgown now."

As they removed the last of her petticoats, her chemise and pantalets, Cathryn was scarcely aware of their half-envious scrutiny of her young body. Her mind kept harking back to the wedding ceremony itself. It had been a brief, unornamented affair, over quickly. She had been stricken with sudden apprehension during the final prayer and when she turned up her face to receive her husband's hasty kiss and saw it was indeed Basil's familiar countenance instead of the lean, hawk-like one of her dreams, she had been flooded with a torrent of emotion which she told herself was relief.

Janet dropped the nightgown of fine white lawn over her niece's head, pulling it down over her shoulders and hips. It was long-sleeved and rather high-necked, trimmed with a modest amount of delicate lace.

"Looks a wee bit plain, don't ye think?" Elizabeth was asking the others.

"Basil picked it out himself," replied Janet sternly. "You know he wouldn't choose anything unseemly."

"Reckon not," agreed the old woman. "Sometimes I wonder if he'll even know what to do with a bride! Especially such a lively young one!"

Janet's reprimand was lost in another wave of lascivious laughter, and Cathryn found herself blushing crimson. Quickly her aunt started shepherding her toward the bed, and helping hands pulled back the coverlets and pushed her between linen sheets. The last part of the ritual involved the brisk brushing of her long hair, which was left unbound, and

31

the pouring of a glass of claret for the bride.

As they urged her on, she tipped up the glass and drained it. Somehow she felt it might help her get through the next hour.

The women spread the covers over her, tucked them about her, and hastened from the room, leaving only one candle burning on the small bedside stand. As their noisy chatter died away, she felt terribly alone. Up to this point she had been very matter-of-fact about her wedding night, for she knew all the facts of life and accepted certain things as inevitable. She assumed Basil would be considerate and gentlemanly, and doubted very seriously if he would be a demanding or sensuous husband. Perhaps, she thought wickedly, I'll conceive immediately and he will prefer to leave me in peace for nine months!

Far off down the street she could hear singing and fiddle playing, and knew her bridegroom was being escorted to his home. Basil had already made it known he did not care to be delivered directly to his bridal bed, as most grooms were; that he preferred the wedding guests to simply say farewell at the front door. A few had grumbled at his prudish attitude, but all had agreed to do as he wished.

Cathryn was glad, because she was no longer certain she could have endured the lewd comments and bawdy jokes of her husband's friends and relatives. How she would have hated them coming into the bedchamber to place him into bed beside her!

Soon the group of men started moving away down the street, calling out last minute advice that made her ears burn. When their catcalls had died into silence, she heard Basil's slow tread on the stairs. He entered the small dressing room adjoining the master bedroom, and she lay listening to the muffled sounds of his disrobing.

I can't face him! she thought wildly. Then she fought down her panic, admonishing herself for being such a silly coward. She knew she must control her skittishness and conduct herself in a proper manner. Basil was taking so long in his dressing room that she began to wonder if perhaps he wasn't a bit nervous, also.

Cathryn closed her eyes quickly as she heard footsteps approaching the door to the room where she lay. She couldn't force herself to watch her new husband walk across the room to her and wished she had extinguished the candle.

The door opened and closed quietly, and she heard Basil's footsteps cross the carpeted floor and stop beside the bed. She knew he was looking down at her, so she forced a shaky smile to her lips and opened her eyes to greet him.

Standing there in her husband's place was the black-haired man who'd spoken to her up at the shieling hut. Her eyes grew wide, and she opened her mouth to scream. Instantly, his hard hand clamped across her face and he said, close to her ear, "I wouldn't scream for help if I were you. You'd just be wasting your breath and upsetting your new husband."

She twisted her head, trying to fight off the stifling hand, but he held her firmly. "Hush, now, lass. There's no one here to help you. The housekeeper's gone, you know . . . and your husband seems to have found himself in something of a predicament."

She raised stricken eyes to his, but he laughed softly and shook his head. "Nay, I haven't harmed the spindly old man. I've just trussed him up like a scrawny Christmas goose. Now will you promise to behave if I take my hand away?"

After a few seconds, Cathryn nodded, and he lifted his hand. She gathered the bedcovers close about her chin and tried to slide as far away from him as she could. He rested one knee on the bed and surveyed her intently, hands on hips. She was very much aware of the aura of animal strength about him, and even more aware of the hard glint of anger in his narrowed eyes as they rested on the wide gold ring on her hand.

"Why did you do this damnable thing, Catriona?" he asked quietly.

"What are you talking about?"

"This . . . this marriage. I thought we had an agreement."

"Agreement?" she cried. "I agreed to nothing! You made a lot of rash statements that had nothing to do with me."

"They had everything to do with you," he interrupted. "I asked you to marry me."

33

"I thought you were insane — that I'd never see you again. And besides, I was already betrothed to Basil. So, you see, I could never have agreed to marry you."

He leaned closer, his eyes burning. "Why didn't you tell me about this Basil?"

"Would you have listened?"

"Perhaps not. But you should have told me about him, and given me the chance to do the honorable thing."

He towered over her, and she shrank from him, terrified by the fury of his anger. There was a dangerous tenseness about him and at that moment she didn't doubt for a second he was an outlaw.

Again he was dressed in black, but this time he had a plaid of red and black tartan flung over one shoulder, fastened with a silver brooch depicting the head of a snarling wolf. Cathryn's eyes widened at the sight of it.

"So you are the thief who's been stealing our sheep and cattle," she exclaimed. "You're the one they call 'Wolf', aren't you?"

"That's right, love. I should have introduced myself before. However, it does seem you have heard of me."

"Oh, yes, to be sure! I know what an outlaw you are! I've heard how you make a living for yourself and your men."

"But there are many other things about me that you don't know, Catriona. It will be my pleasure to acquaint you with them during the long winter ahead."

"What do you mean?"

He smiled broadly at her surprise. "I mean, lass, that I am still planning to take you back to Wolfcrag with me, husband or no. I want you, and I shall have you, even if I have to carry you like a sack of meal over my shoulder all the way."

"You are mad! Stark, staring mad!"

"Easy. I hadn't intended to start your lessons in respect and manners until we were home, but, if need be, they can start right here and now." He made a move toward her and she put out a restraining hand.

"Please . . . oh, please, leave me alone. I don't know what you want or why are you are harassing me, but please, I beg of you, go away and leave me alone!"

34

"I thought I was doing the honorable thing, Catriona, when I came to you and made my intentions clear. I asked you to marry me, and you didn't refuse. You let me ride away thinking you would be waiting when I returned."

"I didn't! I told you not to come back, that I wouldn't marry you."

"I thought you were angered by my haste and were only being coy. You didn't tell me about Basil."

Reaching out one lean hand, he grasped her arm and jerked her across the bed toward him, until they were face to face. "How do you think I felt when I rode up to that shieling hut this evening to claim my bride and the old woman there told me who you were and that you were probably already married to a man old enough to be your father?"

The rage in his face frightened her so much she closed her eyes and refused to look at him. He shook her violently and raved on: "I sat up there on the hillside and watched you come out of the kirk arm in arm with that pompous old turkey and I could gladly have ridden down and killed you both. Luckily for you, I stayed where I was until I had regained my senses, and by lying in wait for your virginal bridegroom, it seems I have at least prevented the consummation of your ridiculous marriage."

"But I am married, and there's no way you can change that," Cathryn cried. "If you don't release Basil and get away from here, you'll only end up getting yourself killed."

"Lass, you don't seem to understand what I'm saying to you. I am taking you back with me to my castle in the Highlands. It angers me greatly that you have done this stupid thing, but what is done is done. We'll just have to make the best of it. We've got to get out of here." He tossed back the covers and pulled her out of the bed and onto her feet. As she stood before him, clad only in the thin night-gown, he let his appreciative gaze rove over her figure from head to toe. She shivered under his intense look, and he drew her close, moving one hand along the curve of her spine and up to her neck.

" 'Tis a shame I haven't the time to appreciate you in your wedding night finery, love." He flashed her a wide smile.

35

"Perhaps later."

Before she could fling herself away from his clasp, he had picked her up in his arms. With one hand he held her head tightly, so her face was pressed into the woolen plaid he wore, and with the other arm he held her legs so she couldn't struggle.

Swiftly, he carried her down the stairs, and though she could see nothing, she sensed he left the house by the back entrance. She felt the frosty night air striking her skin through the gown she wore and heard the hollow ring of his boots on the street. He only carried her a short distance before she heard a man's voice call out softly, "Hist! Here I am, lad."

The man set her upon her feet for just an instant—long enough for him to mount his horse, and in that space of time she saw the red-haired man named Owen. He had obviously been holding the other's horse, waiting in this back alley. As he encountered her eyes, he sheepishly looked away.

"Up you go," murmured her kidnapper, reaching down and pulling her up onto his horse. He settled her in front of himself and then wrapped his warm plaid about them both. With a nod to his henchman, they began riding out of the village. Cathryn fought off the lethargy brought on by shock and tried to throw herself off the horse. The stranger only tightened his grip on her and warned her to behave, his voice a low growl.

"You can't do this!" Cathryn was close to tears, but she struggled to remain calm. Somehow she had to let someone know what was happening. She opened her mouth to scream, but he seemed to sense her intention, for he reined his horse to an abrupt halt and covered her mouth with his, silencing her completely. He finally raised his head and waited to see if she would try to scream a second time. She met his challenging gaze with a scornful stare, but kept her lips tightly shut.

He chuckled. "That's better. You're learning not to fight me."

She was too angry to think of an answer to this, and, tossing her head, turned away.

36

His fingers closed around her chin and he easily turned her face back to his.

"This is all your fault, you know, so you needn't be angry with me. I wanted you for my wife — now you'll have to be my whore."

Then they were moving again, the huge horse's pounding hooves carrying them further and further into the black and starless night.

The next few hours were always to remain blurred in Cathryn's memory. At first the two horsemen kept to the main road leading out of the village, but after a time they left that roadway and veered off onto a narrower one, heavily shadowed by encroaching trees and undergrowth.

Seated across the saddle in front of her kidnapper, Cathryn had begun the journey holding herself stiffly upright, avoiding any bodily contact with the man. Eventually, however, as the rough jolting of the ride tired her, she felt her back muscles weaken, and she could no longer keep herself from sagging against him.

At one point, as they galloped wildly down the darkened lane, some night bird, startled by their violent passage, flew up from the bushes, shrieking in alarm. Cathryn started in terror and immediately felt her captor's arm tighten about her waist, drawing her back against him. She struggled briefly, then abandoned herself to the security of his grip. Her mind was clouded with fatigue, and the will to resist had suddenly deserted her. She must have dozed then, for later, much later, she stirred sleepily and found herself snuggled in his arms, half-turned toward him. She roused up, pushing away from him, and as the heavy plaid slipped from her shoulders, she felt the sharp bite of a much colder wind. Reluctantly, she raised a hand to tug the woolen garment around her shoulders once again, her eyes straining in the darkness to ascertain their whereabouts. It seemed they were now riding along the ridge of some high plateau which swept out before them, empty and desolate, except for several grotesque formations of granite, shadowy and unreal in the thin moonlight. Overhead the sky was filled with ragged bits of clouds, being shuttled wildly along in front of a rising tide of chill wind, and far below them were bottomless oceans of heaving pine forests, unbroken by any light.

Cathryn couldn't remember ever seeing a more eerie scene, and for one brief moment, she almost believed herself to be the victim of a horrible nightmare. But, no, the power in the arms that held her and the warm breath of the man close behind her was most definitely real.

It wasn't long before the first drops of an icy rain began to fall. The drops were caught up by the moaning wind and hurled savagely into their faces. The man on the horse with her turned his head and shouted something back to the one who followed. She couldn't catch his words, which were lost in the wind, but almost immediately he was guiding his horse off the roadway and into a group of towering boulders.

He slid off the horse, pulling his plaid and her with him in one quick movement. Behind him she could see the huge red-haired man also dismounting. They led their tired horses back into the rocks to a sheltered corner where an overhang protected them from the driving rain. While the bigger man tended the horses, the younger one removed himself from the plaid he shared with Cathryn, and began scraping together enough brush and sticks to build a small fire. The three of them gathered close to it, hands held out to its small warmth.

From a leather saddle bag, the black-haired man pulled out some dry oatcakes and passed them to the others. Cathryn's pride dictated that she forego refreshment, but after a first haughty refusal, her unexpected hunger took over and she took the oatcake, eating it with great relish. The redhead took a flask from under his cloak, and after a mighty swig, passed it on to his companion.

The dark-haired man threw back his head and lifted the flask, swallowing deeply. Then he said, "Here, lass, have a swallow. 'Twill help warm you." She felt the flask against her lips, and obediently she drank. At once her throat and nostrils were filled with liquid fire and she choked and gasped. Fighting for breath, her eyes full of stinging tears, she cast a withering glance in his direction.

"What is that?" she managed to whisper.

"Scotch whiskey, my dear." His eyes were amused, his laugh low. "What did you expect to find in a Highlander's flask?"

She had her breathing under control once again, and was beginning to experience a most warming sensation. She could almost understand the value of the drink to the men who spent so many hours out in nasty weather. Still, he might have warned her. . . .

Out beyond the light cast by their small campfire, the rain and wind had both increased furiously. The mournful keening of the wind seemed to go right through Cathryn and she shivered uncontrollably. The man was beside her in two steps, lifting the plaid from her shoulders and pulling her gently back under the protecting rock ledge.

"Come, Catriona," he said, tossing the brightly-colored cloak down onto the ground. "We're going to stay here a while to rest the horses. We might as well get a bit of sleep ourselves."

As soon as she grasped his intention, she whirled away. "You can't expect me to sleep here with you!"

"And why not? I'm certain you would enjoy it much more than sleeping over there alone. Either we share this plaid or you fight off the night chill by yourself." Then, lowering his voice for her ears alone, he added, "I wonder if you are aware of what a charming picture you make standing there in your bride's nightgown, silhouetted against the firelight? I don't need to tell you what enjoyment the sight brings to my eyes, but should I mention the pleasure it's giving my friend Owen?"

She uttered a small cry of dismay and all but leaped into the concealing folds of the plaid. He dropped down beside her, covering them both with the top layer of the voluminous garment. He settled himself comfortably, then murmured, "Relax, love. I haven't any great inclination to rob you of your well-defended virtue at this time. It's too cold, and I'm too tired."

She turned a hostile shoulder, but after a bit, she moved

slightly toward him and asked, "Won't you tell me who you are?"

"Aye, I suppose it would be more seemly if we had been properly introduced, seeing as how we are about to spend your wedding night together."

The hard heel of her foot caught him painfully in the shin, and he grunted in surprise.

"Tsk, tsk, love, you must learn to control that temper of yours."

"Can't you just tell me your name and be done with it?" she snapped.

"I am Revan MacLinn, at your service, ma'm."

"MacLinn? A name well-known in the Highlands, I suppose."

"Without doubt. I will acquaint you with more details of my illustrious family history at some later date. And, of course, it goes without saying that you must also tell me all about your own family, though I doubt there could be much of an illustrious nature to tell. Lord, I never thought to steal a woman from that family!"

Cathryn bristled angrily. "As you very well know, the Campbell name has long been an honored one in Scotland. I am related to some of the most notable men in this country's history."

"And also to some of the most unscrupulous and scheming, if you don't mind my saying so."

"I do mind!" she hissed through clenched teeth. "This whole incredible situation is degrading enough without you bringing your personal prejudices against the Campbells into it."

"You're right, of course, sweetheart. We'll let it go until another time. Now we must rest while we have the chance. But don't think the day won't come when we have to get this family business out into the open."

She opened her mouth to protest, but he put his lips close to her ear and whispered, "Shh, love. Go to sleep now."

Angrily she tried to pull away from him, but he slipped one arm around her body and hugged her tight against him. She drew up both knees to kick at him, and he countered by flinging one lean leg across the bottom half of her body, neatly pinioning her. She refused to speak another word to him, and after lying rigidly for a while, she found herself relaxing bit by bit, drawn to his animal warmth in spite of herself. Just before she drifted off to sleep, the thought came to her that this had been her wedding day. How strange it was for her to be here, somewhere far from home, lying next to the unprincipled rogue who had virtually snatched her from the arms of her bridegroom only hours after the marriage ceremony that made her Mrs. Basil Calderwood!

Basil — she hadn't thought of him for hours. She wondered guiltily if he was still bound and gagged where Revan MacLinn had left him. Most likely he wouldn't be discovered until morning when Mrs. Mettleton would come to wake them for breakfast. How angry he would be!

Cathryn couldn't imagine her father's consternation when he learned of her disappearance. She knew his initial reaction would probably be to form a search party, but how could he possibly know where to start looking for her? Although Basil had undoubtedly gotten a good look at Revan, she knew he could not know his identity; even if he had noticed the wolf's head brooch as she had done, it would be of little help. If the outlaw had eluded the English soldiers for this long and was still known to them only as "the Wolf," she had little hope of believing a small band of vigilantes led by her father and husband could find him and bring about her rescue.

But I can't despair, she told herself. Tomorrow I will be able to think of some way out of this nightmare. Tomorrow. . .

Later, rousing slightly from an exhausted sleep, she thought she heard the far-off howl of a wolf. The eerie sound drifted up from the depths of the valley below, a haunting and lonely cry. Shivering, she pressed closer to the slumbering form beside her and was once again asleep.

The threesome continued their journey just after sunrise the next day, following a hurried breakfast of more oatcakes and Scottish whiskey. This time Cathryn sipped more cautiously, disliking its taste but anxious for its warmth.

By mid-morning the stark look of the mountain plateau had given way to the lush green of forests, and the trail they followed began climbing steeply. Cathryn knew they were well into the Highlands now, and she marveled at the beauty of primitive mountains and rock-rimmed gray lochs, wild and wind-tossed.

Each time they descended into a forested glen, she thought they would surely reach their journey's end, but on they went. She lost count of the number of streams and rivers they crossed. Some of them were narrow and trickling, others wider, deeper, spanned by bridges. All of them were foamy and brown with peat.

Their horses scattered coveys of partridges, causing them to flee their nests in fear of the deadly hooves, for the riders had long since abandoned any marked roadway and now followed some secret trail known only to them. Cathryn tried to mark their way in her memory, but it was impossible. There were too many stands of dark green pines thrusting up against too many similar skylines of faintly purple mountains and the darkening gray of lowering clouds.

The afternoon had grown very late before she had her first look at Wolfcrag Castle. They had been riding slowly along through a densely overgrown forest region, when she realized they were entering a long deep glen. High on either side were steep walls of rock, rising straight up to obliterate the last rays of sunshine, making the glen a dark, seemingly evil place.

The path they now followed began to rise up under them and it soon became apparent they were beginning to scale a narrow rock ridge that cut through the center of the glen, paralleling the cliffs on either side.

The path was so steep and narrow Cathryn began to understand a little better why the government troops had had so much difficulty in ferreting out the lair of the notorious Wolf. If ever they happened upon this track after long weary hours of crossing endless Highland wasteground, they would have to ascend single file, something which would surely go against military grain, and even then, how could they be sure their Lowland ponies would ever survive the climb? One misstep and the animal and its rider would be hurled to their deaths on the wicked rocks below.

After one quick glance downward, Cathryn was grateful for the strong mountain-bred stallion beneath her and, despite her wish to feel otherwise, for the muscular arms of Revan MacLinn, who still held her tightly in front of him.

Breaking what seemed hours of silence, he now spoke, his voice close to her ear. " 'Tis a shame you must first see Wolfcrag in the gloaming, Catriona, for it will seem a gloomy sight to you. I would have wished for sunshine and the singing of birds to welcome you, but it seems there is only nightfall and mist. You must not feel frightened of my castle, for it will welcome you by and by, and in time, you will feel at home here."

Too bone-weary to deny his words and perhaps start another argument, she said nothing and gazed in silence at the castle which towered before them. It was indeed an awesome sight.

Jutting up from the granite ridge upon which it had been built centuries earlier, it was almost one with the rock. From where they sat surveying it, Cathryn could not tell where the rock ended and the castle began.

High gray stone walls all but obscured the main portion of the central keep, and the battlements, towers and crenellated heights looked vast and forbidding. This was a Highland fortress, never meant to lift a welcoming, hospitable face to the casual visitor.

Before them stretched a narrow wooden bridge, its planks spanning a deep rift in the rocky ridge. Were the bridge not there, it would be impossible to gain access to Wolfcrag. At the far end of the drawbridge was an impressive main gateway, flanked by guard towers and completely closed off by a heavy iron portcullis.

Revan MacLinn startled Cathryn by throwing back his head and shouting, "Remember the MacLinn! Remember the MacLinn!"

At the sound of this battle cry, several men appeared on the other side of the main gate, and she could hear muffled shouts. Immediately the grinding sound of working machinery reached her ears and the portcullis was slowly raised.

It seemed the bridge swayed ominously under their weight, but the distance across the gaping abyss wasn't great, and they were soon riding through the entranceway and into a wide, cobbled courtyard.

Cathryn thought people must have poured out of every doorway in the yard, bringing torches to light their way, shouting, laughing and asking questions of Revan MacLinn and Owen MacIvor. Most of them pretended to ignore her, but she was very much aware of the curious, furtive glances in her direction. It shamed her dreadfully to have to appear before them in nothing but her nightgown and borrowed plaid, her hair uncombed and her face unwashed. She wouldn't allow herself to dwell on what they must think of her, for surely they knew the circumstances of her being there.

Revan jumped lightly from his horse and tossed the reins to a stable boy who stood waiting. "I'll deliver Warrior into your hands, young Donald, and trust you to take good care of him. He has carried a double burden for many miles, and were he less strong, might not have survived the strain."

The black-haired stable lad smiled and nodded, showing a great gap in his front teeth. It was plainly evident he would consider it a privilege to do his laird's slightest bidding. Cathryn stared at the boy, surprised to find such a cheerful youngster in the midst of an outlaw band. It would seem the men must have their families here with them then. That would mean other women . . . allies, perhaps.

She turned to find Revan's eyes upon her as he patiently waited to help her dismount, and in the flaring torchlight, they were amber.

"Let's go inside, Catriona, out of the damp night air. I imagine you are tired beyond belief."

She was tired, too tired to protest when he reached up to take her in his arms and carry her across the yard and up a curved stone stairway, past a massive iron-studded oak door and into a large hall.

A young serving girl stood in the doorway, watching their approach with wide, curious eyes. As they passed through the doorway, she bobbed a half curtsy and bade the laird welcome home. She secured the heavy door behind them and watched with interest as Revan set Cathryn down in the castle's Great Hall.

Aware of the girl's bold stare, Cathryn hugged the plaid to her and raised her head proudly. She would keep her dignity despite her bare feet and tangled hair, she told herself.

"Elsa, you're embarrassing the lady with your curiosity," scolded Revan, smiling. "Be a good girl and tell me where I can find my mother, and then fly off and fetch us some dinner!"

The girl blushed and giggled as he winked at her, and Cathryn was disgusted at the obvious devotion he inspired in a servant. Her manner was far too intimate to suit Cathryn.

The girl was quick with the information that his mother was to be found in the Drawing Room, and when she had skittered off to the kitchens, Revan caught Cathryn's hand and pulled her to his side.

"How do you like Wolfcrag Castle so far, love? Does not the spacious Great Hall welcome you with its grandeur?" He laughed down at her and to avoid his eyes, she turned to scan the huge room in which they stood.

Lit only by two torches mounted on the wall near the entrance, the far recesses of the room were lost in shadows. The high gray stone walls she could see were decorated with somber displays of weapons, both ancient and modern, all of them absolutely outlawed by the king. The heads of stags, crowned by magnificent antlers, stared at her with baleful glass eyes, which seemed to bore right through her. Long oaken tables were set against the walls, and a dying fire glowed in the one gigantic fireplace. Carved above the mantel was the family crest, the wolf's head looking lifelike in the flickering firelight. She could just make out a Latin inscription, but before she had time to distinguish the words, a voice rang out somewhere above them.

"Revan! You're back!" Cathryn's gaze was attracted to the young woman who came rushing down a curving stairway to throw herself into Revan MacLinn's arms. "Oh, darling, I've missed you so!"

Cathryn watched in amusement as the tall, striking brunette flung possessive arms around Revan's neck and pulled his dark head down to her own level. Standing on tiptoe, she pressed her voluptuous body against his lean-hipped frame and kissed him fervently. Over the girl's shapely shoulder, Revan raised his eyes to look at Cathryn with a look of such comical surprise that she could have laughed aloud at his obvious discomfort. However, she merely smirked at him, folding her hands demurely, as though prepared to enjoy the continuation of his dilemma.

Revan quickly disengaged himself, his hands on the girl's shoulders setting her away from him, none too gently.

She pretended to pout, pursing her full red lips. "Aren't you glad to see me, Revan? You always have been before."

Then, as though just realizing there was someone else present in the room, she turned and looked at Cathryn, widening her dark eyes in surprise.

Cathryn was certain the girl's performance had been for her benefit, but she couldn't think why. Was it supposed to matter to her if her kidnapper kissed another woman? She was welcome to him, Cathryn thought with vengeance.

"Please don't let me interrupt you," Cathryn murmured. The girl looked from one to the other, her black eyes demanding an explanation of Revan.

"Catriona, this is Darroch. And Darroch, this is the girl I told you about, Cathryn . . . Campbell." He grinned suddenly. "I guess it would be Calderwood now, wouldn't it, love?"

Before she could answer, the girl called Darroch broke in to say, "Campbell? Revan, are you out of your mind?"

"Most likely," was his even reply.

"I never really thought you would do this." The girl swept Cathryn with an acid gaze, then turned her back abruptly. " 'Twill only cause trouble all around, and well you know it."

"Aye, and I know full well where most of that trouble will

46

start, Darroch."

Their eyes seemed to be locked in some strange, private battle, and Cathryn was glad she was not involved in their argument. She understood very little of what they were saying, and cared less, for by this time, she was nearly swooning from exhaustion.

Revan slipped an arm about her shoulders and for an instant, held her close to his side. "We'll speak of it later, Darroch. Right now I'm going in to see my mother and then Cathryn and I are going to have supper and go to bed."

He was sweeping her along the hall with him, toward a closed door, but she had enough time to catch the look of pure hatred Darroch flung at her.

In the next room, Margaret MacLinn was seated in a brocaded chair before a lively fire; she had obviously been working on a tapestry stretched in a frame before her, but at the moment she sat staring into the flames, her needle forgotten. As the door closed behind them, she turned her head. Seeing Revan, she got to her feet, her face losing its sad, vacant look and starting to glow with life.

"Son," she exclaimed, "it's so good to see you safely home."

With quick strides, he crossed the carpeted floor and threw his arms about her. Over his shoulder, the lady's eyes caught sight of Cathryn and she said, "I presume this is the young lady you told me about?"

"Aye, this is Cathryn."

Something in his tone caused his mother to study him with a questioning expression on her face.

"You see, Mother, when I told you I was riding south to claim my bride, it seems there were some things I did not know about the lady."

"You have always been rash and impetuous, Son, so that comes as no surprise to me."

"Will it come as a surprise then to learn she is a Campbell?"

At his mother's shocked look he went on. "That is, she was a Campbell."

"So you are already married?"

"Nay . . . we're not married. She is married."

The older woman pressed one slim hand to her forehead in confusion. "Revan! What on earth are you trying to say to me?"

"When I arrived at the hut where I thought my bride lived, I discovered she was Cathryn Campbell, a chieftain's daughter, who lived in a fine house down in the village. But by the time I got to the village, I found she was Cathryn Calderwood, having just been married to a man at least twenty years older than she."

"Then, how is it she is here at Wolfcrag?"

"It seems I must be the bearer of bad news, madam. Your son has once again stepped beyond the boundaries of the law. Perhaps the limit of decency, if you will. I've just stolen this lovely bride from her husband."

Revan MacLinn's mother gasped and let herself sag backwards into a chair. "You've kidnapped her?"

Revan was grinning as though he felt pride at his own daring. "Aye, that I have. But you're not to worry, Mother. No one knows who took her, and certainly no one followed us from the town. The fools were all too busy getting drunk to celebrate the mating of an innocent young girl to an old goat to see what was happening. It may be days before they sober up enough to even miss her!"

"I thought she was to marry you . . ." his mother began.

"So did I, so did I. But it appears I was wrong in thinking I had made a bargain with the lady. On the very afternoon I arrived to claim her, she was promising herself to another. Though she played me false, a MacLinn could never admit defeat. Rather than return empty-handed I brought her along." He turned to look at Cathryn, one thick black eyebrow quirked. "After all, had I not announced to my entire clan I was off to bring home a bride? No, there was really nothing for it but to steal her."

"You are serious, aren't you, Revan?" His mother looked pale and drawn. "You truly have taken another man's wife?"

"As much as I wish I could tell you differently, it is so. I'm sorry my plan didn't work the way it was meant, for I desired to marry the lass and not just possess her without benefit of clergy. However, the fault is hers, and it matters not to me.

48

'Tis not the first law I have broken."

Incredibly, his mother laughed. "No, 'tis not," she agreed. Then she approached Cathryn, her serious gray eyes taking in the girl's untidy appearance. "My dear," she said, at last, "we do have so very much to talk about, but I know you are tired and hungry. Our talk can wait till morning. Right now I will have one of the servants show you to a room where you can have a hot bath and some supper. Then, in the morning, I will be up to speak with you."

The girl, Elsa, was summoned and briefly introduced to Cathryn. "I want you to arrange a nice hot bath for Miss Cathryn, Elsa, and then bring her some supper on a tray. Take her to—"

"Take her to my room," cut in Revan smoothly. The servant's bright eyes darted to Mrs. MacLinn's face, but when she said nothing, Elsa nodded and started off up the stairs.

Revan's mother bid Cathryn goodnight and urged her to follow the young serving girl. It was only after she had left the warm firelit room, docilely following Elsa up the curving staircase to the second floor that she realized she hadn't spoken a word to either Revan or his mother since her arrival at Wolfcrag.

A wooden tub filled with steaming hot water was placed in front of the fireplace, and Cathryn soaked in it until the water began to cool. She was stiff and aching in every joint, and the bath had been soothing and relaxing. She dried herself with thick rough towels, then slipped into a clean white nightgown she assumed belonged to Revan's mother. Elsa rummaged through a huge oak wardrobe until she found a robe of dark brown velvet which Cathryn gratefully put on over the gown. Despite the blazing fire, the room was vast and chilly. The robe was too large for her so she had no doubt it belonged to Revan, and she wondered idly if she would have to go on wearing borrowed clothing.

Elsa brought her a supper tray, and then left her alone to enjoy the first good meal she had been served since her own wedding supper. The thick hot soup and freshly baked bread tasted delicious to her. When she finished eating, she sipped the small glass of red wine, thankful for its relaxing effect upon tense and strained muscles.

Just as she felt herself nodding off to sleep in the big high-backed chair, the door to the room was thrown open and in strode Revan MacLinn. Cathryn leaped to her feet, upsetting the supper tray and shattering the delicate wineglass on the hearthstones.

"My, my, love, you are clumsy in your haste to welcome me," he taunted softly.

"I had not thought to welcome you, Sir," she replied stiffly.

"Surely you can't be afraid of me, then?"

"No, not that either," she lied, putting one hand on the back of the chair to steady herself.

The tall man walked toward her, and she fought down panic. He came very close to her, his eyes upon her face, their expression unreadable.

His eyes — they fascinated her, mesmerized her in much the same way a serpent is said to fascinate its victims. She could not seem to move away from the powerful gaze of those compelling eyes with the strange amber glints deep within them.

The eyes of a wolf, she thought wildly, savagely stalking its prey. She was afraid of him, and yet . . .

When he put out one hand to touch her face, she flinched but did not move away. His fingers stroked downward along the curve of her cheek, gently tracing the lines of her mouth. He bent his head and covered her mouth with his own, starting a trembling somewhere inside her — a trembling born of fear, she told herself. Fear, and nothing more.

He lifted his head. "I'll not bother you tonight, lass. You'll need a little time to rest and acquaint yourself with your new surroundings. Right now you are in a state of shock, and I don't think you have quite grasped all that has happened to you." The expression in his impelling eyes intensified and his voice grew husky. "And, my dearest Catriona, I want you to be very much aware of what is happening when I make love to you. 'Twould be such a waste otherwise."

50

Once again his lips claimed hers in a long, slow kiss. "You taste of red wine, love — your sweet kiss may make me drunker than the Highland whiskey has ever done." As he bent to kiss her again, she turned her head away and his burning lips touched her throat. She gasped in dismay as some new and disturbing emotion coursed through her. Perhaps she, too, was a little drunk on the red wine.

"You are afraid of me, aren't you, sweetheart? I don't want that; so, I will be prepared to wait. But only for a bit. You'll find I'm not a patient man."

Cathryn said nothing as she watched him cross the room toward the door. Just before he went out, he paused to say, "Catriona, I'd like to explain to you about Darroch . . ."

Her small chin came up. "You owe me no explanations."

"This is not the best time, no doubt, so I will leave it for later." His eyes gleamed with amusement. "I wager it will give us something to talk about during the long nights when we are lying in that curtained bed over there, too exhausted from . . ." Before he could finish his statement, he saw Cathryn swoop to seize the soup bowl on the floor at her feet. Just as she threw it at him with all her remaining strength, he slammed the door shut and the bowl shattered to pieces against its studded width. Outside in the hallway, she could hear his rumbling laughter, and it seemed the sound stayed with her while she climbed into the huge bed and surrendered herself to sleep.

Chapter Three

When Cathryn awoke the next morning, she found herself in a furious temper. Gone was the meek and mild girl of the evening before. Revan MacLinn was right — she had been in a state of shock. Why else would she have so calmly let them discuss her and order her about, their words passing over her head, leaving her untouched? Why else had she so willingly done their bidding, with no word of refusal?

The shock was gone now, at any rate, and they would find dealing with her this morning quite a different matter.

She sat up in the large bed and stared about the room where she had spent the night. It was a comfortable chamber, with a definite masculine air, and, she admitted grudgingly to herself, rather an attractive place.

At one end of the long room were high, wide windows, at the moment covered by heavy drapes of MacLinn tartan. They matched exactly the tartan bedspread on the bed where she was sitting. The tartan was predominantly red and black, with wide bold stripes. It looked rather gay and magnificent against the somber stone walls of the room. Again, Cathryn made the admission grudgingly. For nearly half her life, since that spring of 1746, tartans had been outlawed, and she had seen very few of them outside those in military usage. This was the first private home where she'd seen the tartan displayed so prominently, and she was drawn to its unusual beauty. Perhaps it was due to her Scottish blood, for the English certainly believed the tartan had a special appeal for the Scotsman. It might be that the bright colors and dramatic design recalled to them something of their savage ancestors and the blood-stirring deeds strewn throughout early Scottish history.

Along the opposite wall of the bedchamber was a mammoth stone fireplace, again decorated with the wolf's head emblem. Under and along either side of the snarling animal were rows of Scottish thistles, their stone leaves intertwined to form a border around the entire mantelpiece. Below them was carved a band of words, presumably the MacLinn motto. It read: "Above all, faithfulness."

Rather a strange motto for an outlaw, thought Cathryn wryly. Her eyes were drawn to the two high-backed chairs set in front of the fireplace. The remains of her supper tray were scattered on the floor in front of them, and for a satisfying moment, she let herself dwell on the remembered sound of the soup bowl crashing against the nail-studded door. She only regretted not being able to crash it against Revan MacLinn's arrogant head!

Between the two chairs, which were covered in some sort of black leather, was a small table, its surface littered with books, which she had not noticed the night before. Indeed, they seemed to be unusual items for an outlaw's bedchamber, also. Though Cathryn had been well educated, as most Scottish children were, she had never been allowed to read her father's books.

Her mind piqued, she tossed back the covers and ran lightly across the faded red carpet, settling in one of the chairs, tucking her bare feet beneath her. The fire had all but died, and the room was filled with icy drafts.

The books seemed to be mostly Highland histories and wildlife studies, but among them she discovered two or three recent novels, currently popular in Edinburgh and London. She wondered how they came to be in his possession.

For a moment, her mind was intrigued with the image of Revan MacLinn, finding time to escape the wearying business of cattle raiding, to visit some select little bookshop in order to purchase the latest best-selling books! A very interesting picture indeed, she thought, a droll smile lifting her lips.

Cathryn laid the books aside and went to one of the windows. Pulling back the heavy drapes, she looked out on what must be the back side of the castle. From this height, the view was dramatic. The castle seemed to be perched right at the edge of a sheer granite cliff whose walls ran straight down to the rough, choppy waters of a gray sea-loch. The white-tipped waves pounded incessantly at the foot of the rock wall, and Cathryn envisioned them eating away at the cliffside, until someday the wall would crumble, dumping Wolfcrag and its inhabitants into the icy depths of the water.

Far away, in the distant mists, there were more mountains, piled one upon another, blending with the gray of the rain-lashed sky. Shivering, Cathryn turned away from the dreary scene, dropping the heavy curtain and shutting out what little light had filtered into the room.

Quickly, she crossed to the door, thinking to look out into the hallway to see if anyone was about. She would like a blazing fire and some breakfast, and above all, some decent clothing to put on. To her surprise, she found the door locked and her way barred. The anger she had experienced upon awakening flooded back, consuming her in its heat.

How dare they lock her in like a criminal? she raged. After all, just how far could she have gotten in the state she'd been in?

Looking about for something to make noise, she caught sight of a pair of tall black boots standing in the corner near the wooden clothespress. Snatching up one of them, she began beating on the door with it, making a deafening noise.

Before long, she could hear someone working frantically with the key on the other side. The door was flung open to reveal the consternated face of young Elsa, the servant girl.

"Och, ma'm," she gasped, her eyes wide. "What is wrong? You gave me such a start!"

"I want out of here," snapped Cathryn haughtily. "I demand to know why I've been locked in this room like . . . like some animal!"

It was fairly evident the girl knew little more of her situation than she did herself, but she tried to make an answer. "Perhaps the laird didn't want you to be disturbed, miss. I overheard him telling his mother you were to be left alone to sleep as late as you wanted."

"Well, I'm awake now and I want a fire and some food. And some clothes!"

The girl looked uncertain. "Yes'm," she replied, her eyes darting toward the dying fire on the hearth. "I'll send up someone to do the fire while I get your breakfast. I will speak to Mrs. MacLinn about clothes for you to wear."

She started backing out of the room, pulling the door shut. Cathryn grabbed the handle and pulled back.

"Don't you dare lock this door again!"

It was plain Elsa had been given orders, and Cathryn supposed the girl would rather face her wrath than that of Revan MacLinn. Her struggles with the wiry little maid were useless, for the door was slammed and the key quickly turned in the lock.

Furious, Cathryn again pounded on the door and when there was no response, she began screaming as loudly as she could. Her throat was raw and strained with the effort before there was any sound outside the door. This time it opened to reveal a very agitated Mrs. MacLinn, who stepped inside and faced Cathryn, carefully keeping her back against the door.

"Please, my dear, you must stop acting like this. I know you are terribly upset, but screaming isn't going to help."

When the screams had ceased and Cathryn seemed ready to listen to her, she went on. "There will be someone here in a moment to build up the fire, and Elsa has gone for your breakfast. While you are eating, I will gather some clothing for you. Then we shall discuss this matter of your abduction . . ." Here her voice faltered, as though she had great difficulty in speaking the word.

"I don't want to discuss it," cried Cathryn. "I just want someone to return me to my home."

The older woman made a soothing gesture with one thin hand. "Oh, dear, Cathryn, I know what you must be feeling. But I . . . well, I just can't believe my son is going to let you go that easily. I feel certain he would never have risked so

55

much to bring you here if he had entertained any idea of letting you go home."

"Well, I won't stay!" Cathryn's green eyes flared with anger. "There is no way he can make me stay!"

The woman before her wrung her hands and murmured, "Oh, dear." Raising her eyes to Cathryn's blazing ones, she ventured another sentence. "It seems you do not know my son well, or else you would realize how very efficient he is at achieving what he desires." At the sound of the last word, she reddened and dropped her eyes.

Cathryn took advantage of her embarrassment by reaching out and firmly moving her out of the way. Before the surprised woman could react, Cathryn threw open the door and started into the hallway—right into the arms of Revan MacLinn.

"Well, well," he chuckled, holding her at arms' length to study her. "Once again I am astonished at your haste to welcome me."

Ignoring his words, she burst out furiously, "I demand to know why I was locked in this room!"

"To keep you from rushing downstairs in your nightgown and making a fool of yourself, love," was his quiet reply. "I knew you weren't going to remain docile for long, and I thought to spare you a little embarrassment when you regained your temper." He grinned broadly. "I'm relieved to see it has returned to you intact. Quite unharmed, I would say."

"Oh, yes, you may be sure I have regained my temper. And my senses! I am not going to stay here any longer. I demand you send me home at once."

"So, you demand it, do you?" He was greatly amused, she knew, and it only served to fan the flames of her anger higher.

"I do. I also demand some decent clothes to wear."

Her head went up as she felt his eyes raking her figure in the rumpled nightgown.

"Madam, I see nothing wrong with your present apparel," he said in amusement.

"Oh!" She stamped her foot and turned her back on him.

She couldn't help it—he made her feel so absurd and childish!

"Dinna fash yerself, lassie," he said, with a deep laugh in his voice. Then, abandoning the Highland brogue, he turned to his mother. "Mother, you can return to your breakfast now. I'll see that things are taken care of here. And, if you will, you might speak to Darroch about some clothing for Catriona. She'll have to make do with borrowed things for a few days."

"Are you sure Darroch will comply with your wishes?" Mrs. MacLinn's question was rather pointed.

"Aye, she'd better," he growled.

His mother nodded, but the expression on her face remained uncertain. As she left the room, Revan called after her, "Send Owen in with the wood in a few seconds, won't you?"

As soon as the door closed behind her, he scooped Cathryn into his arms and, carrying her swiftly across the room, dumped her unceremoniously onto the bed.

"You'd best get under those covers until MacIvor has come and gone. I fear he may be growing too accustomed to seeing you in your nightgown!"

Cathryn did as she was told, relieved to see the man did not intend to join her in the wide bed. Pulling the covers up about her chin, she watched as the giant red-haired Owen tramped into the bedchamber, arms full of wood for the fire. He dumped it into the wood-chest beside the fireplace, then proceeded to rebuild the dying fire.

"How's that, laddie?" he asked, dusting his hands on the rough leather trousers he wore and standing back to admire the bright, leaping flames.

"You've earned the maiden's gratitude forever."

At his words, Owen could not prevent his eyes from darting to where Cathryn lay. His slow grin at seeing her in his master's bed, and the significant look he cast at Revan MacLinn, brought a burning blush to her face. No doubt, word that she had spent the night with MacLinn would be making the rounds of the entire castle before the hour was out! Cathryn burned with frustrated indignation!

As the big man was leaving the room, in bounced Elsa with a breakfast tray. At the sight of Owen MacIvor, she smiled pertly and tossed her curly head. "So you've been demoted to stablehand and errand boy, now? Carrying in the wood, indeed!" Her teasing words brought a leer to Owen's broad, homely face.

" 'Tis a sight of you I'm after, lass," he boomed. "I haven't been home long enough to catch so much as a glimpse of your saucy face."

Elsa deposited the tray on the table by the fire, pushing the books aside. Straightening, she grinned broadly at Cathryn and exclaimed, "I'm not so sure 'twas my face you missed!" Both men roared with unrestrained laughter.

Once again Cathryn was shocked by the maid's familiarity and considered her manner far too bawdy to be seemly. She was annoyed to feel another blush rising to her cheeks.

Meanwhile, the little maid pranced back across the room, her freckled nose high in the air. Owen followed as surely as a hunting hound follows the scent of plump young partridges. At the door, he gave her bottom a mighty whack and she squealed in delight.

"I'll be seein' you later, lad," he said, winking over his shoulder at Revan, who stood watching the pair with a broad smile on his face.

He shut and locked the door after them, and turned to Cathryn, "Get up now and eat your breakfast, Catriona."

"Do you intend to stand over me while I eat?" she demanded.

"Indeed, I do."

"Then, I'm not hungry, thank you."

He chuckled. "Don't be so pigheaded, darling. 'Twill only spite yourself. Come on now, get up."

"Didn't I just say I was not hungry?"

He approached the bed. "Get up and stop acting so foolish." It seemed he had reached the end of his patience with her, for his voice was steely, and his hands, as he stripped the covers from her, were strong and rough. He seized a woolen blanket and, pulling her to her knees in the bed, wrapped it around her.

58

"Coming to breakfast, love?"

"No!"

Without another word, he lifted her, blanket and all, in his arms and carried her to the fire. He dropped into one of the chairs, settling her across his lap. Keeping one arm tight about her, he used the other to pull the little table around in front of him.

"Catriona, since you act like a baby, I am forced to treat you like one," he stated grimly. As soon as she saw what he intended to do, she began to squirm and struggle. "Be quiet!" he thundered. Startled by the loud order, her efforts ceased for a moment and she looked at him with huge, heavily lashed eyes.

"Porridge first, love." He calmly went on with his actions. She watched in fascination as he dipped up a spoonful of hot porridge. She saw it was served in the northern manner, the cream and porridge being in separate bowls. Dipping the spoonful of porridge into the bowl of cream, he lifted it to her mouth. She turned her head abruptly, refusing to open her lips. The spoon relentlessly followed, smearing the cereal across her face.

"Take a bite, Catriona," he ordered, and again she jerked her head away. Once more the spoon followed, smearing the sticky mixture along her jaw. She glared at him with the most hateful expression she could manage.

"We'll try again," he said calmly, as he dipped up a second spoonful of porridge. She refused it, throwing her head up and back against his shoulder. The oatmeal splattered down the front of the blanket, and Revan gave her an angry shake. "If you do not behave and start eating, I swear I will force it down you and then bathe you myself, treating you like the messy child you are!"

She saw by the intent look in his deep-set eyes that he was entirely serious. The thought of him giving her a bath was appalling! She could just imagine the pleasure the arrogant, self-assured beast would receive from that!

"If you let me feed myself, I will eat," she muttered furiously. Instantly, the spoon was in her fingers, but when she started forward off his lap, he tightened his grip.

"Stay where you are, lassie. I think it best that I keep a close eye on you."

It was humiliating, but it seemed there was no alternative. After a few mouthfuls, Revan handed her a linen napkin from the tray and instructed her to wipe her face.

"Here, love, you aren't doing it properly. Let me." His sinewy hand took the napkin from her grasp and he gently removed the remaining traces of porridge from her face. Stiffly she thanked him, then returned to her breakfast. She was ashamed to seem so greedy in front of him, but told herself she would need her strength, and ate all the food on the tray.

Revan pushed the little table aside, then rose so suddenly with her still on his lap that she thought she would fall, and one arm quickly encircled his neck. He stood for a moment, seemingly enjoying the feel of her in his arms, then crossed the room and laid her once again among the tangled bedcovers.

"Stay here until someone comes with your clothes," he instructed. "After you're dressed, I'll be back to take you on a tour of Wolfcrag."

Abruptly he left the room, and once again she heard the sound of a key in the lock. Feeling stronger after eating, she experienced the upsurging of anger once again. As soon as she was properly dressed, she would inform him she had no wish to see Wolfcrag—indeed, had no wish to do anything other than return home.

The next time Cathryn heard the key turning in the lock, the door was opened by the black-haired beauty who had greeted Revan so warmly. She shut the door behind her, making a great show of locking it and dropping the key into the pocket of the blue gown she wore.

"I've brought you some clothes to wear," she said, her dark eyes very thoroughly taking in the sight of Cathryn amidst the tumbled bedcovers. She tossed a pile of clothing down at the foot of the bed, then came closer to Cathryn. "Why did you come here?" she asked bluntly.

Cathryn sat up indignantly. "Because I was kidnapped and forced to come here! Don't ever think it was my choice."

"What spell have you cast over Revan?" the girl called Darroch asked, menacingly. "Where did you meet him?"

"It really isn't any of your business!"

The girl's eyes hardened. "Oh, but it is, you know."

"I don't see how . . ." Cathryn sighed. "It seems I can understand very little of what has happened. Your laird is certainly the most evil man I've ever known!"

Darroch's laugh was unbelieving. "Revan?"

"You can't expect me to think very well of his methods of wooing a bride," Cathryn stated flatly. "I have never known such an arrogant, unscrupulous . . ."

"Hush up, you ninny," snapped Darroch. "I think it is you who are the fool."

"Oh?"

"Yes, indeed. You had the chance to marry Revan, or so I've heard belowstairs. What sort of a fool would reject him to marry an old man?"

"Basil is not that old! Besides, I know Basil, and I had only seen this MacLinn twice, and he didn't exactly make a favorable impression."

"Owen tells me Revan saved your . . . shall we say, 'virtue'," Darroch went on. "Is that true?"

"Yes, I suppose so," Cathryn replied. "But of what use was it to save me from his band of men, only to abduct me for his own pleasure?"

Darroch's gaze sharpened. "You mean he has raped you?" she asked boldly.

"Not yet, though he has made it very plain that is his intention. The man has no morals."

"You will find that Revan makes his own laws. His word carries great weight in this district, and though you scorn and ridicule him, there are some for whom rape wouldn't be necessary. There are many who would leap at the chance to be his woman."

"Yourself among them?" countered Cathryn.

"Myself among them." Darroch's flat statement seemed almost threatening, and Cathryn felt that battle lines had somehow been drawn.

"Then, my sympathies to you and to them . . . in fact, to anyone who must live under the black shadow of this . . . this bandit they call 'the Wolf.'"

"And have ye not noticed what a bonny man is the laird?" Darroch's voice was mocking, full of Scottish burr.

"Not to me. I wish someone would listen and understand me when I say I have no desire to be here at Wolfcrag, and certainly no desire to stay with Revan MacLinn. All I want is to go home."

Darroch ignored her words entirely. The audacity of her next question made Cathryn gasp in shock. "Will Revan be coming to your bed tonight?"

"God forbid!" she exclaimed. "He'll never be coming to my bed, if you must know! I'll kill myself first!"

Darroch laughed. "You are a fool! Take my word for it."

She turned to leave the room, tossing a last cutting remark over her shoulder. "Mayhap Revan will come to his senses before too much longer. Your screaming and pounding have the whole place in a turmoil, and surely he cannot help but see what a childish nuisance you truly are!"

The door slammed on Cathryn's irate retort, and she tried to calm herself by examining the clothing Darroch had lent her.

Holding up a gray woolen dress, she fought down disappointment. It looked as though it were made for a child and would almost certainly be too little for her. The undergarments were clean, but worn and patched, and the slippers had seen far better days. The shawl was faded, but she decided it would be useful to help cover the top of the gown which was definitely not going to fit properly. At least these clothes would be preferable to the nightgowns she had been forced to wear for the last two days.

As she had foreseen, the dress was considerably too small. It gapped down the back between the fastenings, and the low front just barely covered her breasts. The skirt was short enough to show her ankles. The ugly black slippers, which proved to be too large, slapped on the stone floor with each step she took.

She found a comb on the oak dressing table and combed the tangles from her long bronze hair. She had just finished and was tossing the shawl about her shoulders when a knock sounded at the door and Revan stuck his head around its edge. "All dressed, love? Ready for our stroll?"

Harsh words crowded to her lips, but suddenly she thought better of refusal. It was a chance to get outside this room, so she said nothing and joined him in the hallway, allowing him to take her arm.

"I thought you might like to see more of your new home," he was saying as they started down the broad stairway. "I know your means of arrival here at Wolfcrag has been strange to say the least, but I'm convinced that if you give yourself a little time, you'll understand why I love it so." He looked down at her. "Perhaps you might even learn to love it yourself."

Just as they reached the bottom of the staircase, several men crowded forward. Obviously, they had been waiting in the Great Hall to see Revan and set up a clamor about some urgent business with their laird.

Revan gestured to a high-backed wooden bench, and said, "Sit here and wait for me, love. I won't be a minute."

He herded the men toward the fireplace at the other end of the room, and Cathryn could hear muffled references to sheep and cattle. She wondered briefly if they were discussing the very animals stolen from her father, husband and their neighbors.

She turned her attention to the narrow slitted windows set into the thick wall at the end of the staircase. Outside in the courtyard she could see a number of people going about their daily chores. There were children carrying wood or going to the well with buckets, women scolding them in Gaelic as they hurried in this door or that, pursuing their own interests. She wondered where they all lived, what they did with their time.

Across the long room, Revan was giving the men rapid, terse instructions, handling their problems in a calm, capable way. As her gaze swept over the group of men, she became aware of a small side door just down the length of the

63

hallway. It was ajar, apparently having been opened and then forgotten by one of the servants. Cathryn decided to try slipping through the partially opened door to make a run for her freedom. She knew she might not get far — she had no way of knowing how she would get out of the courtyard, but just for the moment, she was determined to try. Anything would be better than meekly waiting to see what was going to happen to her.

Quietly, she left the bench and crept down the hallway, not making a sound. No one noticed her until just as she was sidling through the door. One of the men with Revan saw her and called out in surprise. Before she started running, she caught a glimpse of Revan's astonished face and saw it fill with anger.

She was well into the courtyard before he caught her. The cobblestones were still wet from an early morning rain, and she slipped and nearly fell as he grabbed her arm. The shawl she was clutching slid to her waist and she heard his shocked exclamation as he saw her half-bare back.

"For God's sake, Catriona, what are you wearing?"

She faced him defiantly, tears of frustration welling in her eyes. "I'm wearing what I was given. What else do I have?"

He held her in front of him and his eyes missed no detail of the dress. She closed her own eyes in mute misery when she felt his intent gaze on the bodice. She knew the fabric was strained to the limit, and her breasts were nearly bare under his avid scrutiny.

Her eyes flew open at the harsh sound of his breathing. He was furious! She wondered if he would strike her.

Instead, he bent swiftly and picked up the shawl, handing it back to her. It was then she realized his fury was not directed at her.

"Come, love," was all he said as he pulled her back inside the hall. They hastened back up the stairs, and Cathryn was surprised to find they did not stop at the door to the bedchamber where she had slept, but went down the hall to another door.

Revan knocked loudly, then threw open the door without waiting for an answer. Darroch stood in the center of the room, her eyes unfathomable pools.

"What in hell are you up to, Darroch?" raged Revan, thrusting Cathryn in front of him. "Look at this wretched assortment of clothing you gave the girl to wear."

"I only assumed you wanted her to have something I no longer have a use for," Darroch returned smoothly. "Surely you did not expect me to give her one of my better gowns?"

"Darroch, I doubt that you could have squeezed your charming, but ample proportions into that dress when you were thirteen!"

Cathryn had never seen such a malevolent expression as the one which crossed Darroch's beautiful features. Her eyes blazed so that Cathryn thought they would surely scorch Revan MacLinn's face, but he confronted her unflinchingly, and went on with his violent tirade.

"I would make a wager this dress belongs to one of the serving girls. Would I be correct?"

"And what if you are?" Darroch challenged. "Is it so shameful of me not to want to give up any of my own things to this . . . this unwelcome stranger?"

Revan took a menacing step toward her. "I have brought her here to stay, madam, and well you know it. This is my house and everything in it was purchased by me . . . including your precious clothing. Don't you forget that!"

He strode to the large wardrobe at one side of the room, and throwing it open, began rifling through the gowns inside. He tossed one of dark green and another of pale saffron onto the bed.

He faced the outraged Darroch again, saying, "Now you find some decent underthings and a pair of shoes that fit, and bring them to my room within fifteen minutes."

He gathered up the dresses, then, taking Cathryn's arm, left the room. One quick backward glance was enough to tell her how angry the other woman really was. Had she been Revan MacLinn, she was not sure she would have turned her back on Darroch.

"I'm sorry for her shameful behavior, love. I didn't realize how she might treat you."

"Doesn't it seem strange to you," she asked, as he shut the

door of his room behind them, "to apologize for Darroch's behavior, but not your own, which has been infinitely more reprehensible and unjustified?"

Her words seemed to clear the glowering look from his face and he grinned suddenly. "Lass, dear, the moment I first saw you standing on that hillside, I knew any action I took to make you my own would be justified."

"Even kidnapping?" she asked, her voice dripping venom.

"Yes, even that." He moved closer, his hands circling her waist. "You must know that, when a man finds his woman, the only person in the world who can make him whole, there is no law or circumstance that should keep them apart."

"But, don't you suppose poor Basil also thought he had found his perfect mate?" she asked, in an attempt at reasoning.

The expletive he uttered was short and ugly.

He had just lowered his mouth to hers when the door opened and Darroch stepped inside. At the sight of Cathryn in Revan's arms, she stopped short.

She tossed down a bundle of clothing. "Here are the things you required," she said stiffly. After a moment, she turned and left the room, and Cathryn was dismayed. Now that Darroch had seen her so serenely accepting Revan's embrace, she would never believe Cathryn's fierce protestations that she had no desire to be at Wolfcrag with him. She had probably lost her one hope of escape, for she'd had the feeling Darroch would have been more than willing to do whatever she could to help her leave the castle.

Angry with herself as much as with Revan, she twisted away, out of his arms.

"Don't be embarrassed," he said. "Darroch has to see us together sometime."

She turned on him in fury. "Why don't you get out of here and leave me alone? Don't you understand I can't bear the sight of you? I just want to be left alone!"

He clamped his jaw shut on the reply he would have made. "Very well, Catriona, if that is what you want. As far as I'm concerned, you can remain alone until you begin to realize the value of a little companionship." He turned to walk away, then paused and looked back at her. "Feel free to inform us when you desire to be more sociable."

He moved angrily out of the room, locking the door behind him. Cathryn sank down on the bed . . . now what? Was she ever to be allowed outside these four walls again? Was she to be starved to death? Locked away and forgotten forever?

Her chin came up and she straightened her shoulders. Well, if the alternative was to crawl to Revan MacLinn and beg his forgiveness, then she would stay here until she died! Asking for his company was unthinkable, and she vowed never to do it. Never!

Chapter Four

Cathryn was shocked at how quickly her resolve crumbled. Seemingly, all it took to make her reconsider her wish to be left alone was the enticing aroma of roasting meat drifting up from the kitchens below. Imagining the castle's inhabitants gathering for their evening meal, she was stricken with a sharp pang of self-pity.

She had been locked in the room all day with nothing to eat or drink, so now that night had fallen, it was only natural she should begin to think longingly of food. Fortunately, there had been plenty of wood to keep the fire burning brightly, and she had spent the greater part of the afternoon sitting near the hearth, curled into a chair, reading and dozing. Now she became restless. Her head ached, and her empty stomach rumbled and growled. The wonderful cooking smells made her mouth water. She clenched her hands and paced the floor. She was so hungry she felt faint, but how humiliating to give in so quickly! No, it would never do . . . she would not give Revan MacLinn the pleasure or satisfaction of seeing her humble herself. She had to remain firm at all costs.

She wandered to the high windows at the end of the room and peered out into the gloomy night. The wind was keening and howling along the battlements above. It made her shiver to hear it. Down below, somewhere in the unrelieved darkness, was the sea, dashing against the rocky shore.

She hugged herself, feeling a chill that went clear to the bone. The Highlands, she thought. What a dreary and

68

hateful place!

Just at that moment she heard someone at the door and whirled to face Revan. Obviously he was no longer angry, for his dark face was lighted by a huge grin. He seemed very pleased with himself, and immediately, Cathryn felt her anger surging up inside her. It was lessened only a little by the sight of a tray in his hands.

"Ah, Catriona, I trust you are not contemplating throwing yourself from that window! 'Tis a long way down, I assure you."

"You needn't worry."

"I'm relieved." He strode across the room and set the tray on the table by the fire. "Come, here's your supper."

"What? Food for me? To what do I owe this unexpected pleasure?"

"To the good-hearted generosity of my mother," Revan replied. "Frankly, I thought starvation might be a good method of taming you, but my mother declared it a shameful way to treat a newcomer to our home. All things considered, I suppose she is right. Still . . . if you wish, I can take the food away."

"No!" Cathryn hadn't meant to speak so quickly, and the look of surprise on her face caused the man to throw back his head and laugh heartily.

"Can it be that my unwilling hostage is coming around to a more agreeable way of thinking?"

She refused to answer, letting her gaze drop to the carpet at her feet.

"Well, perhaps my mother is wiser than I in this matter." He shrugged. "I'm willing to try it her way for a while."

Cathryn wished he would go away and leave her to her meal. She refused to enter into a battle of words or wits with him tonight. If she held her tongue, surely he would give up and go away.

"I'm willing to make a bargain with you, my dear."

This announcement startled Cathryn, and her eyes flew to his face. "What sort of bargain?"

"If you will promise to behave and come out of this room to take your place in the household, I will promise to leave you alone for the next few days." He gazed intently at her for a long moment. "Do you understand what I am saying?"

Embarrassed, she turned away. "Yes, I understand."

"You must, however, show a little more respect for your chieftain — no more attempts at escape! I don't like being a laughing stock."

She shrugged her slender shoulders.

"A few days should allow you ample time to adjust yourself to your new home and the people in it. Then you can occupy your mind with more . . . urgent matters."

She turned to face him. "Is there any way I might convince you to let me go home again?"

"None."

She sighed. "Then it really doesn't matter much what I think or want, does it?"

His hands were warm on her shoulders. "Catriona, believe me . . . I didn't bring you here to harm you. All I ask is that you give me a chance to prove you can be happy at Wolfcrag."

When she didn't answer, he gently raised her chin with one firm hand. "You will feel better after you've had something hot to eat. Just remember while you dine that you were fed only through the intervention of my mother. Tomorrow I think you should pay her a visit to thank her and get better acquainted."

"To thank her? For feeding a hostage?"

"Not only that, love. If it were not for her, I would be taking off my boots right now, preparing for a long and arduous night here with you."

"Oh, you're disgusting!" Cathryn whirled away, but he caught her arm and turned her to face him once again.

"Be that as it may," he chuckled, gaining obvious pleasure from baiting her, "but at least I have offered to play the gentleman . . . for a few days. Now kiss me goodnight like a good lass and I will leave you alone to enjoy your meal."

"I don't want . . ."

He moved swiftly. Her words were silenced by his mouth, moving softly against hers. His strong hands grasped her shoulders, then slid slowly downward to caress her back,

70

holding her closer against him. At first she resisted, but his strength was so superior she finally gave up the effort. By complying with his wishes, she sought to hasten his departure. He lifted his face from hers and for a long moment stared solemnly into her eyes. Then he gently kissed one corner of her mouth and murmured, "That's better, Catriona. You are indeed learning the futility of fighting me. Now I'll leave you until morning. Goodnight, love."

As soon as he had gone, locking the door behind him, she flew across the room to her meal. There was more soup, crusty bread and slices of roast chicken, all of which tasted delicious. A good meal and Revan's promise to give her a little time were rapidly restoring her sense of well-being. She was filled with a new determination to get herself out of this situation before it became any worse. Suddenly she decided if she had to gain time by playing along with Revan MacLinn, that was exactly what she would do. Craftiness and a strong will were the only weapons she had at hand.

Tomorrow they were going to be astonished at how meek and malleable she had become, and by the day after that, they were going to be even more astonished to find her gone. That should give her time enough to devise a way to leave this pile of cold gray stone they called Wolfcrag Castle far behind!

Cathryn was awakened the next morning by the sound of the key in the lock and the bustling entry of the serving girl, Elsa.

"Good morning, ma'm," the girl chirped brightly. " 'Tis a wonderful day, for there's a bit of sunshine!"

"Yes, I suppose that is unusual for this part of the world," Cathryn said dryly.

"Especially at this time of the year. Aye, we can have weeks of wind and rain, even snow, and then suddenly, out comes the sun to remind us of how lovely the land can be."

Cathryn stretched lazily, too sleepy and contented to even speak ill of the Highland weather. She felt more like her old self than she had since coming to Wolfcrag. She threw back the bedcovers and reached for the velvet robe.

"I've brought you some hot water so you can wash up, and in a bit, someone from the kitchen will be up with your breakfast. Oh, and I'm to tell you that when you are done with eating, the MacLinn will come to show you around the castle." Here she cast daring eyes at Cathryn and grinned impishly. "That is, he says, if you'll promise to behave and not try to run away from him again."

Cathryn stifled the impulse to tell the girl exactly what she thought of Revan MacLinn's comments, but no, that was not part of her plan. From this moment forward, she was going to be very docile and obedient.

"I will try to be ready by the time he arrives," was all she allowed herself to say.

Elsa cocked her pert head to one side and studied Cathryn thoughtfully. "Excuse me for saying so, Miss, but you're so young and beautiful . . . and yet, they say you prefer an old man to our bonny chieftain. I can't believe that is so."

Cathryn swallowed her anger again. "Elsa, surely that is none of your affair!"

"No," the girl answered cheerfully, "but if it was me, I'd leap at the chance . . ."

"But then, it isn't you, is it?" Cathryn's reply was curt, but Elsa only grinned and bobbed a quick curtsy.

"I'd best be about my other chores so you can wash up while the water is hot." She left the room quickly, and Cathryn noticed she did not lock the door. Evidently they had decided to trust her. Encouraged by that fact, she washed hurriedly, flinching against the chill of the room, and scurried into one of the gowns Revan had chosen for her.

The saffron color was complimentary to her bronze hair and green eyes, and she was very pleased with the image she presented in the cheval mirror. She had never seen a full-length reflection of herself before, as the only mirrors in her old home had been small ones, fastened high on the wall. Mirrors led to vanity, her father had believed, and she was certain Basil felt the same way. Still, she did enjoy seeing herself as others saw her, and knew instinctively she looked much better in this gown than she had in the odd assortment of clothes Darroch had first given her to wear. She slipped on ankle-high boots of untanned hides and was immediately glad for their soft warmth. She had no other shawl but the drab one she'd worn earlier, and though it wasn't very pretty, it served to keep away the chill.

Her breakfast was brought in by a young girl she had not seen before. Too shy to speak, the girl cast an admiring look at Cathryn as she set the tray on the fireside table, then hastened from the room.

Cathryn attacked the food with a healthy hunger, glad her captors had decided against starvation. She was nearly finished with the meal when Revan strode in.

Again, he was dressed in black, armed with pistol and dagger, and with the MacLinn plaid draped across one broad shoulder. She noticed it was secured with the wolf's head brooch fashioned of silver. He stood over her, hands on his hips, but somehow he didn't look quite so threatening this morning.

"Have you finished your breakfast, then?" he said politely.

"Yes, I have." Cathryn stood up from the table. "I understand I am to be allowed to see something of the castle this morning."

"As long as you keep your end of our bargain and do not try anything rash."

"I have abandoned all such ideas, sir. I think my efforts to escape would likely be thwarted anyway."

"You are right on that score, Catriona. While you were locked in this room, I made the rounds of the castle and informed everyone that I would deal harshly with anyone who lets you escape. I think you may roam freely, as long as you are content to stay within the walls of Wolfcrag. I trust my clansmen to look after you."

"Yes, well, I have no intention of trying to escape again." She swallowed deeply, hating the taste of the lie in her mouth. "I have learned the futility of such an act."

"Good." He stepped close to her and she stiffened, fearing some unwanted intimacy. Instead, he merely took her arm and turned to walk to the door. "I think we shall climb to the tower above us first, and perhaps walk along the battlements. 'Tis the best way to get an over-all view of Wolfcrag and the countryside surrounding it."

A few yards down the hallway was the steep, narrow stairway that twisted up through the tower. Revan pulled her along behind him, as there wasn't room enough for the two of them to walk side by side. At one landing he stopped to explain. "This is the topmost floor of the castle. It contains only private bedchambers and suites belonging to the family members and officers in the clan. We won't invade their privacy by stopping here."

On up they went, until the stairway ended abruptly with a small thick door, arched at the top and heavily studded. Revan unlatched the door and flung it open, stepping out onto the walkway. Cathryn stepped out behind him. The sun was shining brightly, but up there the wind was steady and cold. It tossed her hair about her head, momentarily blinding her. She caught her toe on an uneven stone and stumbled against the man. A strong arm tightened about her, holding her steady.

"Ah, the Scottish wind! A devil to be reckoned with," he chuckled.

Cathryn shivered and pulled the thin shawl closer about her shoulders. Revan deftly unfastened the wolf's head brooch and wrapped his plaid around the two of them, binding her body close to his. With his right hand he reached up, gathering all the flying strands of hair to hold them securely at the nape of her neck.

"Now you can enjoy the magnificent view," he said.

Cathryn was very aware of the feel of his body next to hers and of the warmth of his hand resting on her neck. She tried to ignore both as she raised her eyes toward the misty Highland hills. She caught her breath at the unexpected loveliness of the autumn morning.

Revan was watching her closely. " 'Tis no' such a bad place to call home," he said teasingly. He walked her a few steps further. "And if it's a glimpse of water you want, look over this way."

He turned her in another direction and there was the sea, huge and restless, darts of sunlight glinting off its moving

74

surface. Along the rock-strewn shore the waves splashed and played.

Cathryn was delighted with the view. As much as she loved the gentle rolling hills of the country where she had grown up, she was forced to admit a grudging admiration for this wild and untamed scenery.

No wonder these Highlanders are so rough and primitive, she thought. The very land in which they live forces them to be! They are tempered by demonic winds, angry seas, and rugged mountains. It would take a special breed to survive here, and who could argue their need for strength and fierceness, even cruelty?

Revan began to walk her along the battlements. "This castle was built here about four hundred years ago, by the first MacLinns to settle this coast. In all that time it has never been invaded by an enemy force. It is a natural fortress, and the only way to get to it is through the long narrow valley there." He pointed out the very glen through which they had ridden only days before. "It is so well hidden that few ever find their way to it. Then, if they do, they cannot cross the chasm running along the face of Wolfcrag unless we lower the drawbridge for them. Once past the bridge, there is the portcullis. On the opposite side of the castle, there is only the sea, and cliffs so steep a mountain goat cannot scale them. Wolfcrag is truly impregnable. The only way it can ever be lost is through internal treachery."

"Why are you telling me this?" She looked up at him. "To discourage any hope I might have of rescue?"

"Aye, I thought it best you know how remote we really are. Don't waste your time dreaming of a rescue party riding up the glen. Even if they could find it, they'd never gain entry to the castle."

She shrugged and managed to keep her voice light. "Then I shall not expect to be rescued."

"My, how meek you've suddenly become!" His teeth gleamed whitely through his beard. "Forgive me if I mistrust that meekness somewhat."

"I assure you, sir, I care very little whether you trust me or not. I am only saying that a person of normal intelligence

75

realizes when the odds are overwhelmingly against him."

"Well spoken! And I would truly like to believe you mean what you say." With an abrupt change of mood, he moved her back down the walkway until they were directly above the courtyard.

Below them was a scene not unlike that in many small villages. Men and women went about their work, calling out to each other, their voices ringing in the clear air.

"Do they live here?" Cathryn was curious about the life of the clansmen, and thought it time for a change of subject.

"Yes, many of them live in the cottages surrounding the courtyard. At the time the Clearances began, when your honorable king was burning people out of their homes, most of my clan came here to live. It was the only way to keep them safe. After all, following Culloden, a great many of the families consisted only of women and children. Some of the luckier ones whose men survived the battle, live outside these walls in their own crofts, but in times of trouble, they, too, come inside Wolfcrag to live."

"How do you support all these people?"

"We farm the land around the base of the castle, and we have a fleet of fishing boats. And," here he grinned wickedly at her, "we do manage to sell a few cattle here and there."

"Cattle you steal! Not exactly a living you can be proud of," she retorted.

He only laughed. "We do raise some cattle of our own, you know. In fact, we have quite a large herd of Highland cattle. Sometimes in the autumn we ride out on raids just to annoy the king and his haughty subjects, though I must admit, it does help to increase our profits at the livestock markets."

"What a horrid way to live!"

"I'd be willing to wager you would find a cattle raid very exciting if you ever lost your prudishness long enough to engage in one. We Highlanders look upon them as great sport."

"I'm sure you do." Cathryn tossed her head and winced as her hair tightened in his restraining grip. "And just because I have never known men who flaunted their lawlessness before doesn't make me a prude!"

"Catriona, you are indeed a self-righteous little prude, whether you think so or not, but I intend to change all that . . . and very soon."

She broke away from his steady gaze. "What . . . what are those thatched buildings over there?" she asked, pointing out several low buildings huddled together along the far side of the courtyard.

"Those are the stables," Revan replied, his mouth twitching with laughter, as he recognized her intent. "We have some very fine horses here."

"Will I ever be allowed to ride?"

"Oh, I should think so. Naturally, you would have to have an escort."

"Naturally."

"It's growing chilly up here," Revan said. "Let's go in." They re-entered the castle through the arched doorway. Once inside, Revan helped her disentangle herself from the folds of the plaid.

"Now shall we see the other parts of the castle?" she asked.

"Yes, but before we go belowstairs, I'd like you to spend a few moments with my mother." A grim look seemed to settle over his features. "She will be in her bedchamber. Indeed, for the last ten years or so, she has rarely seen fit to spend much time outside that chamber."

"Why is that?" Cathryn asked, as they began to descend the narrow stairs.

"I think she lost interest in life after Culloden."

"Then, your father was killed in the battle?" She looked back at him, her curiosity aroused.

"Aye, and my two older brothers as well. The shock of it nearly killed my mother, and would have done, I believe, if she had not felt such responsibility toward me. I was very young, and suddenly the chief of a shattered clan. There was much to be done during those first few weeks and months after Culloden."

His face had lost all expression, and there was a bleakness, a hardness in his eyes.

He can hardly bear to speak of it, she thought, surprised

77

at the depth of emotion he must be hiding behind that careful mask.

"You were too young? That is why you weren't at Culloden?"

"Yes, so young I was forbidden by my father to go. I hated being left and hated it more when they didn't return. I should have been with them!"

"Oh, nonsense!" Cathryn snapped. "Just what purpose would that have served? Getting yourself killed for a useless cause . . ."

He turned to face her. "That's enough," he said, very quietly. She realized immediately the foolhardiness of further speech. She clamped her mouth shut and waited for his next words. "Now we will go in to see my mother and you will be pleasant and cheerful, and under no circumstances will you ask for her help in any way. Do you understand?"

"Yes, of course. Don't you think I know how hopeless that would be? Your mother very clearly bows to all your wishes, so I'll seek no aid from that quarter."

"Good." He nodded curtly.

Margaret MacLinn's room was at the opposite end of the corridor from her son's. When Revan knocked on the door, her clear voice bade them enter. She was seated in a cushioned window seat, her needlework before her. Behind her were high windows with a view of distant forests and mountains.

At first Cathryn thought the room was lovely, for its stone walls were completely covered with brilliant tapestries gleaming with jewel-like colors. It took her a few seconds of careful scrutiny to realize they chronicled the MacLinn history, from the construction of the castle onward. With a start, she noticed the last tapestry was a horrible lifelike representation of the Battle of Culloden. A fallen chief, wrapped in the MacLinn tartan, was depicted, dying with a smile on his bloodied face while his piper stood over him, obviously playing a MacLinn lament. Cathryn felt nauseated at the awful reality of the picture. No wonder Revan's mother was so melancholy. Choosing to live in the past and subjecting herself to this grisly reminder of her husband's death was enough to drive her mad.

She looked questioningly at Revan, but he avoided her gaze and pushed her forward toward the lady at the far end of the room.

"Good morning, Cathryn," she said, warmly. "I hope you slept well."

"Yes, of course. I'd like to thank you for the food you had sent to me. I appreciate your kindness."

"My dear, you are more than welcome. Now, won't you sit here beside me so we can get to know each other a little better? You don't know how much I have looked forward to the day Revan would bring home a bride . . ." She broke off abruptly, casting stricken eyes at first her son, and then the girl beside him.

Far from being upset, Revan laughed heartily. "Don't look so shocked, Mother. In a sense, I have brought home a bride. She just isn't mine!"

Cathryn's cheeks burned, and she found it very difficult to maintain her docile pose.

"What I mean to say," Revan's mother went on, her voice strained, "is that it will be nice to have another woman in the castle — someone I might talk to and spend time with. The other women here are simply too busy, and Darroch isn't the type to sit with me for a while. Revan, why don't you go off and attend to business or something." She waved her hand airily, and it greatly amused Cathryn to see him dismissed like a child.

He only smiled good-naturedly, happy to indulge his mother.

"Very well. There are a few things I need to discuss with Owen. I'll return in thirty minutes or so."

"That will be fine," Margaret answered, turning her attention to Cathryn, who was seating herself obediently.

Revan's tall figure crossed the long room, his quick stride causing the plaid to flare out behind him. He closed the door, and they could hear his booted footsteps ringing down the stone corridor.

"Now that Revan is gone, we can talk," Margaret said. "I want to know if you are really all right."

"As much as can be expected," Cathryn replied.

"I know you have been very upset and unhappy, and I sympathize with you. I'm just glad you decided to come out of that room and talk to us."

"I had little choice in the matter."

"No, I suppose not," the woman said gently.

"You know, the thing I simply cannot believe is how all of you think I am the unreasonable one—that I am the one causing the problem! Doesn't anyone see that your son is the guilty person in all of this?"

"I can understand why you might feel that way, but . . ."

Cathryn interrupted, "Can't anyone reason with the man? Surely there is someone in this place who realizes the seriousness of what he has done."

"He has always been somewhat rash, I admit . . ."

"Rash! Don't you think kidnapping another man's wife goes a little beyond being rash?"

Margaret MacLinn flinched at the harsh words, and Cathryn felt contrite. It would do no good to alienate the one person who had shown her any compassion since she'd come to Wolfcrag. She laid a hand on the woman's thin arm and said, "I'm sorry! I shouldn't speak of your son in that way. I am afraid I let my anger get the best of me."

"Please, don't apologize! I am the first to admit you have the right to feel fear and anger. I only want to advise you to let your anger go and give Revan the chance to . . . to make you happy."

"I am another man's wife. It isn't a matter of whether I could be happy here or not. It's a legal matter, even a moral one."

"You know, Revan never acts without being prepared to suffer the consequences of his actions. He has surely weighed both sides of the issue and decided the risk was worth the gain. As I said, he can be rash, but he will stand behind his decision to the death."

"And you are willing to let him?"

"I know you must think I am very complacent or worse, but the truth of it is, I have lost the will and desire to rail against fate. Revan made his decision and carried it out. I speak honestly when I tell you there is nothing I can say or do to change that. Therefore, knowing that, I won't waste my energies arguing pointlessly." She spread her hands in a helpless gesture. "Oh, I might win small concessions for you, such as persuading them to feed you or let you have more freedom, but, my dear, Revan means to have you as his . . . his mate, and nothing will stand in his way."

"But surely you can't just blindly ignore such a blatant abuse of the law?"

"If you were a Highlander, you might understand a little more clearly. Here, Revan is the law. He makes the rules and no one defies him."

"That is wrong! He is a subject of the king just as much as I or anyone else," Cathryn cried.

"Not to our way of thinking, my dear. I know it must be difficult for you to accept, but we are so remote here that the word of the king has very little meaning. We keep to the old ways — the ways that were supposedly destroyed at Culloden. There are enough of us left, too entrenched to be ferreted out by the king's troops, to keep up the old ways until we are all dead and gone."

"You may choose to live like that, but I do not. I'm part of a much more modern world. I shouldn't care to live in the past."

"You may come to find, as many of us have, living in the past can sometimes be more rewarding than living in a so-called modern world. In the past, a man's word could be trusted; people weren't turned out of their homes in the name of politics and killing wasn't done just for the sake of killing."

"Please, I don't want to argue against your way of life, nor do I wish to have to defend mine. I only want to go back to the life I had before I met your son."

Margaret sighed deeply. "I wish I could tell you that is possible, but, frankly, I don't foresee Revan allowing it. I really think you have to try to adapt yourself to life here at Wolfcrag. It would be easier for you."

"How can you think that would even be possible?"

"May I tell you something?" Margaret asked. At Cathryn's

nod, she went on, "I, too, was brought to Wolfcrag as a captive bride . . ."

Cathryn's despair deepened. If Revan's own father had set such an example, no wonder he saw nothing wrong with carrying off any woman he wanted!

"How barbaric!" she murmured.

Margaret smiled, and for an instant, Cathryn caught a glimpse of the beauty she must have been in her youth. Her face softened and glowed, her light brown hair framing it to make a charming picture. Shadowy gray eyes looked inward, shining with some remembered emotion.

"Yes, I thought so, too, at first. I was so frightened, you see. I knew nothing of men, especially huge, fierce Highland warriors who rode into unsuspecting villages to steal whatever they wanted—cattle or crops or women. My father was away, and we were helpless against them. I shall never forget my first sight of Duncan MacLinn. Aye, he was a handsome, bonny man, though he scared the life out of me! He was seated on a giant black horse that reared and pawed the air. I was standing in the doorway of my home, startled by the shouting and the sound of so many horses running through the streets. He saw me there and rode up beside me. I was so terrified of his horse that I didn't grasp his intent until it was too late. Later he said he loved me at first sight, but just didn't have the time for a gentle wooing! He swept me up onto the horse and brought me here to his castle."

"Oh, how horrible! What . . . what happened then?"

"I was treated kindly, I assure you, but Duncan was quite firm. I was to become his bride and never return to my own family. I cried for days, nearly out of my mind with fear. One day I got tired of crying and because I had no other choice, I took a good look at this man who proposed to become my husband. He was as magnificent a man as I had ever seen—so tall and strong, with the blackest hair and a face carved from Highland stone. I thought about how patient and gentle he had been, despite my cowardly ways. I began to respect him for that, and I suppose that was the day I started to love him."

For a moment she was very quiet, remembering, then she

82

went on. "And love him I did, Cathryn. Aye, it must be a sin to love someone that much."

"But, your poor mother and father! What did they think? Did you ever see them again?"

"Oh, yes, certainly. Duncan refused to let me leave Wolfcrag until we were legally married, but as soon as that was accomplished, he took me back to my village to visit my parents. They, too, were easily won over by his charm."

"And there was no retaliation?" Cathryn asked.

"No, none. My mother and father were often guests in our home, and even my brothers grew to admire Duncan."

She turned to look at Cathryn. "You see, what at first had seemed a cruel twist of fate became the best thing in my life. Who is to say your own situation might not also turn out that way?"

"But it's not at all the same!" Cathryn jumped to her feet and began pacing up and down in front of the woman. "Maybe years ago Highlanders could go on raids and steal a bride and no one would say him nay. But today it is against the law and no one in his right mind would condone such an action. And, have you forgotten? I'm already another man's wife. That fact cannot be excused or overlooked."

"Remember, Cathryn, even if someone somewhere wanted to enforce the law — wanted to find you and take you home, how would it be possible? No one knows who kidnapped you, or where you were taken. Even if they searched for the rest of your life, it is highly unlikely they would ever find you here."

Cathryn buried her face in her hands. "Stop it! Don't torment me!"

"No, child, I don't intend to torment you. I'm only telling you there isn't any sense in battering yourself against a stone wall. Take my advice and face the fact you are here to stay. If you try to make the best of it, who knows? You may begin to feel at home here."

Cathryn's green eyes grew stormy. "As much as you might like to believe that fairy tale, I can assure you right now I will never give up trying to find my way home. And nothing on earth could ever induce me to fall in love with your odious son!"

"What does odious mean?"

Startled, Cathryn and Margaret turned to see a beautiful little girl standing there. Her tiny heart-shaped face was surrounded by a soft mass of smoky black curls, and her dark eyes were wide and questioning. "Are you having a fight?"

Margaret laughed gently. "No, Meg, 'tis only a discussion. And it really isn't polite for you to interrupt."

"I'm very sorry. I didn't mean to bother you, but Mother sent me to ask if you could help me with my stitching." From behind her back she presented a crumpled piece of soiled linen, a snarl of colored threads criss-crossing its surface.

"Oh, dear, it certainly is tangled this time!" said Margaret MacLinn, shaking her head. "Meg, I'm beginning to think you will never make a needlewoman."

At the child's forlorn expression, she hastened to add, "Never mind, I'm positive we can have this back to normal in no time."

This caused the little girl to smile again. She tilted her face to have a better look at Cathryn.

"Are you the lady my mother says screams all the time? She says you are worse than a baby!"

"Meg! How rude of you!"

"I didn't mean to be rude . . ." she began.

"Of course, she didn't," broke in Cathryn. "After all, she did hear her mother say it." Looking down at the child, she asked, "Who is your mother, dear?"

"Her name is Darroch . . ."

"Ah, yes, I have met her then. And you know, I expect I was acting worse than a baby!"

"Sometimes I act like a baby, too, but it is only when I am ill or frightened. Were you frightened of something?"

Cathryn was completely enchanted by the exquisite little girl. Never in a thousand years would she have expected to find such a treasure in this crude place.

She found she couldn't take offense at the child's candid questions.

"Yes, I was very much afraid. But I am better now. This

lady has been very nice to me, you see . . ."

"Oh, of course! Grandmother is kind to everyone," the child said proudly.

Grandmother? thought Cathryn. How can that be?

Her eyes looked from one to the other, and, indeed, there was a similarity in appearance.

Margaret MacLinn caught the questioning look, and asked quietly, "Didn't you know?"

"Know what?" Cathryn asked, puzzled.

"Meg is Revan's child. I . . . I assumed he had told you about her."

Cathryn raised her chin to hide the surprise she felt. "No, he failed to mention the fact he had a child."

Margaret looked rather distressed. "I can't believe he hasn't told you! It's a pity you found out in such a way."

"Oh, believe me, it couldn't matter less."

"Do you know my father, too?" Meg asked. "Don't you think he is a very handsome man?"

Cathryn could not allow herself to tell the innocent child what she really thought of her father, so she smiled a small, tight smile and nodded.

"Darroch and Meg live here in the castle so the child can be close to Revan," Margaret explained. "They've never married, you know."

"Really, it doesn't matter."

"Well, Revan can tell you about it later. I'm sure he will want to . . ."

Cathryn interrupted the older woman. "Please believe me when I say it is of no interest to me. I must compliment you on the rare beauty of your little granddaughter, but, truly, I don't care to know her life's history."

"Very well, Cathryn."

"Now, if you will excuse me," Cathryn said, "I think I would like to go back to my room for a while. I still feel a bit weary and think I should rest for a time."

"As you wish, my dear. Perhaps you would like to take your meals in your room for the rest of the day? It might be easier for you to face the others when you feel better."

Cathryn could discern nothing but sympathy and concern

in the other woman's face. She hoped her own did not reveal any of the turmoil of emotion she was feeling inside.

"I'd like that very much. Thank you." She crossed to the door. "Oh, would you please inform your son where I have gone and tell him I will see him later?"

"Certainly."

Just at that moment Revan entered the room, followed by a large dark-colored hound. Seeing them, the child cried out, "Father!" and flung herself into his arms. Laughing, he swung her high in the air.

"Hello, Meg, I've been looking for you! And see who has been helping me look — King George!" He indicated the dog, whose tail was wagging joyously at the sight of the little girl.

Taking advantage of Revan's meeting with his daughter, Cathryn slipped out of the room and hurried down the hall to her own chamber. She slammed the door behind her and flung herself on the bed, surprised at the strength of her anger.

What kind of a man was this Revan MacLinn? Worse even than she thought, obviously. How could he have allowed any woman to bear his child out of wedlock? Now she began to understand why Darroch hated her so, and it would seem she had every right to do so.

Somehow this further proof of his black character and immorality made it even more imperative that she escape, and soon. A man who could have such a callous attitude toward a woman he bedded would have no qualms about kidnapping or worse.

Revan must have managed a hasty retreat from his mother's room, for suddenly, there he was, standing over her.

"You!" she hissed. "What do you want?"

"What has happened to your good humor, love? I suspected it was only an act all along. Now am I to be subjected to a dose of your usual spitefulness?"

She sat up on the bed. "Why did you follow me?"

"I was curious to know what you thought of my daughter," he said easily.

"Are you quite certain she is your child?" Cathryn spit.

86

"She is really quite lovely and seems so mannerly and intelligent!"

His laughter filled the room. "God, but you've a wicked tongue, Catriona. But then, 'tis one of the things I like best about you."

"Why din't you tell me you had a child?"

"It couldn't possibly make any difference, since I am not married to her mother."

Cathryn bristled. "And just what kind of man refuses to marry the mother of his child?"

A cold light glinted in his amber eyes. "You are not qualified to pass judgment, love, until you know all the facts."

"Decency is decency, even here in this desolate wasteland."

" 'Tis true. But the fact is, decency had nothing to do with the situation at all."

"I can't understand a man like you."

"Yes, I know. It would seem a virile, red-blooded man would be beyond the realm of your experience. I doubt Basil Calderwood ever had a lascivious thought in his life," he replied mockingly.

"Of course not. He, at least, has morals and integrity!"

"I can assure you, my love, if you had seen the man in his night shirt, morals and integrity would not have been nearly enough!"

Cathryn howled in fury and sprang at him, clawing for his eyes. He simply caught her wrists in his hands and shoved her back onto the bed, throwing himself full-length on top of her. She twisted and struggled, made furious by the excited light in his eyes, and by his soft amused laughter.

"Let me up, you hateful beast!"

"Not a chance. I'm having entirely too much fun."

Her struggles increased as she thrashed about trying to unbalance him. He positioned his long legs on either side of hers and pressed her deeper into the softness of the bed. Alarmed by the feel of his hard body against her, she abruptly stopped fighting and lay still, her eyes closed. He waited a few seconds, then raised himself so he could look into her face.

"Now, I will tell you the truth of it, Catriona. The child is mine and though you may not think such an emotion is possible from an inhuman brute like myself, I do love her dearly. I do not happen to love her mother . . ."

Through clenched teeth, Cathryn muttered, "I don't care."

"Yet you act as though you care very much. Surely you realized there would have been other women before you . . . ?"

She stiffened, too furious to even think of a retort to fling at him.

"Darroch and I were lovers once, but it was with the understanding it was for our mutual pleasure and nothing more. I made it perfectly clear to her she was not the type of woman I would marry."

"No, of course not! She was someone good enough to warm your bed, someone good enough to sacrifice her virginity and virtue . . ."

He laughed harshly. "Believe me, love, Darroch was no virgin when she came to me, and she possessed very little virtue—all the more reason for me to indulge in the relationship. Somewhere along the way, she became more emotionally involved than I, and sought to coerce me into marriage by producing a child. I meant it when I said I would not marry her. She was a fool to think a babe would make any difference. I would not be forced."

"No, you're too selfish for that."

"You are no doubt right. At any rate, I have given the child my name and a home, and I have grown to love her very much. But not even for her could I marry Darroch. No man could know happiness with that witchwoman. I only allow her inside the walls of this castle because I think Meg should know her mother. Not that it will ever do her much good. I fear maternity isn't Darroch's strong point."

Through her closed eyelids Cathryn could feel his burning gaze.

"Now, look at me, love," he commanded softly.

"No! Get off me and let me up."

"As soon as you look at me."

After a moment, he released her wrists. Suddenly she felt

his hands unbuttoning the bodice of her gown. Her eyes flew open in startled surprise.

"Ah, I thought that would get your attention soon enough! There is one more thing I would say to you, Catriona. Rest assured that Darroch poses no threat to you nor Meg any threat to our children . . ."

"You pig! Oh, I hate you! I really do!" she screamed. "Get off me and let me up."

"Anything you say, love. I just want to put your jealous mind at ease." He shifted his weight from her body and stood up. For a long time he stood looking down at her, hands on hips and an odd expression on his face.

"One thing I don't understand," he finally said. "Why doesn't the same disregard for convention that made me steal another man's wife now make me simply throw her down and rape her without further ado? Why was I blessed with so damned much patience?"

Before she could make some scathing reply, he whirled and was gone, slamming the door after him.

The rest of the day proved to be uneventful, for which Cathryn was grateful. Her emotions were so mixed and tangled, she no longer knew how she felt about anything. She stared into the fire for hours on end, trying to think of a way to get out of Wolfcrag.

No matter how she thought, it always came back to one person—Darroch. She alone had a valid reason for wanting Cathryn gone from the castle. Her possessive attachment to Revan might overcome any fear she had of him and prompt her to help with an escape plan.

Late in the afternoon, Cathryn went in search of the woman. She wandered down to the Great Hall without meeting anyone, and as she was trying to decide where to look next, she caught sight of the child, Meg and her hound playing near the fire.

"Hello, lady."

"Please call me Cathryn, won't you?"

"All right, and you can call me Meg. My real name is the

89

same as my grandmother's—Margaret Elizabeth MacLinn—but that's confusing, she says, so everyone calls me Meg."

"Meg is a very pretty name, I think."

"Thank you. Do you like my dog's name?"

Cathryn had to smile, in spite of herself. "It seems a bit treasonable, but it is a very dignified name."

"Sometimes we call him 'King' for short," Meg explained. She fondly patted the old hound, who lay at her side seemingly content just to be near her.

"Are there other children here for you to play with?" Cathryn asked, suddenly curious.

"Oh, yes, there are ever so many! My special friends are Rob and Ailsa, but Mother doesn't like for me to play with them too much."

"Why not?"

"Well, she says I shouldn't forget I am the chieftain's daughter, and that I am better than them." She frowned. "But I don't understand what she meant, do you?"

"No dear. No one is better than someone else. Perhaps your mother was mistaken."

"I'm sure she must be. Robbie and Ailsa are awfully good—better than me most of the time." A mischievous gleam lighted her eyes, and Cathryn realized she was her father's daughter, despite her feminine appearance and charm.

"Meg, speaking of your mother, I would like to visit her. Can you tell me where she is right now?"

"Come with me, and I'll take you to her. It isn't far."

Led by the child, Cathryn passed through the drawing room into a small sitting room. Darroch was relaxing in front of a cozy fire with a cup of tea. She was obviously surprised to see Cathryn.

"You have wandered a bit far afield, haven't you?" she asked.

"I wanted to talk to you," Cathryn began, then nodded toward the child, "privately, if possible."

"Meg, go up to your room and change your clothes for dinner. And see that infernal hound stays downstairs in the hall!"

"Yes, Mother." She gave Cathryn a quick look. "Can I come to see you later?"

"Meg, don't be a nuisance!" scolded her mother angrily.

"Oh, no, she's not a nuisance at all," Cathryn protested. "Please do come to see me, Meg. Do you know how to find me?"

"Yes, you're staying in my father's room. I'll come up after supper, shall I?"

"That will be fine. I'll see you then."

Obviously, Darroch did not like being reminded Cathryn was sleeping in Revan's bedroom, for her manner became quite brisk and curt.

"What could you possibly want to speak to me about?" she asked, in an icy voice.

"Look, Darroch, I'm beginning to understand why you are so against my coming here. I can't blame you!"

"Yes, I've heard you were rather upset about the child."

"I couldn't believe any man would treat a woman in such a manner! How cruel of him to let you go through that ordeal . . ."

"In all fairness to Revan," Darroch said drily, "I knew from the start I was taking a chance. I tried desperate measures, and they didn't work. It's simple as that."

"You Highlanders amaze me," Cathryn exclaimed. "Don't you ever get emotional?"

"Oh, my dear, you don't begin to know the depth of emotion running through the heart and mind of a Highlander. It may be slow to appear, but God help us all when it does. It doesn't matter if it's anger or greed or passion, it burns with a glorious flame!"

"Then, weren't you angry with Revan?"

"He made his position clear from the first. Any anger over the matter must be directed at myself." She shrugged. "And, when all is said and done, at least Meg has provided me with the opportunity to stay close to Revan."

"I can't pretend to understand your feeling in the matter, but I suppose it makes no difference."

"None at all," Darroch agreed.

91

"I want to know if you believe I was brought here against my will?"

Darroch laughed sharply. "Your screaming and pouting has made that fairly clear. Frankly, I am surprised Revan has humored you this long. He isn't an overly patient man, I can assure you."

"Yes, so I've been warned. That's really the reason I wanted to talk to you. I'm afraid of what might happen if I stay here much longer. All I really care about is getting back to my home, to my husband. I can't imagine how distraught and worried he must be. I'd like to return to him . . . unharmed, if you understand my meaning. Darroch, you are the only one who can help me!"

"How can I help you?"

"I know you don't want me here, and your reasons are excellent ones. If you can help me find a way out of Wolfcrag, I'll get back to my home, and your own life can return to normal."

Darroch looked thoughtful. "You make good sense, I must admit. In the seven years since Meg was born, Revan has never shown the interest in another woman that he has toward you. I fear he is completely serious when he says he means to keep you here. It would be very dangerous to plot against him."

"I'm not afraid of him! It's just that there is no way I can get outside the castle walls without help from someone."

"And you are correct in assuming I am the only one with reason enough to risk helping you. I confess, I'd like to see the last of you. But . . . the plan would have to be a foolproof one. I can't risk being found out by Revan."

"Do you think you could come up with something?" Cathryn asked. "Isn't there some way?"

"There may be, but I'll have to think on it for a while. Tomorrow would be a good time to act, because I heard Revan telling some of the men he would be gone most of the day on business. With him out of the castle, our chances would be much better."

Cathryn felt the stirring of hope. "Do you think you can devise a plan, then?"

"I am certainly going to try, believe me. I'll come to your room first thing in the morning and let you know what I have planned."

"I'm so grateful, Darroch. I knew I could count on you."

"There is one condition, however."

Darroch's voice was as hard as her eyes.

"And what is that?"

The dark-haired woman arose from her chair and came close to Cathryn.

"If Revan foils your escape plan, you must never implicate me. If you do, I will kill you, I swear."

Cathryn allowed her scorn to show in her voice. "Do you think I am so dishonorable? I will claim total responsibility, and Revan would never know anyone else had a hand in it."

"Just as long as you understand I can't take the chance of having him find out I was a party to this plot."

"I understand perfectly. I'll . . . I'll look forward to seeing you in the morning."

Darroch watched the other woman sweep out of the room, a pleased smile on her face and her shrewd mind already busy plotting. It would suit her quite well to see the last of Cathryn Calderwood.

Chapter Five

The morning brought another day of sunshine and Cathryn hoped it was a good omen. Revan came into the room while she was still in bed to inform her he would be gone most of the day and that, when he returned, he would complete her tour of the castle. His mind seemed occupied with thoughts of the day's business, and he failed to take note of the furtive excitement in her eyes.

Almost as soon as he was gone, Darroch appeared, carrying Cathryn's breakfast tray.

"Here," she said, thrusting it at Cathryn. "Eat heartily, for this will be a long day."

"You've thought of something?"

"Aye, I have a plan. Not completely foolproof, but the best I can arrange on such short notice."

"What are we going to do?"

Darroch sat down on the edge of the bed. "Can you ride?"

"Of course."

"Good. I am going to loan you a riding habit, and the two of us are going out for a little gallop this afternoon."

"How will we get past the gates?"

"Leave that to me," Darroch answered. "I will persuade the guards at the gate that it is all right. I will make them believe I can handle a little fool like you. Then, during our ride, a small accident will befall me, and you will, unfortunately, make your escape. By the time I regain consciousness and make my way back to the castle, you will be far south of here, riding for home."

"It sounds wonderful!"

"I'll slip into the kitchens right after the midday meal and find you some provisions. Let's see, you will need a warm plaid, also, as the weather may decide to turn nasty, and . . . well, I'll see to everything. You just wait here and, for heaven's sake, try to act normally."

"Thank you, Darroch. This means so much to me."

"Your gratitude may be premature, you realize. Don't thank me until you're safely away from Wolfcrag."

"May that be soon!"

After Darroch left, Cathryn ate her breakfast, too excited to be hungry, but practical enough to know she would need the strength the food provided. She dressed in the saffron gown again and settled herself with a book to wait out the long hours of the morning.

The book was interesting enough, but her thoughts were so turbulent and scattered she kept losing the thread of the story and finally laid it aside. Strangely enough, now that she had hope of leaving Wolfcrag, she began to think of the people here she might regret never seeing again.

Not Darroch and never Revan MacLinn, but Margaret, certainly, for she was a sweet woman with an aura of tragedy about her that was rather intriguing. And Meg—in an incredibly short time she had started to grow very fond of the pretty little girl. Perhaps she sensed a kindred spirit. Heaven knew, she had had a lonely enough childhood herself— maybe that was where the attraction lay.

She thought about the child's visit to her room the evening before. True to her word, Meg had come up the stairs to see her, bringing with her, in great secrecy, the dog, King George. The three of them had sat near the hearth for two hours, until Elsa came searching, saying it was time for Meg to go to bed.

She had been so cheerful and earnest, and so entertaining with her tales about the people and events at Wolfcrag that Cathryn regretted her being taken away to bed. And now she was planning to leave the child without so much as a goodbye. Still, it couldn't be helped. It would be too risky for anyone to know her plans.

At midday, Elsa appeared at the door with an invitation for her to join the other ladies for luncheon downstairs. As much as she would like to have declined, she knew it would seem more natural if she did not.

The meal was served in the small sitting room where she had talked to Darroch the day before. Seated around an ornate little table were Margaret MacLinn, Darroch and Meg.

"I'm glad you are joining us, Cathryn," Margaret said. "Meals are much simpler affairs when the men are gone, and you'll find this room far cozier than the drafty dining hall."

Cathryn looked about her, admiring a room that somehow she would not have expected to see in so remote a castle. She had been too intent on drawing Darroch into her escape plans to notice very much about it last night.

The walls were plastered and whitewashed, and over the fireplace were several colorful portraits of the MacLinn ancestry. A tartan carpet covered the floor, matching the drapes at the long rows of leaded glass windows. The sofa and chairs were a royal red, with polished oak trim. A tall clock ticked away in one corner and on the opposite wall were shelves of books.

It was a lovely, warm room — inviting and restful. Cathryn envied the MacLinns the use of it. Somehow, it made every room she had ever lived in seem cold and lacking in spirit.

"Isn't it pretty here?" Meg asked, noticing Cathryn's careful survey of the sitting room.

"Why, yes, it's one of the nicest rooms I've ever seen," Cathryn answered truthfully, seating herself at the fourth side of the table, which was laid with shining china and silver. She wondered if all the lovely items in the household were the result of yet more of the Highlanders' raids.

The serving girl was busily putting bowls of hot broth before them, and when she had gone, Darroch gave Cathryn a meaningful look and remarked, "It is truly a fine day, isn't it?"

"Oh, yes," Cathryn replied, taking her cue. "Do you think

. . ." She looked pleadingly at Margaret MacLinn. "Would it be possible for me to go for a ride?"

Margaret considered the request gravely. "As you know, my son is away from Wolfcrag today. I'm not at all sure he would want you to do such a thing."

"But he assured me I would be allowed to ride—with an escort, of course."

"Well, I am not certain there is anyone here who would be willing to take the responsibility," Margaret said.

"I suppose I could serve as her escort," Darroch cut in smoothly. "I have been entertaining the idea of going out myself. The weather has prevented riding for several days, and I am feeling the need of some fresh air."

"I don't know . . ." Margaret's uncertainty showed in her expression.

"We can stay within sight of the castle," Darroch stated. "What objection could Revan possibly have to that?"

"None, I suppose," his mother replied. "But I think it best to discuss it with the man at the gate."

"Oh, I shall," promised Darroch. "I certainly have no desire to go against Revan's wishes, though I just don't see how a simple ride could cause any harm."

Soon the second course, a meat pie with vegetables, was brought in, and the conversation turned to everyday matters.

When the meal was finished, Darroch announced she was going to go down to the courtyard. "I'll speak to the men in the stables and see if they won't saddle two horses for us. If no one objects to our ride, I will bring you a riding habit, Cathryn."

Cathryn nodded agreement and went to her room to wait. There was nothing she had to do to prepare for flight, for she had no personal belongings and no desire to take away any reminders of Wolfcrag.

After what seemed a lengthy wait, Darroch appeared, a riding habit and a woolen plaid thrown over her arm.

She tossed them to Cathryn. "Hurry, put these on."

Stripping off her gown, Cathryn asked, "Didn't anyone try to stop you?"

"The stable boys wouldn't dare," Darroch said, with a haughty toss of her head. "And as for MacQueen at the gate, I simply bargained with him. He seeks the favor of his chieftain, but fortunately, he hungers for my favors even more."

"Oh, heavens, what did you have to promise him?" Cathryn was shocked at the casual way Darroch spoke of bargaining.

"It doesn't matter, I don't intend to keep my end of the bargain. But, by the time MacQueen finds that out, you will be gone, and I will be recuperating from my accident, and under Revan's protection once again. He won't dare try to force the issue."

"I do hope you aren't putting yourself into any danger by helping me."

"I wouldn't take that chance, no matter how much I want you gone. Oh, in the beginning, Revan will be furious—perhaps even with me—but if I seem sufficiently wounded, he will have to believe my story, and the only thing he can be angry about is that I was fool enough to take it upon myself to escort you. Now, are you ready? We can't afford to lose any more time. Revan might decide to return to the castle early, and to make this work, you have to get a good head start on him. If he thought he could overtake you, he'd ride out immediately. He's a very stubborn man and does not give up his possessions easily."

"I'm not his possession," Cathryn snapped. "And I don't intend to be." Buttoning the jacket of the riding habit, she suddenly paused. "What if we meet Reven on the trail?"

"We aren't likely to," Darroch answered. "His business was taking him to the fishermen's crofts that lie north of the castle. He'll come and go by another path."

"Good." Cathryn draped the plaid across her shoulders, using another of the clan crest brooches to fasten it. As soon as she was able, she planned to discard the plaid and the pin, both painful reminders of her stay in the MacLinn household.

The saddled horses were waiting in the courtyard. As they mounted, they were met by a grinning hulk of a man

Cathryn surmised to be MacQueen. He laid a casual hand on Darroch's thigh and, though her mouth tightened, she said nothing.

"I've had my men raise the portcullis," he announced. "See that you don't go far or stay outside too long. If anything happens, the MacLinn will kill us all."

Darroch's voice was icy. "Don't worry! We'll stay within sight of the castle at all times. If you see something amiss, it will only take you a matter of minutes to get there."

She spurred her horse and rode forward, through the open gateway. Her heart in her mouth, Cathryn followed, keeping her eyes meekly downcast. Once they were free of the confining walls of the castle and crossing the narrow bridge, she could have shouted in exultation.

The sun felt warm on her back and she was free! Getting home was bound to be an ordeal, but at least she was on her way.

The two of them rode slowly single file until they were safely past the steep trail and onto the path leading through the wild glen. Looking back at Wolfcrag, Cathryn could see they were being watched by figures standing on the battlements.

"How are we going to make my escape look realistic?" she finally asked.

"When we get a bit further along this path, we will stop, and I will dismount. I'll make a great show of looking at my pony's hoof as if something is wrong. Then it must appear that we get into some sort of argument, and you will raise your riding crop and strike me. The blow will take me by surprise—I will stagger backward, fall and hit my head on a rock. By the time they see I am hurt, you can be gone. You'll have to hurry, for our plan succeeds or fails according to the speed of your departure."

"How can I pretend to strike you with the riding crop and make it look real?"

"I've thought of that, and I'm afraid there's nothing you can do but actually strike me."

"But I might hurt you," Cathryn exclaimed.

"As much as I hate to say so, it will only give credence to

my story. If you can hit me hard enough to leave a mark, Revan will have to believe you overpowered me. Otherwise, he might find it difficult to believe my tale of woe. Don't think I like putting myself into this position, but it has to look convincing."

Cathryn was doubtful, but if the plan was to work, she would have to go along with whatever Darroch said. Somehow, she would so much rather have applied the riding crop to the wide shoulders or smirking face of Revan MacLinn!

They rode on for about ten minutes, then Darroch reined up her horse to dismount.

"Now, make this look real! A misstep here could ruin everything." She slid to the ground and began to examine the horse's foreleg. "You have food in that saddle pouch and your plaid to help keep you warm. If you ride straight to the end of the glen, then bear southward, you will eventually come to some scattered villages. Anyone there can set you on the right road to the Lowlands. Just don't linger, for Revan may be right behind you. You'll either have to rest your horse or purchase a different one. I've put some gold into the pouch, also. From now on, you're on your own. I hope you make it safely, for all our sakes."

Cathryn fingered the riding crop, wondering when she should strike the blow. She was reluctant to use it and had to admire Darroch's courage as she dropped the horse's foreleg and turned to face Cathryn.

"I don't know how to thank you, Darroch."

"By going back to your husband and staying out of Revan's life," replied Darroch. "Make sure you aren't such an easy victim next time."

"I have no intention of ever setting eyes on Revan MacLinn again. If he should follow me home, my husband will kill him . . . or I will!"

Darroch laughed mockingly. "You know, I truly believe you are stupid enough to mean what you say. Only an idiot would treat a man like Revan the way you have . . ."

"How dare you?" Cathryn gasped.

"I dare because it's the truth. You are too blinded by your prudery and maidenly ways to see he is twice the man others

100

are. Including your precious husband! You know, it's a good thing you never shared a bed with Revan—you're not woman enough for him! How quickly he would tire of your childish, whining ways. In all these years he has never tired of me, I can assure you."

Cathryn raised the riding crop and, without thinking, brought it slashing across one side of Darroch's face. Blood welled instantly, and the woman screamed out in pain. Shocked at her own action, Cathryn was motionless for a long moment, then spurred her horse and began a mad gallop down the glen. Darroch's final words echoed in her ears.

"Damn you to hell!"

One quick glance backward told her Darroch was now lying on the ground, skirts spread around her.

Quite an actress, she thought sourly, then gave up her mind to the task that lay ahead. Leaning forward in the saddle, hugging the horse's neck, she rode as she had never ridden before—toward home and safety.

Cathryn was unaware of the storm building until she heard the distant rumble of thunder. For the past two hours she had really been aware of nothing except the straining animal beneath her and the thump of her own heartbeat. Every mile took her further and further from the nightmare of Wolfcrag and that thought sustained her.

At last she dared stop a while to rest the horse. She had left the sheltered enclosure of the deep glen, and now found herself on a rather desolate tract of moorland. She slid from the horse, glad of the opportunity to rest her aching back and shoulders. Leading the animal to a nearby burn to drink, she cast a wary eye at the clouds overhead.

The sky to the northwest had darkened considerably and a bank of high-piled clouds forecast heavy rain. She loosened the plaid and wrapped it around her for warmth, knowing the night ahead was going to be a long, cold one.

From the saddlebag she took a bannock and ate it quickly, then stooped to drink from the icy burn. Casting a fearful glance behind her, she felt it was time to move on. She had come too far now to risk being overtaken by the MacLinns.

She eased her tired body onto the horse's back and began to ride again, though at a somewhat slower pace. The animal was showing signs of exhaustion, she was afraid, and it was unlikely she could replace it until morning. It was nearly dark now and few people would be willing to take in a stranger who appeared out of the night. Besides, she dared not throw herself on anyone's mercy just yet — she might still be on MacLinn land, and they could possibly recognize her. Not that she had seen any crofts or cottages thus far, and certainly no villages. This was a Godforsaken corner of the world, to be sure.

As the sun disappeared behind the billowing mass of storm clouds, a cold wind sprang up, and the first promise of rain was in the air. Cathryn tightened the plaid, pulling it up over her head, and rode on. Soon it would be dark, and with no moon, she might not be able to travel further. She had to put as much distance between herself and Wolfcrag as possible.

An uneasy silence greeted Revan and his men when they rode into the courtyard. He knew something was amiss as soon as he dismounted and handed the reins to the stableboy. MacQueen, far from being his usual blustering self, was standing just inside the gates, hat in hand, looking every inch the guilty culprit.

"Is there a problem, MacQueen?" Revan asked easily.

The man could not meet his eyes. "Aye, lad. That Lowland bitch has attacked Darroch and escaped."

"What!" Revan's voice thundered and the bigger man quailed before him. "What the devil are you saying?"

"Just that. The red-haired gal slashed Darroch across the face with a whip and rode away. We tried to follow her but she had the jump on us."

"She was on a horse?" The chieftain's tone was deadly.

MacQueen swallowed hard. "Yes, sir . . . the two of them went for a ride and something happened to Miss Darroch's mount. When she got off to have a look, the other girl hit her in the face with her crop and got away. Miss Darroch is hurt pretty bad."

Revan's face hardened—his thick brows drew together in a straight line. "Where is she?" he rasped out. "I want to see her. Now!"

"We took her to the doctor's cottage. You'll find her there."

Without another word, Revan turned and strode to a small cottage located in a far corner of the courtyard. With a brief knock at the door, he pushed it open and entered.

"Darroch?" he boomed.

The doctor, a short, rotund fellow with a wisp of gingery hair on an otherwise bald head, stepped into his path and said, "Now, lad, easy. You'll find Darroch in an uncertain condition at best. She's had a bad blow to the head, and as for her face—well, see for yourself."

Revan turned to the figure struggling up from a cot in the dark corner. Darroch's voice came out of the darkness with pitiful weakness.

"Revan, is that you?"

"Aye."

"Oh, Revan, how could I have been so stupid? I didn't realize what a ruthless bitch she could be. Look what she did to me!"

He stepped closer and was appalled at the angry red wound running the entire length of her face. "Cathryn did that?" he asked, taken aback.

"I can assure you she did," cut in the doctor. "It will be a lucky thing if we can get this wound to heal without leaving a permanent and disfiguring scar."

"She was brutal, Revan. I didn't have a chance of stopping her."

"Why in the hell were you out riding in the first place? Who gave you permission to go?"

"We were all taken in by her meek attitude. Ask your mother! When we were having our midday meal, an innocent remark was made about the weather being nice, and Cathryn inquired so sweetly about going out for a short ride. I . . . I thought it would be all right if she had an escort. You yourself told her it would be."

"I'm aware of that. Go on." His voice was expressionless and Darroch wished the room was not so dark. She would like to have seen his face as she told her story.

"I spoke to MacQueen about it, and he agreed it would do no harm for us to ride out, as long as we stayed within sight of Wolfcrag. And we did, I swear it! It's just that, when she hit me across the face, it took me so by surprise I fell backward, striking my head on a stone. I guess I fainted or something, because the next thing I knew, MacQueen and his men were there and Cathryn was gone."

"MacQueen is a damned incompetent half-wit!" Revan raged. "And you, Darroch! Blast you for a meddling, interfering busybody. I'm going after Cathryn now, and if I don't find her, you had better be out of my reach, for, so help me, I won't be responsible for my actions."

The door slammed behind him, shaking the cottage to its foundation, but Darroch only smiled a small, painful smile. He would get over his initial anger eventually, and with his precious Cathryn gone, sooner or later, he would turn to her again.

"Owen," Revan shouted as he stormed across the courtyard, "round up six or seven men to go with us and find us some food. Get the stablehands to saddle fresh horses — we're going after Catriona. MacQueen, don't think I've forgotten you. Come with me while I change and tell me your version of the story. And, by God, man, it had better be good!"

Cathryn thought she would never be warm again. For the last two hours the rain had poured down steadily, drenching her to the skin. The woolen plaid was sodden, its heaviness dragging against her shoulders. Each step she took was torture; her boots had long since been battered by the stony ground on which she walked and her feet were badly bruised.

If only she hadn't stopped to rest that last time, she thought. Completely exhausted, she had unintentionally fallen asleep, propped against a boulder. When the rain awakened her, the horse was gone. Thinking it had just wandered a short distance away, she searched for it, straining her eyes in the darkness, tripping over the tough roots of heather and gorse, occasionally falling. In her agitation, she had lost her way entirely and no longer knew which direction she was headed.

Confused and frightened, she only knew she had to find shelter somewhere until the rain stopped, and the sun came up. She was so cold! If only she had the means to start a fire . . .

She scraped back wet strands of hair that blocked her vision. Her fingers were so cold they felt numb, and her head was throbbing intolerably. She had to find a place to rest.

Just then the ground beneath her feet gave way and she was slipping knee-deep into the icy mud of a Highland bog. Sobbing in terror, she fought the mud and slime, throwing her body back toward firmer ground. With the last bit of strength she possessed, she managed to drag herself a small distance from the marsh, but she was unable to go on.

As she lay there, no longer conscious of the wet grass beneath her face, a vision of her childhood home came into her weary mind. There was her father, looking so stern and angry, not at all happy to see her. In her joy at seeing him, she tried to call out his name, but her voice was only a whisper. She reached out a hand to him, and he disappeared. Her clutching fingers wrapped around some hard metal object and she brought it close to her eyes, trying to see what it was. It was the wolf's-head brooch — it must have fallen off the plaid in her struggle. She stared at it unseeingly for a long moment, then closed her fingers around it and slept.

The last sound to pierce her consciousness was the distant howl of a marauding wolf, somewhere in the rain-shrouded night.

When the sun rose in the morning, it shone on a world covered with heavy frost. Every blade of grass was encased in

105

a coat of ice and the breath of men and animals came out in huge steaming clouds.

Revan MacLinn rode quietly, his eyes moving back and forth over the landscape ahead. Behind him his men exchanged looks of despair; they knew him well enough to know he was not going to give up this search easily.

Indeed, he would have driven them all night long, had not Owen MacIvor found the words to convince him it was best they take shelter from the elements. They had spent the last half of the night huddled in a cave with their horses, a small brush fire putting forth a brave glow and a little warmth. The men were glad for the chance to rest and eat, but Revan spent the time pacing back and forth at the mouth of the cave, stopping now and then to stare out into the black night.

As soon as light started to creep into the sky, he urged them to get mounted so they could start the search again. Now, more than an hour later, they had found no sign of the girl, and all but their chieftain had given up hope.

At first the trail she left had been an easy one to follow, but with the onset of night and the heavy rains, they had no way of knowing if they were even traveling in the right direction. It was pure madness to go on.

Finally, Owen MacIvor reined in his horse beside Revan's and summoned his courage to speak. "Lad, it's no use. If she got this far, we'll not catch her. Don't you think we'd best turn back for the castle? The men are tired and cold—there's no point in going on."

"Aye, you are no doubt right, Owen. Why don't you take the men and return to Wolfcrag?"

"And you?"

"I'll keep looking a while longer."

"We'll not return without you, Revan. It's crazy for you to go on."

"Mayhap you are right, Owen, but I can't give up just yet . . ."

At that moment one of the men behind them let out a shout.

"Look! Over there—I see something."

Looking in the direction he pointed, Revan seemed to come to life. "It's her horse! That means she may be nearby—perhaps she is injured. All of you, get off your horses and walk this area on foot. We have to find her."

The small group of men dismounted, spreading out to cover every inch of the marshy ground.

"Here she is, Revan," shouted Owen, a few minutes later. "Over here!"

Revan was beside him in an instant. He stopped short at the sight of the slim, plaid-wrapped body lying in the high scrub. Quickly he made his way to it and knelt down.

"God forbid, she's not dead, is she?" asked Owen.

Revan felt her throat for a pulse. Her flesh was cold to his touch and the pulse was feeble. "She is breathing, but just barely. We've got to get her back to the castle."

He scooped her into his arms. "Owen, strip off that plaid. It's soaked clear through. I've got a dry one in my saddle-bags."

The big Highlander gently eased the woolen garment from around the unconscious girl. As he lifted one arm, he caught the gleam of silver. Opening her clenched fingers, he saw the MacLinn crest.

Closing her hand over the brooch again, his eyes met Revan's. "What do you make of that?" he asked.

"I don't know, Owen. She probably wanted to keep it near to remind her just who was responsible for her ordeal." He smiled wryly. "I have much to answer for this time, my friend."

Chapter Six

They were seen approaching the castle and the portcullis was raised in one smooth motion. The horses' hooves clattered on the stones of the courtyard, and stablehands ran to hold the animals while their weary riders dismounted.

Owen MacIvor leaped from his horse and took Cathryn's still form from Revan. As soon as Revan's boots hit the cobblestones, he reclaimed her and strode toward the front entrance, calling out orders as he went.

"Owen, find the doctor and send him to my room. Donald, see to the horses — Dougal, go tell the cook these men require a hot breakfast!"

The front door swung open as he neared, and Elsa stood aside to let him enter the hall. She gasped in shock at the sight of Cathryn.

"Oh, lord, sir! Is she dead?"

"She soon will be, Elsa, if we don't do something." He started up the stairway. "Can you bring some hot water, towels and a nightgown to my room right away?"

"Oh, yes, sir. Right away!" Elsa caught sight of one of the kitchen girls lingering near and called out, "You, Jeanie! Go with the master and open the door to the bedchamber. Help him get the lady to bed."

She sped away on her own errands, while Jeanie flew up the stairs, darting around Revan to throw open the door.

"Mind the fire, Jeanie," Revan said as he laid Cathryn on the bed. "It will have to be kept burning brightly."

While the young girl busied herself stirring the fire and

throwing on more wood, he began to strip Cathryn's soaked and ruined clothes from her body.

He pulled off the torn boots and tossed them aside. His jaw tightened at the sight of her bruised feet. He rubbed them gently between his two hands, dismayed at how icy they felt.

As he unbuttoned and removed the riding habit and tore away her camisole and petticoat, he thought her body could have been carved from marble, it was so cold and lifeless. He pulled a blanket from the bed and wrapped it around her.

Elsa hurried into the room with a steaming basin in her hands and a pile of linen cloths draped over her shoulder. Revan pulled a small table close to the bed and took the basin of hot water from her.

"I've brought a nightgown for her, but I expect we had better get some of that mud off the poor wee lassie," fussed Elsa.

"Aye, it would appear she spent a considerable amount of time in the bog," Revan said grimly. He pulled the blanket away and Elsa began cleansing Cathryn's feet and legs. After she finished with the washing, he took the towels and rubbed the chilled limbs briskly, tucking the blanket around them again.

While Elsa washed the girl's arms, Revan picked up her right hand and gently loosened the fingers from the silver brooch, which he laid aside on the bed table. The wolf's head was imprinted on the palm of her hand like a brand. Somehow the sight of it caused a powerful emotion to rise within Revan and he flung himself away from the bed, almost angrily.

"Where in hell is that blasted doctor?" he raged.

"Here, lad—right here," panted the stout physician, rushing into the bedchamber clutching a small leather bag. "Calm yourself! You'll not do one whit of good by ranting and raving. In fact, you'll be most helpful if you'll clear out for a bit and let me have a look at the young lady."

"You may need my help . . ." began Revan.

"You can best help by going downstairs and getting yourself something to eat. Have some whiskey while you're at it. Elsa can put the girl into a nightgown and then I'll make my examination. I'll soon be down to talk to you."

Margaret MacLinn was waiting for him as he left the bedchamber.

Anxiously, she laid her hand on his arm and said, "Thank goodness you found her, Revan. How is she?"

"As of this moment, I fear she is more dead than alive."

"I am certain the doctor will know what to do, Son," Margaret soothed. "Where did you find the girl?"

"Lying in the frozen mud along the edge of a bog," he answered flatly. "The little fool had lost her horse somehow and was wandering about on foot—in the rain and dark! Good God, what must she have been thinking of?"

"Sometimes people do senseless and foolish things in their desperation."

"Yes, and she was made desperate by her fear of me. You don't have to remind me," he said bitterly.

"Don't blame yourself, Revan. If we are going to start pointing the finger of guilt, I myself will be called to account. I should have put an absolute end to the idea of Cathryn and Darroch going out on a ride. Despite her attitude, I should have known she had not yet given up the idea of getting back to her husband."

His face darkened so at her words that she hastened on. "And you cannot deny the part Darroch and MacQueen played in all of it. No, we are all to blame in some way or another."

"Who brought her here against her will? Who kept her here, knowing she hated and feared me? No, if she dies, it isn't any of you who will be to blame."

Knowing there really was nothing more she could say, Margaret urged her son to join the rest of the men at breakfast. Together they went down to the Great Hall and, as they entered, all talk and laughter ceased. Each man looked furtively at his chieftain's face, and no one dared risk speaking to him. Even Owen remained silent for the time being.

Revan refused food but poured out a measure of Scottish whiskey and stood drinking it in front of the fire, one booted foot on the hearthstone, staring into the flames. He didn't move until the doctor came in some time later.

"Well?" he asked, breaking the uneasy silence.

"I can't deny the truth, Revan. The girl is gravely ill. So ill, in fact, she may not survive until evening."

"What in hell are you trying to tell me?" he thundered, clutching the front of the shorter man's shirt.

"Now, lad, I'm doing all I can . . ." Somehow the fear in his eyes registered in Revan's anxious brain and he loosened his grip.

"Sorry, man, I'm out of my mind with worry. I know you're doing all that can be done."

"Aye. She was exposed to some very harsh weather and her lungs sound extremely congested. Her breathing is very labored and will no doubt get worse before it's over. I've put some salves and unguents on her chest and covered them with a poultice. We'll keep a steaming kettle of herbs on the fire to help ease her breathing. I've mixed up some medicine she'll have to be given regularly, every few hours. I'll send my wife up to help look after her. Della's the best nurse I know."

"Is there anything else we can do?" Revan asked.

"We've got to keep her warm. That's very important."

"How long do you think it will be before we know if she is going to get better?"

"I'm afraid to say, lad. The fever will be on her by nightfall, and after that . . ." He shrugged. "She'll need all her strength to fight it. If she can't . . . there's nothing we can do."

Revan ran a distracted hand through his thick black hair. "I see."

"And now, you and all the men who were out in the foul weather last night should get some rest. We don't want anyone else coming down with a fever." He shook a finger at Revan. "You look pretty ragged, so I'm warning you, take care of yourself."

"I will, I will," Revan said impatiently.

"I've given the girl her medicine, and Della will come up in a couple of hours to dose her again. Young Clint MacLinn's wife is in labor with her first child, so if you need me, send someone to his cottage."

When the little man had bustled out of the castle, Revan returned to his room. As soon as he stepped inside the door, he could hear Cathryn's slow and labored breathing. The air was warm and humid, redolent of sweet herbs. Elsa was standing over the girl, straightening the bedcovers.

"You can go now, Elsa," the man said. "I'll stay here with her."

"You'll call if you need something?"

"Aye. I'll call."

Revan pulled an armchair close to Cathryn's bedside and sank into it. He kicked off his boots and lay back his head, letting weariness overtake him.

The sound of someone moving about the room woke him a few hours later. He saw a tall, elegant lady stirring the fire and checking the pot of herbs.

"Della, is that you?" he asked, sitting up. Someone had thrown a blanket over him while he slept, and now it went sliding to the floor.

"Oh, Revan, you're awake! I'm sorry, I should have been more quiet." The woman crossed the room to stand before him, but his attention was turned to the still form in the bed.

"Your husband boasted that you were a good nurse. I hope there is something you can do for Cathryn."

Together they studied the waxen face, surrounded by vivid bronze hair spread over the pillow. Long dark lashes made heavy shadows on her cheeks, and there was no trace of her usual rosy coloring.

"I'll do what I can, but at this stage of the illness, we can only wait—and pray."

Cathryn stirred slightly, and a tremor seemed to shake her frail body. A moan sounded from between pale lips.

Revan jumped to his feet and stood over her. His fearful eyes seemed to burn right through Della MacSween.

"What is it? What's wrong?"

"Don't be alarmed. As my husband told you, the fever will grow worse tonight and, when it does, you must expect the

112

poor girl to be restless. She may even become delirious. Patients often do with the ague, you know. She will have bouts of chilling and shaking, and while it will seem particularly horrible to you, she very likely won't remember any of it when she recovers."

"You mean if she recovers, don't you?" Revan asked grimly.

"Don't think that way! The worst thing you can do is give up hope. Keep a good attitude and all will turn out well in the end." Her kind eyes sparkled. "Of course, as I said, it never hurts to pray a little in the meantime."

"Pray? I hardly have to tell you that is something of which I have very little knowledge."

She laughed softly. "Then, there is no time like the present for getting better acquainted with the process. Believe me, it will stand you in good stead. Now, I have administered her medicine, so I think I should go see if my husband needs any help with the birthing. I'll leave you to watch over Cathryn until I can get back."

She gave him a steady look. "You won't be alarmed by the fever, will you?"

"No doubt I've seen worse in battle," was his clipped reply. Della MacSween nodded briskly and made her departure. It was her experience that the fiercest warriors, who risked their own lives without a qualm, were the first to grow fainthearted when called upon to witness the suffering of someone they cared about. She doubted if Revan MacLinn would be any different!

In another hour, Revan found he couldn't remember ever having had a more harrowing experience — on the battlefield or off — than he was having watching Cathryn struggle against the illness that possessed her.

He paced the floor and cursed, furious at his helplessness. As the fever took hold, she thrashed about in the bed, sometimes calling out deliriously and sometimes seized by terrible bouts of shivering.

Straining to catch her words, Revan knelt by her bedside

and leaned over her, smoothing her tangled hair away from her burning forehead.

"What is it, Catriona?" he murmured. "What do you want?"

"Cold! I'm so cold," she moaned. "The rain . . ."

He wrenched open the chest at the foot of the bed and dragged out another blanket which he spread over her. The doctor had emphasized the importance of keeping her warm, he knew.

He tossed more wood onto an already blazing fire, at a loss as to any other way to make the room warmer.

Cathryn was muttering again, tossing her head from side to side. Her teeth were chattering so she could hardly get out the words, but Revan was stricken to hear her say, "Please don't let me be cold. I'm freezing!"

Finally, in desperation, he stripped off his own clothes and, pulling back the mound of bedcovers, crawled into the bed beside her, gathering her close in his arms. He must try to warm her with the heat of his own body.

At first she struggled, her fever-clouded mind warning her something was amiss. At last, however, as his warmth began to envelop her, she relaxed and snuggled close against him.

He rested his chin on the top of her head, holding her in the firm curve of his arm. Her hair was soft and fragrant as it swirled around him.

Revan sighed. How many times had he imagined just such a scene as this? How ironic that it should happen under these circumstances. As Cathryn grew quieter, he let his thoughts wander and finally drifted back into an uneasy sleep himself.

Della MacSween found them sleeping thus when she reappeared at nightfall. Revan opened one eye to see her standing over them, her handsome face lighted by a wide smile.

"I'm not sure this is what the doctor had in mind, but I must admit, it seems a very effective way of keeping the lady warm."

"To tell you the truth, I couldn't think of any other way to

114

do it," Revan said with a smile. "I never knew playing nursemaid could be such a pleasant task!"

"Well, I warn you, not everything we nurses are called upon to do is pleasant. As a matter of fact, I have come to perform one of the more unpleasant duties—getting the patient to take her medicine. It tastes vile, I can assure you."

From the table she took a corked bottle and spoon. Opening the container, she poured a dark liquid into the spoon.

"Now, if you will just hold her gently, I'll slip this into her mouth. No doubt it will be easier this way."

Revan's arm supported Cathryn's head and Mrs. MacSween easily tilted the liquid down her throat. She coughed once or twice and turned her head, but didn't open her eyes.

"How long will she go on sleeping?" Revan asked in concern.

"It's very difficult to tell, but don't worry. My husband thinks it is generally a good sign."

"At least she is resting a bit more peacefully than before."

"Due to your fervent ministrations, no doubt," teased the doctor's wife. "You really should tear yourself away for a while, however, and go have something to eat. You don't want to become ill, too, and your mother tells me you haven't eaten anything all day."

" 'Tis true," he replied. "And to be honest, I think I am beginning to feel ravenously hungry."

"A good rest can do that," she agreed. "Would you like for me to stay with Cathryn while you are gone?"

His smile was swift and, she thought, very charming. He sat up in the bed, carefully settling Cathryn's bronze head back onto the pillows. "I'd appreciate that very much. I won't be long . . ."

He began to toss aside the bedcovers, but she cast one quick look at the pile of his clothing on the floor and cried, "Wait! I'll just step outside until you're dressed."

He grinned. "As you wish, Della."

Revan took time for a good meal and a few words with Owen MacIvor, then resumed his watch in the sick room, taking a bottle of whiskey and a glass up with him.

Cathryn was just the same when he returned, though again, Della MacSween urged him to stop worrying.

"It always seems worse to the onlooker," she stated. "Cathryn may seem to be in great pain to you, but I promise, she won't recall much of what is happening now. If she can make it past this first night or two, I think she will be just fine. She sounds like a strong-willed young lady from what I've been told."

"Aye, she is that," Revan said wryly.

"Darroch has told me something of the girl," Della went on. "After her injuries, she spent the night in our cottage and as she talked, she explained Cathryn's situation."

"I'm sure that was a very enlightening conversation."

The woman couldn't help but laugh. "Yes, it was indeed. You know, I can't recall anyone ever standing up to Darroch before. That is why I say your Cathryn must be very strong-willed."

"By the way, how is Darroch? She took a nasty blow."

"More to her pride than otherwise," Della said dryly. "Still and all, the wound will be a long time healing. My husband gave her some salve she can use to prevent a scar on her face. What she will do about the scar on her pride, none of us care to speculate."

"Yes, she cared little for Cathryn from the beginning. Now . . ." He shrugged. "I'll have to worry about that later, I suppose."

"Indeed. Now, I must go. Shall I come back at midnight to give her more medicine or do you think you can manage?"

"I'll manage. But should she get worse, I'll send someone for you and your husband."

"Very well. Now, have a good night's rest if you can."

When she was gone, Revan settled into his armchair and poured a glass of whiskey. This he sipped as he stared alternately at the fire and at Cathryn's feverish face.

Just before time for her medicine, the chilling began with renewed vigor, and she cried out several times. The sound of

116

her terror-stricken voice cut right through Revan, and it frustrated him because he could do nothing to ease her nightmares.

Supporting her quaking body, he forced the medicine between her feverish lips and held her as she swallowed it, coughing painfully.

As the mellow chimes of the old clock on the corner desk rang out, he stripped off his clothes and once again crawled underneath the covers beside her. Through the long night when she was wracked with chills and fever, he held her close and comforted her in soft Gaelic phrases. Once, as he was drifting off to sleep after one prolonged bout, he smiled to himself to think how outraged the fiery Cathryn would be if only she knew his naked form was stretched so close beside her, holding her in such an intimate embrace!

There was very little change in Cathryn's condition for the next several days. Someone was with her every moment, keeping up the fire, seeing to her medicine, and bathing her hot forehead. Now she alternated between fever and chills, so for a while the blankets would be piled high, and then, one by one, removed. A harsh, hacking cough began to plague her, but, again, the doctor said it was encouraging.

"I feel it means the congestion is loosening up somewhat," he explained. "We'll keep using the unguents and keep the air moist with herbs. So far it seems to have done only good."

He and his wife spent a great deal of time in the room watching over Cathryn, and Revan grew used to depending on them. He remembered the first time he'd met them — he had thought them a very odd pair; the doctor seemed much older than his wife and was a short, pudgy, nondescript sort of fellow, while Della was tall, slender and quite comely in a reserved and quiet way. However, he noticed how well they worked together and how much each respected the other.

Revan sighed heavily. That was the way it should be between a husband and wife. The way it had been with his own parents. The way he had wanted it to be for himself. Perhaps it took a patience he didn't have — or perhaps it was

117

strictly a matter of luck, after all.

He was grateful to Doc MacSween and his wife, for their encouragement had helped him get through some very bleak hours. If Cathryn lived, he knew he had them to thank.

One afternoon as he sat by her bedside reading, a knock sounded at the door, and Darroch entered the room. She came close to the bed and stood watching Cathryn with an undecipherable expression on her face—a face still marred by the thin red line running down one side.

"So you brought her back?"

"Did you doubt it?"

"I hoped you wouldn't find her," she said honestly. "It would have been best if she had found her way home."

"I know where she lived. What makes you think I wouldn't have gone there to bring her back?"

"Someone there would have stopped you, Revan, surely. Having regained their treasure, I'm certain they wouldn't have given her up so easily a second time." She turned her dark eyes on his face. "Do you know, she told me she would kill you herself if you tried to take her from her home again?"

A broad grin lighted his bearded face. "She did, did she?"

"Oh, Revan, you fatuous dolt! You look as if you think her words were unusually charming or clever."

"Unusually spirited is more like it. It amuses me that someone so small and weak should have every confidence that, should the need arise, she could slay me single-handedly!"

His laughter rumbled, further irritating Darroch.

"Does this scar on my face look like the handiwork of a small and helpless person?" she demanded. "Not likely. I think your precious Cathryn is more vicious and capable of treachery than you give her credit for. If I were you, darling, I wouldn't turn my back on her. Not as much as she hates you!"

"Did she tell you she hated me?" he asked, interested.

"Oh, yes, in very clear language. And it does me a great deal of good to see you groveling at the feet of a beautiful woman who doesn't want you. One who won't obligingly fall into your arms."

"As you once did, my dear?" His eyes narrowed.

"Yes, unfortunately, as I once did." She came close to him. "And as I would again, if given the chance."

"Sorry, Darroch, that kind of thing is in my past. You know I've always been honest about the kind of woman I want to marry. Now I have found that woman, and I intend to lead a different type of life."

"Saving yourself for her alone?" she sneered.

"Surely you can't have forgotten the MacLinn motto — 'Above all, faithfulness'?" he asked, lightly.

"How trite," she mocked. "You know, you and this Cathryn may just be perfect for each other after all — you are both the biggest fools I have ever met. She because she doesn't want you, and you because you can't accept the fact she will never love you."

"You are right, I'll never accept that. Do you think I would have gone to so much trouble, risked so much, if I wasn't certain we were meant to be together?"

"Somehow she has blinded you, Revan. I don't know how or whether you'll ever regain your senses or not, but if she stays here, nothing is ever going to be the same."

He shrugged. "She stays, no matter what."

"Then, mark my words, you will be sorry! Have you never read the Bible tale about Samson and Delilah? Well, Revan, that's your Delilah lying there in that bed! And you can be certain of this — someday she is going to shear you closer than a Highland sheep!"

"Much to your enjoyment, of course."

"Of course."

Darroch turned to leave the room, but paused in the doorway to say, "If she should awaken, tell her I was asking about her and that I will be back to see her — sooner or later." One hand went up to caress the weal across her face. "We have a great deal to discuss."

After a full week had passed, the fever and chills were gone and, though she sometimes slept restlessly, Cathryn seemed much better. The doctor assured Revan she was recovering,

119

though slowly, and warned him not to be too impatient.

"Let her rest and sleep all she can. Awareness will come back to her shortly, I promise."

Now that she was so improved, Revan began sleeping in the small dressing room which adjoined his bedchamber. Though he missed spending the nights by her side, he knew it would be disastrous if she should fully awaken while he was in her bed.

There were times now when she would open her eyes, but the things she saw were yet in her mind and not in the room with her. Once or twice she had called out for Basil, and when that happened, Revan left the room in a silent rage, though why he should be jealous of the older man he didn't know.

As Cathryn improved and grew stronger, he returned to the business of the estate, which he had neglected far too long. He knew she would be in capable hands with either Elsa or Della MacSween in attendance. It also pleased him that, most afternoons, his mother and Meg went in to stay with Cathryn.

When Cathryn first opened her eyes, she didn't know where she was. Nothing at all looked familiar until she saw the MacLinn tartan blazing at her from the darkened corner. Tartan drapes!

Her heart sank, and she let her head drop back onto the pillow.

I must have been dreaming, she thought wearily. I thought I had gone home.

A cool hand was applied to her forehead and a calm voice said, "Hello, Cathryn. Are you feeling better?"

"Who are you?" Cathryn asked in a weak voice.

"I'm Della MacSween, the doctor's wife. I've been helping to care for you while you've been ill."

"Have I been ill?"

"Very ill, indeed. For a time, we weren't sure you would survive. You certainly frightened Revan."

"Revan?"

"He has been here day and night, watching over you."

Helpless tears trickled out of Cathryn's eyes and ran down her pale cheeks.

"I just wanted to go home!" she wailed.

The lady sat on the edge of the bed and took Cathryn's thin hands.

"Oh, my dear, please don't cry. You should be happy you are so much better."

"But you don't understand . . ." Her huge silver-green eyes fastened on Della's face in desperation as memories began flooding her confused mind. "I wanted to get away from Revan MacLinn so much! And I . . . I think I hurt Darroch terribly. I never meant to strike her so hard."

"Don't worry, she's fine. Truly."

"I'm glad," Cathryn murmured. "Was . . . was Revan very angry?"

"No, only anxious to find you. He saved your life, Cathryn, by riding after you. A few more hours in the open and there isn't any medicine that would have made you well again."

"I would have died?"

"Without doubt. Be thankful Revan came after you, that he cares so much for you."

Cathryn's head dropped wearily back onto the pillows and she closed her eyes for a long moment. When she opened them again, she asked, "Do you know how I came to be at Wolfcrag, Della?"

"Aye, I expect everyone knows the story by now."

"What would you do if you were me?"

"I'm not certain, my dear, but I am enough of a romantic to think—to hope—that all will turn out well. The important thing right now is for you to rest and stop worrying about the future. It will take care of itself."

Cathryn's eyelids were beginning to droop, and she yawned sleepily. "Della, make me a promise, please."

The doctor's wife patted her hand. "What is it, dear?"

"Don't tell Revan I woke up . . . not just yet . . ."

Della tucked the covers around the sleeping girl, shaking her head. She really didn't know whether to pity or envy her.

For nearly a week, Cathryn, with Della's help, carried out her deception. She still slept a great deal, but each day felt stronger, and soon she was sitting in a chair for a few minutes at a time or walking the length of the room on Della's arm.

Elsa brought up food, sworn to secrecy but puzzled over Cathryn's reluctance to face Revan MacLinn. Taking Della aside, she had asked, "Why is she so afraid of the laird? Was he not at her side day and night, taking care of her?"

"Yes, Elsa, that's true. What you don't understand is that the fever has left her very weak and confused. She just isn't thinking normally yet."

Elsa's eyes were round. "Oh! Well, perhaps it's best for a while longer."

Della knew the plot would soon have to come to an end one way or another. Elsa could easily let the word slip, or someone in the kitchen might become aware that the patient was consuming a considerable amount of solid food now. Naturally, her own husband was beginning to get suspicious. Occasionally he would look in on Cathryn, and though he said nothing, there was a speculative gleam in his eye. Of course, it was most likely Revan himself would figure it out, as he came into the room often during the day. When he appeared, Cathryn's eyes were shut tightly and she lay rigidly beneath his concerned gaze. Sometimes, seeing the look in his eyes, Della had to bite her tongue to keep from blurting out the truth. In her opinion, it was time for Cathryn to face him. Then, when he had gone and Cathryn dared to open her eyes, her relief at not finding him still there so evident, Della would always decide—a few more days.

One dark afternoon when there was more than a hint of snow in the air, Della decided to leave early. "If I linger too long, the storm will begin, and I have several errands to do, so perhaps I should be going."

Cathryn was beginning to be bored with her convalescence and having places to go and errands to do intrigued her. "What sort of things do you have to do?" she asked.

"Well, I must make sure the two elderly sisters who live next to us have enough firewood to last out a storm, and I want to check on the new baby who was born while you were so ill. He seems healthy enough, but his mother is very young, with no one to advise her. And I have baked some bread for old Ian . . ."

"You do so much, Della. I admire that more than I can say."

Della was wrapping herself in a woolen plaid. "There is much to do. When you are better, if you like, you can help. I promise, I can find many things to occupy your time."

Cathryn smiled wanly. "I'll think about it."

"You do that. Now, do you want me to see if Margaret is free to sit with you?"

"No, I'd like to be alone for a while, I think. Maybe I'll get a book and read. I'm getting awfully tired of this bed!"

She smiled ruefully, and Della laughed.

"You know what you can do about that, don't you?"

"Yes, but I'm just not ready. Not yet."

"Anything you say. If I can't get back to see you this evening, I will look in on you tomorrow."

When she had gone, Cathryn threw back the covers and slipped on her borrowed robe. She was still a little wobbly on her feet, but it felt so good to be up and walking about! She went to the window to look out and was surprised to see a few fat snowflakes drifting past the glass panes. A gray mist hovered about the castle, and she could see no further than its four walls.

She crossed the room and selected a book from Revan's desk. It would be a nice diversion, she decided. She settled into the high-backed chair by the fire, glad of its intense heat, and tucked her cold feet beneath the robe.

She became engrossed in the book and had read for about twenty minutes or so when she heard footsteps and male voices outside in the corridor. She flung the book aside, hearing it strike the wood chest. Tearing at the robe, she dropped it as she scampered to the bed and threw herself into it, pulling the covers up to her chin. Her eyes snapped shut and she tried to slow her frightened breathing.

The door was opened quietly, and she felt someone approach the bed. The silence seemed to go on forever.

Finally, a hearty voice said, "Well, it would seem the lass is regaining some color at last!" It was the doctor.

A masculine hand rested briefly on her cheek, and then she heard Revan exclaim, "Good God, man — she's burning up! The fever must be returning!"

"What's that you say?" the doctor cried. "Impossible!"

Now she felt his hand touching first one side of her face, then the other. His voice then sounded from the foot of the bed. "Let me just check something here . . ." He quickly lifted the blankets and grasped her feet in both hands. "Ah, yes, just as I suspected. Cold feet."

"What does it mean, MacSween?" Revan was clearly agitated. "Is something wrong?"

Cathryn could hear a low chuckle. "Step out into the hall a second, lad, and I'll give you my professional opinion."

She heard the door close softly and knew, somehow, she had been found out.

Outside the door, the doctor let his amusement show through at last.

"What the hell is so funny?" Revan stormed. "Is she having a relapse or not?"

"Not exactly." At the younger man's confused expression, the doctor went on. "I've been suspecting this for some time now. I think Cathryn is fully recovered and just pretending to be ill. My guess is she doesn't want to face you and any anger you might feel over her attempt to escape."

"But her face," Revan protested. "I tell you, it was burning hot."

"Indeed it was . . . on the left side. But the right side was as cool as you please."

"What would cause something like that?"

Amused, the doctor said, "Well, my guess is that the young lady was out of her sick bed, perhaps sitting by the fire reading."

Light was dawning in Revan's astonished eyes. "And the heat of the fire only struck one side of her face?"

"Yes, and she must have been barefooted, for her feet were icy. Had she been in bed all along, I'm fairly certain they wouldn't have felt so chilled. And, son, haven't you noticed she's no longer the thin child she seemed during her illness? I'd wager someone has been bringing her more than cups of tea and hot broth! And, I'm afraid I know exactly who that someone is."

"Della?"

"Aye, she's the very one I had in mind."

"Cathryn must have convinced her I'm a beast, also, or, I swear, she would have told me Cathryn was better. She knows how worried I've been."

"It's a puzzle how these women stick together, Revan."

"But it doesn't make sense . . ."

"Ah, you're beginning to know women better!"

Revan rubbed his beard thoughtfully. "Aye, and the more I know them, the less I understand them."

The doctor laughed loudly and thumped him on the back. "So true, my boy, so true. And there is nothing we poor men can do but keep struggling along, trying to understand them, and when we can't, just loving them anyway."

"Sounds like a mighty task."

"Aye, but not a thankless one, at least. It's all worth it, you'll find. Now, I'd best be off on my rounds, and you had better go in there and decide how to deal with your patient."

"Lord knows how I'll do that."

Cathryn was prepared for his anger, but not his silence.

When he came back into the room, he quietly seated himself in the chair at her bedside. Long moments dragged by, and yet he said nothing.

It was so unnerving Cathryn could feel a blush creeping across her cheeks, and her eyelids twitched with the effort of staying closed.

Finally, after what seemed an endless wait, she opened one eye cautiously and met his sardonic, and not very amused, gaze. Her eyes both opened wide at the look, then shut tightly.

"Catriona," he said, as if to a naughty child, "what do you

think you are doing?"

She looked fearfully at him again, saying nothing.

"Didn't you think I would be pleased to find you recovered?"

She tried her best to look innocent . . . and questioning.

"Doctor MacSween says you were probably well enough to be sitting by the fire just before we came in. Is that true?"

She shook her head, her eyes solemn.

"You're denying you were out of bed?"

She nodded.

"For God's sake, can't you talk?"

"Y-yes."

"Yes what? Yes, you can talk or yes, you deny being out of bed?"

"I wasn't out of bed," she whispered.

"Oh?"

"I swear it," she said, a bit louder.

Revan jumped up from the chair in which he was sitting and walked to the fireplace. He looked about for an instant, then seemed to find what he was looking for.

He came back to the bed with a book in his hand.

"Weren't you sitting by the fire reading this book, Catriona?"

"No," she lied.

He seemed to accept her word. Turning to lay the book on the bed table, he said, "Then Elsa must have had it. I just couldn't believe she would have treated it so badly — tossing it down on the floor! She knows how precious books are here in the Highlands. Her carelessness will have to be punished, I'm afraid."

"Punished?"

"Clan chieftains have that perogative, you remember."

"How . . . ?"

Revan pretended to think over the matter. "Oh, nothing too severe. Perhaps a couple of lashes from Owen's whip, no food for a day or two."

"For dropping a book?"

"Aye, she must learn to be more careful with my property." He made his lean face stern.

Cathryn sat up in bed, shocked. "How cruel! That seems to be going too far, even for you!"

He laughed easily. "Don't overtax your strength, my love."

"Damn you! You know very well I was the one reading the book! Elsa had nothing to do with it."

He raised one thick eyebrow. "You? In your weakened condition? Impossible."

"I'm not so weak as you might like to think, sir! And, yes, I sat in that chair and read that book, and gave it a toss when I heard you approach. Now perhaps you will punish me with a few lashes."

"Yes, perhaps." He came close to her. "You, too, must learn to be more careful with my property." He ran a lean finger down her cheek and across her lips. She tossed her head angrily. "You nearly killed yourself, Catriona."

"Next time maybe I won't be so unlucky as to survive!"

"There will be no next time. Make no mistake about that, love."

"You will have to guard me every second then."

"I can think of worse ways to spend my time."

With an angry gasp, Cathryn flung her head back onto the pillow, burrowing under the covers.

Revan paced back and forth at the side of her bed for a few moments, then announced, "I've decided on your punishment, love. We will save the whip for another time. I think I've hit upon something you will think is even worse."

She peered out at him, not certain if he was serious or not.

"Tomorrow evening my friends and neighbors are gathering at Wolfcrag for a little banquet in honor of my birthday. Now that I know how fully recovered you are, I will also expect you to be there."

"I won't be up to something like that!" she protested weakly.

"Oh, yes, I think you will. Elsa can help you dress — wear the green velvet gown. And, I warn you, if you haven't made an appearance by eight o'clock, I will come up and get you, even if you have to attend in your nightgown."

Cathryn's protest was cut short by the slamming of the bedroom door.

Outside, Revan hesitated. Perhaps he should go back and apologize, tell her she didn't have to come to the banquet after all. He hadn't meant to get so carried away by his anger. All the time Cathryn had been ill, he kept promising himself he would find a way to tell her he was sorry about disrupting her life, even putting it in danger. He would search for ways to explain himself to her, to win her gently. But, damn it all, the truth of the matter was that he couldn't be in her company for two minutes without getting into an argument. Her childish obstinance made him lose all control. Still . . .

Just at that second, the book crashed against the door with a loud, rending noise. Despite himself, he laughed and went on down the stairs with a lighter step.

Chapter Seven

Cathryn was a little miffed at the lack of sympathy she received from Della MacSween the following day. The doctor's wife only smiled when Cathryn told her she had to attend the banquet.

"I will be there myself. Perhaps we will be seated together."

"You don't understand! If Revan thinks I am well enough to sit through a lengthy meal with his friends, he will see no reason why I shouldn't . . . well, why I shouldn't take up other household duties."

"And mayhap you should, dear. If you are going to be at Wolfcrag indefinitely, you will find it very boring with nothing to do."

"I know you are pretending to misunderstand me, Della MacSween! But I'm certain you know just exactly what I mean." Cathryn stamped one foot in anger, feeling quite betrayed by her new friend. "The last thing in the world I want is for that man to . . ."

"Shh! Someone is at the door," warned Della.

It was Margaret MacLinn followed by a woman Cathryn did not recognize.

"Cathryn, I am so thrilled to see you up and about! Revan told me you will be joining us this evening for the banquet. I'm delighted."

"I'm really not certain I feel up to it," Cathryn said.

"Oh, of course you do. You have been ill for so long, it will be wonderful for you to have some excitement." She turned to the lady beside her. "This is my seamstress. She is going to make you some new clothes. It's past time you had something to wear other than nightgowns and borrowed dresses. Morag will want to take your measurements if you don't mind."

Cathryn shrugged. It really made little difference to her.

Margaret continued, "First, why don't you get into the dress you will be wearing tonight and let Morag pin it so she can take in the seams? It will look much nicer if it fits properly, and since your illness, you are more slender than ever."

Cathryn sighed, defeated. It seemed she had no allies left.

A few hours later she was standing in front of the mirror, eyeing her reflection critically. There were few signs of her illness left — just slight hollows at the base of her throat and under her cheekbones. Her natural color had returned and was enhanced by the dark green of the gown she wore. Morag had done an excellent job of fitting the tight bodice to her figure, making the dress look as if it had been made for her.

Earlier in the afternoon, Margaret MacLinn had sent her granddaughter with a pair of earrings she wished Cathryn to wear this evening. They were very old, and probably quite valuable — lovely, deep green emeralds in antique gold settings. Cathryn was touched by the gesture and pleased by the way the jewels looked with her dress. She pinned her thick hair on top of her head in order to show the earrings off to their best advantage.

It was now a few minutes before eight o'clock, and she knew it was time to go down to the Banqueting Hall. She regretted having to go alone. Of course, if she delayed any longer Revan would probably come looking for her, and she preferred to enter alone rather than on his proprietary arm. Gathering her courage, she left the relative security of the bedroom and went down the stairs.

She was assailed by the lively droning of the bagpipes as she neared the Great Hall. It was a curious sound and one she had not often heard. A piper stood at the castle entrance, piping in the guests in accordance with old Scottish tradition. A tradition it was now highly treasonable to observe, she thought grimly.

As she passed through the Great Hall, she felt the eyes of those gathered there upon her, but she only lifted her head higher and nodded as she passed each one. From the hubbub of noise coming from the next room, it seemed most of the guests had already assembled in the Banqueting Hall.

She hesitated a moment on the threshold, searching for some familiar face. She felt as though she were about to step into a scene from some distant time — a time when Jacobean gentlemen and their ladies met to honor the Old Pretender and plot a means of returning the Stuarts to the British throne. A time when it was yet honorable to be a Highlander, and men were free to wear the tartan and had no need to take it from its hiding place to wear on special, secret occasions.

The Banqueting Hall was a magnificent room with ancient stone walls and a high, heavily beamed ceiling. The MacLinn coat of arms was boldly emblazoned on the chimney breasts of the fireplace, and a length of MacLinn tartan was brilliant against the polished wood of the banqueting table which ran down the central portion of the hall.

Overhead were hanging chandeliers fashioned of stags' antlers entwined to support thick white candles, though even the light of a hundred candles was not enough to illuminate the far corners of the room. The deep window recesses and the Piper's Gallery were heavily shadowed.

But the scene was made most dramatic by the guests themselves, each of whom was wearing his own clan tartan. Of course, the red and black of the MacLinn was dominant, but there were others scattered throughout the crowd, and Cathryn could not deny they made a proud and brave sight. In her young lifetime, she had never seen anything like this.

Suddenly, she became aware of the intense gaze of a man standing near the fireplace. With a jolt she realized it was Revan MacLinn.

With a few words to his companions, he started across the floor to where she stood.

This was a Revan Cathryn had not seen before. He had dressed for the occasion in the traditional kilt of Dress MacLinn tartan. His snowy linen shirt had falls of lace at the throat and wrists, and his black velvet jacket gleamed with silver buttons. A sporran made from some light-colored animal hung at his waist, supported by a silver chain. The swinging edge of the kilt struck him at the center of the kneecap, and below that, his strong legs were covered with finely knit hose. The jeweled hilt of a dagger was plainly visible.

Far from being the rather feminine fashion she had always imagined it to be, Cathryn decided the kilt was a very manly garment. To her way of thinking, the Highland outlaw looked more dangerous dressed for this evening's entertainment than he had when clothed in rough homespun and leather.

His black hair was tidier than usual, she noticed, no longer tied back with the leather thong. It had been trimmed and brushed until it shone like ebony. His eyes were truly amber in the candlelight, and the expression was, as usual, amused. White teeth gleamed against the dark beard, and his smile was just as disturbing as the first time she'd seen it.

"Catriona," he said, taking her hand and drawing her into the room, "you look as though you've never seen a man in a kilt."

"As you must know, I have not. Do you forget such things are against the law?"

He answered, "But the kilt is still worn in Edinburgh. Surely you've seen it there?"

"You forget, I am from a small village. There the men wear only breeks. I have never been to Edinburgh."

His warm glance fell upon her face. "That is something we shall have to remedy, my love. There is much to see and do in that lovely city. I shall enjoy showing it to you someday."

She kept her face as expressionless as possible. She was not going to let him goad her into an argument in front of all these people.

But he didn't seem intent on fighting. On the contrary, his mood was jovial and pleasant. He made a sweep of the room, Cathryn on his arm, introducing her to his friends and neighbors. Some of them she had met previously, but most were strangers. All of them welcomed her to Wolfcrag and seemed genuinely glad to meet her.

It interested her to see there was no division of the classes here. Owen MacIvor, looking huge and menacing in his kilt and jacket, was as much an honored guest as the most influential aristocrat. The doctor and his wife were treated as well as the highest officer in the clan.

Soon it was time to be seated at the long table, and Cathryn found herself on Revan's right. He was at one end of the table, with his mother at the opposite end. Doctor MacSween was beside Cathryn, and Della was just across the table. Cathryn was relieved to be close to the couple, for she felt she knew them better than anyone else in the castle. Nowhere did she see Darroch and wondered at her absence.

As the meal commenced with the serving of a barley-broth, Revan leaned close to her and said, in a low voice, "You look very beautiful tonight, Catriona."

She inclined her head in acknowledgment of his compliment, then replied, "And you, sir, look very much the gentleman." Half-under her breath, she added, "Naturally, looks can be deceiving!"

She wasn't sure he heard her until he threw back his head and laughed heartily.

Again, he leaned close to whisper, "A lovely red-haired woman makes a fine disguise for the devil, my dear."

Her head came up quickly, a retort on her lips, but she saw several of the others at the table watching them. No doubt they looked the loving couple, bright head and dark so close together, their words low and intimate. Not anxious to further the image, she turned an abrupt shoulder toward Revan and began a conversation with the doctor. Maddeningly, she heard Revan's low chuckle and knew that, once again, he had correctly interpreted her motive.

The next course, a delicious poached fish, was brought in from the kitchen to the accompaniment of the pipes and the pleased applause of the diners. Approval was even louder for the following course, which proved to be roast venison.

Wine was being served with the meal, but after dinner, Cathryn suspected, the natural Highland exuberance would be mixed with the potent Scottish whiskey, making the evening a noisy, uninhibited affair.

Toward the end of the meal, a young man in MacLinn tartan began to play soft music on an unusual stringed instrument he set on a stand near the fireplace.

"What instrument is that?" Cathryn asked of the doctor.

"Why, that is the clarsach, the Highland harp. Do you approve of its melodious sounds?"

"Yes, it sounds very beautiful. What is the song he is playing? It's unfamiliar to me."

The doctor smiled. "As well it should be, Cathryn. 'Tis an old Jacobite air."

Jacobean or not, the melody was very stirring, and before much longer, the hum of conversation had died, and the silence in the room was broken only by the haunting refrain. Even Cathryn felt moved, with the weak tears still so prevalent since her illness close to the surface.

The young man strumming the harp suddenly began to sing and in a moment first one voice and then another joined him, until the room echoed with the sound.

Revan leaned close. "They say this song brings tears to the eyes of Bonnie Prince Charlie each time he hears it."

His words brought Cathryn back to reality, spoiling the magic of the moment. "As it should!" she hissed. "I hope it serves to remind him of the black day he took an unprepared army of fools into battle where they were hopelessly outnumbered . . ."

Revan interrupted, his teeth clenched, "And helplessly slaughtered by Butcher Cumberland, acting in the name of the almighty king!"

"You Highlanders were plotting against him," was her angry rejoinder. "He had to protect his government."

"That's not the point, my dear," Revan said acidly. "It was not his government. He was not the rightful heir to the throne. James Edward Stuart was!"

"If it were possible, I'd almost like to see you Scots under his rule now! You deserve each other." Her voice rose. "And have you not heard how your precious bonnie prince spends his time these days? Lolling about with his mistresses and drinking himself insensible. A fine king he would be!"

Revan's eyes blazed, and his hands clenched and un-clenched, as if he longed to feel them about her throat. "You had best shut your mouth, my lady!"

Something about the silence in the room finally registered with them, and they lifted heated faces to meet the aston-ished eyes of all those seated around the table.

Revan coughed lightly to cover his embarrassment and stood up, lifting his wineglass.

"Let us toast our good king over the water!"

Exclamations of approval rang out, and the entire com-pany got to its feet, wineglasses raised high. Only Cathryn remained seated, her face set and stubborn. She knew Della MacSween was frantically signaling with her eyes that it was not an intelligent thing to do, but she was too angry to pay any heed. After all, what could Revan MacLinn do to her in front of his guests?

"Cathryn," he warned, his voice a low growl, "stand up and drink."

"I refuse." She looked directly into his eyes so he could be certain she would not be intimidated.

" 'Tis not your place to refuse," he snapped. "I order it."

"Don't forget, I am a Lowlander, and you are not my chieftain. I refuse to be a party to this."

Embarrassed, the doctor cleared his throat and said kindly, "Oh, come, come, my dear—it's only a simple toast."

"There is nothing simple about treason, sir." This time her voice was loud enough to be clearly heard throughout the room and several shocked gasps sounded. She pushed back her chair and stood up.

"All of you must know this is treason! Why do you persist in this foolishness? Why must you keep romanticizing a drunken fool who led you to disaster? Why do you go on commemorating a battle you lost? You lost!"

Revan's hard hands clamped around her shoulders, and he shook her until bright strands of hair came unpinned and tumbled around her hot face. She thought he would slap her, and her eyes dared him.

"Have you lost your mind? Are you still feverish? These people are my friends and guests in my home. You have no right to speak to them in such a way, and I demand an apology on their behalf!"

"I can't apologize for speaking the truth," she stormed, her head still whirling from the rough shaking he had given her. "I won't."

His eyes narrowed. "You can and you will. Immediately."

She stood her ground, aware of how dangerous the moment had become. She was still too angry to be frightened.

"Catriona, let me advise you. Make your apologies and drink the toast. Otherwise, the consequences will not be to your liking."

"Your threats are not enough to make me go against everything I have been taught to believe in."

"My threats are not empty, however. I mean what I say — you had best begin your apology."

A deep voice came from near the end of the table. "Ah, Revan, an apology isn't necessary. The lass is right — she comes from a different district, one where they do not see things the way we do. Let's forget it."

Without taking his eyes from her face, Revan answered, "I cannot forget insults to my friends so easily. At least she will drink the toast."

"I will not . . ."

Revan was lifting his glass high once again. His voice was clear and strong. "A toast to our King James, and to his courageous son, Charles Edward Stuart!" He drained his glass in one draught and set it back on the dining table. All around him, the others were lifting their glasses and drinking.

"I'll not drink this toast, Revan, no matter what you say."

"You will, madam, most definitely."

His strong fingers grasped her jaw, holding it in a vise-like grip. Before she could wrench away, he lifted her goblet with his other hand and put it to her lips. She choked and swallowed, unable to move her head away. She could feel his brutal hand bruising her face, but she was powerless against his strength. The blood red wine trickled down her chin and throat, staining the front of her gown.

When the glass was empty, Revan replaced it on the table and said. "Now, musician, let's have another ballad."

Cathryn looked at the faces around the room. Some were shocked, some pleased, some pitying. She took up the lace napkin at her place and used it to dry her face and mop the spilled wine from her dress. Then, laying the napkin aside, she calmly turned and began walking out of the room.

There was no sound as she crossed the floor, though she was quite certain every eye was on her. It was a relief that Revan didn't come after her or try to stop her. Her humiliation was complete without a further scene.

As she walked through the door and began to hurry across the Great Hall, the stunned silence behind her was finally broken. She heard a masculine voice proposing a toast to Revan on his birthday, and then the harp music began again.

It was well past midnight when the first guests began to leave, their farewells ringing out in the icy night air as they crossed the courtyard. Most of these people lived within the walls of Wolfcrag; those who had come from any distance would spend the night.

Though Cathryn had heard a few feminine voices in the hallway and assumed the ladies had come upstairs to bed, enough noise yet issued from the lower floor of the castle to indicate the men were still celebrating the occasion. She was grateful, for she had no wish of any further confrontation with Revan. Though, of course, she knew the confrontation would have to come, sooner or later. She had defied him in front of his clansmen and had insulted not only him, but all of them.

She continued pacing to and fro in the bedchamber, wrapped in the velvet robe, her ruined gown tossed carelessly into the corner. She would never wear it again, she vowed. Nothing could make her re-live the humiliation of

137

this night!

She longed to be able to lock herself in the room, but the key was nowhere to be found. It would be mere foolishness to try to barricade the door, even if she thought she could move any of the heavy furniture.

No, it simply wasn't worth it. If he came seeking revenge, there was nothing she could do to stop him.

Later she fell into an uneasy sleep in one of the chairs by the hearth. The muted tones of the old clock told her it was two in the morning, but downstairs, the music went on.

The stealthy opening of the dressing room door awakened her and brought her to her feet.

Revan ducked his head and entered the room through the small doorway, shutting it carefully behind him. When he saw Cathryn watching him, he started to grin.

"Catriona, my love, take off your clothes."

"What?" His voice had been so quiet she was not sure she had heard him correctly.

"I said," he repeated, moving toward her, "take off your clothes. I am here to exact my revenge." His speech was slurred, his movements slow and ungraceful.

"Don't be ridiculous!" she snapped. "You are drunk!"

"Haven't I told you before, a Highlander never gets drunk?" He lurched against her and both of them fell in a heap on the rug in front of the fire.

"How obliging you are, sweetheart," he murmured, lips against her hair. "But don't you think the bed would be more comfortable?"

Angrily, she shoved his heavy body off her own and scrambled to her feet. "I think you should go to bed, yes, but don't expect me to join you there."

He rose, a little unsteadily, and began unbuttoning his jacket. This he tossed across the back of the chair. "You know . . . you know you'll have to bed with me sooner or later, don't you?"

"I propose we make it later," she said scornfully. "Much, much later."

"You have a sharp tongue, woman!"

She started across the room and he followed her, saying, "Do you know what people are saying about me?"

She shrugged to show her indifference. He went on. "They think I have become weak. And do you know why they think that?"

"No, why?"

"Because of you, that's why." He grasped her arm and pulled her to him. "Because of that little display downstairs tonight . . . my God, Catriona, I should have beaten you right then and there."

"Don't you think humiliating me before all those people was punishment enough?"

"And what about the humiliation you caused me?" He seemed to be having difficulty making his eyes focus properly. He was clearly more inebriated than she'd thought. "Never has a clan chieftain been so treated!"

"The days of power and respect for clan chieftains are gone," she reminded him quietly.

"I beg to differ, love. I am about to exhibit my own power over you, the lowliest wench in my household!" As he bent his head to kiss her, she pushed him away, causing him to sprawl drunkenly across the bed. His kilt was knocked askew, exposing naked thighs. Cathryn caught her breath and turned away, the sight of his near nudity shocking her.

He laughed most heartily. "Aye, I forgot ye little Lowlander lassies know nothing of the Highlander's kilt! Didn't ye know, love, that a true Scotsman wears nothing underneath?"

"Not only didn't I know, I find I don't care very much."

"Then why don't you look at me when you say it?" he laughed, tauntingly.

"I am unaccustomed to half-dressed men who have had far too much to drink accosting me in my bedroom," she stated.

" 'Tis my bedroom, which you always seem to forget," he grumbled. "Damn it, why doesn't this blasted bed quit spinning?"

At those words, Cathryn turned to look at him. For a second she enjoyed the misery on his face, but then she realized he was about to become very sick.

Quickly she threw herself to her knees and started groping under the bed for the china chamberpot, which she thrust under his nose just in time. Revan was suddenly so ill she took pity on him, despite her best intentions to stand back and enjoy his suffering. She sat on the bed beside him and held his head as he retched and heaved, brushing his hair from his eyes with her fingers.

"If my men could see me now," he gasped, still managing a wry smile, "I'd never, never hear the end of it. 'Twill make an entertaining tale for you to pass on to them . . ."

"Nay, I'd not use this against you," she said feeling a grudging compassion for him.

He smiled weakly and laid his head against the cool pillows. "It's true," he muttered. "I never was so weak before — never, until you came here."

Instantly he was asleep, robbing Cathryn of the chance to remind him it had not been her idea to come to Wolfcrag.

She covered the chamberpot and set it near the door. Then she pulled off Revan's shoes and lifted his feet and legs onto the bed, keeping her eyes very carefully averted. Before pulling the bedcovers over him, she deftly removed the dagger from his stocking. She stood looking down at the sleeping man for a long moment, then opened her hand to look at the bejeweled dagger lying against her palm.

She was very much aware that, since coming here as Revan MacLinn's captive, there had been a number of times she would gladly have held just such a dagger and had him at her mercy. She sighed. But not now, not tonight. For the first time she had seen him vulnerable, and she had been in the position of being strong. It pleased her to be able to make the choice of whether or not to do him harm. She smiled to herself, left the dagger on the bedside table, and blew out the candle. She would finish the night in the narrow cot in Revan's dressing room.

Chapter Eight

It was mid-morning when Cathryn awoke. The castle seemed strangely silent with none of the usual noises. She supposed events would be somewhat altered by the lateness of the dinner party the night before. Perhaps the castle inhabitants would lie abed most of the day.

She put on the robe, smiling to herself. If the rest of them left the party in conditions similar to Revan MacLinn's, it would most likely be a very solemn place today. Well, she would go in search of something to eat and then look for Meg. No doubt it would be lonely for her with the adults resting.

Unfortunately, her only gown was in the bedchamber next door and she would have to risk waking Revan to get it. She certainly couldn't wander about in her nightclothes.

She opened the door to the bedroom very carefully, frowning at the slow creak it made. She could see Revan on the bed, amid a tangle of bedcovers, arms flung wide. She waited, but he gave no sign of hearing her. She eased the door all the way open and quietly slipped through.

As she tiptoed past the bed to the wardrobe, she could hear his even breathing. She had just removed the saffron-colored dress and was turning to flee, when he opened his eyes, yawned and stretched, and sat up in bed.

"Oh!" she exclaimed in surprise.

"Surely you weren't going to leave without saying 'good morning'?" he remarked, eyeing her with his usual sardonic humor.

"Why, I didn't want to wake you," she answered sweetly. "I thought you might be feeling somewhat indisposed this morning."

He grinned. "Sorry to disappoint you, my love, but I feel wonderful!"

"Well, you weren't feeling wonderful last night," she snapped.

"Oh, that—" He shrugged. "I might have known you would bring that up at the first opportunity."

"I was only expressing concern," she murmured, still reveling in her feeling of power over him. She toyed with the idea of trying her hand at a little simple blackmail. Flashing him a coy look, she said, "Of course, I'd never mention it to anyone . . ."

"Mention what?" he asked, though his tone told her he knew very well what she meant.

"Why, your clumsy arrival in my bedchamber and your subsequent illness. It would not be a very flattering portrait, would it?"

"No, indeed, love."

"It's certainly not a thing a man would want his kinsmen to know about. Why, what would those fierce Highlanders think if they knew their highly regarded leader had passed out in the company of the enemy, leaving himself unarmed and at the mercy of anyone with a grudge against him? Would that inspire their confidence?"

He shook his dark head, a look of controlled mirth on his features. "Not likely! But you know, Catriona, I am hurt you consider yourself my enemy. I had not realized the extent of your hostility."

"Let me assure you, it is limitless."

"And yet, you left the dagger on the table instead of through my black heart. How do you justify that?"

She turned away, refusing to meet his eyes. "I really can't explain it. Perhaps I just couldn't bring myself to take advantage of you when you were in such a vulnerable position."

"Aye, that's just how I felt when I spent all those long hours in bed with you during your illness."

She whirled to face him. "What did you say?"

"I believe you heard me correctly."

"You spent hours . . ." Her voice faltered.

"In bed with you, love. That's right." He grinned broadly, making her think he had never looked more wolf-like.

"But . . . but, why?"

"Oh, for strictly medicinal purposes, I assure you. Poor lass, you were in the throes of delirium and shaking with chills. I could think of no better way to warm you."

Her eyes widened and became very dark. She averted her face and asked, "No better way than . . . what?"

He laughed. "I only lay beside you to warm you with the heat from my body."

One hand crept to her throat and she lowered her head a little, relieved.

"Oh," she said in a very small voice.

"Of course," he went on, carefully watching her, his smile growing wider, "I was completely unclothed at the time."

"I don't believe you!"

"That's your privilege, of course. But if you'd like to know whether or not I'm lying, just speak with Della MacSween. She'll tell you the truth."

"The MacSweens knew about it?" she cried, turning on him again. "And did nothing?"

"Once again, you seem to forget — I am their chieftain and they do not question my actions."

"How could you?" she stormed. "How could you? I was desperately ill, with no way to defend myself. You took advantage of me."

"Yes, to your way of thinking. To my way of thinking, I used great restraint."

"Your way of thinking is depraved and lewd," she spat.

"Mayhap it is more honest than yours," he retorted.

"What do you mean?"

"I try to see things as they are, while you persist in twisting everything."

"I do not!"

"Oh, but you do. Did you not read some hidden motive into my reason for getting into bed with you?"

"You know very well there is only one reason a man like you gets into bed with a woman!" Suddenly she turned crimson and covered her face with her hands. "Oh, look what has happened to me! You are making me as crude as everyone else around you. I . . . I seem to keep saying and doing such awful things."

He chuckled. "Yes, you do, but mayhap we can strike a truce. If you wish, I will solemnly promise never to breathe a word of your indiscretions to your Lowland kin and, in return, you must promise to forget about last night and my moment of weakness."

"It seems a rather one-sided bargain to me," said Cathryn.

"One-sided?"

"Of course. It will be no great hardship for you to refrain from spreading evil gossip about me because you have no plans to ever see my kith and kin again and well I know it. But, of course, what thief or outlaw ever made a bargain in good faith?"

"Do you forget your own recent bargain, madam? You conveniently forget that I kept my end of it, while you did not."

Unable to deny what he said, she kept silent.

"Did I not honor my promise to leave you alone, Catriona? Answer me!"

"Yes, I suppose you did, but . . ."

"Aye, I kept my word, but you, what did you do? Made another attempt to escape, nearly bringing disaster down on all of us. And it seems evident that your promise to behave was never made in good faith. So don't preach to me about the honor of a thief, my lady."

"Very well," she murmured, clutching the velvet gown to her and avoiding his steady gaze. "Now, if I may, I would like to go and get dressed."

"Yes, go on."

Then, as she started across the room, his voice came again. "One more thing, Catriona. I think I should warn you that the bargain of which we were speaking is now no longer in effect. After all, why should I play the gentleman when you have no intention of being a lady?"

144

Dismayed at his meaning, she protested. "Why can't we strike another bargain? I swear I will be honest this time and do as you ask."

"While you make your plea very charmingly, love, I do not think I care to be put off much longer. I think it's best we just agree on one thing."

Cathryn hesitated. "What is that?"

He flung himself back onto the pillows, hands behind his head, and gazed up at the beamed ceiling with a thoughtful look on his face. "Your state of virginity is about to come to an end."

"We shall see about that," Cathryn snapped, striding angrily out of the room.

Behind her, she heard him say, "Oh, yes, indeed we shall."

As soon as she was dressed, Cathryn seized the drab, borrowed shawl and hurried down the stairs and out the front door. She made her way directly to the doctor's cottage, speaking to no one in her haste. Her frantic knock was promptly answered by the doctor.

"Here, what's wrong, lass?"

She pushed past him, into the sitting room where a cozy fire glowed in the fireplace and several lamps were lighted against the darkness of the winter morning. Della MacSween was sitting in a rocking chair before the fire, a pile of dark yarn on her lap. She laid aside her knitting needles as Cathryn came in.

Standing up in alarm, she asked, "Is someone ill?"

"No, it's not that." Cathryn looked from one to the other of them, then burst out, "How could you have let Revan MacLinn force himself upon me while I was sick and helpless?"

They looked at each other in amazement, then Della began to smile. "Why, Cathryn, he didn't do anything wrong."

"What do you call it then?"

"Lass, he was only trying to help," the doctor cut in. "That is, if you are talking about what I think you are talking about."

"Aye, she is," Della nodded.

"Couldn't you have insisted on some other way? He tells me he was naked!"

Della put an arm around Cathryn's slender shoulders and led her to the sofa. "Believe me, we were trying everything. You were smothered in blankets, Elsa brought hot bricks for the bed, the fire was blazing. When Revan became so desperate he could think of nothing else, he got into the bed with you and shared his body heat. That's all there was to it. When I found him like that, I just couldn't bring myself to reproach him because it was working. You were warmer."

"I can't bear to think about it," Cathryn cried, burying her face in her hands. "I . . . I feel so compromised."

"No need to, my dear," Doctor MacSween reassured her. "Revan was only acting on your behalf, and no one outside Della and myself knows anything about it."

"He taunted me about it just now," Cathryn wailed. "How could he have done such a thing with noble intentions and then turn around and use it against me?"

"How has he used it against you, dear?" Della asked with concern.

"He is threatening me."

Della sat down beside her and asked calmly, "Why would Revan have any need to threaten you?"

Cathryn felt a large lump rising in her throat and suddenly, she just couldn't get the words past it. Her gray-green eyes brimmed with tears.

"What is it, girl?" Della persisted. "Has something happened?"

"I . . . I can't talk about it!"

Della's eyes met those of her husband over Cathryn's head. "Adam, why don't you go make yourself a cup of tea?"

"Better yet, why don't I take myself out of here? I need to go check on two or three patients, anyway. I'll be back in an hour or so."

"Thank you, dear," Della said, as he grabbed up his plaid and went out the door. As soon as he was gone, she shook Cathryn gently and said, "Now, stop crying and tell me

146

exactly what is going on."

Cathryn brushed aside the tears with a shaking hand and whispered, "Della, I'm afraid Revan MacLinn is going to force me to . . . to become his mistress. He has more or less given me his word on that!"

"And you are unwilling?"

Cathryn flounced off the sofa and exclaimed in an angry voice, "Good Lord, yes, I'm unwilling! Why would I be otherwise?"

Della shrugged. "I don't want to sound unsympathetic, Cathryn, but if that is his intention, I feel there is very little we can do about it."

"You must have some influence on the man. Your husband is a doctor — can't he reason with him, convince him it would be a grave mistake?"

"Would it really be such a tragedy?" Della asked quietly.

"It would make me an adulteress," Cathryn answered. "Isn't that rather tragic?"

"Ordinarily, yes, but in this case, where your marriage is in name only, where there was no great affection, perhaps it might be different."

"How dare you suggest there was no love between Basil and myself! What do you know about it?"

"Only what I have been told, of course, but, Cathryn, for God's sake — look at yourself."

"What do you mean?"

"You are a young, beautiful woman, full of life and passion and emotion. From what Revan tells me, Basil Calderwood is a pious, stingy stick of a man without enough fire to light a candle! I can't forget how outraged Revan was when he saw the man your father had chosen for you." Her eyes sparkled. "I thought he would never stop ranting and raving."

"When did he speak to you of my husband?" Cathryn asked stiffly.

"That first evening after you'd arrived. He came to see us and talked far into the night. He asked our advice on how to deal with the situation. He acted out of rash indignation, on the spur of the moment, and once he had you here at

147

Wolfcrag, he suddenly didn't know how to handle the dilemma. He wanted to coddle you like a precious child and yet, he wanted to punish you for not wanting him, for marrying someone else."

"This is so insane, Della. When Revan spoke to me about marriage, how could I take him seriously? He was a reiver, an outlaw — someone I had only seen once before. I knew nothing of him, and he knew nothing of me. He made his proposal, if that is what it can be called, not knowing anything of me or my life. Had it been a normal situation, I would have informed him of my engagement. It just seemed like a prank, a joke. I didn't take him seriously. No one would!"

"Well, I'm afraid Revan did. True, had he known who you really were, and had he been prudent enough to check into the details of your life, it might have been different. But I doubt he would have given it up as a lost cause — he just might have used different tactics. Once he saw you, it didn't take him long to decide you were the perfect mate for him."

"It isn't up to him to decide something like that," Cathryn protested. "I should have a say in the matter, also."

"May I ask you something?" Della said quietly.

"Of course."

"Did you have any say in the matter of your betrothal to Calderwood?"

Cathryn looked down at her hands. "No," she finally said, "not really. It was my father's wish, and I have been raised to be a dutiful daughter. Naturally, I wanted to do as I was told."

"Didn't you ever question his reason for choosing someone like Basil?"

"I knew his reasons, of course."

"Will you tell me what they were?"

"I'm sure you will not think they are very good reasons," Cathryn began. "My father is one of those unfortunate men who cannot seem to hold onto money. He likes his little luxuries and . . . and he has an appetite for gambling. So, you see, he was often in debt and being harassed by his creditors. Basil has a great deal of money, and the two of

148

them struck up a bargain."

"With you as pawn?" Della asked dryly.

"That's not how it was."

"It would appear that way to me, Cathryn. Your father sold you to the highest bidder. That is what Revan suspected, and it seems he was right. I know how you feel about being brought here against your will, but think about it! Can you really think life here would be any more unpleasant than life as Mrs. Basil Calderwood?"

"Della, I thought you were my friend. Of course, I realize you have known Revan much longer, but I thought there was a special bond between us. I truly expected you to see my side of this." Cathryn's eyes were stricken, making Della contrite.

"There is a special bond between us. I feel very close to you, and that is why I dare to speak to you this way."

"You cannot think you are helping me by casting aspersions on my father?"

"No, I don't mean to do that. I only want you to really think about your life, and how it could be different here at Wolfcrag. Different, and possibly better. There are good people here, and I feel you could be happy among us."

"I can't deny there are some wonderful people here," Cathryn replied, "but it's not my home."

"Do you really miss your home that much?"

"Of course I do! I had no chance to say goodbye to my father or my friends. I was taken against my will, and I have been kept here against my will. You cannot expect me to feel happy about that."

"No," Della agreed, "Revan's methods were definitely lacking in finesse. But he had no choice; he had to act quickly."

"It's very frightening to be at the mercy of a man you do not know," Cathryn pointed out. "He seems so brutal at times."

"Revan is not a brutal man, and well you know it. A brutal man would have had his way with you long ago, not caring about your thoughts or feelings at all. You have held Revan off a good deal longer than I would have thought possible."

"I beg of you, Della, please help me now."

"Cathryn, are you afraid because you don't know what to expect?" Della asked gently.

"No, it isn't that. It's . . . I'm just afraid of Revan MacLinn. He isn't like any man I've ever known, and I don't know how to deal with him."

"Is he so unpleasant compared to your husband?"

Cathryn spread her hands. "It isn't a matter of unpleasant. It's my life we are discussing. What happens to me when Revan MacLinn has tired of me? How can I go back to my home then? I have to consider the scandal and my future. All those things matter a great deal to me."

"Revan's commitment would be a long-lasting one, I'm certain, but I must admit, he has placed you in a position where you are not to be blamed for thinking of such things. Perhaps the two of you should sit down together and discuss all the sides of the issue. Mayhap Revan has not looked at this from your point of view."

"It's possible he has not, but Della, I vow, we couldn't discuss it calmly. If we speak together for longer than a few seconds, it seems we are arguing."

"I know, love. It was very apparent at the banquet last night."

Even Cathryn managed a small laugh. "What a disastrous evening!"

"You certainly made one thing very clear to all of us, however."

"What is that?"

"There is a great deal of passion between the two of you."

"Della, that is the first totally senseless thing I have heard you say," Cathryn admonished, a little shaken by the other's words.

"Yes, I frequently lapse into romanticism. My husband is forever telling me so. I apologize."

"No matter. But, seriously, Della, what should I do?"

"I'm not sure there is anything you can do, but why don't you spend some time considering whether or not you would actually prefer your life as the wife of someone like Basil Calderwood." As Cathryn started to protest, Della held up a

150

firm hand. "All I ask is that you be honest with yourself. In the meantime, possibly Adam will speak with Revan and suggest the two of you have that serious discussion. Perhaps you could make him understand how you feel."

"Perhaps . . ." Cathryn sounded very doubtful.

"And now I am going to fix us some luncheon if you will stay."

"Oh, yes, I'd like to. I had forgotten how hungry I am." A dimple flashed as she smiled brightly, and Della thought how difficult it would be for Revan MacLinn to carry on a serious discussion with so much beauty to distract him.

"And, Cathryn, I have to ask one more thing before I'm done. How is it you seem to have overlooked the fact that Revan is an extremely handsome and virile man? He's young, strong, powerful—certainly all the things most women search for." She started out of the room, but paused long enough to toss one further comment back over her shoulder. "Just be glad I'm a happily married woman, or I would be a formidable rival for his affections!"

Later in the afternoon Cathryn went in search of Meg and found her in the nursery with her dog, playing with an odd assortment of dolls. The nursery was a long, pleasant room located on the same floor as Revan's bedchamber, but in the opposite wing, next to the room where Darroch slept.

"Hello, Cathryn," the little girl smiled. "Want to see my dolls?"

"I'd like to. Where did they all come from?" Cathryn spread her full skirts and sat on the floor beside Meg.

"This one was my mother's, and these used to belong to Grandmother when she was a little girl. Aren't they lovely?"

One or two were genuinely lovely, though well-worn. Several of them were very tattered, and one had bandages on both legs and around its head. Cathryn picked it up, smiling.

"What has happened to this little fellow?" she asked.

"He was injured in a fierce battle," Meg explained seriously. "He was fighting the horrible English, you see."

"What does a child like you know about battles and fighting?"

"We read about famous battles sometimes in Father's history books," Meg explained.

"Surely you cannot read?"

"Well, only a little. My father is teaching me to read and write, but I don't know any big words yet."

Here was yet another side of Revan MacLinn! Perhaps Della is right, Cathryn mused. There may be more to him than I have allowed myself to see.

"I can write my name," boasted Meg. "Would you like to see?"

"Why, yes, I would."

The child scrambled across the room to some shelves where she found a slate and some pieces of chalk. She settled herself beside Cathryn again and began laboriously printing her name on the slate.

Later she got some books and Cathryn read her stories from Scottish history. The child knew most of them by heart and added details, impressing Cathryn with her knowledge. The MacLinns were still intent on raising faithful little Jacobites, it would seem.

She so enjoyed her afternoon with Meg that she asked the child's nurse if she might stay and share her supper before the fire. The nurse agreed and Meg was delighted. The two of them had a merry time, tossing tidbits to the hound and laughing at his antics.

"Will you come and play games with me tomorrow, Cathryn?" the child asked.

"Of course I will. What sort of games do you like to play?"

"Do you know how to play 'Hide and Seek'?"

"Why, yes, I played it when I was a little girl like you."

"We could play that tomorrow. It's one of my favorite games because there are so many places to hide in Wolfcrag. When we go into the Banqueting Hall, I will show you the secret tunnel."

"Secret tunnel?"

Meg's dark eyes glowed with excitement. "Yes! It goes from the castle down to the beach. A long time ago when the castle was under siege, the ships would come into the cove and smuggle in food and supplies through the tunnel. That's what Father told me. I know how to open the door, too."

Cathryn considered this thoughtfully. "Well, Meg, I would dearly love to see that. Tomorrow we will go have a look at it, I promise."

"Don't tell my mother, please. She says I can't go into the tunnel to play. It's too dangerous."

"Dangerous?"

"Some of the supports are too old and could fall in. But I don't go into the tunnel very far. Sometimes I hide there when Robbie and Ailsa are playing with me. They never find me there."

Cathryn laughed. "Don't you think you are taking an unfair advantage?"

The child looked at her with solemn eyes. "What does that mean?"

Just then a tall figure standing in the doorway stepped out of the shadows and crossed the room, to Meg's delight.

"Father! Have you come to read with me?"

Revan MacLinn knelt beside her, scratching the dog's ears. "I surely have. But mayhap you are tired of reading, little one." He cast a questioning look at Cathryn. "I see the two of you have already been at the books."

"Yes, Cathryn read to me, but I'm not tired. I want to read some more."

Cathryn rose to her feet, smoothing her skirt with nervous hands. "I think I will just leave you two alone, then," she murmured. "I will see you tomorrow, Meg."

"Goodnight, Cathryn. Thank you for coming to play with me."

"I enjoyed myself very much. Goodnight."

As she stepped past Revan, she felt his eyes on her, but wouldn't let herself look in his direction. She heard him say, "I will see you later," and knew his words held more than a little threat.

She paused outside Meg's door and took a deep breath.

What was she going to do? If something didn't happen, it would seem she would lose her chance for reasoning with Revan. Perhaps she should go back to the MacSweens and try throwing herself on their mercy again. It hadn't worked very well the first time, but she was at a loss as to what else to do.

As she left the doorway, she heard a voice speak her name softly. It seemed to come from the shadowy staircase winding up to the tower. She took a few steps in that direction.

"Who is it?" she asked.

"Cathryn! Come here," the voice repeated.

Impatiently, Cathryn started up the steps. At the first turn she collided with Darroch.

"Oh! Darroch, you startled me," she exclaimed. Then, for the first time, she saw the angry red scar she had made with the riding crop. She swallowed painfully. "How awful! I'm so sorry about hitting you."

"Are you?" Darroch's glittery gaze was menacing, and the smile on her red lips was mocking and hard. "Then why haven't you come to see me to make amends? Why did you make me find you?"

"As you must surely know, last night was the first I have been out of my bedchamber since I was found and brought back here. I thought to see you at the banquet."

"I chose not to go," Darroch stated. "Can you imagine why?"

"Yes, I think I know why. But surely the scar will fade."

"The good doctor assures me it will, but it is taking an interminably long time. You didn't have to strike me so hard, Cathryn, and you didn't have to hit me in the face. That wasn't our deal."

"I know and I'm very sorry. I just got so angry with you — now I can't even recall the things you said to me, but you must be aware of how you goaded me!"

"I risked everything to help you and that is how you thanked me. Why did you do it?"

"I told you, I just got so angry I lost my head and struck out blindly. I truly meant you no injury."

Darroch stepped to the same level as Cathryn. She was

154

clearly the stronger of the two and, suddenly Cathryn feared her. She moved away a bit, finding her back against the cold rough stone of the wall. The stairway was quite narrow and lighted only by a flaring torch set into a bracket at the foot of the stairs. The light just barely reached the level where they stood.

"I think I know why you slashed me so viciously," Darroch went on. "I've given it a lot of thought while I have been recuperating, and it seems you could only have had one motive."

"Motive?"

"Yes. I think you were afraid Revan would turn to me for comfort when you were gone, and you tried to spoil my looks so he would look elsewhere."

"That's ridiculous, Darroch. I was running away from the man. Why should I care to whom he turned?"

"That's what I can't understand. You claim to hate him and yet, I wonder . . ."

"I hoped he wasn't angry with you."

"He was angry with everyone, but he could never prove MacQueen and I plotted with you. He threatened and stormed, but we stuck to our stories and he finally gave up, though I know he is suspicious."

She came closer and Cathryn backed away, going higher up the stairway.

"After all I risked, you couldn't even make it out of MacLinn territory, you fool!"

"I don't know what happened. I tried to do just what you told me, but somehow I got so tired and then I got lost . . ."

"Did you tell Revan I was in on your scheme?" Darroch demanded, her voice harsh.

"No, I swear I didn't."

"How can I be sure?"

"Has he told you I implicated you?"

"He hasn't had the time to speak to me, as you know very well. For the last two weeks he has done nothing but wait by your bedside. Perhaps you planned it that way all along."

"Don't be preposterous," Cathryn exclaimed.

"Preposterous?"

155

"You're a fool if you think I'd do anything to keep myself in the presence of Revan MacLinn!"

"How dare you call me a fool?" Darroch's hand flew up and struck Cathryn a stinging blow across the face. She gasped and ducked back, losing her footing and falling to her knees.

"I owe you that and so much more," Darroch cried. "If I ever find out you so much as breathed a word, I will kill you, just as I promised." She dealt Cathryn another sharp blow. "It would be so easy to kill you. I could push you down these stairs right now, and no one would ever know it wasn't an accident. I would enjoy it immensely . . . yes, I'd enjoy making you pay for what you did to my face!"

She laughed harshly.

"If you'd enjoy living a bit longer," said a quiet voice behind her, "you'll reconsider what you are doing." The enraged woman whirled to see Revan standing there, a scowl on his face.

"Revan, surely you can't deny my right for revenge? Look what she has done to me."

"Darroch, I have very little doubt that you deserved every inch of that scar. I think you would be ill-advised to speak of revenge again. The matter is over and done, and I suggest you forget it and stay away from Cathryn. I warn you, never lay a hand on her again!"

For a few seconds they glared at each other, and then Darroch pushed past him and went down the stairs. They could hear the door to her room closing with a crash.

Cathryn was still cowering on the stairs. Fearfully, she met his amber eyes. He stood over her, hands on his lean hips and a thoughtful expression on his face.

He reached out a strong hand and pulled her to her feet. Gently he touched her cheek where Darroch had slapped her.

"Are you all right, love?"

Shakily, she brushed a bronzed strand of hair from her eyes and straightened her shoulders. "Yes, I'm fine. Thank you."

His eyes took in her disheveled appearance, slowly rang-ing over her body. She grew uneasy, but could think of no way to get past him on the narrow staircase.

Finally he said, "Catriona, I have come to your rescue for the last time without a proper reward."

"What do you mean?" she breathed.

Swiftly, he swung her up into his arms and, going down the steps two at a time, carried her into the wide hallway and toward his bedchamber.

Chapter Nine

Revan MacLinn kicked the door to the bedroom shut behind them and set Cathryn on her feet. From his shirt pocket he took the door key and turned it in the lock.

"What are you doing?" Cathryn raged. "Let me out of this room."

"No, lass, I've made up my mind. You'll not be leaving until morning, and then," he smiled roguishly, "mayhap you won't want to."

Cathryn started across the room toward the small dressing chamber, but Revan moved faster, locking the door before she could wrench it open.

"It's fortunate the locks take the same key," he grinned. "I'll just put it up here for safe-keeping." He laid the key on top of the tall wardrobe, out of her reach.

"Have you lost your mind?" she stormed.

"No, just regained my manhood, sweet. I've been too easy with you; I can see that now." He sat on the edge of an armchair and began pulling off his boots. "Had I tamed you from the beginning, none of this nonsense would have taken place."

"Revan, what are you doing?"

"What does it look like I'm doing?" he asked, standing up and beginning to unlace his shirt.

Cathryn experienced her first real moment of panic.

Always before, someone or something had distracted him, saving her from the final humiliation. She was starting to doubt anything could save her this time.

"Can't we discuss this reasonably?"

"I doubt it, love. When have we ever discussed anything reasonably?"

He pulled the white shirt over his head and let it drop to the floor. Cathryn started backing away, looking about for some means of avoiding him. He sensed her purpose and laughed.

" 'Tis no use, Catriona. There is no way out for you now."

"You're vile! A madman!"

She felt the window ledge behind her and knew there could be no further retreat in that direction. She sidled along the stone wall and, relentlessly, he followed. At the corner he blocked her escape by placing his hands on the wall, one on either side of her head. When she tried to duck out of his trap, he leaned forward and pressed her back against the cold stone.

His face only inches from hers, he murmured, "Even insults from your lips are exciting. I can barely imagine what it will be like when you begin whispering endearments."

"You'll never hear endearments from me!" she cried.

"Don't be too certain of that, sweetheart."

When he began kissing her, her heart fluttered and leaped, making her fear she might faint. She couldn't allow herself to do that — it would make this too easy for him.

His lips were warm and firm as they covered her mouth, then moved along her throat. As he turned his head to kiss her shoulder, she bit his ear sharply. He let go of her for an instant, cursing in Gaelic.

Cathryn flung herself away from him and ran, trying to hold her full skirts up and out of the way. He caught her easily, picking her up in his arms and carrying her to the bed. As soon as he tossed her onto it, she threw herself to the other side. She slid off the bed, and he grabbed for her, catching the hem of her skirt and causing her to fall heavily onto the floor. He lay across the bed and reached out one long arm, clutching her ankle. With a grip of iron, he dragged her back toward him, causing her petticoats to bunch up around her hips. He smiled appreciatively at the sight of her long, slim legs, but a sharp kick from her free foot struck him in the chest, and he momentarily lost his hold on her.

She was up and quickly away, circling the room, trying to keep some piece of furniture or other obstacle between them. Clad only in tight leather breeches, he followed her with the sure, muscular grace of a wild animal stalking its prey.

Cathryn was breathing heavily, both from fear and exertion. Her breasts rose and fell, attracting the attention of his topaz gaze. Her hair was tumbling wildly down her back and over her shoulders, giving her a wanton look completely at odds with the terror in her eyes.

"This will be easier if you don't fight me, Catriona," Revan stated and made a sudden lunge at her. She gasped in fright and darted away.

He caught one arm and whirled her back against his bare chest, holding her tightly with an arm around her waist. With his other hand he began unbuttoning the row of tiny buttons down the front of her dress. She struggled to free herself, but his hold only tightened, threatening to shut off her breath.

When the last button was undone, he slid the gown from one shoulder, leaving it naked under his burning kiss.

Cathryn moaned and twisted in his grasp, but that did not prevent him from baring the other shoulder and dropping the gown to her waist. Suddenly, with a quick flick of his strong wrist, the dress fell to the floor at her feet, spreading wide in a saffron circle.

He lifted her from the folds of the velvet gown and turned her to face him. Wearing only her chemise and petticoats, she tried to shield herself from his devouring stare.

"Don't be unduly modest, love," he said, his deep voice warm with laughter. "I have seen you in far less, remember."

She flung out a hand to strike his face, but he caught her wrist easily and twisted the arm behind her back, arching her body against his.

Her chemise was loosely laced at the top and her breasts

strained against the fabric as if aching to be free. He put her other arm behind her back and held it there, firmly. Then, with a look that touched her like pure flame, he bent close to her and, taking the ribbon on her chemise into his strong, white teeth, he gently pulled it loose. He nuzzled his face into the gaping top of the garment and slowly kissed the rounded side of each breast. Cathryn's breath came in ragged gasps, and she tried to lean her body away from his.

"Why do you struggle?" he asked. "I will have my way, and well you know it. Let's be done with the fighting."

"Never!" she hissed.

"Ah, Catriona, you are a stubborn woman."

Again his lips moved over her breasts, this time finding and caressing the nipples through the thin material.

"Stop it!" she cried, thrashing her legs and trying to kick him. Feeling his ardent mouth against her body only served to further infuriate her. "You vile, unspeakable creature!"

His face was mocking as it raised to hers. "I adore you, too, my love." His kiss was brutal, punishing her for her angry words. He pressed her so tightly against him there was no use in further struggle.

Keeping her arms pinioned behind her back with one hand, he slid the other to her knees and lifted her easily into his arms, his demanding lips still on her own. Then, as he carried her toward the bed, his mouth trailed kisses from her lips to her throat and along the side of her neck.

"Now," he warned her quietly, "I am going to put you down on this bed, and if you try to run away again, I am going to lift your petticoats and thrash you until you cannot sit down for a week."

"You wouldn't!"

"That's the trouble with you, lass. You never believe I mean what I say."

"Oh, I believe you are capable of the brutality," she spat back at him. "I just can't believe the other people in this castle would let you inflict bodily harm on an innocent woman and do nothing to help her. And, I promise you, if you try to harm me further, I will scream until they all come running!"

"Scream away, love. I have informed my men of our plans for the evening and they will see we are undisturbed. 'Tis not unusual for the Highland wedding night to be a bit noisy . . . and, lass, I do consider this our wedding night."

Cathryn paled. "What do you mean . . . noisy?"

"I mean, the usual weddings in these parts are celebrated with a good deal of *usquebaugh* — Scottish whiskey, if you don't recognize the name — and things can get extremely . . . joyous." Again, his lean features lighted with amusement and his smile gleamed through the dark beard. "If the bride and groom do a bit of whooping and thumping, no one thinks anything of it."

"I was speaking of screaming," she retorted angrily, "not whooping in misguided joy."

"Och, darlin', if you'd only give me the chance, your joy might not be misguided." He pressed a warm kiss on her lips. "And, besides, the sight of Owen MacIvor standing guard outside this door with a dirk and a fierce scowl is enough to discourage even the stoutest-hearted hero who might mistakenly think your screams are other than uncontrolled expressions of bliss."

"Owen MacIvor is outside this room?" she cried, shocked. "Do you mean to say he has heard everything that has gone on between us?"

"I would not be surprised if our activities have been heard by everyone in the castle," he grinned. "So far they have been rigorous, to say the least."

"How could you be so insensitive? Have you no pride or decency?"

"Surely we don't have to discuss that again?" he asked tiredly. "Tonight I will stand for no more lectures on my boorish behavior. Since that's the way you see me, that's the way I intend to be and your lectures will do no good. And now, I'm getting a bit weary of standing here holding you. I would like to conserve a little strength for what comes next, so will you promise to stay put if I let you down?"

She stared defiantly, her eyes a dangerously dark shade of green. "I'll promise nothing."

He dropped her onto the bed. "It doesn't matter," he said

flatly. "You won't go far."

She put her feet on the floor and when he didn't react, she stood up to face him.

"Revan, please let me reason with you."

"Never! I'll promise nothing," he mimicked her words. He leaned forward and, grasping the bedcovers, stripped them back.

She stamped her foot in anger. "Damn you, listen to me!"

His eyebrows went up. "Surely you never spoke that way to Basil?"

She turned her back and covered her face with her hands. She made some muffled reply he couldn't hear. Turning her back to face him, he pulled her hands away from her face and said softly, "I couldn't hear you, love."

"I said it was cruel of you to mention my husband at a time like this!"

"It was cruel of you to take a husband, Catriona. It was cruel of you to not recognize what lay between us from the first."

"You insist on making this my fault," she cried, raising stricken eyes to his. "I . . . I find myself in a situation I didn't create. A situation I don't want, and I'm helpless to do anything about it."

"You will never be helpless, my dear."

Her chin came up and she straightened her shoulders. Facing him boldly, she asked, "Am I not helpless at this moment? Am I not at your mercy? You have just informed me this is so, but for God's sake, Revan, if there is any way I can talk you out of this, tell me what it is!"

His hands went to her shoulders. "All my life I have prided myself on the fact that, once I have made up my mind on a matter, nothing will change it. Therefore, take my word for it, there is nothing you can say or do to dissuade me. But, love, you are mistaken if you think you are helpless. Believe me, you hold all the cards in this game, and you will find soon enough it is I who am at your mercy."

"I don't pretend to understand what you are saying," she replied, scorn in her voice again. She realized pleading or cajoling was not going to work and she steeled herself for further physical resistance. It seemed the only choice left.

He pulled her to him, and as her hands came up to ward him off, she could feel the powerful muscles and crisply curling hair of his chest. His strength was so effortless, so much a part of him that she feared her struggles would be wasted, but she vowed silently to outlast him as long as possible. She could bite and scratch and claw. No, she was not going to make it easier for him. If he took her tonight, it was going to be a matter of rape.

His hands were warm against her skin as he slid them up her arms to drop the straps of the chemise down over her shoulders. As she tried to tug them back up again, his fingers were busy further loosening the lacing down the front. She thrust his hands away and tried to avoid his grasp, but he pushed her down onto the bed, his hands following relentlessly, loosening and tearing at the fabric and lace, pulling it away from her upper body until it lay bare beneath his gaze.

Still she struggled, twisting from side to side and drawing up her knees. He was through with laughter and teasing now, and she sensed it in the altered expression on his face and in his eyes. There was renewed intention as he casually undid the buckle of his leather breeches and let them drop to the floor. With a sudden disregard for Owen MacIvor's listening ear, Cathryn gave a small scream and flung herself to the far side of the bed. She had never seen a naked man before, and the sight of Revan MacLinn's brawny masculinity did little to assure her of her safety.

He reached out a sure hand and caught the waistband of her petticoats, pulling her back toward him. The fabric began to rip and with impatient hands, he tore it the rest of the way, flinging the ruined garments aside. As he lowered himself to the bed, Cathryn began flailing the air with her clenched fists. One of them caught the man just below the right eye, and she almost laughed at his look of incredulous surprise.

"Why, you little she-devil," he groaned, "just be glad I'm a gentleman."

"You! A gentleman?" she panted, hysterical laughter

beginning. She saw a lustful determination in his eyes and felt she would choke in her desperation. She clawed at his chest, leaving ugly red scratches.

"Damn you, Catriona," he said between clenched teeth, "can't you just give in like a good lass?"

"I'll never give in to you!" Now her breath was coming in sobs, and she was barely aware of what she was doing. One hand caught in his thick black hair, and she yanked as hard as she could, feeling satisfaction at his yelp of pain. As he loosened his hold on her, trying to untangle her fingers from his hair, she used her other hand to slap his face with the last bit of strength she could muster.

Instantly, he slapped her back and muttered, "That, my love, was the last blow of the battle. I am through with patience."

And, indeed, as he positioned her body beneath his, he did it with such ease that she knew he had only been playing with her, allowing her to think there was some small chance of escape. Hot tears welled in her eyes, and she choked back sobs.

Dimly, she felt his heavy body over hers, then the deep and burning pain and his quick, hard thrusts. Close by her ear she could hear his voice, murmuring Gaelic words over and over, until, with a deep moan he moved to cover her lips with a violent kiss. As she looked upward into his passion-darkened eyes, she knew he had entered some unknown world of ecstasy, leaving her far behind.

In pain and frustration, she turned her face from his kiss and let the tears flow freely. Later she was aware of him leaning over her, kissing away the tears and whispering, "Catriona, I didn't want to hurt you, but it was your choice to fight me. Next time I promise it will be different."

She turned on her side, lifting a bare shoulder against him. Presently, she heard him sigh and felt the warmth of the blankets as he pulled them over her. He was quiet for a long time, and then she heard his deep breathing and knew he had fallen asleep. A storm of weeping shook her slender body and she buried her face in the pillow, so neither Revan nor Owen MacIvor would hear her giving way to the helplessness she now felt.

Sometime in the early morning hours Cathryn roused up, stiff from lying in one position and shivering with cold. She turned quietly onto her back, trying to ease her aching muscles. As she moved her head on the pillow, she saw that Revan had awakened and was watching her.

"Are you cold, love?" he asked, pulling the bedcovers about them.

She couldn't bring herself to answer, but an involuntary shudder shook her body and Revan, noticing, said, "I'll build up the fire. 'Tis nearly out."

He slipped from beneath the blankets and strode across the room where he stoked the fire and tossed on more logs. Cathryn turned away from the disturbing sight of his nakedness, but the newly rekindled flames leaped high and threw his shadow on the wall, huge and menacing. She closed her eyes tightly, clutching the covers about her chin.

She felt the bed give as he crawled back into it and stretched out his long frame. After a few minutes he turned to her and slipped one arm beneath her head, drawing her close. She stiffened, keeping her eyes closed.

"Catriona," he said softly, "look at me."

She turned her head away and his breath was warm on her neck.

"You knew it would have to come to this, surely? I made no secret of my intentions from the start."

He waited and when she still didn't speak, he raised himself to look down into her face. "Lass, there's naught you can do about it now. Accept it with good grace and mayhap, in a short while, it won't seem such a terrible thing."

She felt his light kisses on her brow, then down the line of her jaw and to her mouth. She tried to control her revulsion and lay as quietly as possible. It was a mistake to think he would become discouraged and leave her alone. Soon she could sense a growing ardor on his part, and his kiss became more demanding.

"Damn, I try to be gentle," he groaned, "but you have

166

made me wait so long it isn't easy."

His voice grew husky and his hands rougher as they caressed her shoulders and breasts. "Catriona, you are so beautiful . . ."

Finally, words were forgotten as he lowered his body over hers and the nightmare began again. In the heat of his passion, as before, he whispered words in Gaelic, his breath harsh in her ear.

Afterwards, he slept once again, but she lay staring into the darkness, quiet tears running down her face and onto the pillow.

A loud knock at the door awakened them the next morning, and Cathryn sat upright in the bed, clutching the sheets and blankets about her.

"Easy, love, 'tis only Owen," Revan murmured.

"Don't let him in! I don't want anyone to see me like this."

Revan stretched and tossed back the covers. "If I don't make some kind of response, the man will be breaking down the door to see if you have planted a dagger in my back."

As he crawled out of the bed, Cathryn ducked back under the covers, saying, "Then, please, close the bed curtains so I will be out of sight."

His laugh was easy. "Whatever you say, Catriona."

He pulled on his leather breeks as the knock sounded again. "In a moment, Owen. Have a bit of patience."

He untied the bands holding the tartan curtains around the bed and pulled the drapes together to hide Cathryn's huddled form.

Retrieving the key from the top of the wardrobe, he unlocked the door to admit the large Scotsman who waited outside.

"Gad, Owen, you needn't have stood guard all night," Revan chuckled ruefully. "You don't look as if you slept much."

Owen's thick eyebrows went up, and he placed ham-like hands on his hips, threw back his curly red head and laughed loudly. "In the name of truth, lad, you don't look as if you had too peaceful a night either! Look at you — I've seen you come out of battle in better shape!"

Revan followed Owen's amused glance to his chest, which was streaked with angry red scratches. Before he could say a word, Owen's laughter rang out again.

"By God, is that a black eye?"

Revan's cheek felt tender to his touch. "Aye, chances are," he agreed, smiling. "And the little she-wolf nearly bit off my ear. A very lively wench, Owen, let me assure you."

"I hung about outside the door long enough to know the truth of that. For a time there I feared for your life! But then, when the crashing and the arguing ceased, I figured you had things under control, so I went off to seek a little amusement myself."

"For your sake, I hope your companion was more amiable than mine," Revan said.

Muffled exclamations came from inside the curtained bed and the two men exchanged amused glances.

"Now, Owen, what brings you to our door so early?" asked Revan, ignoring Cathryn's outburst.

"The morning is half-gone, Revan, and Elsa has been up here twice with some new clothes for Cathryn. And she wanted to know if you'll have breakfast or not. Finally, I sent her down to the kitchens to tell them to start preparing your breakfast, and she said she'd be right back with the clothes. I thought I should warn you." His gaze swept Revan's chest again, then lingered on the pile of torn petticoats beside the bed and an overturned chair by the fireplace. "The lass has a wagging tongue, as you may recall."

"All right, Owen, my friend," Revan laughed. "We'll get presentable. When she comes back, send her on in."

After the door closed, Revan set the chair upright, and gathered the petticoats into a ball and stuffed them into the wardrobe. He pulled out the velvet dressing gown, parted the bed curtains and tossed it in to Cathryn.

"As you no doubt heard, Elsa is bringing you some clothing."

"I heard," she replied, snatching the robe from him and pulling the curtains closed again. "I don't know how you

168

expect me to face anyone."

He bent to pick up her dress, still lying in a golden circle and folded it carefully, putting it into the wardrobe. Then he pulled his own shirt over his head and was just putting on his boots when another knock sounded, and Elsa bounced in, her round face lighted by a big smile.

"Mornin', sir," she beamed. "I've brought some of Miss Cathryn's new clothes. Morag has had all the cottage women sewing day and night, and they have made some things truly worthy of the laird's . . . er, lady." Her smile faltered, but her eyes were as impudent as ever.

Revan only smiled. "Cathryn, come out and see the things Elsa has brought," he commanded.

There was no response from the woman in the bed, so he turned back to Elsa. "I guess the lady isn't interested, Elsa. Do you think you could just distribute the clothes among the other women in the castle?"

"Wait!" Cathryn cried, sticking her tousled head through the tartan curtains. "I . . . I need the clothing, Revan. I have almost nothing to wear."

"Then, for heaven's sake, come on out and look at the things."

It took all her courage to leave the security of the bed and face Elsa's bright and knowing eyes, and Revan had to admire the way she held her chin high, with only one quick glance at the door to make certain Owen wasn't in the room. Wearing the man's robe, which was too large for her, and with her long hair uncombed, she looked like a small and vulnerable child.

Elsa piled the stack of clothing in one of the armchairs, and Cathryn sank to the floor in front of it, her embarassment forgotten in her interest in the new clothes. As she shook out the dresses one by one, she seemed to lose her self-consciousness.

"Oh, look at all these lovely things!" she cried. "I can't believe it." She lifted a soft blue wool gown with a high neck and long cuffed sleeves. "This will be so warm. And this . . . look at this!" She held up an elegant black dress, also of the softest wool.

169

She looked up at Elsa and Revan, her misery momentarily forgotten and her large eyes shining with pleasure. She looked so appealing, Revan took a step toward her, then remembered Elsa's presence and checked his stride.

There were two other dresses for everyday, a caramel-colored wool and a gray velvet, with lace collar and cuffs. There were underthings, as well, and two pair of leather slippers. On the bottom of the pile of clothing was an exquisite green evening gown. Cathryn lifted it reverently. "It's the most beautiful dress I've ever seen," she breathed. "I've never owned anything so wonderful!"

She got to her feet and held the dress to herself, looking at them for their approval. The velvet shimmered silver green, shading to a much darker green in the deep folds. It exactly matched her eyes and made an effective background for her darkly flaming hair. When her eyes caught sight of the look in Revan MacLinn's she felt as though, once again, he had laid his hard, warm hands on her body. She flushed and looked away, a little of her sudden delight fading. Quietly, she folded the dress and laid it with the others on the chair.

"Thank you for bringing these to me, Elsa," she said, smoothing the velvet folds with a small hand. "I must go see Morag today and thank her. Those poor women must have sewn for hours on end."

"Aye, but they don't mind, seeing it was for you."

"But they don't even know me," Cathryn said, surprised.

"Nothing is too good for the laird and his lady," answered Elsa. "They'll all move heaven and earth to please the MacLinn."

Cathryn's eyes fell. "Yes, well, I really don't know what to say, except that I am very grateful. It will be a pleasure to have my own clothing again."

"Morag said to tell you the rest of the dresses will be done in about a week, and she should have your cloak finished by tomorrow."

"There are more?" Cathryn gasped. "Oh, my goodness, I never expected anything like this!"

Elsa grinned broadly. "Your thanks should go to the laird, I'm sure. Now I'll just go down to the kitchen and fetch your breakfast. I'll be right back."

When she had left the room, Revan said, "It pleases me to see you looking happier, Catriona. I feared you might never smile again."

His gently teasing tone irritated Cathryn, but she made no reply, busying herself with placing the new clothing into the wardrobe. As she pulled out the wad of torn petticoats, her cheeks flamed and she threw them angrily into the corner.

"Reminders of a fate worse than death?" he mocked.

"A reminder of the worst night of my life!" she snapped.

He stepped close to her, his big hands closing over her shoulders. "If I thought you really meant that . . ."

"What makes you think I don't?" Green eyes blazed into amber ones. "How could it have been anything but the worst night of my life?"

"You might be surprised at what a bit of cooperation on your part could do." He bent his dark head toward hers. "I suggest we try it tonight . . ."

"I suggest you . . ." At that moment Elsa returned, with a heavy tray in her hands. Revan released Cathryn to take it from her and place it on the table near the fire.

"Will that be all?" Elsa asked pertly.

"I'm truly sorry to bother you further, but would it be possible for me to have some hot water for a bath?" Cathryn asked.

"Oh, yes, ma'm," Elsa nodded. "I'll bring it right away."

As she scurried away again, Revan pulled one of the chairs up to the table and motioned for Cathryn to seat herself. She would like to have refused, but in truth, she was hungry, so she simply sat down and began to eat, paying no further attention to the man. With a raised eyebrow and a half-smile on his lips, Revan pulled up the other chair and set about eating his own breakfast.

They were nearly finished when Elsa came back with two oaken pails of steaming water. She was followed by Owen MacIvor, sheepishly toting a copper bathtub and another pail of hot water. These they placed before the fire at Cathryn's bidding.

"Thank you very much," she said graciously. "I won't bother you again."

Gathering up the dishes, Elsa left the room. Owen gave his master a questioning look, to which Revan replied, "Yes, I'll be along in a few minutes. I'll meet you downstairs."

Cathryn took some soap and towels out of the tub, then poured two of the buckets of water into it. She looked pointedly at Revan, who stood watching her.

"What? You expect me to leave?" he asked.

"I demand it! Surely I'm to be allowed at least enough privacy for my bath?"

"For God's sake, woman, we have just spent the night together," he exploded. "What harm will it do if I choose to sit and watch you at your bath?"

"I will not bathe in front of you," she said firmly. "I refuse."

"So, you're still refusing your laird?" he said, coming close to her. "I would think you'd have learned the foolishness of that."

Her chin shot up, sparks of anger glinting in her eyes. "You are an unspeakable, insufferable . . ."

He caught her arm in a cruel grip. "I have the time if it's another lesson in humility you seek." His voice was steely, dangerous. Her eyes fell before his arrogant gaze.

"No," she murmured. "I . . . I'm only asking to be allowed my bath in private."

"Look at me," he ordered. She raised her eyes again, almost overwhelmed by the fierceness of his. "You may have your bath alone, love, but you do know I could make you do as I wish, don't you?"

She was silent. He gave her arm a gentle shake. "Don't you?"

Mutely, she nodded, feeling the total misery of the night before settling on her once again.

"Just don't forget that fact. Now, I'll leave you and go down to meet Owen. I will see you later today."

He cupped her face in both hands and kissed her lips, very softly, surprising her with his gentleness after the harsh words.

Later, in the little tub filled with steaming water, she

172

scrubbed every inch of her skin, knowing full well she was never going to be able to erase the feel of Revan MacLinn from her body. Somehow, in some inexplicable and distressing way, she felt as if he'd branded her, marking her forever as another of his possessions.

Chapter Ten

Later, when her bath was finished, Cathryn dressed in the blue woolen gown and was combing her hair when someone tapped at the door.

Nervously, she gave a start. She didn't want to see Revan again just yet. Throughout the long night she had dreaded facing him in the light of day, but after they were awakened by Owen's knock, events had occurred so rapidly she hadn't time to become self-conscious. Her pleasure over the new dresses had helped take the edge off her embarrassment and, later, her anger over his assumption she would calmly display herself before him had sustained her until he was gone. Now, the thought of seeing him again filled her with apprehension.

"Who is it?" she asked hesitantly.

" 'Tis me, Elsa. Are you finished with your bath?"

Breathing a sigh of relief, Cathryn replied, "Oh, yes, Elsa, come on in."

As they worked together to empty the water from the little bathtub, Cathryn was aware of the maid's close scrutiny. Finally, she said, "Elsa, please don't stare! It unnerves me."

"Sorry," Elsa muttered, picking up the buckets and carrying them into the privy chamber in the dressing room. Cathryn could hear the water being poured down the *lang drap* and then the girl was back.

"I don't mean to be irritable," Cathryn said, "it's just that I . . . well, I dislike having to face anyone this morning, and you shame me by staring."

Elsa grinned, unable to look stern for long. "Aye, I can see what you mean. 'Tis certain everyone will want a look at you today."

Cathryn whirled away, cheeks flaming. "Then it's true? Everyone knows about . . . about last night?"

The girl nodded gaily. "Oh, to be sure! The MacLinn told Owen, and the word got around quickly. Not much can be secret in a place like this."

"How can I ever face them again?" Cathryn fumed. "Oh! Revan MacLinn is a hateful, selfish brute!"

"Miss, you shouldn't feel that way," Elsa scolded, her voice light, but with an undertone of seriousness. "There's many a lass who'd be honored to have been chosen by the laird."

"Then why didn't he pick one of them?" Cathryn cried. "It wasn't fair for him to make me his if there were so many others who were willing. Does he think all he has to do is command, and I will fall at his feet, ready to adore him?"

"No woman has ever scorned Revan MacLinn," Elsa pointed out, reasonably.

"I have! I do!" retorted Cathryn, her eyes blazing. "He will find that it takes more than a night of forced seduction to win me over!"

Elsa's round face took on a bemused expression as she considered the possibilities of a 'night of forced seduction'. Finally she asked, with only a little hesitation, "Was he not a bonny lover?"

"Oh, Elsa!" Cathryn allowed her disgust to show in her voice. "All the women in this castle must be daft! If you think it would be so wonderful to be . . . to be physically attacked by the great MacLinn chieftain, why don't you just form a line beside his bed? I'm certain the rampant stallion would be happy to accommodate the lot!" She took a few steps away from the girl, then whirled back, saying, "Sometimes I think I'm losing my mind! I am in the most horrible situation, and yet, everyone seems to think I should be honored by his attentions. No one considers my feelings! I have become an adulteress through no fault of my own, and yet, I am the one who will have to pay the price when the day of reckoning comes. It galls my soul to know how I will suffer and how your chieftain will just walk away, ready for his next conquest, with no blame or responsibility in the matter. Can't you understand that?"

175

"I think I know what you mean, Miss, but the MacLinn isn't like that. He isn't going to walk away from you. He looks upon you as his wife, Owen says, and he means to be faithful." She giggled. "No matter how long the line waiting at his bedside, he would show no interest."

"I find that very difficult to believe," Cathryn snapped. "And even if it were true, his faithfulness is misplaced. I am another man's wife."

"I agree, that's a problem," Elsa said solemnly. "But somehow, Revan MacLinn will solve everything."

"You MacLinns have great faith in your chief," Cathryn remarked dryly.

"Indeed. He has brought his people through a great deal, and we feel we owe him our lives."

"It must be nice to be such an adored hero." Cathryn's tone was acid, but Elsa chose to ignore the fact.

"Oh, yes," the girl agreed. "Of course, the MacLinn is worthy."

Cathryn gave up. She wasn't going to get through to the girl, to any of them. They were so accustomed to obeying their leader and thinking his every word was sacred they could never approach the situation from her viewpoint. She was wasting her breath.

Elsa pushed the bathtub back into the corner by the fireplace, saying, "I am supposed to leave this here in case you want to use it again. Now, is there anything else you would like for me to do?" Just then her bright glance caught sight of the pile of petticoats Cathryn had tossed aside earlier. She bent to pick them up, shaking them out. As she saw the jagged tears that went from waistband to hem, she rolled her eyes around to look at Cathryn.

"Shall I take these to Morag to be mended, Miss?"

"No! Burn them. I certainly don't want them anymore."

"Very well."

"However, speaking of Morag," Cathryn said in a meeker tone, "perhaps you could tell me where I might find her? I should thank her for my new clothing."

"I believe she is with Mrs. MacLinn," Elsa answered. "They are doing the handwork on your new cloak."

"Then, as much as I dislike the thought of it, I suppose I should go speak with both of them."

She paused outside Margaret MacLinn's door, summoning her courage, then finally knocked.

The two women were seated by the fire with a length of russet velvet between them. As she approached, she could see they were sewing strips of dark brown fur around the hood and hemline.

"What a beautiful garment!" Cathryn breathed.

Margaret MacLinn smiled. "It's your new cloak, dear. Would you like to try it on?"

Before she could answer, Margaret was on her feet, placing the heavy cloak around Cathryn's shoulders. She pulled up the hood, tucking in bright strands of hair. Stepping back, she looked at Morag and uttered something in Gaelic. The other woman replied, also in Gaelic, nodding and smiling.

"Morag says you are very beautiful, and it is a pleasure to sew for someone who looks like you."

"Thank you," Cathryn said, her hands caressing the smooth velvet fabric. "Tell her it is the loveliest cloak I have ever seen and I will be proud to wear it."

Margaret conveyed the message and the other woman smiled and nodded again. It was quite evident she felt honored at Cathryn's words, though Cathryn could not understand why.

"I came to thank you both for the new clothes," she went on. "I am overwhelmed by your generosity."

"Revan's generosity," Margaret corrected, gently. "My son gave orders that you should have some decent clothing of your own, and he was very specific about what you were to have. He even chose the fabrics and colors."

"Well, I am grateful to those of you who spent so many hours sewing! I can't imagine turning out so much in such a short time."

"Don't forget, there are a large number of women on the castle grounds, and they were all willing to lend a hand. So many people working long hours can accomplish a great deal."

"I am very appreciative, but it wasn't necessary for them to inconvenience themselves so much," Cathryn replied.

"It was no inconvenience. Besides, they all enjoy pleasing their chieftain."

"So I have been informed." Cathryn's tone was dry.

She lifted the cloak from her shoulders and laid it gently across Morag's lap. Laying a hand on the woman's arm, she smiled and said, "Thank you, Morag."

The seamstress' face creased into an even bigger smile as she put her own hand over Cathryn's and said something in Gaelic.

Straightening, Cathryn looked questioningly at Margaret. "What did she say?"

Margaret looked uneasy, but after a brief moment, said, "Morag says you are a very bonny lassie, and it was a lucky day for all of us when Revan brought you here to become mistress of Wolfcrag. She wishes you good fortune and many children."

Cathryn attempted to keep smiling graciously. To Margaret she said, "Don't worry, I won't create a scene. I think there have been quite enough of those lately."

"I'm sorry you are still angry. I thought things might be getting a little better."

"After last night?" Cathryn asked. "Impossible!"

Margaret flushed but met her gaze. "I had hoped Revan would give you a bit more time. He hasn't the patience his father had, I'm afraid."

"I warned you not to expect a romantic ending to this story, remember. There is less chance of that than ever."

"Cathryn, please give him a chance. . . ."

"I have to go now, Margaret. I promised Meg I would come to see her today. I just wanted to thank you for the clothes."

She left the room before Margaret could say anything further. Again, she realized the futility of arguing with any of the MacLinns.

She found Meg in her room playing with her assortment of dolls. The hound, lying on the hearth, raised his head as Cathryn came into the room, but immediately went back to his slumber, satisfied there was no danger to his young mistress.

Cathryn settled herself on the floor beside Meg, thinking she was probably the one person in the entire castle who didn't know of her abasement. Here there would be no avid scrutiny, no knowing looks or half-smiles.

"Did you come to play with me?" the little girl asked, tilting her head to one side.

"I promised I would, didn't I?"

"Yes, but sometimes grown-ups forget or get too busy with other things."

Cathryn felt pity for the child. No doubt she was often shuffled to one side when clan business or household affairs beckoned.

"I always keep my promises, Meg," she said. "Besides, I really do want to see the secret tunnel you told me about."

Meg's eyes lighted happily. "Shall we go down now?"

"Let's do."

Hand in hand, they started to the door. The dog opened one sleepy eye, then wearily dragged himself away from the fire. It was very evident he would have preferred to stay right where he was, but felt it his duty to follow them.

"I'm so glad you remembered me," Meg stated, looking up into Cathryn's face as they went down the stairs. "My mother was very angry this morning and told me to stay out of her sight. I thought I would have to stay in my room all day. But she won't mind if I am with you, will she?"

"I don't know, dear," Cathryn answered honestly. "Perhaps not. We shall just have to avoid her."

"I don't know what was wrong with her," the child continued. "Do you think her face might be hurting her? Grandmother says it does sometimes."

"Yes, I expect that's what it was," Cathryn replied briskly, though she had her own idea about what had made Darroch so irritable. To change the subject, she asked, "Where is this secret tunnel?"

Meg led the way through the Great Hall and into the banqueting room where Cathryn was momentarily chagrined at the memory of the night Revan had forced her to drink the toast to the Stuart exiles. Quickly, she put the feeling aside and concentrated on Meg's next words.

"See this stone?" the child asked. They were standing in the large recessed area by the windows and through the tall glass panes Cathryn could see the rocky beach and swirling gray ocean below them. She dragged her eyes back to the castle wall where Meg's small hand rested.

"I see it. Is that how you get into the tunnel?"

"Yes, you just push here and the door slides open." To demonstrate, Meg pressed against the slightly raised stone and, with a grating noise, a small section of the wall shifted, leaving an opening just large enough to slip through.

"Do you want to go inside?" the little girl asked. "We wouldn't have to go very far."

"What happens if the door shuts behind you?" Cathryn asked, a touch of fear in her voice. Cold, dank air rushed in through the mouth of the tunnel and she could hear the muffled roar of the ocean. It looked like a rather dark and frightening place.

"You can shut the door or open it from the inside," Meg explained. "There is another stone on the other side of this wall."

The child gathered up her skirts and stepped inside the tunnel, followed by her dog. Cathryn went next, ducking low to avoid striking her head on the stones.

The floor of the tunnel was damp rock, quite slippery, and sloping steeply away from the entrance. She supposed it would drop rapidly to the beach directly below them. She noticed a pile of candles on a ledge of stone just above the doorway.

Cathryn followed Meg for a few yards, until the lack of light made it difficult for them to see.

"I don't think we should go any further, Meg—especially if the tunnel is dangerous. I am certain your mother would be even angrier if she found out we came here."

"Yes, she doesn't like the tunnel very much."

"I think I can understand why," Cathryn laughed nervously. "It's so dark and cold!"

"Sometimes when Father is with me, we go all the way

180

down to the water. He doesn't think it is dangerous."

"Nevertheless, I think we should go back now."

"Don't you want to see our little boat?" Meg asked.

"There is a boat?" A sudden note of interest had come into her voice.

"Yes, a very old one. It has a wolf's head painted on the side, and Father used to play in it when he was a little boy. Sometimes we go out in it, and he rows me to one of the islands so we can watch the seals. Wouldn't you like to do that sometime?"

"Yes, but perhaps when it's warmer outdoors."

"I'll ask him if he'll take us this summer so we can see the babies. Wouldn't that be fun?"

"That would be very nice," Cathryn replied. "But right now I am getting cold and want to go back inside the castle."

"All right, but what shall we do next?"

"We could have that game of 'Hide and Seek', if you like. I am certain you will be able to show me a good many other places where you and your friends hide."

"Oh, yes, there are ever so many!" She suddenly looked serious. "Cathryn, I'm glad Father brought you to live with us. You are more fun than anyone in the whole castle."

"Even your father?" Cathryn asked with a teasing smile.

Meg considered for a moment and finally answered, "Yes, just a little bit more fun. He is always so busy being the clan chieftain that sometimes he doesn't have time to play with me."

"Well, I have a good deal of free time," Cathryn stated, foolishly pleased that someone had, at last, rated her higher than Revan MacLinn. "I promise, we shall become very good friends."

As they closed the door to the tunnel behind them, she felt the pricking of her conscience. She knew she was making a promise she might not be able to keep if everything went according to the new plan she was already formulating in her mind.

Lowering clouds filled the western sky, causing the afternoon to turn dark early. Standing at the window watching the last bit of sun being swallowed up by the evening, Cathryn's thoughts were far away. She wondered what had gone on in her home since she had last seen it. It was nearly impossible for her to guess the state of her father's mind, and she hardly dared think of Basil. She glanced down at the gold band on her finger. She knew he would have been furious at Revan's high-handed action, but with no means of retaliation open to him, how had he coped with his frustration? She wondered if the two of them expected to ever see her again, or had they simply gone on with their lives, convinced she was already lost to them? If only she could send them some kind of mental message, to urge them not to give up—to keep hoping and waiting for her return.

Below in the courtyard she heard the noisy arrival of several men on horseback; Revan at their head. He had obviously been away from the castle, so that explained why she hadn't seen him all day. Now, she supposed, the dreaded meeting was inevitable. She remained at the window, resting her forehead against the cold glass, looking out, even though it had now grown too dark to see very much. Lamps and candles were being lit in the cottages, and sometimes a door opened, spilling light onto the cobbled pavement. It made her wonder what life must be like for the people who lived in those small houses so close under the huge shadow of Wolfcrag.

She heard Revan's booted footsteps on the stairs, and soon he had flung open the door and was striding into the bedchamber.

"Cathryn?" He came up behind her and put both arms around her waist. There was a smell of fresh cold air clinging to him and his plaid was damp. He put his mouth on her neck, causing her to twist away.

"Still unfriendly?" he asked, lightly.

She gazed at him, not speaking. There were so many things whirling through her mind that she wanted to say to him and yet, strangely enough, the words just wouldn't form on her lips. For some reason, she was in an odd mood this evening.

He shrugged and began unfastening his plaid. "All right, love. There will be time for conversation later. Now we must get ready to go down for the evening meal."

Throwing the woolen garment across a chair, he went into the dressing room and presently she could hear water splashing into the wash basin. In a few minutes, he was back, drying his face with a towel. His damply curling hair gave him the appearance of a young gypsy.

"Are you ready to go downstairs, Catriona?" he asked, tossing the towel aside.

She shook her head. "I'm not going. I prefer to eat in this room, if you don't mind."

"Oh, but I do mind. My kinsmen will be expecting to see you by my side tonight, and I wouldn't want to disappoint them."

"What about my feelings? Can't you see how I feel about having to appear before them after all that occurred last night?"

"Lass, you have to face them sometime. It might as well be tonight. No one will insult you."

She gave him a level stare. "No one could insult me as you have already done!" She saw his face tighten in anger. "I'm not afraid of being insulted. It's their stares and laughter to which I object."

"Naturally they are curious about their new mistress," Revan began.

Cathryn interrupted. "I am not their mistress!"

"But you are mine," he said quietly. "It all amounts to the same thing."

"That's ridiculous."

"We are going to have to discuss this later, love. I'm afraid they are waiting for our arrival downstairs."

"I'm not going," she declared, glaring at him.

"Why do you persist in making everything so difficult?"

Before she knew what he was doing, he grasped her in his arms and tossed her bodily over his broad shoulder. Holding her tightly about the knees, he started out of the bedroom.

"Put me down!" she cried furiously. "How dare you!"

"You force me to use drastic measures, Catriona."

She pounded on his back with both fists, but it didn't slow his progress down the stairway and into the Great Hall. The hubbub of noise died abruptly as they made their entrance. Cathryn could feel the blood rushing to her face, making it fiery red.

Revan stooped to set her on her feet, then raised a smiling face to the others seated at two long tables.

"I'm sorry we are late. Now you can proceed with the meal."

As the serving girls began passing bowls of soup, he pushed Cathryn into a chair at the head of one table and seated himself beside her.

Leaning close to her, he whispered, "Now see if you can behave yourself properly during this meal. I fear my clansmen may be growing weary of your childish behavior."

"It matters not a whit to me," she retorted, tossing her head. She felt very much like sticking out her tongue at him, but knew that would only verify his opinion of her childishness. Maddeningly, the more he accused her of being childish, the younger and more foolish she felt. He had such an adverse effect upon her, in every way!

"Good evening, Cathryn," Della MacSween said calmly. "You look lovely this evening."

Cathryn turned to the woman seated beside her, again confused with a mixture of feelings. She was glad to see her friend, but resentful the woman had failed in her efforts to forestall Revan MacLinn's physical advances.

"Ah, my good friend Della," she said sarcastically. "The one I counted on to intervene on my behalf! How nice to see you again!"

"Don't be angry, Cathryn. Adam and I did what we could, and you know very well I warned you Revan probably wouldn't listen."

"I should have realized no one in this castle would see my side of the matter," Cathryn muttered bitterly. "I am quickly learning I have only myself to depend upon."

"Oh, Cathryn, that's not true," Della exclaimed. "You're just in a foul mood this evening, and you want to think the worst of everyone."

"Of course I'm in a foul mood! Why wouldn't I be? Last night was a . . . horrible ordeal, and I'm certain I can expect no better tonight."

"You know you are making it worse, don't you?"

Cathryn's eyes glinted in her anger. "I wish people would stop saying that to me! I'm not going to knuckle under and make any of this easier for you. All of you who stand by and see me in this situation and do nothing to help should suffer terrible guilt feelings. You know it's wrong not to help me."

"Why don't you drink your wine, Cathryn? Maybe it will improve your mood."

Abruptly, Della turned away and began a conversation with the person seated on her other side. Cathryn felt uneasy. Perhaps she shouldn't have indulged in that little display of temper. She couldn't afford to lose the one good friend she had made. She reached for the wineglass and took a small sip. Mayhap Della was right, and she should try to improve her disposition. If the wine would help, she would drink it. She tilted the glass and drank the contents. As soon as she set it down, a serving girl was at her elbow to refill it.

"Eat your soup, love," Revan said. "It'll be getting cold."

"I'm not eating, thank you," she replied stiffly.

"Don't try that again, I warn you. Just in case you don't recall, I can and will force you to eat. Is that what you want?"

"No!"

"Then pick up your spoon and start eating," he ordered. " 'Twill be less noticeable than if I have to do it."

The look she gave him was venomous, but he only smiled pleasantly. Slowly, she took up the soup spoon and began to eat. After a few bites, she reached for the wine and drank down half the glass. She was aware of Revan's raised eyebrow and defiantly drained the glass. He said nothing, but she knew he was amused and a bit puzzled over her behavior.

When they were finished with the soup and plates of roasted mutton were being placed before them, Cathryn drank a third glass of wine. Della was right, she thought, the wine did make her feel better — not happy, exactly, just more uncaring.

"Della," she said, her voice low, "you had an excellent idea. This wine is already improving my mood."

"Good. It could stand to be improved."

Cathryn, offended at her words, was quite surprised to hear her own clear laugh ring out. Several of the other diners paused to stare at her, captivated by her gaiety. Revan turned to look at her, realizing it was the first time he had heard her laugh since bringing her to Wolfcrag. The thought was not a pleasant one.

"Tell me what amuses you so, love," he said. "I enjoy seeing you laugh."

"Della keeps scolding me," Cathryn replied. "She's just like you — always trying to make me behave."

Della and Revan exchanged looks over Cathryn's head.

"I think your mood has sweetened considerably," Della said gently. "I really don't think you need any more wine."

"I have only had three glasses," Cathryn argued. "Surely a fourth can't hurt." She held up her empty glass and a passing servant filled it again. Cathryn took a small sip and set the glass beside her plate. "See? I'm going to make this one last."

"Finish your dinner, Catriona," Revan suggested.

"You sound just like my father used to. He always said that . . ." She shook her finger in Revan's astonished face and said in a deep voice. " 'Finish your dinner, Cathryn.' He never called me Catriona. I don't think he would like that name very much."

"Shall I help you eat?" Revan threatened.

"No! Leave me alone. I'll do it."

She picked up her fork and started eating again, stopping between mouthfuls for more wine.

When dessert was served, she declined, but held out the glass to be filled again. Revan took the glass from her and set it out of reach.

"I think you have had enough, love. It's time for us to go upstairs."

"I don't want to go upstairs with you!" she shouted, causing heads to turn all the way down the length of both tables.

Revan's face reddened, and he cast a desperate look at

Della.

"Cathryn, you must be exhausted," Della said. "Wouldn't you like to go up to bed now?"

Cathryn shook her head violently. "I don't want to go to bed with him." She pointed an accusing finger at Revan. "Do you know what he wants . . ."

"For God's sake!" Revan said. "How am I going to shut her up?"

Della couldn't completely control her laughter, even though the man glared at her.

"Why don't you call for some music?" she suggested.

"A good idea!"

The piper was hastily summoned and, almost immediately, the room echoed with the sound of the lively tune he played. Several of the others rose from the table and began dancing, with much shouting and hand-clapping.

"Oh, look at them," Cathryn cried. "I have never seen anyone dancing like that before."

Her green eyes sparkled and her toes tapped in time to the music. Revan couldn't take his eyes off her smiling face. This was Cathryn as he had longed to see her.

"I think we should be going up to our room now, love," he murmured in her ear. She brushed him away.

"Not yet. I want to dance first."

"Do you know how to dance?" he asked.

"No, but I can learn. I am certain I can do that step."

Revan gave a resigned sigh. "All right, I'm willing to give it a try."

"No, no, I don't want to dance with you," she said, pushing herself away from the table. "I think I would like to dance with that man over there." She pointed out a young blond-haired fellow seated across the table from them. At her words, he sprang to his feet and came around the table to her side. She took his hand and they walked away, Cathryn chattering as if she had known him all her life.

Della MacSween felt a pang at the sight of Revan's face as he watched the two of them whirl out among the other dancers. The expression in his eyes was forbidding, and she knew the situation was fraught with danger.

"Revan, don't look like that," she pleaded. "Sit down and act as though you don't mind her dancing with him. After all, it won't do any harm."

"No, I suppose it won't," he admitted, dropping back into his seat. "What is she trying to do?"

Della chuckled. "I'd guess she is trying to play for time. She is worried about leaving with you. Her fear is what prompted her sudden thirst for wine, I do believe."

"Why should she be so afraid of me?" he asked, perplexed.

"Put yourself in her position and perhaps you will understand. This hasn't been easy for her, you know."

"Nor for me," he said, watching Cathryn's laughing face.

"Good heavens!" Della exclaimed, almost angrily. "I wonder when the two of you will begin to think of someone other than yourselves."

His eyes left Cathryn reluctantly. "What do you mean?"

"Oh, never mind. Perhaps someday you will reason it out for yourself. In the meantime, I see my husband approaching, looking very much like he would like to go home."

"I share his thought, I'm afraid."

Again, Cathryn's laugh rang out, and Revan saw her among the other dancers, her skirts swirling high, revealing slim ankles and a shapely calf. His jaw tightened. She was making a spectacle of herself, he decided. It was time to go.

He left his place at the table and strode across the room. Just as he reached the dancers, the music came to a quick halt. The young man with whom Cathryn had been dancing flung himself down on a bench, out of breath and laughing. Cathryn seated herself upon his lap, putting one arm around his neck. Revan advanced on them, aware of the sudden hush in the room and the startled look in the man's eyes as he saw his chieftain towering over him.

Cathryn looked up at Revan, her eyes wide and innocent. "Don't you think Ian is a wonderful dancer? I think he should be properly rewarded." She leaned forward and kissed the astonished Ian full on the lips.

With a growl of anger, Revan grabbed her arm and pulled her off Ian's lap.

"What do you think you're doing?" she laughed, unsteady

on her feet.

"I'm taking you up to bed," he answered. "I think you have entertained these good folk enough for one night."

Once again he tossed her over his shoulder and, to Ian's great relief, swept the room with a smiling look. "It seems my lady was reluctant to come here this evening, and now she is reluctant to leave. However, the hour is growing late and I must insist. As for the rest of you, feel free to stay and dance as late as you please. Piper, start the music again!"

Turning, he proceeded up the stairs. From his shoulder, Cathryn raised her head and surveyed the room full of people. "G'night, everybody!" she called out, then laid her cheek against Revan's broad back and closed her eyes.

Inside the bedchamber, Revan dropped her gently onto the bed, sitting down beside her.

"Good lord, Catriona, you're an aggravating wench! I don't know whether to spank you or kiss you."

She sat up and looked at him, considering. "I shouldn't like to be spanked," she said finally.

With an intent look in his eyes, he bent his face to hers and kissed her, a long and satisfying kiss that started his blood surging. He placed an arm about her shoulders and lowered her to the pillows. Her mouth, which tasted of the wine, parted beneath his lips, and he felt his heart give a painful lurch.

"Oh, Catriona, love," he murmured, his hands moving to the fastenings on her dress. "I can't believe how willing you've become." He laughed harshly. "I should have tried wine a long time ago."

She sat up so he could slide the gown off her shoulders. "I'm . . . I'm not willing," she stated, "just very, very tired."

"Then stand up and take off this dress, and we'll get you into bed."

Obediently, she got off the bed and stood docilely as he took off the dress and began unhooking her petticoats. He heard her sigh.

"I know why you want to get me into bed," she said,

189

shaking one finger at him. "Don't think I don't."

"Do you mind?" he asked softly, stopping to place a kiss on her shoulder.

"Of course I mind."

"You don't seem to mind as much as usual," he smiled.

"Oh, I do—really, I do. I just can't seem to show it."

He stripped away the last of her undergarments and she stood naked before him. She didn't seem to notice and only smiled as his hungry eyes took in every detail of her lovely body.

"My God, but you're a beauty," he whispered.

"Yes, but I'm getting terribly cold," she complained. "And I don't know where my nightgown is."

Revan began taking off his own clothing, but when his hand moved to the buckle on his trousers, Cathryn said, "Don't do that. Let's go sit in front of the fire for a little while."

Surprised by her unusual behavior, but willing to let her have her way, Revan sat in one of the armchairs near the hearth and pulled her down onto his lap. She laid her head on his shoulder, closing her eyes.

"I'm so very tired," she repeated softly.

His hand gently caressed the smooth skin of her back, moving up to cup her head in his large palm. He turned her face to his and covered her mouth with a kiss. She tried to push him away, but her efforts were feeble, and after a moment, she sagged against his chest and let him continue kissing her. His lips moved down her throat, over her breasts and back to her lips, growing continually more ardent.

His warm hand traveled from her neck down the curve of her shoulder to her waist, then rested on the fullness of her hip, drawing her body closer to his. Her soft warmth on his lap made thinking difficult and, for the moment, he let himself believe her sweet acquiescence was the result of some emotion she felt for him rather than the wine she had drunk. It was a heady feeling and one he allowed himself to enjoy without reserve.

She stirred and opened her eyes. "Why are you kissing me?" she asked, leaning away from him to look into his eyes.

"Because it's a very pleasant occupation, love. Don't you agree?"

She shook her head. "No, I don't like it at all." She pressed her lips to his again, then sighed and nestled closer, her head tucked beneath his chin. "See how dreadful it is?"

He laughed softly. "Oh, yes," he agreed, " 'tis fearsomely dreadful." He found her mouth again, his kiss becoming bolder. The feel of her body against his bare chest was having a profound effect upon his breathing and finally, he declared, "We're going to bed, lass."

He rose from the chair, Cathryn in his arms. "Good," she murmured. "I am already half asleep."

He placed her beneath the blankets and as quickly as possible, pulled off his breeches and stretched out beside her. Still she did not turn away or retreat to her side of the bed.

"Cathryn?"

"Hmmm?"

"Shall I make love to you now?"

"No, I don't want you to," she replied, her eyes closed and a dreamy smile on her face. "I just want to go to sleep."

"I think you are lying to me." He bent over her, experimenting with more kisses and caresses. She lay still beneath his touch, neither encouraging nor discouraging him. Something about her passiveness inflamed him and quickly he was ensnared in a passion so overwhelming he could not have controlled it in any event. His body surrounded hers and he was lost to rational thought.

Somewhere, dimly, her mind realized what was happening, but the feeling of euphoria created by the wine persisted, robbing her of any desire to protest. She only wanted to stay in this peaceful state of indifference. Long before Revan uttered one last, terse cry in Gaelic, she had slipped into a deep and dreamless slumber.

Chapter Eleven

Cathryn moved stealthily around the bedchamber, occasionally casting a fearful glance over her shoulder toward the door. Each time she looked, she expected to see Revan MacLinn, his lean frame insolently blocking the doorway, a mocking smile on his face. Her heart turned over at the thought. If he appeared now, it would ruin her entire plan.

It had been a long and nerve-wracking day thus far. She had awakened at noon with the worst headache of her life. It throbbed and pounded each time she moved and even the dim light coming through the windows hurt her eyes. She had lain in bed a long time until Elsa came in with a potion for her to drink.

"Mrs. MacSween sent it," the girl giggled. "She said she thought you would probably be needing it."

Cathryn felt too ill and grouchy to answer. She took the glass of medicine and drank it down, shuddering at its bitter taste. Later, when the severity of her headache began to lessen somewhat, her mind was flooded with half-remembered images from the night before. The last clear memory she had was of herself being whirled about the hall in time to the noisy pipe music, very much cognizant of the burning gaze Revan had leveled in her direction. After that, nothing was clear, but visions of herself sitting unclad on Revan's lap persisted. She was vaguely aware of having tolerated, even accepted, his kisses and caresses. And her tortured mind wouldn't even consider the possibilities of what might have gone on in the big, curtained bed. Her face flamed at the

192

thought of facing the man again. There was no doubt he would be pleased at the chance of recounting every intimate detail. No, she must be gone from the room before he came searching for her.

As soon as Elsa had left, armed with the message that Cathryn didn't feel well and planned to sleep away the afternoon, she had jumped out of bed and hastily dressed. For warmth, she chose the light golden-brown wool dress. Hanging on a hook inside the wardrobe was her new cloak and she gave thanks for it, for she knew she would have need of its warmth. It was a raw afternoon outside and bound to be even colder on the water. Her plan involved rowing the little boat Meg had told her about along the coast until she could find a safe haven, and there was no way of knowing how many hours she might have to endure the wind and sea-spray.

She began pulling her new gowns out of the wardrobe and tossing them onto the bed. She might have to leave without food or other provisions, but her feminine mind rebelled at the thought of leaving her new clothes behind. All but the green evening gown, she sadly decided. It was simply too bulky to fit into a manageable bundle. Regretfully, she smoothed its soft folds one last time before putting it back into the tall chest. Perhaps she could have a copy of it made when she reached her own home.

She folded the other dresses into a pile which she tied up in a linen sheet. It would be awkward to handle, but she was determined not to leave without it.

She quietly opened the bedroom door and looked up and down the hall. Fortunately, there was no one around. Shouldering the bundle, she slipped down the stairs and into the main room of the castle. It was silent and shadowy; she seemed to have chosen an ideal time to make her departure.

The Banqueting Hall was also empty, she saw with relief. Only a few more seconds and she would be outside Wolfcrag. Once she was into the tunnel, the chances of her being found were very small. She pressed the stone as she had seen Meg do, and the wall again shifted, revealing the passageway.

With a last look, she stepped into the tunnel, pulling the

bundle of clothing in after her. Before closing the door she reached for a flint and candle, glad of the flickering light they produced. As the door grated shut behind her, she felt very much alone and half-fearful of the cold dark that lurked just outside the brave circle of light cast by the candle. It was not pleasant to think of lingering in the dark tunnel for any length of time.

She moved slowly, placing her feet cautiously on the damp and slippery floor. As she had suspected, the tunnel sloped downward sharply and as she went further into it, it seemed the steep pitch almost propelled her headlong. It was with relief she noticed steps had been hewn into the solid rock where the way was steepest, allowing the walker to slow his pace.

Cathryn moved through the tunnel for five or ten minutes before she noticed a gradual lightening and then it wasn't long before she made a turn and could see the not-too-distant end of the passage. Under her feet, the stone floor leveled out and gave way to deep sand. The roar of the ocean was now much louder.

As she burst out of the tunnel onto the open beach, the wind caught her hair and whipped it about her head. It billowed the warm cloak and tugged at the sheet-wrapped parcel she carried. The candle was immediately extinguished and since she no longer needed it, she dropped it in the sand.

There was a crescent of sandy beach, edged on either side by huge rock boulders. The only way out of the cove was by water, unless she wanted to retrace her steps through the tunnel. Turning to look behind her, Cathryn felt dwarfed by the massive structure of the castle. It seemed to rise skyward straight from the sand, its base being formed by the same granite boulders that denied escape from the beach. She shivered violently, partly from fear and excitement, and partly from the wintry wind that seemed to chill her very soul.

Once again shouldering the bundle, she started across the sand to where the little wooden boat waited. It was slightly tilted to one side, high up on the beach where the wild tides couldn't get at it. Cathryn tossed the clothing into the boat and stood surveying it with a thoughtful expression. It was not going to be easy for her to get it into the water, but she had to try. It would take considerable time, she feared, for the sand was deep and restricting, and the boat would have to be pushed a rather long distance.

Placing her hands on the bow of the boat, she lowered one shoulder and shoved it with all her strength. The boat barely budged, but on the next push, it shifted an inch or two. She straightened, judging the distance to the water's edge, then, with a sigh, bent to her task again.

"If I offer to lend a hand, would you mind telling me what the hell you think you are doing?"

In the split-second before she whirled to face him, Cathryn realized Revan was furious. When she did turn, one hand flew to her throat in fear at the look in his eyes. Flames seemed to flicker in their amber depths and, for an instant, she felt engulfed by their hot rage.

"Revan!"

"Yes. I take it you are surprised and not too pleased to see me."

"I . . . I" Cathryn abandoned her attempt at an explanation. It was quite obvious he was beyond listening to it anyhow.

"My God, woman, just what do you think you are doing?" Each word was rapped out angrily, to be caught by the gusting wind and whipped away. "Is it your intention to kill yourself?"

"It is my intention to leave this castle by any means available," she answered, chin high. "That shouldn't surprise you."

"Your intentions don't surprise me," he replied, "but your methods continually amaze me. I knew what you'd try the moment Meg came and asked me about taking the boat to see the seals. I've been waiting for you to make your move, all the while telling myself you'd have more good sense. I hadn't thought you so stupid."

"Stupid?" she cried, stung.

He grabbed her shoulders and spun her about. "Yes, stupid! Look out there!" An imperious hand gestured toward

195

the gray swirling waters of the sea. "Do you see the water? See how it's churning and blowing? Now, how in the name of all that's holy did you expect to keep a boat afloat in that?"

She clamped her lips together, refusing an answer.

"Providing your puny strength could have managed to launch the boat, you'd have capsized within minutes, and with all those heavy clothes on, you'd have been dragged under and drowned before anyone knew where you were."

"Maybe it would have been for the best!" she screamed at him, wrenching away from his tight grip. "Mayhap that would have solved all the problems."

"Don't be an ass."

"I'm not an ass!" she blazed.

"You can't think this was your most intelligent plan?"

"I saw a way to get away from here and I took it," she retorted.

"You preferred to risk your life rather than humble your stubborn pride?"

Her green eyes sparked at him, contempt curled her lip. "I'd prefer to be dead than to stay here as your whore!"

She saw the flash of incredible anger in his face and fear prompted her to move away from him. She turned and started striding down the length of the beach, knowing there was nowhere to go, only knowing she must remove herself from his reach.

"Catriona," his voice barked. "Come here."

Heedless, she kept walking. With a roar of anger he went after her, a strong hand clamping down on her elbow and dragging her to a halt.

"You know as well as I do there is no place for you to go, so don't try running away from me again."

"I won't stand here and be lectured."

"Lectured? Why, I should beat your damned superiority out of you here and now. I should punish you in some way you won't soon forget."

"You have already punished me beyond endurance by forcing your hateful, unwanted attentions on me."

"Madam," he growled, "I warn you—matters could rapidly become much more unpleasant."

"Threaten me all you want," Cathryn yelled at him, "but nothing could ever be more unpleasant than the last two nights in your bed! No punishment on earth could be worse than that!"

It took all her courage to face the look in his eyes, but she stood her ground, her heart thumping painfully with the knowledge that she might be pushing him beyond the limits of his endurance. However, at that moment, she felt she would almost welcome his hands about her throat. Oblivion might be a preferable solution.

"Damn it all to hell!" he exploded. "You make me furious, Catriona. I don't know when I have ever been so riled by another human being. That night at the banquet I thought I was mad enough to beat you, but let me tell you, it wasn't a patch on the rage I am feeling at this moment. You drive me out of my mind with your idiotic plans for escape and your careless disregard for your life or mine."

One big hand came down on her shoulder, nearly causing her knees to buckle under her. He turned her body and with a rough shove, propelled her toward the tunnel entrance. "We're going back inside the castle," he informed her, as she stumbled forward.

"Then you will have me horse-whipped, right?" she gasped scornfully.

"I haven't decided what to do with you," he replied, his words coming from between clenched teeth. "So far nothing has worked. It's obvious I am going to have to try more severe methods."

She went down on one knee in the sand and when he stooped to pull her up, she flung back one hand, striking him in the face. As he lost his footing, she leaped up and attempted to run. He sprang at her, his heavy body felling her full-length on the damp sand. He grabbed a handful of her long hair and jerked it painfully.

"I'm through with these childish games, love," he warned. "I suggest you decide to behave yourself for once in your life."

"Ouch! You're hurting me," she whimpered.

His hold on her hair tightened. "Good. I intend to. Now, get up."

As he got to his feet, he kept his hold on her hair and she scrambled to her feet as best she could, tears of pain springing to her eyes.

"If I have to keep you under lock and key until you are an old lady, I'll do it, so help me, God! I may have to hobble you or chain you to the bed."

Stumbling along in front of him, Cathryn's breath was coming in sobs. "That would be convenient, wouldn't it?" she sneered.

"Aye," he snapped back.

She lost her footing again and this time, as she half-turned to look back at him, she blurted out, "What is wrong with you anyway, that you cannot seem to find a woman without kidnapping and abusing her?"

"Don't infuriate me further, Cathryn."

" 'Tis true, you aren't exactly handsome, but there must be some other terrible thing I don't know about."

"Silence!"

She smirked at him. "Does insanity run in your family? Or is your virility at question?"

He bellowed in pure rage. "That does it," he shouted. "Damn you, that does it!"

He gave her a hard shove that sent her sprawling in the sand. Before she could make a move, his long hard body was covering hers, his hands ripping and tearing at her clothes.

Real panic closed in on her, bringing swift regret at her angry words. "Stop it," she cried. "You're hurting me."

Heedless, his hands tore at the fastening on her cloak, then spread it to either side of her twisting body.

"Revan!"

"Oh, so now you want me to be the gentleman again? Now you're sorry you egged me on, insulting and taunting me?"

"Yes, yes, I'm sorry—honestly I am!"

"Nay, you enjoyed making slurs against my sanity and my manhood. I'm tired of your ill-mannered observances. I may be insane—God knows you have done your best to make me so—but I shall be most happy to prove my virility."

His hands roamed over her breasts, hurting her, punishing her. Then they moved downward, grasping her skirts and pulling them out of his way.

He wasn't teasing her, she realized. He was deadly serious. She had goaded him into an action beyond his control. Becoming thoroughly frightened, she began to cry and try to fend off his hands.

"Lie still," he thundered. "You asked for this. I've no doubt but that this is what you've wanted all along."

"No, Revan, please no!"

She sensed he was loosening his own clothing and she made a desperate effort to twist away. He thrust her back down, her head striking the ground with a hard thud and her hair spreading out in the clinging sand. Beneath her she could feel the wrinkled folds of her new cloak and a stone digging painfully into her shoulder blade.

"You are hurting me," she repeated, pushing against his chest. She could feel the chill air against her naked legs, but it was suddenly diminished by the warmth of his body as he lowered it over hers.

"I really don't care if I am," he rasped. "You accused me of treating you like a whore and, if I am not mistaken, this is the sort of thing you had in mind. I was a fool to think I could win you over with patience or kindness or romantic kisses. I should have done this from the very beginning!"

"Please, please stop . . ."

"Oh, damn you, Catriona," he moaned, "why do you keep trying to run away from me?"

His strong body seemed to pound her into the sand and, in her acute misery, her mind clutched one thought and held it. As she turned her head from side to side, her eyes blinded by scalding tears, she whispered, "My cloak—oh, my new cloak!"

Revan didn't look at her as he straightened his clothing and helped her to her feet. Still crying, she shook as much loose sand as she could from her cloak, then slipped it on to conceal her rumpled gown. Revan strode back across the beach to retrieve the bundle she had left in the wooden boat, and then, roughly grasping her arm, he pushed her back

199

into the tunnel.

He didn't stop to pick up the candle she had dropped, so she assumed he had walked its length in darkness many times before. She slipped and stumbled, and clung to his arm, which could have been cast from iron, it felt so hard and unyielding. She thought he must still be furious with her and, chastened, she did nothing to further provoke him. She was at a loss as to how to deal with this latest violent mood.

He made a rapid check to see if anyone was about before they left the secret tunnel. A hard hand on one elbow, he steered her up the stairs and into his bedchamber, releasing his hold as soon as they were inside the door.

He tossed down the parcel of clothing and said, "I'll send Elsa with hot water for a bath. I expect you might like to wash some of the sand from your hair. I'll go have a bath and change of clothing myself, then I'll instruct someone from the kitchens to bring up our supper. I think we must have a long talk this evening, Catriona."

Abruptly, he was gone, leaving her to puzzle over his words. Wearily, she hung away her cloak and opened the bundle, putting away her other things. Her escape had been short-lived, it seemed, and now she was at a loss as to what would happen next. A wave of hopelessness washed over her, making her feel just as much as if she were drowning as those high, gray ocean waves might have done. No more tears would come, just the awful empty feeling of failure.

Later, sitting in the little copper bathtub filled with scented hot water, she began to recover some of her resilience. It might take longer than she'd like, but someday some opportunity for escape would present itself, and Revan MacLinn wouldn't always be right there to prevent it.

As she thought of him, the door to the dressing chamber opened and in he walked, wearing a fresh white shirt open at the neck, black trousers and boots. A gold chain about his neck glinted in the light from the fireplace, catching her eye. He seemed to have completely recovered from his earlier temper, for his face was devoid of anger. He seemed his old self, amusement playing around his mouth, his eyes bold and a bit arrogant as they moved over her sitting in her bath.

She realized he was staring and hastily crossed her arms to cover her bare flesh. He laughed lightly.

"Don't let me disturb you, love. Go on with your bath, I will just sit here and enjoy . . . the warmth of the fire."

He pulled one of the chairs nearer the hearth and dropped into it, resting one booted foot on his knee. He stared into the flames, seemingly oblivious to her. Finally, after a few uneasy glances in his direction, Cathryn began to soap her hair with a square of lavender-scented soap.

She stole another quick look in his direction but he still stared at the flames, completely ignoring her ablutions. Reassured, she lifted both arms and began working the thick lather through her hair.

Watching her from the corner of his eyes, Revan knew she did not know what a beautiful picture she made. Her skin was highlighted by the golden glow of the fire, and the movement of the flames accentuated the shapeliness of her lithe arms and firm breasts. He swallowed hard — it took a lot of effort to appear nonchalant and disinterested.

Cathryn reached for the small pitcher standing on the floor beside the bathtub. She kept her head tilted back to prevent the soapy lather from running into her eyes, and her fingers moved blindly, trying to locate the pitcher. Revan finally seemed to notice her difficulty and got out of the chair to assist her.

"Here, is this what you need?" He put the pitcher into her searching fingers, and she gasped at his sudden nearness.

Uneasily, she replied, "Yes, thank you." She kept her head back, but moved her eyes sideways to look at him. "Please don't stare at me."

"Sorry," he muttered, moving away. He kept his back to her, looking into the fire once again. He could hear the splash of the water as she dipped up pitchersful and poured it through her hair, rinsing away the soapsuds. Her shadow moved on the wall, making a lovely picture he enjoyed watching.

Finally, she was satisfied with the cleanliness of her hair and she twisted its length, wringing out the excess water. Leaving the wet twist of hair hanging over one shoulder, she went on with the rest of her bath, soaping her arms and legs and rinsing them with clean water from a nearby bucket. As she squeezed a spongeful of fresh water over her shoulders, she again sneaked a quick look at Revan MacLinn. She had yet to figure out his current mood; he was neither angry nor lecherous, only quiet and rather somber.

At last her bath was completed and, with the water cooling rapidly, she was ready to get out. She thought about simply asking the man to leave the room, but feared it would be the start of another argument between them. After a few minutes, she reached for a towel and stood up, and wrapped it hurriedly about herself. He didn't appear to notice her, so she blotted the moisture from her skin and moved to the wardrobe where she pulled out a nightgown. With another hasty glance in his direction, she turned her back and dropped the towel, sliding the nightgown over her head as fast as she could. Revan thoroughly savored the view of her slim back, rounded buttocks, and long, tapering legs before turning back to the fire and pretending indifference. In a few moments, she shyly came near the fire, wearing his velvet dressing gown, a brush in her hand.

"Do you mind if I sit here to dry my hair?" she asked timidly.

He shook his head and moved away, dropping back into his chair once again.

Cathryn used the towel to dry her hair a bit more, then began pulling the brush through the long, tangled strands. She leaned forward toward the heat of the fire, fluffing out the strands as they dried. As she brushed, she wondered what was going on in the mind of the dark-haired man sitting opposite her. Where, she asked herself, would the events of the evening lead? She had seen him in many moods, but, to be honest, this was the most inexplicable of all, and she had no idea what he was thinking.

Revan kept his sober gaze on the bright bronze hair as it dried beneath the hypnotic motion of the brush. Finally, not really sure what prompted him, he left his chair and went to kneel beside her.

"Here, let me," he commanded softly, taking the brush

202

from her. Surprised, she didn't resist, though her body stiffened a bit at his sudden approach. He began pulling the brush through the fiery length of her hair, slowly and carefully. It was thick and lustrous, and as it dried, it sprang away from his touch with as much independence as its mistress usually showed. A smile hovered about his mouth.

"Catriona," he began abruptly, "about this afternoon . . ."

He could see her back tighten and her obstinate chin go up.

"I don't know what to say, except that you provoked me beyond all reason."

She looked at him, her expression considering, as if willing to listen to what he had to say. Surprised, he went on. "I did not mean to hurt you, but I cannot apologize either. You took a chance, but you knew what you were doing and 'tis only proper that you suffer the consequences of your actions."

She nodded, at a loss for words, and as yet unwilling to start any more disagreements with him.

He laid one warm hand on her thigh, drawing closer to her. His other hand dropped the brush and came up to curl around her waist. She drew back slightly, but kept her eyes on his face, a little wary. He leaned toward her, raising his face to hers, the odd expression still lighting his eyes. At that moment, a brisk knock sounded at the door and he sat back on his heels, disgruntled.

"What do you want?" he shouted gruffly.

"I've brought your evening meal, sir," came the timid reply. With a sigh and a wry grin, he got to his feet and walked to the door, where he opened it and took a well-laden tray from one of the kitchen girls.

"Well, the timing leaves something to be desired," he admitted, "but the food does smell good."

He placed the tray on the table between the chairs and began uncovering the various dishes. There was a steaming bowl of chicken with barley and mushrooms, a crusty loaf of bread and a wooden dish of fresh butter, some fruit and a bottle of wine with two glasses.

"Pull up your chair, lass, and let's have our supper," Revan said, uncorking the wine. "Shall we start with wine—I know how much you favor it."

His laughing eyes rested on her face and, despite herself, she smiled and blushed, embarrassed by the thought of her indiscretions the night before.

"One glass and one glass only tonight," she vowed, taking a small sip.

He chuckled. "Whatever you say."

She took the plate he handed her and spooned the savory chicken onto it, returning it to him. Taking the second plate, she spooned out a helping for herself. She sliced the tender bread with the knife he offered her and was lavish with the sweet butter.

As they ate, Revan mused on the picture of false domesticity they made. Admittedly, Cathryn was only being docile and compliant because she was as yet uncertain of his mood, but he had to sympathize with the part of himself that wished there could be many other such evenings as this stretching out before them.

Cathryn had not realized the extent of her hunger, for this was her first meal of the day. She kept her vow of drinking only one glass of wine, but she had two helpings of the chicken and two slices of buttered bread. She knew it amused Revan to see her with such a hearty appetite, but she didn't let it deter her.

"It does me good to see you eating so well, lass," he laughed. "It makes a mockery of your declaration you'd rather be dead . . ."

"Please don't start on that topic again," she pleaded. "Couldn't we have just one hour when we are not fighting?"

He leaned back in his chair, considering her gravely. "Aye, that would be a nice change, wouldn't it?"

She had to smile a little. "Yes, indeed."

"Do you think it's possible?" he asked after a while.

"What? For us to get along for an hour without an argument?" she questioned.

"Aye."

"Well, I rather doubt it," she said, so seriously that they both had to laugh.

204

Suddenly his amber eyes grew serious. "Catriona, what do you really think will happen to us?"

Her glance fell to her hands, twisting nervously in her lap. "I don't know," she said finally. "But I think somehow I will go home again. I mean, I cannot imagine staying here and doing battle with you, year after year."

"Are you so sure we would always be doing battle?" he asked gently.

"It would seem that way to me. I have been here quite some time now, and we haven't done very well in getting along, have we?" Her gray-green eyes probed his, seeking an honest answer. His own gaze fell before hers, and he shook his dark head.

"No, not very well."

Cathryn pushed back her chair and began stacking the dishes onto the tray. "And then, this afternoon . . ." Her voice trailed away. "It was a horrible experience as far as I'm concerned."

"Aye, as far as I'm concerned, also," he agreed.

As she moved about the little table, he watched her, his amber eyes shadowy in the dim light. After a time, he reached out one firm hand and caught her wrist.

"Come here, lass," he ordered, in a low voice. She looked at him, startled, but saw nothing dangerous in his look.

He drew her closer to him until she stood between his knees. "I want you to answer me as honestly as you know how, Catriona. Do you promise?"

She nodded, uncertain as to his meaning.

"Do you think there would ever be a time when you could learn to . . . well, to hold me in some affection? I mean, in time, after we have worked through all the fear and anger and recriminations? Sometime in the future when we've had the chance to solve all the problems with which we seem to be faced."

She was silent for a long time, staring down at the muscular hand still clasped about her wrist. Its strength impressed her, the obvious virility of it vaguely frightened her. She moved her arm slightly and he released her.

"Answer me, lass. Do you think you could ever be fond of

me?"

She turned away. "I . . . I truly do not think so, Revan." Her voice was so low he could barely hear her. She was aware of him standing up, close behind her, and then his voice came again, beside her ear.

"And why not, love?"

"For several reasons," she said quietly. "We could start with the fact that you are a Highlander, and I come from the south. We were raised in very different ways, and the things you believe in are things I have been taught to despise. And then, you are an outlaw, living in hiding from the authorities. What kind of life would that be? I would treasure my freedom too much to have to exist in such a way. And, most importantly of all, I have a husband who is waiting for me. I exchanged marriage vows with him, and he is the one to whom I owe my loyalty and obedience."

"And what about your love?" Revan moved to stand in front of her, raising her face with one finger beneath her chin. "Where does that come into the matter?"

She dropped her eyes. "All right, I will admit I do not exactly love Basil. I think that is something that comes with time. I think most marriages are that way — in the beginning, there is mutual respect and admiration, and, with the passage of time, these things deepen into love."

He gave a short, harsh laugh. "You paint a very dismal portrait of marriage, my love."

"Only to your way of thinking, perhaps."

He sighed. "Perhaps."

Abruptly, he turned away from her and said, "Are you tired, Catriona? If so, why don't you go on to bed? I think I will sit here by the fire for a while and mayhap read a book. I have had little time for reading lately."

She was frankly astonished at his suggestion, but after a bit, sensing he was completely serious, she took off the dressing gown and slipped beneath the covers. She lay staring at the ceiling thinking about this latest turn of events, but eventually her eyes grew heavy, and she could no longer ward off the lethargy overtaking her. Just before she dropped off to sleep, she caught a glimpse of Revan, seated in his chair, the book on his lap forgotten as he stared unseeingly into the fire.

It must have been hours later when she was awakened by a deep and searching kiss and the feel of his strong hands on her shoulders.

"Revan?" she murmured, sleepily. His body felt cold to her and she shivered. He drew her closer, saying something in Gaelic.

She felt his hands caressing her back and sliding lower to cup her buttocks and pull her even closer to him. As she started to protest, his mouth covered hers again and, suddenly, she was only conscious of his lips on hers as an unexpected weakness spread throughout her body and threatened to overcome her. He put one leg across her body and his skin no longer seemed cold. She felt the heat of his growing passion and almost flinched at his burning touch.

One hand unfastened the high neck of her nightgown, pulling it off her shoulder and slipping inside the garment to stroke her breasts, teasing them into excited peaks. She gasped as new sensations coursed through her body.

She pushed against him, but weakly. His strength was not violent as it had been earlier in the day, but it was just as undeniable. She gave up any proposed struggle and lay quietly beneath his touch. She was astonished at the depth of her arousal, especially after her cruel and utter humiliation at his hands just a few hours before. She had no means of analyzing her totally unpredictable reaction to the man.

He covered her face and neck with hot, sweet kisses, and his hands seemed to be everywhere, taunting and stimulating her, drawing her out of herself, releasing a flood of passion throughout her entire being. She was amazed and horrified to feel her body arching against his, eager for his touch. Her arms crept up about his neck and her mouth opened under his kiss.

He circled her waist with his hands, drawing her into the ultimate embrace. Just as she felt his body claim hers, reality asserted itself and her passion flared and died. It was too late

207

to deny him, she knew, but at least she had regained her own reason, though that did not make her feel any better as he crushed her to him, swept away on the tides of his own passion. Somehow she felt cheated and unfulfilled and very much ashamed of herself for feeling that way.

When next she awakened, the gently exploring fingers of dawn were creeping in through the tall windows, casting a feeble light on the room and its contents. Opening her sleepy eyes, she was surprised to see the other side of the bed was empty. Raising up on her elbows, she could see Revan, back in the armchair, a wineglass in one hand, his eyes still gazing intently into the golden depths of the dying fire.

Chapter Twelve

Cathryn had just finished dressing the next morning when Elsa appeared at the door with a summons from Revan. He was waiting for her in the sitting room downstairs. She thought that was unusual, for never before had he been reluctant to present himself in the bedchamber.

She studied her reflection in the mirror, admiring the new black wool dress with its high collar. She was glad the neckline hid most of the bruises which had appeared on her neck and shoulders this morning. The sight of them brought back the memory of Revan's violent rage the day before, filling her with an unsettling emotion. How could he have been so angry at first, then so gentle later? There was much about Revan MacLinn she did not understand.

He was standing before the fire when she entered the sitting room, turning at the sound of her footsteps.

"Good morning, Catriona," he said, rather formally.

"Good morning."

She stood waiting for him to continue, all the while aware of his intense stare which swept her from head to toe. At last he spoke, "I've been thinking about our situation, love. I think it is time we resolved the problems."

"Oh?" She looked at him in faint surprise, eyebrows slightly raised. She wondered where this conversation was leading.

"To tell you the truth, I have given it a great deal of thought since yesterday." He turned back to the fire, hands clasped behind his back. After another long moment, he said, "I have decided to take you home."

His words were so low she thought she must surely have imagined them. Quickly crossing to his side, she said, "What did you just say?"

He bent his dark head to look down at her. "I said, I have decided to take you home. That is, if you still want to go."

He turned away from the sudden blaze of joy he saw in her eyes.

"Revan," she exclaimed, "do you mean it? You aren't just tormenting me because I made you so angry?"

"No, I'm done with tormenting you, love. And the look on your face answers my question more clearly than any words. When can you be ready to leave?"

"I . . . I don't know. It wouldn't take me very long to gather up my things." She paused, eyes raised to his face. "That is, if I am to be allowed to have the clothing. Perhaps there is someone here who might need it?"

"It's yours to take, lass."

"I should like a little time to say goodbye to your mother and Meg, and to Della . . ."

"If you can accomplish all that this morning, we can leave right after the midday meal."

"So soon?" Cathryn clasped her hands. "Oh, I can't believe this is happening!"

"I'll go find Owen then, and we'll prepare the horses and choose a few men to accompany us."

He started from the room, but she reached out a hand to touch his arm as he passed. He came to an abrupt halt.

"Revan, won't you tell me why you've suddenly come to this decision? After all this time?"

His smile was wry. "I'm not sure I know, love. It seems strange to me, also."

His burning amber gaze moved over her face, and it seemed he was struggling to find the proper words to go on.

"When I brought you here, I suppose I was arrogant enough to think I could win you over and make you want me as much as I wanted you. I flew in the face of convention, not really stopping to consider the possible outcome. I was fool enough to tell myself your resistance was only temporary—that sooner or later, you would come to see things my way."

He walked to the windows to stand looking out at the cloudy day. After a moment, he continued speaking. "Mayhap that is my trouble—I've been too accustomed to having my own way, with no one saying nay to me. You intrigued me because you had the nerve to stand against me, despite the odds. Your efforts to retain your virginity amused me, I must admit, because I never stopped to think about it from your point of view. After all, you were raised to be a lady and, I suppose, the issue was a much more serious matter to you. It wasn't right that I took so high-handedly what you alone should have been allowed to give to the man of your choice." Here he gave her a half-mocking glance, one eyebrow raised. "Of course, I shall never understand your choice of a man, but that has little to do with it."

He came close to her again. "I should never have assumed I knew what you really wanted. It wasn't until yesterday that I finally faced the truth." He kept his face carefully devoid of emotion.

"Knowing what the Scottish seas are like at this time of year, you preferred to take your chances in a fragile little boat rather than stay here. You told me you would rather be dead than accept my advances, and it would seem you were telling the truth, as much as I would like to think otherwise. I have never lost my self control as I did yesterday on the beach, and that disturbs me greatly. How could we go on this way? You would never give up seeking a way to escape me and, the longer we are together, the more uncertain my temper becomes. What possible good could come of that?"

He grew silent again. After a moment, Cathryn said, "You sat up most of the night. Is this what you were thinking about?"

"Aye, though it would seem I have left the thinking a bit late. And who knows how long I might have deluded myself if it wasn't for something you said last night that finally pierced my arrogance and forced me to study the situation in a truer light?"

"What did I say?"

"That you didn't think you would ever be able to feel any affection for me," he replied flatly. "I have to believe you were being as honest as you could be and that doesn't leave me much hope you are going to have a change of heart and suddenly decide to settle happily at Wolfcrag." He put his hands on her shoulders and stared deeply into her eyes. "Though there was one brief moment last night when I swore you were responding to me . . ." He paused, obviously waiting for her to confirm or deny his statement.

Cathryn took a deep breath. To say she had not felt some emotion at his touch would be a lie, but if she gave him any reason to believe he had nearly broken through her defenses, he would never let her go. She carefully composed her face before meeting his intense look.

"I . . . I felt no response," she declared, then, at the look in his eyes, hastily added, "I'm sorry if I have hurt you."

He dropped his hands and his laugh was harsh. "It doesn't seem right for you to speak of hurting me after all I put you through. Nay, lass, you have nothing to apologize for. On the other hand, it seems I have a great deal . . ."

"If you allow me to return home, there is nothing further you need say or do. That is all I ask."

"Very well, love. That, at least, I can and will do. Now I must start preparing for the journey. It will be long and difficult in this weather, but we dare not wait much longer, for once the heavy snows begin, our glen could easily become impassable."

"Revan," she said quietly, "I am so happy! I truly don't know how to thank you."

"The fact that we can be done with fear and hatred is thanks enough for me, Catriona. In truth, I was growing weary of the battles."

"As was I."

For a long moment their eyes met and held. His were dark with some unnamed emotion and hers bright with unshed tears, though why she should feel like crying she did not know. He took a step forward and, suddenly, she was clasped tightly in his strong arms, her head close against the expanse of his chest. For an instant, she thought it had all been a jest

212

and that now he would mock her in his usual sarcastic manner, but he did not. He only held her, his arms like bands of iron and his heart thumping rhythmically beneath her ear, for a long, silent moment. Then, abruptly, without another word, he released her and strode out of the room.

It did not take Cathryn long to prepare for the journey home. Once again, she folded her dresses into neat piles to be placed in the saddle pouches. As soon as that was done, she donned her cloak and crossed the courtyard to Della MacSween's cottage.

Della seemed pleased to see her and invited her inside.

Cathryn grasped the other woman's hands and exclaimed, "Della, guess what! I'm going home!"

Della's bright smile faded instantly. "What are you saying?" she asked.

"Revan told me this morning that he intends to take me home. Isn't it wonderful?"

"Revan is taking you home?"

"Yes!"

Della pulled her hands away and walked to the fireplace, as if suddenly chilled. She glanced back over her shoulder at Cathryn. "What brought this about?"

"I'm not certain," Cathryn answered. "Mayhap he grew tired of fighting with me."

"Mayhap. Still, 'tisn't like Revan to give up so easily."

Cathryn's face took on an anxious expression. "You don't think he is only tricking me, do you?"

"If he told you he was taking you home, you can rely on it. But . . ."

"Yes?"

Della faced her again. "Why would you want to go, lass? Why?"

"How can you ask?" Cathryn cried. "I want to see my father, to set his mind at ease about my welfare. And, of course, there is Basil."

"Oh, of course, Basil," Della said dryly. "What about Revan?"

"What do you mean? What about Revan?"

"Do you just forget about him? Can you forget about him—after all that has happened?"

Cathryn looked down at her hands. "I will remember him always, naturally." Her shoulders straightened and her eyes blazed momentarily. "After all, he has changed my life considerably, in many ways. I fear it won't be easy to overlook that."

"Have you no feeling for the man?" Della asked quietly, her blue eyes resting on Cathryn's face.

"Not the sort you mean, Della," was her reply.

"Then, this must be a happy day for you," Della said stiffly.

"Indeed it is. We are to leave right after the midday meal, so I have come to say goodbye to you and to thank you for being my friend."

"Yes, well, I wasn't aware our friendship was to be so short-lived, but perhaps it is for the best."

"Della, are you angry with me?" Cathryn asked, stung by the other's tone.

"No, lass, just disappointed. I think I expected something else from you."

"But what?" Cathryn was puzzled.

"As we Highlanders say 'Dinna fash yourself, lassie'. Just have a safe journey home and . . . and a good life with Basil."

"You sound as if we will never see each other again," exclaimed Cathryn.

"It is unlikely we ever will, my dear. Remember, you are returning to your old life, and there is no room in it for those who must live outside the law. Our friendship would be impossible, I'm afraid."

"Surely there is some way we could communicate—or meet again?"

"I don't see how," Della said in her calm voice. "When we say goodbye, I fear it must be forever."

Cathryn's eyes filled with tears. "Della, don't be like this. You only seek to punish me because I want to go home."

"It pains me to stand by and see you making a foolish mistake," Della said flatly. "That is all."

"You don't understand!"

"No," Della said, taking Cathryn's arm and moving her toward the door. "I truly don't. And now we should say goodbye. I don't want to be responsible for delaying your journey."

She opened the door, and Cathryn felt herself being put out, gently but firmly.

"Della, please . . ."

"Goodbye, Cathryn. A safe journey to you."

The door was closed before Cathryn could say another word. For a time she stood looking at the weathered wooden planks, thinking she should knock and try to reason with Della. Finally she shrugged and walked away, not seeing Della's unhappy face watching from the window.

It was no easier saying goodbye to Margaret MacLinn. As soon as Cathryn entered the older woman's bedchamber, Margaret was crossing the room toward her, hands outstretched.

"Oh, my dear, Revan tells me you are going away."

"Yes, he has agreed to take me home to my father," she answered, distressed by the look on Margaret's face.

"I don't understand . . . what has happened?"

"Revan didn't tell you his reasons?"

"Nay, and I wasn't going to pry, not the way he looked when he told me. I hoped you would explain."

"I'm not certain I can, Margaret. I only know he made up his mind last night and informed me of his decision this morning. I am well pleased, of course."

"Are you truly, child?" Margaret's eyes were full of pain as she searched Cathryn's face.

Cathryn looked away. It didn't seem right that her good fortune should be so disagreeable to everyone else. It seemed no one shared her joy.

"Yes, I truly am. You can't have forgotten how I've planned and plotted to get back to my own people?"

"I had hoped you were growing fond of us," Margaret said in a sad voice. "I allowed myself to believe you would forgive

Revan and grow to love him."

"A relationship begun under such adverse conditions rarely breeds love," Cathryn pointed out. "I know it is true your own married life began in such a way, but you must admit it was a miracle it turned out as it did."

"Mayhap you are right," the older woman sighed. She put her arms around Cathryn and hugged her briefly. "I had so hoped you and Revan might also be blessed."

Cathryn pulled away to look into Margaret's face. "Sometimes it would be nice if things worked out the way we wish they would. But remember, you wished for one thing and I wished for another. It isn't possible for the fates to please both of us."

"Then you are happy about the way things turned out?"

"I am happy to be going home," Cathryn stated. "I must admit, I will miss those of you here at Wolfcrag who have been so kind and generous to me. I don't believe I could find truer friends anywhere. I shall dislike giving up that."

"I have grown used to seeing you about the castle and it will seem strange when you are gone. I had thought to finally see Revan settled and happy."

"Oh, but you will! I know he will soon find someone else. Believe me, it won't be long until you see him happily wed and perhaps the father of many sons."

"For his sake, I hope so," Margaret said. "And, if you truly wish to return home, then I am glad for your sake. No matter how much we will miss you, you would never be content here if your heart bides elsewhere. 'Tis best you go now before any more time goes by."

"I won't forget you, ever," Cathryn said, kissing Margaret's cheek. "You have been very kind to me. Thank you for that."

"I hope you will be happy, lass."

"And I hope you will be granted your wishes for your family."

They smiled at each other, then embraced again.

"I had better go find Meg now," Cathryn said. "I want to say goodbye to her, too."

Margaret bowed her head. "Cathryn, I hope you will understand what I am about to say. Revan asked me to tell you he would rather you didn't let Meg know you are leaving. He thinks it will upset her far too much. He has asked me to explain to her after you are gone."

Cathryn felt stunned at the prospect of leaving without saying farewell to the child, but she knew she must respect Revan's wishes. "Very well," she murmured, turning away. "It will be difficult for me to go without seeing her, but perhaps you can tell her goodbye for me. Tell her I will miss her very much and . . . and I hope to be able to see her again someday. Will you tell her that, Margaret?"

"Yes, I will tell her."

"Bless you."

Margaret laid a slim hand on her arm. "Remember us with some affection, Cathryn. I pray your stay here has not been completely unhappy."

Tears stung her eyes. "I shall remember many things with gratitude, you may be sure. And now, goodbye Margaret."

"God go with you."

After a hastily eaten noon meal, Cathryn met Revan and the small band of men who were to accompany them in the courtyard. She looked about in vain for Della, but there was no sight of her. Cathryn was dismayed their friendship must end in such a way.

She was just preparing to mount the docile little mare Revan held for her when a voice cried out, "Cathryn!"

She turned to see Meg dashing out of the castle, followed by her harassed-looking nurse. Meg ran straight to Cathryn and into her arms, sobbing loudly.

"Why are you leaving? Where are you going?"

Cathryn knelt to hold the little girl, her anxious eyes raising to Revan MacLinn's. He stepped close to his daughter.

"Meg, you must stop this at once," he said.

"But why is Cathryn going away without telling me goodbye?" Her eyes were huge and tear-filled and the sight of them made Cathryn's heart turn over.

"Oh, darling, I wanted to say goodbye to you, but . . .

217

well, your father thought it might make you too sad. I left a message with your grandmother."

Meg clung to her, still sobbing. "Why do you have to go?"

"I haven't seen my father for a very long time, Meg. He doesn't know where I am. Can you imagine how sad your own father would be if something happened to you? Don't you think you would want to go right home and let him know you were safe and well?"

Meg searched her face and seemed to decide she was making sense. "Will you come back after you have seen your father?" she asked.

Cathryn's eyes faltered under the child's direct gaze. "I . . . I'm not sure, Meg."

Meg looked up at her father. "Will you make her come back, Father?"

Revan shifted his feet, looking uneasy. "That will be up to Cathryn, Meg."

"Oh, please come back, Cathryn. Promise you will?"

"I can't promise, dear. I . . ."

Meg began to wail aloud in her misery. "Then I will go with you and make you come back!"

"Nay, lass," said her father, gently.

"I want to go with you to take Cathryn to see her father. I want to make sure she comes back."

Revan stooped and swung the little girl up into his arms. With one hand he brushed away her tears and smoothed the hair back from her flushed forehead.

"Meg, 'tis impossible. The weather is too cold and the journey too difficult for you. I want you to stay here with your grandmother and keep her company. And I promise, if Cathryn should decide she wants to come back to Wolfcrag, I will bring her back to you."

"But what if she doesn't want to come back?"

"Then there is nothing we can do," he said softly. "The decision is hers. Now you act like a grown-up lady and tell us goodbye, then go inside where it is warm."

She put her arms around his neck and hugged him. "Please be careful, Father, and hurry home. Do everything you can to make Cathryn come back with you."

He placed her on the ground again, and she turned to Cathryn, who was still kneeling on the cobblestones.

"Goodbye, Cathryn. Please come back."

"I can't promise you that, Meg, but I can promise I will never forget you or the games we played. Someday, when you have learned all your letters, maybe you can write to me and tell me how things go at Wolfcrag."

"No, just come back," the child said stubbornly.

They hugged, a quick, hard embrace, and Cathryn set the little girl away from her. She smiled and said, "Goodbye for now, Meg."

Revan assisted her onto the horse's back, then swung up onto his own mount. As they clattered over the stones and out through the main gates of the castle, Cathryn turned to wave one last time at the forlorn figure of the child. It seemed strange to be setting out on such a hoped-for journey with tears blinding her eyes, and her heart heavy within her chest. Somehow she had not foreseen that leaving this place of captivity would be so painful.

Once they were outside the boundaries of the long, narrow glen, the wintry wind hit them with full force. A faint stinging moisture was in the air, a definite promise of snow.

At one point, Revan halted the group, and each of his men-at-arms unlashed the extra plaids and furs they had strapped behind their saddles, putting them on against the increased chill. He swung down off his horse and approached Cathryn carrying a blanket made of wolf pelts sewn together.

"Here, Catriona, let me wrap you in this. 'Twill keep you much warmer." He reached up to lift her from the saddle and, when she stood on the ground before him, draped the blanket around her, pulling it close about her head and shoulders. Then he easily picked her up and set her back on the saddle, tucking in the blanket around her legs.

"Thank you," she said, not certain he could hear her above the wind. He nodded and handed her the reins, then remounted his own horse and the party moved on again.

By late afternoon the wind had calmed and a thick swirling fog descended to shroud the countryside, making the bare trees look like grotesque creatures rising beside the path. It was a quiet, eerie world with no noise but the muffled drum of the horses' hooves and the creaking of the saddles.

Cathryn did not see one landmark that looked familiar to her; she recognized nothing from either her first journey to Wolfcrag or her ill-fated attempt at escape. No wonder the government men had never located Revan MacLinn's stronghold, she thought, for it was extremely well-hidden. They traveled over so many miles of granite boulders and scrub-covered hillsides that, before long, it all looked just the same. Cathryn marveled that Revan and his men could find their way so easily and shuddered to think of her own foolhardiness in trying to find her way through this wilderness without a guide. Her chances of making it home, or even surviving, for that matter, had been very small, indeed.

It had grown rather dark when they came upon the crofters' cottages. A glad cry went up from two or three of the men, for they knew Revan intended to spend the night there and they were glad of the opportunity to rest and have a meal.

Revan brought his stallion beside Cathryn and shouted to her, "We're going to spend the night in these old crofters' cottages. We can build a fire and cook supper, then get a good night's rest."

Cathryn nodded, grateful for the chance to rest her tired, aching muscles. It would be heavenly to be inside four walls again, away from the weather.

The cottages were obviously deserted, though a well-worn path passing close in front of them testified to the fact they were often used as resting places for weary travelers. They were some distance apart, with a crumbling stone stable set between them. Revan and the others led the horses into the shelter provided by the stable and began to unstrap the saddle bags and unearth supplies needed for the night.

"Owen, will you get a fire started in the far cottage?" Revan asked. "Cathryn can go with you and spend the night there."

"Where will the others stay?" Cathryn questioned.

"The men will sleep in the first cottage. We'll get a fire built there and cook the meal. Someone will come for you when it is ready. For now, you'd better get in out of the cold."

She was surprised to be given the cottage to herself and wondered whether it was for her privacy or if it was Revan's way of trying to punish her. Then a thought occurred to her, making her jaw tighten in anger. Of course! If she were in a cottage alone, it would be less obvious if he were to slip away from the others and join her.

Well, she thought, as she followed Owen's large figure through the swirling mist, I will show him I am not that grateful! It insulted her that he would yet assume she was willing to share a bed with him.

Inside the bare cottage it was so dank and cold she almost changed her mind. Perhaps there would be an advantage to having someone to sleep with. Owen had gathered an armload of scrub and now he set about building a fire in the circle of stones in the center of the floor. He worked silently, never glancing in Cathryn's direction. She stood watching, impressed by his skill. He tended the small initial flicker until it flamed bright and strong, then left the hut to find wood with which to feed the fire throughout the long night.

Stepping to the window, Cathryn looked out to see the men scurrying about, tending the horses, gathering wood and taking supplies into the other cottage. The window was covered with some sort of animal skin stretched taut over the half-rotted wooden frame. It was strong enough to keep out the blustering wind and opaque enough to see through. Still, the figures she watched were distorted, giving them a weird appearance. Something about the deserted cottage disturbed her and made her shudder. She moved away from the window and stood closer to the fire.

She sighed with weariness. It had been an eventful day. She unrolled the blanket of furs onto the floor by the fire and sank down on it, holding out her hands to the flames.

Tomorrow sometime she would be home. She tried to imagine her father's reaction. A small smile lighted her face at the thought of their reunion. The smile died as she thought of Basil, for some reason. Inwardly, she felt he was going to be a bit more difficult to appease than her father. No, she reasoned with herself, 'tis only my own guilt at being unable to return to him as a virgin bride. She could only hope he would be understanding, or, better yet, never bring up the issue. After all, he was a gentleman, and it was entirely possible he might choose to treat the matter discreetly.

Owen returned with the wood and, shortly afterward, one of the men came to escort her to the other cottage for the evening meal. There were slices of fried meat, cheese, bannocks, and steaming mugs of tea, as well as the usual Highland whiskey. Cathryn declined the whiskey, but gladly accepted everything else. A day of vigorous exercise in the open air had made her ravenous.

The men ate greedily, saying little, and as soon as their meal was done, began making pallets on the floor where they would sleep. One or two of them were already snoring by the time Cathryn had eaten her fill. She helped gather up the eating utensils and, as she handed them to Owen, announced that she, too, was going to retire for the night.

"Wait, I'll walk you back to your cottage and see to the fire," Revan instructed.

Cathryn protested. "Oh, no, it isn't necessary! I can do fine on my own."

" 'Tis no trouble, lass," he began, but she didn't wait to hear his words as she pulled open the sagging door and slipped out into the night.

Outside the cottage, she had to pause for a few seconds to get her bearings. There was no moon yet and the low clouds made the darkness almost impenetrable. When her eyes had adjusted somewhat, she started off, struggling to hold her cloak against the icy gale which had sprung up again. She had taken only a few steps when her toe struck a half-buried stone and she pitched forward, landing on all fours and bruising her knees painfully.

"Damn!" she muttered, feeling like howling with the pain. A deep laugh sounded beside her and strong arms lifted her to her feet. Her face was only inches from that of Revan MacLinn.

"You shouldn't be so stubborn, Catriona," he said, pulling her cloak about her. "If only you'd have waited a moment, I might have been able to prevent this little mishap."

She could no longer hold her anger in check.

"I didn't want you to accompany me, sir! I wanted to give you no excuse to end up spending the night in my cottage."

His voice was harsh. "Look at me!"

Obediently, surprised at the tone of his voice, she raised her eyes to his. "I thought we had agreed to be done with the fighting, love. I had no evil intention, and it pains me you should think so little of my honor."

"You weren't planning to . . . to stay with me?" she asked hesitantly.

"I am returning you to your husband, remember? It was my decision to relinquish any claim I might have had on your charms. Indeed, I would be a brute to do anything less." His laughter was easy, his face more relaxed. "Of course I wasn't going to force myself upon you, lass."

"Then I apologize. I am sorry I suspected your motives."

He placed a firm arm around her shoulders to steady her, and they moved down the dark, stony path to the far cottage. Once inside, he busied himself with the fire. Watching him, Cathryn was suddenly overcome with drowsiness and even the hard little pallet at her feet looked inviting.

Revan straightened and threw a quick look around the firelit room. Satisfied that all was well, he said, "I will leave you now so you can get some sleep. I'm afraid we will have to be up and on our way at dawn if we hope to reach your home by nightfall tomorrow."

"Yes, I suppose so." Cathryn stifled a yawn. With a quick grin, Revan started for the door.

"Goodnight, Catriona."

When he had gone, she lay down, fully dressed, and pulled her cloak and the heavy fur blanket over her. She stared into the golden flames for a minute or two but was soon lost to sleep.

A scratching, scrabbling noise awoke her some time later. She opened her eyes instantly, but lay still, trying to ascertain what had made the sound. It came again, from behind her, and she stiffened in alarm. Hardly daring to breathe, she waited until she heard it a third time. Garnering all her courage, she turned slightly in her bed and peered into the darkness behind her. The fire had burned down somewhat, so the shadows were deeper. She saw nothing and was just beginning to feel relieved when a movement outside the window caught her eye.

The moon had come up and cast a watery light in through the window. As Cathryn watched, a bony arm reached up and rapped against the pane, its fingers clawing and scratching. She leaped to her feet, prepared to run, and then reality asserted itself and she realized the bony arm was only a tree branch, and the noises came from the wind tossing it against the side of the hut. She laughed shakily, hand over her heart, and sank back into her bed. She was so relieved she hadn't raised an alarm, for Revan would never have overlooked such cowardliness.

She lay for a long time, unable to go back to sleep, her mind drifting aimlessly. Once she watched a beetle of some kind crawl out from a crack along the door and proceed on a laborious journey all the way across the room.

After a while, sleep overcame her again, but it was a troubled sleep, affording little real rest. When she began to dream, she knew she was dreaming, but the reality of it still terrified her. She saw herself seated on a horse, surrounded by Revan and his men, riding down into her village. A crowd of people had gathered to welcome her, and she smiled warmly at them, so happy to be among familiar faces again. Then she saw her father running toward her, and she spurred the horse to ride closer to him. Just as he was within speaking distance, Basil appeared from nowhere, wearing a black cape that billowed out behind him. His thin face was distorted with anger, his bushy brows drawn together into a straight line. He shoved Hugh Campbell out of his way, causing the older man to fall beneath the hooves of Cathryn's

224

horse. She screamed a warning, but it was too late, and she saw her father's blood staining the stones of the street. Sobbing, she threw herself from the horse to kneel beside his lifeless body, but Basil's bony hands were upon her, pulling her to her feet and shoving her down the street toward his house. His housekeeper stood in the doorway, her mouth wide and ugly in a horrible laugh. Cathryn cast a pleading look over her shoulder at Revan, but he sat motionless on his huge horse. With a mocking smile, he slowly shook his head and called, "Sorry, love, but you made your choice."

Basil dragged her into the house and to the parlor where a great fire was blazing. He threw her to the floor and stood over her, his eyes full of hatred and contempt.

"Harlot!" he shouted. "Adulteress!"

She blithered words like an idiot, trying to explain — trying to make him understand. He wasn't listening and her panic increased. He turned away and she saw him pulling a black glove over one long, thin hand. When he looked at her, his face was twisted into an evil expression.

"You must be punished, Cathryn. You must pay for what you have done."

"What are you going to do?" she asked fearfully, her heart thumping so loudly she knew he must be able to hear it.

"I'm going to brand you as the adulteress you are!" He reached down a gloved hand and picked up a metal object lying on the hearth. It glowed red-hot and, as he turned to her, she could feel the heat on her face.

She thought he was going to brand her on the forehead, as she had once read primitive people had done to punish adulterers, but instead, he put out his ungloved hand and ripped her dress, baring her breasts. Then, with a fanatical laugh, he thrust the hot metal against her skin and she felt as though she was being torn apart by the pain. Her screams of agony filled the room again and again. Basil, still laughing, stepped away from her, and her horrified eyes fell to the blackened mark on one breast. It was a perfect imprint of the snarling wolf's head that appeared on the MacLinn crest.

"Now all your life you will wear the brand of the man who ruined you!" cackled Basil. "And everyone will know you for what you are—the whore of an outlaw!"

Cathryn sat upright on the pallet, the dream breaking apart and letting her regain the reality of the chill, dark cottage. She was shaking and there were tears on her cheeks. So real had the dream been that she still felt the searing pain and loosened the bodice of her gown just to prove no brand existed.

"Catriona!" At that moment, Revan burst through the door, pistol in hand. He was followed by Owen wielding a dirk whose blade flashed dangerously in the firelight.

At the sight of Cathryn sitting upright, her eyes wide and frightened, Revan dropped to his knees beside her. "What in God's name happened?"

She looked from one to the other, puzzled. "What do you mean?"

"You screamed, lass—enough times to wake the dead!"

She buried her face in her hands. "Oh! I'm sorry to have bothered you. It was only a nightmare."

Revan breathed a deep sigh. "Thank God. I thought you had been attacked by outlaws or something!"

Cathryn laughed ruefully. "Can that happen to a person more than once in a lifetime?"

Behind them, Owen's deep laugh rumbled. "Nay, only if ye are verra unlucky, lass!" His white teeth gleamed in his broad face. "I'll go tell the others that nothing is seriously amiss, Revan."

"Good. I'll be along in a minute or so."

When the man had gone, Cathryn apologized again. "I really am sorry to have caused you so much trouble. I haven't had a bad dream since I was a child."

"It must have been a fearsome one," Revan remarked, reaching forward to straighten her dress. "What was it you dreamed?"

"Oh, I really don't remember now that I'm awake." She refused to look into his eyes, but evidently her expression was innocent enough to placate him.

"Well, you must have been very frightened."

She swallowed hard. "I was," she admitted. "It was silly of me, but the dream seemed so real!"

"Do you think you can go back to sleep now?"

"I'm almost afraid to try," she answered, "yet I know I need the rest to get through tomorrow. My only choice is to attempt it, I guess."

"You do have courage, lassie," Revan said, his voice low and oddly caressing. "Is it any wonder that it shakes me so badly when I do see you really afraid? 'Tis so out of character for you."

He took hold of her shoulders and pushed her gently back down on the pallet. Then he put the covers around her once again, tucking them tightly about her feet and legs.

"I don't think you should sleep alone, Catriona. This old cottage is spooky, I'll warrant, and it might be some company would help you rest easier." He got to his feet.

She half-raised, about to make her protest, when she saw him turn and start toward the door. Over his shoulder he said, "I'll send Owen back to stay with you. You can trust him with your life."

She let her head drop, puzzled. She had expected Revan to use her fear as reason enough to force himself upon her. The old Revan would have, she suspected—but this was a new and completely different Revan. She wondered if she would ever figure him out.

It wasn't long before Owen returned, carrying his bedroll and looking a little sheepish.

"Sorry, lass," he mumbled, tossing the blankets down on the other side of the fire. "This wasn't my idea, but young Revan would have it no other way."

"I know," she said. "I hope it isn't too inconvenient for you. To tell you the truth, it will be a comfort to have some company. I'll try not to wake you again."

After that she lay quietly, waiting to hear the snores she assumed would accompany Owen's slumber. Outside the wind wailed and moaned, and she wondered if she would ever get the sound of it out of her head. The eternal wind of the Highlands!

"Cathryn?"

"Yes?"

"Were you asleep?"

"No, just lying here listening to the wind. Does it ever stop blowing?"

The big man chuckled. "Not often." There was a long pause, then he spoke again. "Lass, there's something I'm wanting to talk to you about, if you'd allow it."

Cathryn sat up to look at him, surprised by his words. "What would you say to me, Owen?"

The Highlander abandoned his bed to sit closer to the fire, also. She could tell by the anxious expression on his face that he had something important to say and was uncertain how to go about saying it. He hesitated a long time before starting to speak.

"Lass, you know you have the means to destroy Revan, don't you? Nay, not just Revan — all of us."

"But how?"

"You know his name and where his castle is located . . ."

"You know I could never find Wolfcrag again in a thousand years," Cathryn exclaimed.

"You might not be able to pinpoint it exactly," Owen pointed out, "but you could lead the soldiers to a general vicinity. Who's to say they might not get lucky and stumble across it? Or, mayhap they will use threats or bribes and find someone with a suspicious mind to give them ideas? You know more about the location of Wolfcrag than even you realize, girl."

She shook her head. "I only know that it's deep in the Highlands . . . at the end of a long, narrow glen . . ."

"And that it overlooks the west coast of Scotland," Owen reminded her. "Understand, Cathryn, all those are things no one has known before. How long do you think it would take an army of determined men to march along the coast? That is almost certainly going to bring them to the MacLinns."

"Don't you think Revan should have considered all that before he kidnapped me?" Cathryn asked, with some spirit.

"Of course he should have," Owen agreed. "But he was bewitched! Out of his mind. Nothing any of us said could have stopped him."

"What do you want me to do?" she asked quietly.

"Would you think I asked too much if I asked you not to

228

mention any details about the location of the castle? Or if I asked you not to reveal the 'Wolf's' name?" His anxious eyes bored into hers until she had to look away.

"How can I make them believe I knew nothing of my whereabouts?" she asked.

"Couldn't you make them think you were taken into the castle in darkness? That all you ever saw from the battlements was forested land?"

"Lie to them, you mean?"

He dropped his head. "Aye, that's what it would amount to, I suppose."

"And am I to lie to them and say I never heard this 'Wolf' called by his Christian name? Do you think anyone would believe that?"

"Make up a name," Owen suggested. "Use some common name that would throw suspicion away from Revan. You could do that, surely?"

"And what about the clan name? What do I tell them about that?"

"All right, I'm asking you — hell, I'm begging you — lie about everything! Do what you can to protect the lad. He knows himself he is putting all of us into danger by taking you back, but he won't listen to reason. We tried to convince him to stay at Wolfcrag where it was safe, but no, the stubborn fool wouldn't hear of it. Said he was the one to kidnap you and it is only right he be the one to return you to your family."

"It is the honorable thing to do, Owen," Cathryn stated. "Of course, I hardly need to mention that if he had done the honorable thing in the very beginning, none of us would have such problems."

He nodded. "You might be right, but now it matters not. The lad intends to take you straight to your father's arms and be damned to the consequences. Once he is seen and a name put to him, his safety is in grave danger."

"What if I persuade him to let me ride into the village alone?" Cathryn said. "Then no one would see him, and even if the villagers do learn his name, you would all be on your way home again. It might curtail your raiding somewhat, but I can't think that would be such a tragedy. 'Tis time you all learned to obey the law."

She saw the start of a twinkle in his eye. "Does this mean you are willing to consider what I'm saying?"

"Don't look so relieved, Owen. I've agreed to nothing. After all, why should you think I owe Revan MacLinn anything? Why should I want to help him?"

"You know yourself that without his aid, you'd never have gotten home again. You'd have either lived out your life among the MacLinns or killed yourself in some fool attempt at escape. Now I don't know how you ever talked Revan into risking everything to bring you home, but it seems to me you owe him a great deal."

Cathryn sighed. "Yes, I know you are right. You may not believe this, but I am just as amazed as you about Revan's reasons for letting me go home. I suppose none of us will ever know what made him decide to do it."

"Lord knows you hounded him about it often enough," Owen said, his voice full of amusement. "In truth, however, I think you could have raged on and on about it, and he still wouldn't have paid you any heed until it was his own idea. And I have my suspicions about what it was that caused him to change his mind . . ."

"Won't you tell me, Owen?"

He shook his shaggy head. "Nay, 'tis for Revan to tell you, if he ever thinks he should. And, after all, 'tis only a suspicion."

"You think he tired of my bad temper?" She smiled hesitantly.

"Nay, I think he may have felt himself becoming too fond of it. But, lass, I'll not say more . . ."

After a time, she said, "Since you think it is important, I will do what I can to throw as little light as possible on Revan's true identity. I suppose I do owe him that much, though why I feel that way is beyond my understanding. After all, he has caused me a great deal of suffering and anxiety, just because of his careless, thoughtless actions."

"He thought he was acting for the best," Owen stated simply. "He let his emotions get the best of him. I have never known the lad to do that before."

"I hope he never does it again," she said with feeling.

"Aye, the poor lad has learned a lesson, I ken."

"Why do you sound so sad?" she asked, gazing at his face. He looked like such a strong and ruthless person, but Cathryn was beginning to suspect a deep streak of compassion within him.

"It troubles me to see Revan unhappy, if you must know." He shifted his big body, uncomfortably. "We've all blamed you, to tell the truth. Now I don't know what to think. You seem like a real lady, so mayhap Revan's method of wooing was at fault. Maybe you have acted the only way you knew how."

"None of you ever realized how truly frightened I was," Cathryn said, eyeing him through the flames.

He threw back his head and laughed loudly. "By God, you never showed it, lass! I'll never forget the night at the banquet. You stood up to the MacLinn in a way I would never have dared do. And the looks that passed between you, why they were hot enough to send the whole room up in a blaze!" His laughter died, and he shook his head, as though confused. " 'Twas that night I thought you would make your peace with each other."

" 'Twas that night Revan came up to his room staggering drunk . . ." Cathryn began with asperity. Suddenly, her promise to Revan never to use that night against him loomed large in her mind, and she broke off the words before she could speak them.

"And the battle raged on?" Owen finished for her, his eyes full of amusement at the thought.

She smiled. "Yes, the battle raged on."

"And ye never did make your peace with each other, then?"

"Oh, we did manage one conversation with no insults or arguments," Cathryn replied, still smiling. "The night before Revan told me he was going to take me home, he seemed almost a changed man. Suddenly, it didn't seem difficult to talk to him without screaming."

"He's a fine lad," Owen said. "It just took ye a long time to find it out."

"Mayhap his virtues are easier for you to appreciate, Owen," she said gently, "since you were never his hostage."

"Nay, that canna be. In a manner of speaking, I am his hostage and have been for many years now."

"What do you mean?"

"Lass, I am what the Highlanders call a 'broken man.' You yourself should know that the MacIvors are a Campbell clan . . ."

"I never thought of it!" Cathryn exclaimed, eyes wide.

" 'Tisn't something I boast about," he commented. "Years ago I was accused of poaching deer on one of the Campbell estates. I hadn't done it and didn't think the accusation would amount to much. Suddenly I found myself on the way to the gallows. The old Campbell laird had decided to make an example of me." Anger sparked and glowed deep within his eyes at the memory. "By God, even my own clansmen wouldn't come to my aid. In another minute I'd have been swinging if it hadn't been for Revan MacLinn. He and some of his kinsmen were out on a raid when they saw the Campbells hauling me to the gibbet and decided to interfere. They were overfond of harassing the Campbells anyway, and what seemed a bit of fun to them, saved my life. I swear, Revan looked like an avenging angel that day, bearing down on the crowd, riding that big black stallion, sword swinging over his head. Nothing has ever sounded better to me than his voice shouting the MacLinn battle cry!"

"And so they rescued you from the lynch mob?" Cathryn prompted, as the man fell silent, remembering.

"Indeed they did. I threw myself on their mercy and the MacLinns took me under their protection, making me a 'broken man' and the mortal enemy of the Campbells. Lord, was I shocked when I saw how young the MacLinn chieftain was. I knew if he had that kind of boldness then, he was destined to be a great chief. I swore to myself then and there I would be his man to the death."

"Do you still feel such strong loyalty?" she asked out of curiosity. She was not used to men with such ferocious emotions. In fact, the men she had grown up around had rarely shown any emotion at all. She had believed that was a masculine trait, but now, sitting in this isolated mountain shack, looking across the fire at Owen MacIvor, she was confused. His rugged face fairly glowed with devotion for his young chief and, as he had told his story, he had all but seethed with emotion. No one could possibly accuse Owen of being less than masculine. Perhaps the Highlanders truly were a breed apart, not to be compared to any men she had previously known.

Suddenly she was recalling the words Darroch had once said to her: "Oh, my dear, you can't begin to know the depth of emotion running through the heart and mind of a Highlander. It may be slow to appear, but God help us all when it does. It doesn't matter if it's anger or greed or passion, it burns with a glorious flame!"

Cathryn was beginning to understand just what the other woman had meant. Obviously, the flame of Owen's loyalty burned on, diminishing little through the years.

"Aye, the loyalty is there forever. I tell ye, if need be, I would lay down my life for the lad. Under the circumstances, he could have made me his slave. Instead, he made me his friend."

Cathryn was silent for a long time before speaking. "And you thought it would be the same with me?" she asked gently. "Just as Margaret MacLinn thought."

"Aye," Owen agreed. " 'Tis what we hoped for. It would have pleased us to see Revan happy, but . . ." He spread his big hands. " 'Twas not meant to be."

Cathryn hunched her shoulders and stared into the depths of the fire. Conflicting emotions dwelt within her at that moment, but she hesitated to try and express them. Most of them she truly didn't understand anyway. All she said was, "It was not all bad at Wolfcrag, Owen. I think I learned some things there . . . things about how other people live. And I met some wonderful people, too." She sighed. "It will be with me for a long, long time."

He raised one thick eyebrow. "Are ye certain you're doing the right thing by going home, lassie?"

"I must go home!" she cried. "I've got to set my father's

mind at rest, and I have to try to explain things to my husband. Can't you see it is the only choice I have?"

He sighed heavily. "I suppose so, but it seems a hard thing . . . for the both of you."

"It is for the best. I truly believe that."

" 'Tis what Revan said to me, but I think you are both only trying to convince yourselves."

He reached for his blankets, drawing them about his huge frame. " 'Tis late. We'd better get what sleep we can."

"All right, Owen. Goodnight."

After a while she heard him say, "Thanks, lass, for protecting Revan. Just don't let him know I asked you."

The next day was miserably cold, but still the snow held off. The riders and their animals pushed themselves to the limit of their strength. They eventually left the rough high country and started the final trek across a more gently rounded landscape.

At dusk, they halted on the crest of a hill and, her heart hammering painfully, Cathryn saw the lights of her village spread out below them.

Home! She had come home!

Revan brought his horse close beside Cathryn's, a little distance from the rest of the party. He spoke to her for the first time all day.

"Would you mind if I have my men wait here for me? It might prove a little dangerous for them to ride into the town."

"If you don't mind, I would prefer to ride in alone, anyway," she replied.

"Nay, I will go with you," Reven said flatly. "I wish to confront your people and tell them what happened. I want to make certain they don't blame you."

"That is kind of you, but it isn't necessary. You would be taking too much of a risk by facing them."

"I have done it before, remember." His amber eyes were

234

lighted by the smile that had been rare the last few days. "I have no fear of the Campbells."

Her obstinate chin went up. "Don't let's begin another argument just as we are about to say goodbye."

His smile faded. "You are right, Catriona. It would be best if we could part on amiable terms."

"We can, I assure you. I am very grateful to you for seeing me safely home."

His look was intense. "Gratitude is a poor substitute for what I had hoped from you, lass."

She raised her head a bit higher and, choosing to ignore his words, she went on, "It has been a long, cold journey and has taken you away from your family. It was good of you to do it."

"I owed you that much, at the very least."

"Now that we are here, I would ask you one more thing only."

"What is that?"

"Let me ride down alone. When I have reached my father's house, I will send someone with the mare and then you can be on your way before anyone gets a good look at you."

He leaned forward to look into her face. "Do you think I'm afraid?"

"No, I know you are not. That is the danger. You must remember, even if you don't fear for yourself, you have others with you for whom you are responsible. I would not like to have that on my conscience."

"Does that mean you have overcome your raging desire to see me lying at your feet, wounded and humiliated?" His white teeth flashed in the near-darkness.

"I . . . I" The old anger was there, quickly to the surface. She swallowed and began again. "Yes. I have no further wish to see you or any of your men injured."

He shook his head in wonder. "You make me think I should have held out for just a bit longer. I swear, Catriona, you are starting to have some feeling for me."

She turned her head haughtily, not letting him see her eyes.

235

"Nonsense," she said curtly, causing him to laugh.

"Are you certain you want to ride down alone? Do you think it will be all right?"

"I'm certain, on both counts."

"Don't bother sending back the mare. Keep her as a reminder of Wolfcrag Castle and all who dwell within. Think of us sometimes, will you, lass?"

She blinked quickly, afraid her tears might spill over, embarrassing her. "Of course I will think of . . . of all of you. I will miss Meg and your mother. And . . ." Here her voice nearly broke. "I think Della was quite angry with me when I left. I am sorely distressed about that. Please tell her I am sorry."

"I will. She is a good woman and will understand."

"I suppose I should go then and not keep you waiting here in the cold. May you have a safe journey home again."

He laid one strong hand over her arm. "Catriona, I wish you happiness with Basil." At the expression on her face, he said, "Nay, don't think I mock you! I am only admitting what you have told me many times . . . he is your lawful husband, the one you chose to wed. I can't deny my pride suffered greatly when you refused me, but at least I have gotten to the place where I can honestly say I hope you will find happiness with the man. You . . . you aren't afraid to face him?"

She thought his eyes would burn right through her, his gaze was so intense.

She shook her head slightly. "No, I'm not afraid. I will make him understand somehow."

"Mayhap I should come with you . . ."

She held up a hand. "No! Truly, it will be all right, Revan. There is no need for you to put yourself into jeopardy."

"I only hope I haven't put you into jeopardy," he replied.

"I will be fine."

"Will you allow me to kiss you goodbye?"

"If you wish."

His hand was still resting on her arm. Now he moved it upward along the line of her throat and took one bright strand of hair in his fingers, bringing it to his lips. Now his

lean, hard hand slipped behind her head, causing her hood
to fall back, showering her shoulders with a fiery fall of hair.
His fingers tightened and he leaned close to cover her mouth
with his. The heat of his face against her own drove away the
chill of the night air and suddenly seemed very comforting.
The kiss was deep, but gentle. She was so stirred she could
not move away. Finally, with a barely discernible moan, he
tore himself away and straightened his shoulders.

"I never meant to hurt you, Catriona. I hope you believe
that."

"Yes, I do." Her voice was quiet.

"Goodbye, love. Take care."

She turned her horse and began the descent to the village
street and her father's house. Once she turned to look back at
them, but already they were barely visible—just dark shapes
huddled at the crest of the hill. She turned her face toward
home.

Chapter Thirteen

Cathryn guided the horse she rode through an empty village street. Although she knew most of the villagers would be at their evening meal, somehow she had not expected her homecoming to go quite so unnoticed.

She reached her father's house at last, sliding wearily from the saddle to brush the wrinkles from her skirts and straighten her cloak about her shoulders. She tied the horse to the post by the front gate and made her way down the path.

There was no light in the entry hall, but she easily found her way. Standing just inside the door, she savored the feeling of being home again. The familiar sounds and smells of the house were just as she remembered — the slow ticking of the old clock standing in the corner near the stairs, the scent of the beeswax polish the housekeeper used, the smell of good food cooking. Cathryn breathed it all in, then smiled at her own nostalgia. After all, she hadn't been gone so very long. It was just that the tumultuous events of the last few weeks made her feel so removed from the life she had lived here.

From the back of the house she could hear the clatter of dishes and a voice or two. Her father would be having his supper, she suspected. Not knowing how to announce her arrival, she began walking the length of the darkened hallway toward the dining room.

Standing in the doorway, she took in the sight of her father seated at the table, enjoying a bountiful meal by the light of the old silver candelabra that had stood in the center of the mahogany table since her earliest memory. Feeling foolishly sentimental, she stepped into the light, tears glistening in her green eyes, and said, "Father?"

The man seated at the table looked up, disgruntled at being interrupted at his dinner. When he caught sight of his daughter, he dropped his fork and half-rose in his chair. "Cathryn! For God's sake, where did you come from?"

She began to laugh and cry at once as she crossed the room toward him, arms outstretched. Instead of rising to embrace her, he dropped back into his chair heavily.

"Why did you come back?" he asked.

Cathryn came to an abrupt halt, letting her arms fall to her sides. "What do you mean, why did I come back? Aren't you glad to see me? Don't you even care that I am all right?"

Slowly he pushed back his chair and got to his feet, shuffling to her and enfolding her in a quick hug. "Sorry, Daughter, I didn't mean to seem unwelcoming."

"Well, I suppose it was something of a shock for you to see me suddenly appear," she laughed, a little unsteadily.

"Yes, yes it was." Turning toward the door at the opposite side of the room, he called out, "Mary! Come here."

The maid appeared so quickly that Cathryn was certain she must have been eavesdropping, but it didn't lessen her pleasure at seeing the girl again.

"Hello, Mary," she said, smiling.

"Oh, lord, Miss Cathryn, you've come home. I'm so glad to see you," she cried, throwing her arms about her young mistress and giving her a hearty squeeze. "We were so afraid we would never see you again."

"There were moments when I was afraid of the same thing," Cathryn admitted.

Hugh Campbell cleared his throat. "Enough foolishness, ladies. We have some business to attend to. Mary, send the kitchen lad to fetch Mr. Calderwood immediately, and then bring in a plate for my daughter. I daresay she has need of a little nourishment from the looks of her."

When the girl had left the room, her round eyes lingering on Cathryn's as if she were trying to convey some important

239

message, Cathryn removed her cloak and seated herself at the table. Patting the chair beside her, she said, "Sit down, Father, and tell me how you have been."

"How do you think I have been?" he answered acidly. "I wonder if you can even begin to imagine . . ."

"I am certain you were worried and I am sorry for that. There was no way I could get a message to you or let you know I was well."

He ran a thick hand over his face and, for the first time, Cathryn thought he looked older and unwell. "Why did you do it, Cathryn? Whatever possessed you?"

She sat back in her astonishment. After a brief moment, she asked, "What do you mean? I did nothing."

"I wish I could believe that . . ." He broke off his statement as Mary appeared with a plate for Cathryn. Placing it in front of her mistress, she stood uncertainly, as if she would like to speak.

Annoyed, Campbell said, "You may go now, Mary. We'll call if we need you."

Cathryn laid a restraining hand on the girl's arm. "Mary, why are you working in the kitchen now?"

The girl looked quickly at Campbell, then back to Cathryn. She said in a small voice, "When you left, there was no need for a personal maid . . ."

Campbell interrupted. "I told her she would have to go to work in the kitchen or find a position with someone else. I couldn't afford to pay her to sit around in the event you decided to return home."

Cathryn stared at her father. "Did you have so little faith I would come back?"

Mary patted her hand. "I always knew you would be back, as soon as you could. That is why I stayed on, so I could see you again."

Cathryn smiled at her. "I'm so glad you did, Mary. It would seem you are happier to have me home than my own father."

"Now, Cathryn, what do you expect?" the man blustered. "You have caused me a good deal of trouble by your damned nonsense."

She grew very still. "What nonsense do you mean, Father?"

"This nonsense of running away with an outlaw or whatever the rogue claims to be. You have put me into a very precarious position." The stocky man began to pace the floor, pulling on his beard. "You can believe Basil has made things as difficult for me as he could. He has threatened to ruin me if I don't . . ." He cast a quick look in her direction. "Well, as you have probably known since it was decided you were to marry Basil, he has fairly well controlled my purse strings. When he wants, he can make my existence very unpleasant."

"I don't understand," Cathryn finally said, her head beginning to throb. It had been such a long, exhausting day. Somehow, at the end of it, she had expected a happy reunion with her people, some food and a night of rest in her old familiar bed. Things had taken an unexpected turn and they promised to get worse. Suddenly, the eeriness of her nightmare was upon her once more.

"I don't understand," she repeated wearily. "What is it Basil wants you to do?"

Mary cautiously cleared her throat. "Miss, Basil Calderwood has been telling everyone that you . . ."

Just then, hurried footsteps sounded in the hall and, as Cathryn rose to her feet, Basil Calderwood appeared in the doorway. He was dressed in the usual black, his cape hanging in great folds from his thin shoulders. He slowly pulled black gloves from his hands as he studied her. Not knowing how to greet him, Cathryn remained silent, returning his look without blinking.

Finally he spoke. "So! You decided to return to us, my dear. Has your lover tired of you so soon?"

Cathryn gasped. "My what?"

"Your savage Highland lover," he sneered. "The outlaw who so conveniently snatched you from your marriage bed."

"I don't know what you are trying to say," she stated, though she was filled with dread.

"Just this," Basil said in cold, clipped tones. "You and your secret lover concocted this scheme—this plot—to extort money from me." He came close to her, his small eyes

241

gleaming wickedly. "Isn't that why you are here? To demand funds?"

"Of course not!" she exclaimed. "I have come back to stay."

"And what sum does your outlaw plan to demand to allow me the privilege of having my wife back again?"

"What are you saying?" she asked, bewildered by his unexpected accusations.

"That you tried to make fools of your father and myself. I did not suspect you of being that sort, Cathryn, I must admit. Your innocent air and amiability threw me off guard. It wasn't until you were gone we began to find out what kind of low creature you really are."

"Low creature?" She whirled to look at her father. "What is he talking about?"

Before Campbell could make a reply, Basil Calderwood went on. "I don't know just when or how you met this fellow they call the 'Wolf', and I am not sure what prompted you to hatch such a fiendish plot against me, but I can assure you, it is not going to work. You may have tricked me into marriage, but I am going to extricate myself from that and, in any event, you will not see so much as a penny from me."

He strode across the room toward the fire, slapping his gloves against one skinny thigh. He stared into the flames a few seconds before he turned to face her again.

"I suppose you had a good laugh at my expense, Cathryn. You let me go through with a very expensive wedding, knowing all the while I was making a fool of myself in front of my friends and neighbors. Then, at the most humiliating time possible, your lover attacks me and makes off with you, in what was supposed to look like a very realistic kidnapping. He has kept you away a long while, during which time we were to have fretted and worried about your safety. Now he sends you back with demands for money to prevent him from taking you off again. I have no doubt that even if we paid whatever sum he asks, you would soon be gone again anyway. Am I correct?"

Cathryn was so shocked by his wild theory she couldn't make herself believe he was serious.

"I will not be your blackmail victim, Cathryn. I do not

242

intend to pay out good money to keep you with me or, for that matter, to assure that you stay away from me now that your reputation is so hopelessly soiled."

"Basil, can you really believe any of what you have just said?"

"I'm not a man to make accusations lightly," he said righteously. "I have a reputation to maintain, and I intend to look after it properly, despite what you have tried to do."

"I have not tried to harm you or your reputation, Basil," she said quietly. "I certainly have not tried to harm my own father. There was no plot; there is no demand for money. The man who . . . who held me simply relented and brought me home."

"And you expect us to believe that?" he asked scornfully.

"It is the truth."

"Can you deny the Highlander was your lover?"

"Of course!"

"How do you explain the fact you knew each other when he came to take you from my home?"

"But we didn't know each other . . ." she began.

Basil held up one long, thin finger. "Ah, my dear, don't forget, I was only in the next room, clearly able to hear your conversation. It was most evident you had met before and, if memory serves me correctly, the man spoke of having proposed marriage to you. Hardly something one does with a stranger, wouldn't you agree?"

Cathryn turned to her father. "I admit we had met briefly, up in the pastures. He and his men were stealing animals, and they ventured onto our land. I was out alone when his men surrounded me. I . . . I would have been at their mercy, but the outlaw came to my rescue. The only thing is, he decided he had taken a fancy to me himself, and . . . well, he did propose marriage. But you must see, I didn't take him seriously. How could I? I was engaged to Basil, our wedding only a short time away. I let him think what he wanted because I was afraid of him and didn't want to anger him. The next day I returned home, and I truly had no idea he was mad enough to come back for me. That is why it seemed we knew each other, Basil."

"Oh, I think it was rather more than a passing acquaint-ance, Cathryn. After your hasty departure, your father and I rode up to the pastures to talk to Elspeth. We figured she would know the truth of the matter. Of course, she pro-claimed your innocence, but everyone knows the old woman is overfond of you and would do anything to protect your name. However, we had a little look around in the hut and found all the proof we needed. Tell her what we found, Hugh."

Cathryn raised stunned eyes to her father's face, already knowing what he was going to say.

"I'm sorry, Daughter, but the evidence is damning. We found your torn dress and a man's cloak, hidden beneath your bed."

"But you don't understand! When the outlaws first ac-costed me, one of the men was drunk and tried to lay hands on me. I struggled and my dress was torn. When their leader came to my rescue, he gave me his cape to cover myself with. I didn't want to worry Elspeth, so I hid them and forgot all about them."

She looked from one to the other of the men, knowing her story made little difference to them.

"Father, don't you believe me?"

He shrugged. "Perhaps you are telling the truth, Cathryn. Your tale could as easily be the truth as what Basil is saying. It's just that . . . well, I'm sorry, my dear, but I simply can't afford to believe you." He couldn't meet her eyes. "I am not getting any younger, and I have to think of myself, of my welfare."

"Are you telling me that Basil is paying you to turn against me?" Her voice was incredulous, and her father had the grace to look ashamed.

"You have placed us both in an intolerable situation," Hugh Campbell said, trying to explain what she obviously did not understand. "You have to realize what Basil went through, having the whole town know he had been ill-handled by that rogue. You can guess what sort of jests were made about his bride disappearing on her wedding night. It hasn't been easy for the man, and I can fully appreciate his

244

wanting to place some of the blame on me. After all, I should never have indulged you the way I did while you were growing up. I have failed to teach you responsibility, it seems. Yes, I can understand Basil's anger with me."

"And he has shown his anger by withholding some of the money he was so generous with when he was trying to buy me from you," she stated acidly.

"Watch your tongue, Daughter. Don't make this worse."

"How can it be worse?" she asked forlornly. "I was the innocent victim of a ruthless kidnapper, and you are refusing to believe any part of my story. You want me to be guilty, don't you?"

"Ridiculous," Basil said shortly.

"No! It's easier for you to think I was plotting against you than to admit you were bested by another man. You have to put me at fault just to salvage your pride!"

Basil's scowl deepened. "I think you had better curb your tongue, as your father suggested."

Cathryn laughed bitterly. "If only you knew what I have gone through to get back home. I must say, my welcome hasn't been precisely what I anticipated."

"Let me assure you, your welcome isn't complete yet." Basil smiled, an evil expression on his face.

"What do you mean?"

"I ordered your father's kitchen boy to rouse the villagers and have them gather in the street. We are going out to greet them, and you will confess your part in this scheme to them. All I want from you now is for you to clear my name by admitting your guilt and letting the townspeople know of your duplicity."

"I will not explain myself to the people of this village. If you don't choose to believe me, there is no reason to shame myself before them, also."

"You will stand before them and admit your guilt, madam. You will publicly confess to your crimes and give me the proof I need to obtain a legal divorce from you. That is all I ask."

Cathryn's eyes were blazing. "All you ask? Do you think this is some small favor you are requesting? I refuse to stand

245

in front of these people and tell them I have committed some crime I haven't."

"I am not asking you to take the blame for a crime you did not commit," he said, a rude smile on his lips. "I feel certain you have committed the crimes of which I speak."

"I won't do it, no matter what you think," she said stubbornly. "And, surely, my own father would not stand by and see me thus humiliated?" She looked questioningly at him, and though his eyes fell, he said, "You have to do this, Cathryn. You cannot expect Basil to wish to stay married to you, and you know the church has strict rules concerning divorce."

"It is essential that you publicly announce our marriage was never consummated," Basil stated. "And a brief statement of confession as to your sins will be quite enough. Then I shall obtain my divorce and hopefully, never have to lay eyes on you again."

"And you, Father, after you have aided Basil in this legal matter, will you want to see me again? Would you be so good as to tell me what plans you have made for me?"

"In the old days, miss, you would have been banished from your clan and from your home," Basil reminded her sarcastically. "You would have been turned away with no money or aid from your kinsmen, to roam the land like the strumpet you have become."

"Is that to be my fate, then?" She studied her father.

"It remains to be seen," he finally replied. "General Whitton wishes to question you about this Highland outlaw. I'm afraid, daughter, your fate rests in his hands, and his mercy will no doubt be tempered by the amount of valuable information you care to give them about your . . . your abductor."

"And you will do nothing to help me?"

"What can I do? Just tell me that? My hands are tied. You put me into this position, so don't blame me if I am powerless to help you."

"We have wasted enough time," Basil suddenly announced. "I can hear the crowd gathering, and I think it is time for your public announcement."

"I won't do it!"

Basil's claw-like hand closed over one arm, and he yanked her toward him, viciously. "You will do as I say, madam, or you will regret it mightily." Grabbing up her cloak, he tossed it around her shoulders, then pushed her across the room and down the hall. Hugh Campbell followed, but made no attempt to interfere.

Basil threw open the front door to reveal a good-sized crowd of curious people standing in the street in front of the Campbell house. Some of them held torches aloft, lighting the scene with a sickening clarity. Their faces were avid, eager for excitement. In a country village of this size, events were rarely of a scandalous or sensational nature.

A slight cheer went up as they saw Basil appear, shoving his errant bride before him. They sensed the entertainment was about to begin.

Cathryn felt her mind reeling, unable to grasp what was happening. She stood, head bowed, silent in her shame.

"Good people," Basil called out, "thank you for gathering here this evening. It is only right that you are present to bear witness to the testimony this woman is about to give."

A few catcalls rang on the still air, followed by rude laughter. Basil held up his hand, pleading for silence.

"I want to say to you that I have undergone a great deal of suffering at the hands of this low creature and, lest any of you doubt it, ask her own father. He was just as deceived by her as I . . . nay, as any of us. Cathryn Campbell grew up in this village, but who among us knew her true nature? She must have the soul of a witch to so completely fool all of us with her maidenly ways. Had she appeared other than a sweet young girl, I certainly would never have asked for her hand in marriage. I was committed to doing the honorable thing by her, but it seems honor is something she doesn't understand. My belief is that she saw the opportunity to make a fortune for herself and her ill-bred lover by duping me. However, I refuse to be a party to such trickery. Let the Highlander have her and welcome to him. But not a cent of my money goes with her! I demand a divorce, as is my legal right, and then I do not want to ever lay eyes on Cathryn

Campbell again."

A voice from the back of the crowd shouted, "But I wager ye'd enjoy laying hands on her, eh, Calderwood?" A great wave of laughter rolled forth from the crowd, causing Basil to tighten his thin lips.

"Don't be lewd, man," he cautioned. "I want nothing further to do with this wanton."

"What about it, Campbell?" another voice shouted. "Is what he's sayin' about your daughter true?"

Hugh Campbell licked his lips nervously, flicking a quick glance at Cathryn. She shrugged, defeated, knowing he would say whatever Basil wanted him to say. Her presence or her reaction to his words had no importance now.

"Basil has some evidence in his possession that makes any defense impossible, I fear," Campbell stammered. " 'Tis my shame as well as my daughter's." He took a deep breath and Basil piously nodded his agreement. Hugh Campbell shot another rapid look at Cathryn, but she stood quietly, staring straight ahead and saying nothing, so he deemed it safe to further elaborate upon his own innocence in the whole sordid affair.

"As you all must know, I have been forced to raise my daughter on my own since the unfortunate death of my wife many years ago. I tried to do right by Cathryn, but it seems I failed in some way . . ." He spread his hands in bewilderment. "It must have been simple for her to fool me, I was so trusting. I swear I was as shocked as anyone when I found out what the girl had been up to. I am responsible for sending my daughter up to the summer pastures, so it would seem I am also to blame for her misalliance with the outlaw."

"Nay!" came a harsh voice from the front of the crowd. "Cathryn could see Basil's stout housekeeper, the dour Mrs. Mettleton, standing there. "You are not to blame for the girl's misdeeds, Mr. Campbell. She is one of those doomed to shame. She was born with the bad blood and naught you could do would ever change that. I warned Mr. Calderwood about her time after time! I knew she was nothing but a temptress and an evil woman."

"I want you to know I would never have given my blessing

to a union between my daughter and Mr. Calderwood had I known the truth about her. He is too fine a man to have been treated this way," Campbell shouted.

Basil smiled as the crowd grew restive, voices beginning to raise in agreement. He held up his bony hands, requesting silence. "Friends and neighbors, please! It is not my purpose to ask you to condemn Cathryn Campbell. I very much fear she will find an adequate measure of shame and remorse in the life she has chosen for herself. I want nothing more than to be granted my freedom from a marriage with her. She herself will now confirm there is enough reason for a divorce to be granted."

Cathryn felt every eye upon her, eagerly awaiting her words. She felt sick as her shocked glance passed over faces of people she had once called friends. Why had they turned against her so quickly, with so little thought for her predicament? She nervously wet her dry lips, but the words wouldn't come.

"Cathryn," Basil prompted. "Tell these good folks what you wish to say."

She found her voice then, though it was weak and shaky. "I wish to say nothing, and you know it," she hissed.

Basil's eyes narrowed. "Tell the truth, Cathryn," he said loudly, "was our marriage ever consummated?"

"At least that is something I can admit with pride," she snapped back, and a handful of people close enough to hear her laughed heartily. "Nay, it was never consummated, and who is to say it ever would have been?"

"I warn you madam, you had best keep a civil tongue or this could become very nasty, indeed."

She realized it would do no good to further antagonize Basil, just as she knew the situation had already deteriorated to a point where she was not going to be able to make a case for herself. She had all but lost the battle before it began.

"Will you swear before a court of law it was never consummated?" he questioned.

"Yes," she replied quietly. "That much of what you say is the truth."

Basil turned to the crowd. "You know there are two

reasons for divorce — adultery and willful desertion. Since it is common knowledge my wife has committed both those indiscretions, it will not be necessary for her to say anything further. I think I have clarified my position."

Cathryn's anger finally surfaced, and she shook off the deadly lethargy that had enfolded her.

"How dare you stand there and assume I will let you publicly accuse me of crimes of this magnitude without a word of defense on my own behalf? I protest this entire proceeding! It has no legal value; it is only meant to humiliate and shame me!"

"You deny you deserted me?" Basil cried.

"Of course I deny it! I was kidnapped — taken from your home by force!"

"By a man you knew intimately," Basil sneered. "I ask you, good people, does that sound like kidnapping to you?"

Shouts of "nay" and various obscene observations rang in the air, making Cathryn cringe. Knowing it was useless, she went on.

"I was abducted against my will; I tell you! I did not know the man who took me . . ."

"Even if we believed you were taken against your will, madam," Basil said clearly, "do you now expect us to believe you lived among these outlaws for the past weeks without breaking your marriage vows? Do you think any man here believes you are still a virgin?"

Cathryn gasped in shock, waves of shame crashing over her head.

"You see? She cannot answer with honesty," he cried triumphantly.

"No," Cathryn interrupted, "let me speak . . ."

"We intend to let you speak. Tell us whether or not you are yet a virgin."

"How can you take such pleasure in this?" she whispered to Basil.

He laughed a cold laugh. "In the same way you amused yourself at my expense. I am not a dull clod to sit back and let you make a mockery of my name. Revenge is very sweet, my dear."

"I will gladly give you the divorce," Cathryn said in a low voice, "so why do you think it necessary to conduct this public hearing?"

"It is necessary because I am in no way to blame for what has happened. A divorce is a blot on a man's reputation for the rest of his life. I want the people I live among to know this was forced upon me—that I am the innocent party. That is the only recompense I will have."

"What about my reputation? If you make these people believe I am capable of all you say I am, they will shun me forever."

"Something you should have considered before you embarked on this madness," Basil retorted.

"I didn't embark . . ." Cathryn started, tears of frustration welling in her eyes.

"Enough of this quibbling!" shouted Basil, turning again to the crowd. "The woman now seeks my pity, but I tell you it is I who should be pitied. An honorable man dragged into the courts by a scandal of this nature—a man powerless to save his good name. And all because he was fooled by the sweet smile of a scheming woman."

"A Jezebel! A harlot!" cried out Mrs. Mettleton. "She's the one to blame!"

"I did nothing wrong," Cathryn protested.

"Have you retained your virginity then?" Mrs. Mettleton asked, a gleeful look on her ordinarily sour face. "Or were you the bride of the outlaw?"

Cathryn's desperate gaze swept over the faces of those before her. She knew they wanted her to be guilty. Trying to explain to them she had been taken by force was not going to save her.

"I was kidnapped by the gang of reivers and . . ." Her eyes fell. The crowd grew silent, sensing she was about to say something they wanted to hear. After a long moment, she raised her eyes again and, looking at the black-clad man beside her, she said, "I was held prisoner and kept locked in a room. I was at the mercy of the Highlanders, and it is only through their mercy that I have been returned home."

"And were you returned unharmed, Cathryn?" Basil questioned.

"I am no longer a virgin, if that is what you mean," she said. "I was raped."

"Oh, come now," the man sneered. "Raped, is it?"

"Yes, I swear it."

Basil turned on her in fury. "You tramp! You stand before these good people and expect them to believe you were raped? When they all know you for the harlot you are!"

"I am not a harlot!"

"You, madam, are the worst kind of woman—an adulteress! You are not fit to associate with the decent folk of this village. I would not blame them if they thought fit to punish you themselves."

"Aye, we should teach the strumpet a lesson," agreed a female voice from the back of the crowd.

"In the old days they would have stoned her for what she has done," pointed out Mrs. Mettleton.

"Stone her!" The cry was raised immediately with such fervor that Cathryn felt her skin crawl. The situation was now far past her control, and she began to realize the danger.

A handful of pebbles was thrown her way, striking her across the breast and shoulders. They were too small to be painful, but the action spurred others in the crowd to do likewise. A larger stone grazed her cheek, leaving it sticky with blood. She turned to Basil, expecting him to do something, but the look of barely restrained excitement in his eyes sickened her. He would do nothing to aid her—indeed, the villagers were playing right into his hands.

Another stone was flung, catching her on the shoulder, and she gasped in pain.

"Basil, please help me," she cried.

"What do you expect me to do?" he asked, his voice just barely masking his triumph. "These people hunger for justice."

"You call this justice?"

"Silence, adulteress!" screeched Mrs. Mettleton. "You deserve to be treated like the whore you are!"

At that moment there was a small confusion at the back of the crowd and the townspeople moved aside to let a man on

252

horseback through. Just as Basil Calderwood's housekeeper drew back an arm to hurl a stone at Cathryn, a cruel hand closed on her wrist, causing her to cry out in pain.

"Drop that stone, you trouble-making bitch," a steely voice commanded.

Cathryn lifted dazed eyes to meet the unreadable amber ones of Revan MacLinn. Mrs. Mettleton twisted to see who had accosted her, and when she met the gaze he now turned on her, loosened her grip, letting the stone fall harmlessly to the ground. Revan flung her arm away, as though he'd hated touching her. Without another look in her direction, he moved his stallion to the front of the crowd toward Basil and Cathryn. As the villagers moved away, clearing a circle around them, the torchlight illuminated the riders who formed a ring outside the crowd. They were Revan's men and all were armed. Owen MacIvor, pistol cocked and ready, was only a few yards behind Revan, his narrowed eyes moving from side to side, calculating any danger to his chief.

Revan halted his horse just short of Basil, whose face was contorted by shock. Revan ignored the older man, keeping his eyes on Cathryn. He dismounted slowly, coming to stand in front of her.

"Are you all right?" he asked, reaching out to straighten her cloak, fastening it securely about her shoulders.

She nodded.

He turned to face Basil then, and an expectant hush fell over the crowd as the two men studied each other.

Cathryn had never been so aware of the animal-like strength and grace of the outlaw as she was now, seeing his tall, muscular frame next to Basil. He appeared to tower over the other man, and every inch of his broad-shouldered, lean-hipped body was tensed for action.

"By God, man, you put me in a dangerous mood," he growled in a low voice. "If you give me the slightest excuse, I will be glad to wring your scrawny neck."

"See here," Basil spluttered. "Just who do you . . "

"I repeat, give me the slightest excuse," Revan said. Basil clamped his lips shut. He felt the threat just as surely as if Revan had laid hands on his throat.

"Catriona," Revan said over his shoulder, "I won't leave you here. Will you go back to Wolfcrag with us?"

"Yes," she whispered. "I can't stay here, and I haven't anywhere else to go . . ."

Revan's eyes narrowed and sought out Hugh Campbell, who looked very much as if he would like the earth to open and swallow him. He gulped nervously as the full impact of the angry amber eyes struck him.

"I could kill you for this," Revan said. "If only you knew how often Cathryn has spoken of you and of her home. How could you allow this to happen? You knew the man was telling lies. Is money so damned important to you?"

"It . . . it wasn't that," Campbell stuttered, his voice a scared whine. "I thought he was telling the truth . . ."

"Even if he had been, you were willing to stand by and let them stone your only child! What kind of a man are you?"

"I . . ."

Revan interrupted. "It doesn't matter. I have no time for cowards and weaklings. I'm just sorry for Cathryn that you are what you are."

As he turned, a hand was laid on his arm and a small, feminine voice said, "Here, sir, for Miss Cathryn — for her poor face." He looked down to meet the earnest gaze of Mary, the Campbell's maid. She was offering a damp cloth. He took it and she leaned closer to whisper, "Thank God you came. I thought they were going to kill her. Calderwood has been stirring up trouble ever since she's been gone. Take her with you and don't ever let her come back here!"

He smiled and nodded, then cupped Cathryn's chin in one hand and gently used the cloth to wipe away the drying blood on her cheek. The cut itself was small, and she did not seem to feel any pain from it. Revan tossed the cloth back to Mary, then lifted Cathryn onto the back of his horse.

She twisted the gold wedding band from her finger and threw it at Basil's feet.

Revan stood beside the stallion, holding the reins loosely in one hand and swept the crowd of townspeople with a look of contempt.

"I've heard it said that you here in the south think we

254

Highlanders are savages. I want you to know that nowhere in the Highlands have I ever seen anything more savage than what you have attempted to do tonight. No Highlander would turn against a clansman or neighbor without first hearing both sides of the issue. You didn't even do Cathryn the honor of listening to her. It pleased you more to condemn and punish her. I wonder if you realize how Calderwood has used you for his own purposes?"

A murmur went through the crowd and someone muttered, "Aye, that's what I tried to tell 'em!"

"Cathryn was trying to tell you the truth," Revan continued, his voice strong, compelling them to listen. "She didn't lie when she said she was kidnapped. I took her from her marriage bed by force. It wasn't planned in advance, and she had no idea of it when she went through with the wedding ceremony. We had met previously, and I had proposed marriage, but it was because I thought she was a peasant lass. She had only contempt for me, naturally, and had no way of knowing what I intended. She nearly died in one attempt to escape me and come home. After she made it evident she would never give up trying to get back to her father and husband, I decided it would be best to bring her home. Thank God, I couldn't make myself ride away without coming back one last time to make certain all was well!"

Cathryn sat huddled on the horse, seemingly unaware of what was being said. She had pulled the hood of her cloak over her hair, and her face was hidden in deep shadows.

"One last thing," Revan said. "Cathryn also spoke the truth when she said I raped her. That is precisely what happened and, while I am not overly remorseful about it, I am willing to accept all the blame. Cathryn is not, nor ever intended to be, an adulteress. She would have been perfectly willing to carry out the terms of her marriage contract, though God alone knows why. That was the first sin committed here — giving a beautiful woman like Cathryn to a pious, evil-minded, old miser for his wife. It will be my pleasure to remove her from his reach forever."

"What about my divorce?" Basil asked.

"What about it?"

"Surely you don't expect me to allow her to keep my name?"

"It matters little to me what you do," Revan replied, "just as long as you are no longer free to harass Cathryn with your filthy insinuations."

"I fear they are more than insinuations, sir!"

"Go to hell, old man."

"You two are well-matched," Basil shouted as Revan turned to walk away. "A thieving Highland outlaw and a cheap whore who will lift her skirts for any man!"

Revan whirled and his fist made solid contact with Basil's bony jaw, knocking the man onto his back in the dust. Revan knelt in front of him, one arm across his knee, a deadly-looking dagger in his grasp.

"If you say another word, you'll find my dagger through your throat. I would like to be done with politeness and beat you until you cannot stand, but even I have to admit the injustice of that. You are such a pitiful excuse for a man, it would be no contest. I will walk away this time and leave you crawling in the dirt like the miserable worm you are, but I warn you — if you ever do anything else to injure Cathryn or her reputation, I will kill you and take pleasure in doing it." He rose to his feet and turned to Hugh Campbell. "As for you, I pray I will never treat my own daughter as you have yours. I think you have most likely committed the worst crime of all."

He swung up onto the big stallion behind Cathryn, his arms going around her and his hands taking command of the reins.

A woman in the rather subdued throng spoke up, "Oh, bless us, he's a bonny man! 'Tis no wonder Cathryn preferred him!" General laughter sounded, breaking the mood somewhat.

"See to Cathryn's mare, will you, Owen?" Revan said to the man still waiting in the crowd. Owen nodded grimly.

The townspeople again parted to let the riders through. A few kinder voices called out farewells to Cathryn, but she only turned in Revan's arms and hid her face against his

256

chest, causing his jaw to tighten and his expression to grow even more stern. Owen followed, leading the mare, still looking from side to side, anticipating any move that might be made against them.

As they moved down the village street, the other MacLinn clansmen fell into formation behind them and, with a gathering speed, they rode into the night.

Basil got to his feet, shaking with fury and indignation. "I'll pay a handsome reward to any man who can trail the outlaws and bring me back word of where this . . . Wolfcrag is located. I mean to have my revenge against the lot .of them."

"What kind of reward?" asked one fellow, obviously interested. "It would be a long and dangerous mission and could take some time."

Basil brushed his dusty clothing, his eyes dark with hatred. "I will make it well worth your while," he promised. "You can rely on that."

Chapter Fourteen

They rode steadily for some hours, trying to put as much distance as they could between themselves and the village. The moon was riding high in the clouded sky before Revan signaled them to a halt and announced they would stop to eat and rest.

They found shelter beneath an overhang of rock, deep in a forested area. The men busied themselves with building a small campfire and making a meal on cold bannocks and water from an icy burn.

Revan got off his horse and lifted Cathryn down.

"Well, it would seem I have had to come to your rescue once again, Catriona," he said gently, teasing her. She made no reply, only staring at the ground beneath her feet. Revan cast a desperate look at Owen, who shrugged helplessly.

Unrolling the fur blanket that had been strapped on the mare's back, Revan found a dry spot deep in the shadows, away from the others. Leading Cathryn by the hand, he said, "Here, lie down and try to rest. Shall I bring you something to eat?"

She shook her head, then obediently lay down on the blanket. Revan knelt to tuck it around her. In the darkness he could barely see her face, but he could tell her eyes were wide open and staring.

"Are you going to be all right?" he asked anxiously.

Startled, her eyes flew to his face, as though she had been unaware of his presence. When she spoke, her voice was only a small whisper. He leaned closer to hear her words.

"It was just like my nightmare," she was saying.

"Don't think about it anymore, lass."

"I can't forget it. I won't ever forget it."

"I should never have left you," Revan said, grinding out the words with feeling. "I should have kept you at Wolfcrag in spite of everything."

"I thought they would be glad to see me," she went on, not hearing his words.

"Cathryn . . ."

She sat upright, one hand reaching up to touch the cut on her cheek. She looked at Revan in wonder.

"They would have killed me, wouldn't they?"

He bowed his head, unable to meet her eyes.

She whispered, "They were going to kill me, and my own father did nothing to stop them! I thought he loved me."

"Hush, lass. Don't think about it."

"I was so ashamed and so frightened."

Tears glistened on her face and suddenly, she threw herself down on the pallet and began to cry, the sobs shaking her body.

"There, there," Revan murmured in an attempt to comfort her. " 'Tis best to let the misery out, Catriona."

He lay beside her, an arm across her heaving shoulders, his head close to hers.

"I wish I could do something to make it easier for you," he said, his lips against her hair and the warm, sweet scent of her filling his nostrils. His misery was nearly as great as hers, and he cursed silently, blaming himself for all that had happened.

"What am I going to do?" Cathryn sobbed. "What is going to happen to me?"

He pulled her close, softly patting her back. "Hush, lass, we can talk about that later. For now, try to go to sleep."

She made no effort to remove herself from his arms, so he held her, comforting her until the crying was done, and she had fallen asleep. He pulled the warm blanket around her and went in search of Owen.

He found the man beside the fire, hands outstretched toward the warmth. Dropping down beside him, Revan said, "Christ, Owen! They were going to kill her!"

"Aye, laddie, it would seem so. 'Twas a good thing you decided to go back for her, I ken."

"When I think what would have happened if we hadn't . . ." Revan's face looked murderous. "God damn that pompous bastard to hell! How I would like to have killed him where he stood!"

"Easy, Revan," Owen cautioned. "Ye got the lass away from there; that's the important thing."

"Did you get a look at her?" Revan asked bitterly. "Her spirit is finally broken, I'm afraid. After all I put her through, it took that pair of whoreson blackguards to bring her to her knees. I've never seen her like this—she doesn't hear, she barely speaks, and, when she does, it's as if she's still there, facing that mob." He jumped to his feet and began to pace.

"Like as not, she is in a state of shock, Revan. She'll be better after she has rested."

"I hope so." He ran a hand through his hair. "I don't like the thought of seeing her like this from now on. I feel guilty enough as it is."

"She is strong," Owen pointed out. "In a while, she will be more like herself."

"Can you imagine her feelings when she found out her own father believed her to be at fault? Look at the times she tried to escape to get back to him. Lord, what kind of a man must he be?"

"Selfish, greedy—afraid to stand against Calderwood because he has grown soft and too accustomed to his luxuries."

"It seems a poor enough reason to abandon a daughter," Revan said.

"With the Campbells, it has always been every man for himself," Owen stated. "And it would seem Hugh Campbell is no different than the rest."

"Well, sitting here talking about it won't change anything," Revan sighed. "I suppose we'd better get a little sleep. We

260

can't linger too long."

Owen threw him a quick glance. "Then you have considered the possibility someone from the village may have tried to follow us?"

"I've considered it, but I think it's unlikely. We left in something of a hurry, and Basil was a bit incapacitated, but it won't hurt to be cautious."

"Aye, that it won't. We've taken more than enough chances for one day."

The long-promised snow came the next day, falling softly to muffle every sound and shroud every rock, bush, and tree. The little band of travelers bundled up against the chilling numbness of the storm as best they could and pushed on toward home. It was well after midnight when they approached Wolfcrag, and the snow came steadily, as though it would never stop.

They hailed the sentry, and after a wait, the portcullis was raised. A few sleepy stableboys appeared to help them with the weary horses, but for the most part, the residents of the castle were not aware of their arrival.

Cathryn was glad, for she realized no one would expect to see her back again, and her reappearance was certain to cause a stir. It was something she would have to face tomorrow, but, for the time being, she was grateful to be able to slip quietly inside Wolfcrag, meeting no one.

As she slid down from her horse, she stumbled in exhaustion and nearly fell. Revan steadied her, then, after a look at her drawn face, lifted her into his arms and strode across the courtyard and into the castle.

"Revan, I can walk," she protested weakly, as he started up the stairs.

"It's been a long trip, Catriona, and I know you must be tired and cold. Tomorrow will be time enough for you to start being strong again."

She heaved a big sigh. "Yes, I suppose so. It will be rather a surprise for everyone to learn I have returned to the castle."

As he set her on her feet inside the bedchamber, she gave a

261

small, rueful laugh. "And to think of all the farewells I said All for nothing."

"Worry about it later, lass," Revan said kindly. "For now you should get into bed and go to sleep. It's the best thing for you."

"Will you . . ?"

His mouth lifted slightly. "I'll sleep in the other room tonight, so you won't be disturbed."

She nodded, relieved he had understood her unspoken question.

As he turned to go, she said quietly, "Thank you for all you've done, Revan. I am sorry things turned out this way."

"For your sake, so am I. Goodnight, Catriona."

As he opened the door to leave, he met one of the stablehands carrying the saddlebags containing Cathryn's clothing. He instructed the boy to leave them on the chest near the wardrobe.

"You can unpack everything in the morning," he suggested. "It's late and you need the rest."

Cathryn was too depleted to protest his usual high-handed management of her affairs. It was something she would have to contend with later, she thought, rummaging through the bags for her nightclothes.

She hung her cloak away inside the wardrobe and quickly got out of her travel-stained gown, letting it lie on the floor where it fell. Pulling the nightgown over her head, she relished the familiarity of the bedchamber. She had not imagined she would ever be back inside this room again, and its air of welcome was comforting.

Later, as she lay in bed, she closed her mind to the memories of her father and Basil. It was too soon to start sorting through them — they were still too painful. Maybe in the morning, she told herself, taking a deep, ragged breath. Maybe when she wasn't so tired . . .

In the morning she was awakened by a knock on the door. Before she was fully awake, the door flew open and Meg dashed inside, followed by her grandmother.

You came back!" Meg cried, leaping onto the bed and throwing her arms around Cathryn's neck. "I'm so glad you did!"

Cathryn laughed, but tears sparkled in her silvery-green eyes. It hurt her that this child she had known only a short time could welcome her with unabashed affection when her own father had turned her away.

Meeting the kindly eyes of Margaret MacLinn, she realized the woman had read her thoughts.

"Welcome back, Cathryn," she said warmly.

"Thank you," Cathryn replied. "I'm afraid I have slept very late this morning."

"Don't worry. Revan tells me you arrived sometime in the early morning hours, so I am certain you needed the rest."

"I was so happy when Father told me he had brought you back," exclaimed Meg. "But he made me promise I wouldn't ask you why you changed your mind . . ."

"The important thing now," interrupted Margaret, "is that she is here. We will just concentrate on getting you settled, Cathryn, until you have had a chance to decide what it is you would like to do."

"Yes, I will have to make a decision, won't I? I'm so confused right now . . ."

"No one expects you to make any sudden decisions. Just rest and enjoy yourself, and the problems will take care of themselves one way or another."

After they had gone, Cathryn dressed, donned her cloak and set out for Della MacSween's cottage. Before she could knock, the door was thrown open, and Della seized her in a warm hug.

"Cathryn! How good to see you again. I'd heard you were back and I was hoping you'd come . . ."

"I wanted to see you right away to apologize for the way I left."

Closing the door behind them, Della took her cloak. "No, 'tis I who should apologize. And I do! I have regretted my behavior every minute since you left. I don't know what got

263

into me."

Cathryn's smile faded. "I suppose you heard what happened?"

Della nodded sympathetically. "I don't know what to say."

"It was so humiliating, Della. All I could think of was getting home and then, when I saw my father, I knew immediately something was wrong. He didn't even seem glad to see me."

"You don't need to talk about it, Cathryn," Della said softly.

"I want to tell you. Maybe it will help me understand it myself. I find it very upsetting to see that my entire childhood was based on a lie . . . a lie I've told myself! Oh, I knew my father had some disagreeable traits. He was overfond of gambling and often spent money he didn't have, but he always seemed a doting parent. He was concerned about me, I know he was!"

She moved to the fireplace, holding her hands to the flames. "I had not seen how he has changed the last few years, I suppose. Even when he was arranging the marriage to Basil, I had no idea how his greed had grown. Certainly I was fully aware he needed money, and that my marrying Basil would be a great financial boon to him. But, Della, I never felt bought and sold—not until I went back home and saw my own father stand by and do nothing to help me. Basil's largesse means more to him than I do!"

Della laid a hand on her shoulder. "Don't do this to yourself, Cathryn. It won't help to keep thinking about it."

"I can't seem to stop thinking about it," she said miserably, turning to face the other woman. "I remember how excited I was to be going home and then, in a flash, the scene last night comes into my mind and it's almost like I am still there, facing that crowd!"

"Oh, Cathryn, I'm so very sorry. Revan told us about it . . . I thank God he was there to save you."

"I've no doubt they were going to kill me," Cathryn said in a small voice. "I knew they were going to, and I couldn't even fight them anymore. I was simply too tired."

"And too shocked by your father's actions, I'll wager," the

doctor's wife said indignantly. "And that husband of yours is a very lucky man! There was murder in the heart of Revan MacLinn, you may be sure!"

"He must grow weary of coming to my rescue," Cathryn said, shaking her head slightly. "I still don't know how he came to be there at the right moment . . ."

Della smiled broadly. "Oh, haven't you heard the story?"

"What story?" Cathryn looked puzzled.

"Owen told us, but you must swear never to admit to Revan you know. I mean, he may choose to tell you himself and you have to pretend you knew nothing about it. Do you promise?"

Laughing uncertainly, Cathryn said, "I suppose so."

"Well, it seems that, after you had ridden away into the village, Revan and the others started off in the opposite direction, heading home. They had only gone about a mile when, suddenly, Revan halted his horse and announced his intention of going back."

"Going back?"

"Aye. Owen says he told the rest of them to go on, he would catch up later. 'By God,' he said, 'I am going back for her, Owen. I have given up too easily!' And before they could stop him, he was gone. They followed and Owen tried to talk some sense into him, as he put it, but it was no use. Revan had made up his mind and he was going back to get you."

"Whether I wanted to go with him or not?"

Della laughed softly. "It would seem so. Now, Cathryn, don't start looking so obstinate! You had better thank your lucky stars that he did come back. If you have any doubts, let yourself think about being stoned to death. No matter what you think of Revan MacLinn, you have to admit living with him would be preferable to that."

Cathryn opened her mouth to make a sharp reply, then closed it suddenly. In a few seconds, she said, "Of course you are right. It may take me some time to learn the proper attitude. After all, I have been at odds with the man for a long time."

"It will get easier as you begin to know him better," Della

promised.

"I don't know what will happen now. I can't seem to think ahead at all."

"There's no need, dear. Just stay here and let us be your friends. We'll take care of you, and everything will work out for the best, I'm certain."

"I don't know what sort of a relationship I am supposed to have with Revan now," Cathryn went on, her face anxious.

"Don't worry! He's not a monster. After what you have been through, I doubt if he will force himself upon you. He realizes you need time to decide what you want to do with yourself."

"I'm not sure of that," Cathryn said. "And, even if he does allow me to decide my own fate, my mind is in such a muddle right now that I couldn't make a decision if I had to."

"There will be plenty of time for that later, Cathryn."

"That's what Margaret told me, also. You both have been so good to welcome me back and to advise me. Thank you for that."

"I'm just happy that we have a second chance to get to know each other. I want us to become real friends."

"I'd like that, too, Della."

"If there is anything I can do to help you, please tell me."

"You have already helped me immensely. But I will remember your offer, to be sure. I think I will most likely need a shoulder to cry on from time to time."

Della MacSween's face grew serious. "Cathryn, just don't forget that Revan has broad shoulders, too."

"Will you promise me one thing, Della?" Cathryn asked gently. "Promise you won't try any more match-making between myself and Revan. I know you mean well, but it upsets me."

"I'm sorry and, I promise, no more match-making. Just don't forget he wants to help you, too."

Cathryn wore her warmest dress under the cloak and had on a pair of borrowed fur-lined boots, but she was still chilled by the afternoon winds. She huddled on one of the granite

266

rocks at the base of the castle, watching Meg run and play with several other children. They shouted and laughed as they romped in the feathery snow, their antics bringing a smile to her lips. For a moment, she imagined what it must be like to be so young and carefree, oblivious to the pain and indignities of the adult world.

From her vantage point, she could see for miles down the long glen, but, because of the blanket of snow covering everything, there was actually very little to be seen. A weak sun nipped in and out among the clouds, making the afternoon alternately gray and sparkling silver.

Cathryn had come out through the castle gates with Meg and, for the first time, had felt a sense of freedom on the grounds of Wolfcrag. A narrow footpath circled the base of the castle and Meg led her that way, pointing out a number of things. The child kept up such a happy chatter that Cathryn began to relax. She was not expected to make comments, just to look where Meg pointed, nod and smile. It felt good to let some of the tension of the last two days slip away.

When the other children came out to play, Cathryn sent Meg off, and found a sheltered spot in the mild sunlight where she could watch them. After a time, her mind began to wander.

If she did as Margaret and Della suggested, she knew circumstances would eventually force her to resume her former role at Wolfcrag, that of Revan's mistress and lady of the manor—not quite a wife, but something more than just a paramour. It wasn't what she would choose, perhaps, but after the way she had been received by her own clansmen, it seemed the only choice available to her.

She had no money of her own, and she certainly wasn't prepared to ask the MacLinns for charity. She had no training to enable her to find a position somewhere. With winter closing in, it seemed the most sensible thing to do was to stay at Wolfcrag until spring, at least. And, she told herself, she was not going to be a parasite. If she stooped to letting them feed and protect her, and did nothing to earn her keep, she was no better than her father.

No, that was not her way. She would do the only thing she knew to make herself useful to Revan MacLinn. If, by agreeing to be his mistress. she could serve some purpose, then so be it. As she turned the thought over in her mind, it made her cheeks burn, and she was glad for the chill breeze. It seemed she had gone past the time when she could virtuously proclaim she would be no man's harlot, for she was planning to be exactly that and, circumstances were such, she could do very little else.

She sighed. After all, she owed Revan something. It was only through his intervention that she was even alive. It seemed fair he should have some say in her future. She imagined he would expect her to assume the same role as before, for, in truth, he knew her alternatives as well as she did.

I will make the best of the situation that has been forced upon me, she told herself, shoulders straightening decisively. If I can provide Revan with some measure of comfort and pleasant company, then perhaps I will earn my keep. I will make a life of sorts. . . .

She knew it would be difficult to face the fact she was now his property, whether she liked it or not, her only duty to make his life as pleasant as possible. But she would force herself to do it. Her life was surely worth that much.

I won't think about what will happen when he tires of me, she thought. Perhaps, when that day comes, I will be better able to fend for myself. Until then, I will take this day by day, and not look too far ahead.

Having decided on a course of action, she felt better. Tonight she would go to Revan and start her new life as the mistress of Wolfcrag.

A single candle burned by the bedside, throwing a soft warm light over the bronze hair cascading across the pillows. Cathryn had bathed and dressed in a fresh nightgown, and now she lay in the big, curtained bed, waiting for Revan to appear. She had told him at the evening meal she would like to speak to him, and he had promised to come to the bedchamber as soon as he could.

She wasn't sure how to go about making her intentions clear, but she hoped Revan would assess the scene and understand.

She heard his footsteps coming up the stairs, and then a knock sounded on the door. At her request, he entered the room and closed the door behind him. His surprised glance took in the figure in the bed, and he said, "I'm sorry, Catriona. I didn't realize you would have retired for the night."

She half-rose. "No, don't go. I . . . I need to talk to you."

One black eyebrow shot up and a smile hovered about his mouth.

"Would you mind coming closer?" she asked, her voice tremulous.

"Not at all," he replied, crossing the floor to stand by the bed.

He looked down at her, noting the way the candlelight had shaded her ivory skin with gold, and how the small flame was reflected in the depths of her wide green eyes. Her long hair flowed over the pillows like molten metal, looking warm to the touch.

Forcing himself to maintain a casual attitude, he asked, "Is something wrong?"

"No, nothing. I just . . . well, I wanted to thank you again for what you did for me."

" 'Tis not necessary, Catriona, believe me."

She swallowed deeply, then edged her body a bit further toward the center of the bed.

"Please, sit here for a moment, won't you?"

There was a glimmer of amusement on his face now, but deep within his eyes a small flame began to flicker. He sat on the edge of the bed.

Cathryn drew herself up into a sitting position, bringing her body close to his. She blushed as his bold gaze fell to the lacy bodice of her nightgown. The lace and thin fabric did little to conceal her breasts, and she felt naked under his look. Quickly, before her courage deserted her entirely, she hesitantly put both arms around his neck and drew his head

269

down to hers. She could feel a tremor of shock run through his body as she placed her lips on his. He slipped his arms about her waist, pulling her closer to him, and his warm mouth responded ardently to hers.

When the kiss ended, he put his mouth against her ear and whispered, "It is good to have you back here, love. I don't think I could have done without you."

He covered her throat with heated kisses, then sought her mouth again. Her lips parted under his, further stimulating his desire.

"Your reception is warm, my lady," he murmured. "I only hope you mean it to be."

"Yes . . ."

"Catriona, my love, I don't know what is going on, but it is exceedingly pleasant."

His laugh was deep and throaty as he pulled back to look into her face. Her eyes fell under his amorous stare, and he laughed again, catching her to him.

"You're a beauty, lass, and God knows, a man should never trust a beautiful woman."

His hands moved to the front of her gown, gently loosening the bodice so he could slip his hands inside to cup her breasts. The warmth of his hands made her gasp in pleased surprise, and his palms moving against her hardening nipples made her mind reel with emotion.

He pressed her back against the pillows, slipping the gown from her shoulders. He trailed a line of fiery kisses from one shoulder to the other, stopping occasionally to cover her soft mouth again. His lips then moved to her breasts, teasing and arousing her.

He threw back the bedcovers, then deftly removed her nightgown, tossing it aside. She was unable to disguise her embarrassment when he looked at her naked body and, instinctively, her arms crossed to protect herself from his avid scrutiny. His warm fingers closed around her wrists, and he gently raised her arms over her head, holding them as his dark head lowered, like some swooping bird of prey, to ravish her flesh with burning lips. She twisted under his touch, her eyes closing in sweet agony.

270

A slight chill struck her bare skin as he moved away, and she could hear the unmistakable rustle of his clothing being removed. Tentatively, she opened her eyes, but the sight of his tanned body looming over her caused her to shut them instantly. His image was burned into her mind and she could still see the broad shoulders that tapered to lean hips, the sinewy muscles rippling golden in the candle's glow.

She realized that, though Fate had forced her into this situation, at least she had been fortunate enough to have to give herself to a young and healthy man, one whose skin smelled of some subtle spice and whose breath was clean and warm on her face.

She put out a hand and touched the furry breadth of his chest as he got into bed beside her. She heard his low chuckle.

"If I blow out the candle, will you open your eyes, Catriona?"

"Y — yes."

With the room in darkness, he turned back to her. One hand went to her slim waist, then slid slowly over the curve of her hip and down the length of her thigh. He returned the hand to her hip and pulled her closer against him. The heat of his body warmed her through and through, and she nestled against his chest. His arms went around her, imprisoning her, holding her captive under a kiss that sapped her strength and left her breathless. She sensed his ardor was raging now, seeking to throw off the bonds of self-control, and it frightened her. She knew it would not take much for her own feelings to get out of hand, and that realization cleared her fevered mind somewhat. As he raised his body to cover hers, a small cry escaped her lips and she stiffened.

"Easy, love," he whispered. "I won't hurt you."

Playing the whore was not as simple as she'd thought, she realized, trying to control her riotous thoughts. It wasn't pain she feared, at least not the kind of pain Revan meant. It was the possibility she was committing herself to years of life with this man — a man she really didn't know at all. She couldn't afford to allow herself to have any sort of feelings for him. What would happen when his lust died? What would be her fate then?

"Catriona?" he said suddenly, pulling away from her. "Damn! I think I understand what is going on now. You're trying to repay me for saving your life, aren't you?"

She looked up at him, tears starting in her eyes. "I don't know what I'm doing," she whispered miserably. "I'm so confused."

"Lass, as I have already told you, I don't want your gratitude. There was no need for you to subject yourself to this. I didn't expect it. I . . . I thought you wanted it . . ."

"I only wanted to please you," she said.

"No!" His voice was loud in the darkened room. "I won't have you as my slave, Catriona." He sat up in bed, removing his body from contact with hers. "That isn't what I want."

"You once wanted it . . ." she began.

"That was before," he said grimly. "Now I feel differently."

"Then, what do you want?"

"I want you to think of this castle as your home for as long as you want. And I want you to stop thinking you are obligated to anyone here. You are free to do as you please, free to go where you want. If you decide you want to ride away tomorrow and never come back, I won't try to stop you. I would only advise you to stay until spring when the weather will be better for traveling. No one is going to bother you, not even me. I promise!"

He could feel her questioning gaze on his face, even in the darkness. "Lass, tomorrow you can choose a bedroom of your own, where you can have all the privacy you please. I'll do anything I can to make you feel at ease here." His big hands closed over her shoulders. "Oh, make no mistake," he murmured, his lips against her temple, "I still want you. But not like this. I have to be willing to wait until the day you can come to me out of something other than gratitude. If you ever turn to me in desire, I shall be most happy to make love to you, believe me. Nothing less than that will do, however. Is that understood?"

"Yes," she answered quietly. "But what if it never happens?"

"Then I will have grown old waiting for nothing," he

chuckled. "Nay, lass, 'tis something you can't force. If it is meant to happen, it will."

He turned on his side, pulling her back against him, fitting her body to his.

"Now go to sleep and let me enjoy my last night with you as my bed partner," he said. "I won't make any demands on you and, starting tomorrow, I will behave in as gentlemanly a fashion as I possibly can."

Warmed by his body and relieved by his decision to take the lovemaking no further, Cathryn stayed close to him as she drifted off to sleep. Once she stirred in her sleep, and the man watching her murmured, "Just don't keep me waiting too long, love."

With a heavy sigh, Revan MacLinn buried his face in her fragrant hair and gave himself up to slumber.

In the early morning hours he awoke to find her head still on his shoulder and her slender legs entwined with his. The soft feel of her lying beside him made his pulse quicken, and when she turned in her sleep and stretched out a careless hand, brushing his nakedness, he moaned in frustration and eased himself out of the bed into the cold night air. Silently, he pulled on his clothes and left the room.

With no other thought than to remove himself from the temptation in his bed, Revan walked out the front door of the castle and crossed the courtyard in long, agitated strides. As he neared the gate, the startled sentry sat upright at his post and rubbed sleep from his eyes.

"Is something amiss?" he asked, his hand searching for the pistol he kept close by.

"Nay," Revan answered. "I couldn't sleep. I thought I would take a walk and enjoy a little fresh air."

"Enjoy?" the guard laughed. " 'Tis too frosty to enjoy, to my way of thinking."

"Aye, you may be right," Revan answered, suddenly realizing he had come outdoors without a plaid. The keen wind cut through his clothing, biting at his skin. Still, it seemed an improvement over the stifling warmth of the bedchamber.

The sleepy guard scratched his head and yawned mightily. "It looks like it will be a long winter," he commented.

Grinning wryly, Revan nodded agreement. "Aye, I'm inclined to think it's going to be a damned long winter."

Chapter Fifteen

Cathryn had dressed and eaten her breakfast before Revan MacLinn made an appearance the next morning. She did not know he had passed several sleepless hours on the cramped cot in the dressing room, and it took considerable poise for her to face him after the events of the night before. She felt a warm blush creep over her cheeks as she recalled her clumsy attempt to instigate lovemaking, for, even though she had been more or less rebuffed, she distinctly remembered falling asleep clasped in his arms, close to his naked body. The knowledge that she had protested very little now shamed her.

She felt more than a little relief when he announced his intention of helping her find a bedchamber of her own. Thinking clearly about her situation and making some decision about her future would surely be easier if she were not continually distracted by his amorous advances or his undeniably disturbing physical presence.

"There are a number of empty rooms on the floor above," he was saying as they walked down the wide hallway, "but only two on this floor. The smaller of the rooms is next to my mother and the other is at the opposite end of the castle, next to the nursery. Naturally, if you would care to look at the rooms on the next floor, you would have a greater selection."

"Would it be possible for me to have the chamber near the nursery?" she asked quickly. "I think it would be nice to be close to Meg."

A sudden smile appeared on his lean face, and he threw

275

her an amused look.

"What did I say that was so funny?" she questioned sharply, irritated by his humor.

"It's not what you said, Catriona," he replied. "It's just that . . . well, wait and see."

"Does the room belong to someone else?" she persisted. "If so, I will find another, just tell me."

"In a sense, it does belong to someone else. But here, see for yourself."

They had passed the rooms occupied by Margaret MacLinn, Darroch and Meg, and had arrived at the last room in the wing. Revan unlatched the heavy door and stood aside for her to enter.

She took in the contents of the bedchamber with delighted eyes. It was the counterpart to Revan's room, occupying the same location in the opposite end of the castle. It had the same tall windows as his room, and she was immediately drawn to them. They faced the courtyard, with the wide expanse of ocean beyond. Looking sideways, across the facade of the castle, she could see the jut of Revan's bedchamber at the other end, some distance away.

She whirled to look at the rest of the room. It was a little smaller then Revan's, and decorated in a cozier fashion. Instead of the rough stone walls, there was dark and elegant panelling. The fireplace was smooth gray stone and over the carved mantel was the wolf's head emblem embellished with the delicate Scottish thistle.

In front of the fireplace was a high-backed chair covered in a bright red tartan that matched the drapes, as well as the bedspread and curtains on the four poster bed. An ornate little tea table stood beside the chair, at the moment containing only a small brass lamp and a carved box of polished wood.

In an alcove toward the back of the room was a beautiful walnut desk and chair, and on the opposite wall, a tall bookshelf filled with leather-bound volumes.

"It's a lovely room," Cathryn exclaimed, her pleasure lighting her face.

"But, lass, could you ever feel at home here?" Revan

questioned, a wicked gleam in his eye.

"What do you mean?"

"Well, I should tell you that we refer to this chamber as 'Bonnie Prince Charlie's Room'. Perhaps the Jacobite implications might cost you your sleep at night."

"Bonnie Prince Charlie's Room?"

"Aye, that illustrious gentleman chose to spend a week or so with us at one point in his career, and this is the room where he slept."

"After the Battle of Culloden?" she asked.

"Yes, during his flight to avoid capture by the king's men. For some months he was a fugitive and had to be hidden in various places throughout the Highlands. There was a price on his head—30,000 pounds—but no one betrayed him. Instead, they gave him food and shelter and eventually made it possible for him to board a ship back to France. He stayed here at Wolfcrag for a time before he sailed."

"You met him?"

"You forget, I was one of the few males left in the household," he said quietly. "I was his host."

"So this tartan," she said, indicating the blazing red and green of the drapes, "is the Stuart tartan?"

"Aye, the Royal Stuart. By Highland law it can only be used by royalty, but I doubt if anyone would seriously object to your having this room. As you know, we are not overfond of laws in this castle." He grinned broadly. "Of course, now that you know something about the bedchamber, you may prefer another."

She remained silent, looking around her again, as though trying to conjure up the image of the fleeing and defeated prince. It seemed there was very little of his personality stamped upon the quarters where he had rested so briefly.

Her eyes fell on a tall chest of drawers set along the wall near the door. Above it hung several framed articles, one of which was a colorful portrait of a young man. Cathryn walked closer.

"Is this your bonny prince?" she asked.

Revan joined her. "Aye, so it is. Done when he was very young."

"He doesn't look the sort to have inspired an army," she observed dryly.

"And why not?"

"Oh, I don't know. Perhaps it is because he looks so soft, almost feminine. I shouldn't have thought he would have lasted one day on a military campaign."

"Let me assure you, when he arrived in Scotland, his looks were much changed. He had broadened and matured. They say there was an air of jauntiness about him that made men follow him. Of course, by the time he arrived at Culloden, the jauntiness was gone, and he was already beginning to look like an old man, as in the sketch there."

He pointed out a pen and ink drawing in a tarnished gold frame, hanging beneath the portrait. The contrast was striking; it didn't even look like the same man. The sketch was yellowed and stained with what appeared to be water and possibly blood. It had been folded at some time, and the creases cut deeply into the paper. A bold hand had drawn the prince, draped in a plaid and reclining in the rough heather, obviously resting. The artist's skill had portrayed the man's weariness with just a few lines. Cathryn leaned close to try to decipher the careless signature scrawled at the bottom of the sketch. In addition to the artist's name, there was a phrase in Gaelic and the date, April 14, 1746.

"What does it say?" she asked.

"The artist was Alex MacLinn," he replied evenly, "and the Gaelic is 'Bliadna Thearlaich', 'Charlie's Year', as we Highlanders called it."

"MacLinn?" Cathryn turned inquiring eyes on his face.

"My brother," he nodded. "He did this sketch two days before the battle, and later, when it was discovered among his things, one of our clansmen smuggled it home to us."

"I'm so sorry, Revan. He must have been a very talented artist."

"Aye."

"Will you tell me about your brothers?" she asked softly.

"Sometime, lass."

She turned her attention back to the picture. "Why do you think he wrote that phrase on the sketch?"

"Charlie's Year'?"

"Yes, it seems a strange title for the drawing."

"My own theory is that, by the time this sketch was done, they all knew they weren't going to be victorious. They had begun to realize their own weaknesses and to suspect the strengths of their enemy. Look at the prince's face—it isn't exactly the countenance of a confident man, is it? Nay, they knew it was only a matter of time until they were routed. They knew the end had come."

"The end of 'Charlie's Year'," Cathryn repeated softly, stricken by the sad finality of the words.

Her eyes moved on to a third frame, this one containing a document of some sort. It was written in Gaelic and all she could read was the name 'Alistair MacLean' scrawled by hand at the top.

"What is this?"

"It's an oath the Highlanders were forced to sign after the defeat at Culloden. It followed close on the heels of the 'Black Act', which prohibited the wearing of our traditional Highland dress. The penalty for disobeying that law, by the way, was six months' imprisonment for the first offense, and seven years' transportation for a second offense. In addition to that, men were made to sign this oath."

"Would you read it to me?" she requested.

"I, Alistair MacLean, do swear as I shall answer to God at the great day of judgment, I have not, nor shall have in my possession, any gun, sword, pistol, or arms whatever, and never use tartan, plaid or any part of the Highland garb; and if I do, may I be cursed in my undertakings, family, property; may I never see my wife and children, father, mother, or relations; may I be killed in battle as a coward, and lie without Christian burial in a strange land, far from the graves of my forefathers and my kindred; may all this come across me if I break my oath."

"How cruel!" she cried. "Was it some sort of cruel jest?"

"Aye, a cruel jest, indeed. And the joke was on the poor fools who signed this worthless piece of paper expecting any sort of mercy."

"What do you mean?"

"MacLean lived north of here, fifty miles or so. We had ridden that way hunting when we came across the smoldering remains of his home. The old man, his wife, and daughter had all of them been shot and left where they lay. We managed to give them as decent a burial as we could, and while gathering stones to pile over their graves, one of my men found this oath, caught in a thicket of shrubs. There were other papers, blowing in the wind, but it was this one that attested to the falseness of our conquerors. MacLean had signed the oath, but they were going to turn him out of his home anyway. When he protested, they killed his whole family. It taught me never to trust those in power—lying comes too easily to them. At any rate, I brought the document home and framed it, as a reminder."

Cathryn shivered. "What an awful story," she said. "What an awful oath!"

She could still hear his deep voice reciting the heartless terms of the oath; she knew it would be some time before she could forget it.

"Did you ever sign?" she asked.

His look was scornful. "Never. I'd have died first."

"I can believe that! There is a lot of pride in you, Revan."

"Aye, a lot of pride, indeed. I repesent the last of the chieftain's family, Catriona, and I'm very much afraid pride is about all we have left."

She studied him for a long moment, uncertain what to say.

His mood shifted rapidly. "There are one or two other Jacobite mementoes in the room," he said. From the top of the chest he took a small dagger, the amethysts set into its silver handle catching the light. He pulled the short dangerous blade from its sheath and held it out for Cathryn to examine. The Stuart coat of arms was engraved on the blade. "This belonged to the prince. He gave it to me when he stayed here at Wolfcrag. I spent a lot of time at his bedside, listening to him talk, and I guess he was grateful. As seems the case with great leaders, he was a very lonely man."

"You said you spent time at his bedside. Was he ill?"

"Mostly tired, I think, and dispirited. He was already

depending on a potion, as he called it, which he took quite regularly. He definitely returned to France a broken man."

"Even you have to admit the truth about him," Cathryn exclaimed. "So why do you defend him so? Why is he such a beloved hero to the Highlanders?"

"You don't understand, Catriona. The man himself may be weak, even a failure, if you will—but the thing we strive to perpetuate is the dream he represented. That's all."

"Oh." This was a new thought for Cathryn.

"Over here, in this wooden box, is our most precious remembrance of the bonny prince," Revan said, stepping to the little tea table and opening the box setting there. "When Charles left, he must have forgotten this, as the maid found it in the room when he had gone." His lean fingers lifted a finely wrought gold chain from its bed of deep green velvet. A tiny, lacy cross dangled from it.

"It's beautiful," Cathryn breathed.

"And no doubt rather valuable. We sent word to the prince before he sailed that it had been found, but he instructed us to keep it until he returns for it. So, we placed it in this room, which we keep ready for his reappearance."

Cathryn smiled. "If you think he will be coming soon, perhaps I should find somewhere else to sleep."

"It seems unlikely he will return this winter," Revan said solemnly, though there was a twinkle in his amber eyes. "If you think you can withstand the ghosts here, you are welcome to the room."

Cathryn looked about one more time. "It seems a very cozy room, one where I could feel at home. If there are no objections, permit me to stay here and see for myself whether or not it is really haunted."

"As you wish, madam," he said.

"I will remove my things from . . . from your room right away," she stated, aware of the constraint that had crept back between them.

"I will send Elsa up to help you," he said. "Please let her know if there is anything further you require."

When he had gone, she returned to the windows and looked out at the misty sea. How ironic that she, the

281

rebellious Lowlander of just a few short days ago, should now find herself ensconced in the "Bonnie Prince Charlie Room" and be so greatly pleased to find herself there!

Later, after Owen had appeared to fill the wood box and start a fire, Cathryn and Elsa began the task of moving Cathryn's things to her new room. They hung and folded her dresses away inside the clothespress and placed her shoes and underclothing on the shelves within.

Elsa insisted on polishing the furniture, though not a speck of dust was to be found, and together they made up the bed with clean sheets and a soft, feather-filled comforter. Just as they finished spreading the tartan coverlet over it again, footsteps sounded at the door, and they looked up to see Darroch standing there, a sneer on her handsome face.

"My, you do give the folks here at Wolfcrag a great deal to gossip about," she said. "First, the virginal captive falls into bed with the handsome chieftain, then suddenly, she announces her return home. Just as suddenly, she is back, and now, to everyone's amazement, she moves out of the laird's bedchamber and into one of her own. Each day brings some new and unexpected development."

"Hello, Darroch," Cathryn said mildly. "Won't you come in?"

The other woman laughed and moved to the center of the room, skirts swaying gracefully. "Would you care to explain your circumstances now, Cathryn?"

"Why should I?"

Darroch tilted her head to one side, the light from the tall windows pointing up the thinning, but still visible scar across her face. "Is it true your father threw you out of his house?" she asked.

Elsa looked from one to the other of the women, her eyes wide and uncertain.

"I fail to see that that is any of your business," Cathryn replied coolly.

"Have you finished your housecleaning duties, Elsa?" Darroch asked suddenly, causing the servant to look quickly at Cathryn.

Cathryn nodded. "Yes, you've done everything necessary, Elsa."

Darroch continued. "Then why don't you get out of here and let the lady and me have a private conversation?"

"Should I go, Miss Cathryn?" Elsa asked hesitantly.

"Yes, go on. If I need anything further, I will send word. Thank you for your help."

Elsa sidled out of the room, relieved to be getting away from the tense atmosphere, but not sure she should leave the two of them alone.

"Darroch," Cathryn said, turning back to the dark-haired woman, "if you think I am going to give you a full account of my journey home, you are mistaken."

"Perhaps I have already been given a full account," Darroch smirked. "Don't you think Revan would have told me?"

Stung, Cathryn retorted, "I really don't care if he has, though, if, as you say, he has told you so much, why do you come to me asking questions?"

"I wanted to see how you looked when you spoke of being turned away by your kin. That must have hurt your pride!"

Cathryn only stared at her, saying nothing.

Darroch's laugh bubbled up again. "How I wish I could have been there to see it. After all the boasts and threats you made about the wonderful Campbells, they didn't even want you."

She came closer to Cathryn, her eyes greedy for some sign of distress.

"How did it feel to be called a whore, and by none other than your esteemed bridegroom?"

"Darroch, I should like for you to leave my room now," Cathryn said quietly.

"Your room? How is it possible for you to sound so haughty when you and I and everyone else knows you are only living here on Revan's charity? And now it would seem you aren't even woman enough to repay him in the only way he requested."

"The arrangement between Revan MacLinn and myself is of no concern to you."

283

"Oh, but it is, my dear," Darroch purred. "It is of great concern to me. I have made no secret of my dislike for you, and I have openly admitted I would be well-pleased to have you gone from here. It suits me quite nicely to know you are no longer sharing a bed with Revan, and I would be delighted to assist you in any way to further insure you do not succumb to his charms again. Rumor has it that it was your idea to move out of his room, so may I assume the relationship will not be resumed until you decide it is to be?"

"You may assume anything you please."

"Then let me tell you something that may help strengthen your resolve not to become Revan's mistress."

"What is that?"

"If you should allow yourself to be bedded by Revan again, I shall take Meg and leave this castle. No one would ever see us again, you may be certain." Her full lips widened into a mocking smile. "How well do you think Revan would like never seeing his child again?"

"Why do you always threaten me, Darroch?"

"Because you are such a threat to me and to the things I want."

"I don't mean to be. It was never my intent to take anything from you."

"But you have."

"Do you think I have taken Revan from you?"

"Indeed I do," Darroch answered, her smile gone. "But if you continue with your present role of reluctant lady, I shall find some means of reawakening his desire for me. As long as you stay away from him, all will be well."

"I mean to stay away from him, but not because of your threats."

"It doesn't matter why you refuse him, it only matters that you do. By now, you know me well enough to know I will do just as I say I will. It wouldn't please Revan to find out Meg is gone through your interference."

A hard rap on the door heralded the arrival of Revan MacLinn. As he stepped into the room, his scowl deepened.

"Well, well, Darroch, I wouldn't have expected to find you here—not after I gave you explicit orders to stay away from

Cathryn."

"I merely came to welcome her to her new quarters, Revan," Darroch said smoothly.

"I'm not fool enough to believe that," he snapped. "I suggest you get out of here now and leave her alone. Don't bother to come back again."

Darroch tossed her head angrily and marched to the door. "Anything you say," she snarled, hurling the words over her shoulder. The door slammed behind her, and Cathryn let out a breathy sigh of relief.

"Did she bother you?" he asked. "Elsa told me she was here, starting trouble."

"No, she didn't bother me."

"Yet you seem relieved to have her gone."

"It's just that she dislikes me so much I don't feel I can trust her."

"Nay, it would never be wise to trust Darroch. That much I can say with certainty."

He held out his hand. "Here, I brought you something."

On his palm lay a key, which Cathryn took with a question in her eyes.

" 'Tis the key to this room, Catriona. I thought you might feel safer with it in your possession. Now you don't have to fear unwanted visits from Darroch . . . or anyone."

"That is very kind of you, Revan," she said, thinking of the other times they had argued over just such a key. A sparkle lit her silvery eyes. "Now if I am to be locked in my room, at least it will be by my own choice."

His face remained still but his eyes were warm. "If you persist in looking at me like that, madam, you will find it necessary to keep your door locked."

Cathryn flushed and moved away. She had not meant for the conversation to take this sudden turn. She said the first thing that came into her mind.

"Why did you tell Darroch about my humiliation at the hands of my family?"

"Is that what she told you?" His voice was low.

"Yes, she said you told her all about it."

"When will you learn you cannot believe Darroch?" he

285

asked, putting his hands on her arms and turning her to face him. "Lass, I told her nothing. As a matter of fact, I only gave my mother and the MacSweens the barest of facts. I have no wish to further your pain."

"Thank you for that. It seems I am constantly thanking you for something these days, doesn't it?" A wry smile twisted her mouth.

"No doubt Darroch used her wiles to ply one of my men for information. I will have a word with them," he said grimly.

"No, it doesn't matter. Let them know what happened. Perhaps it is better for them to know the truth than to speculate."

"Aye, there's enough speculation as it is about your new bedchamber. Rumors are flying fast and furiously." He gave a deep chuckle. "Mayhap it will lighten the dullness of winter for them."

"We certainly have kept them guessing, haven't we?" Cathryn couldn't resist the question.

"I repeat, my dear," his smooth voice stated, "guard your glances more carefully. No matter how gentlemanly I plan to be, after all is said and done, I am still a man."

"I am sorry," she murmured, careful to keep her eyes lowered. "I meant nothing by it."

When he had gone, she sank into the chair and gazed deep into the flames of the fire. Instead of being simplified, she suddenly feared her situation had just become hopelessly complicated.

For the rest of the day, Cathryn simply enjoyed the quiet atmosphere of her new bedchamber. She took her luncheon and evening meal there, seated in front of the fire with a book to read as she ate. It seemed much preferable to going downstairs to join the noisy throng gathered in the Great Hall. In a day or two she might feel up to that, but right now she needed to be alone. Solitude was like a balm to her lacerated spirits.

Margaret and Meg had both paid her short visits and,

though she was glad to see them, she also appreciated the brevity of their stay. Della sent word she would come to see her the next day. It was as if they all wanted her to know they were happy to have her back, but were willing to wait until she was ready to make herself a member of the household. It was certainly a pleasant change to be her own person again.

When darkness began to fall, she lighted some of the candles around the room, as well as the small oil lamp on the table next to her chair. However, with the evening shadows came unwanted memories and she found herself gripped by a melancholy that threatened to crush her.

Huddled in the chair, shivering despite the fire, she let herself relive the events of the trip home. Thoughts she had stubbornly kept at bay now crowded in on her and, each time an accusing voice rang in her mind's ear, she cringed, as though facing the hostile mob again. She feared she would never be able to forget how she'd felt then, and prayed she would never be so alone and defenseless again. It frightened her to think how easy it would have been to simply have given up.

She forced herself out of the chair and over to the wardrobe. Perhaps she should prepare for bed in order to take her mind off that horrid scene. She unfolded a night-gown and, taking a candle to light her way, went into the little dressing room which adjoined her chamber. She poured fresh water into the wash basin and washed her face and arms. Slipping into the nightgown, she quickly folded her clothes and laid them on a chair. She then went around the bedroom snuffing out candles, leaving just the one by her bed. She climbed into the bed, grateful for its warmth, and, propped against several large pillows, allowed herself to survey her new quarters with more than a little smug pride. In a few days, perhaps, she might have added enough touches to mark the room as her own. It still seemed a little impersonal, but to her it was a much-longed-for haven.

Across the room, Bonnie Prince Charlie's eyes smiled at her through the gloom. Traitor though he may have been, she thought there was a similarity in their circumstances. Events had made it necessary for them to take refuge in a foreign place, in a stranger's home. Like the prince, she was only biding her time, waiting for some unknown incident to make sense of her life again. An unexpected feeling of kinship with the exiled Stuart sprang up in her, and she knew she would never resent sharing this room with his spirit.

She wondered what his thoughts had been as he had lain in this same bed. No doubt they were even more turbulent and uncertain than her own. At least there was no price on her head, no deaths on her conscience, and no one systematically searching the endless miles of heather for her.

The bed was most comfortable, and she was extremely tired, but somehow, sleep wouldn't come. After an hour or so of tossing and turning, she flung back the covers and got up. She went to the windows and stood looking out toward the ocean, even though there was nothing to be seen except a few weak stars shining in the darkness overhead. As she turned, she could see a light in Revan's room and, as she watched, his shadow fell across the glass. Surprised that he wasn't downstairs with the rest of the clansmen, she watched his dark figure pace back and forth in front of the windows, pausing occasionally to peer out into the night just as she had done.

What was it that bothered him? she wondered. What could be of sufficient importance to cause the MacLinn just such a restless and sleepless night as she was experiencing?

Della arrived for her promised visit early the next morning, bringing with her Cathryn's breakfast tray.

"Just stay right there where it's warm," Della instructed her. "I'll sit here at the foot of your bed while you eat."

"I've never entertained a guest while dining in bed," Cathryn smiled. "I think I'm becoming rather decadent."

Della laughed. "How shameful!" She swept the bedchamber with an admiring look. "This is certainly a comfortable room, my dear. How do you like it?"

Cathryn busied herself with pouring two cups of tea, one of which she handed to Della.

288

"I like it very much. It's good to know I can have privacy whenever I want."

"Don't you find it a bit lonely?"

"Lonely? After the last few weeks, I'm longing for a little loneliness."

Della took a small sip of tea, her eyes innocent above the rim of the cup.

"Still and all, it is a long way from . . . the rest of the household."

"With the nursery just down the hall?" Cathryn asked.

"Well, it seems such an isolated room and so full of old memories. I thought it might have disturbed you at least a little."

"Not at all." Cathryn carefully buttered an oatcake. "The ghosts of Culloden did not walk last night, if that is what you mean."

"It seems someone did," Della said guilelessly. "From our cottage, Adam and I did happen to notice your light — until the early morning hours."

"I didn't sleep especially well," Cathryn admitted. "I was tired from moving my things into this room, and I expect I was still feeling the effects of the journey home. I think I was just too exhausted to sleep well."

"That's all?"

"If you are trying to get me to admit I missed Revan, you may as well forget it. I found being alone quite satisfactory."

Della sniffed. "It would seem your idea of satisfactory and mine are very dissimilar."

"Oh?"

"Indeed. I can't say I would particularly relish spending the night alone, unable to sleep, and surrounded by so many unhappy ghosts! No thanks. I believe I would just as soon have a warm companion with whom I could while away the sleepless hours."

"Della, you promised."

"Oh, all right. If you don't care to discuss Revan, what do you want to talk about?"

"Well, if I am to spend the winter at Wolfcrag, why don't you tell me something about some of the people I am likely

289

to meet? I am quite interested in learning more about the cottage folk."

Later, when Della had gone, Cathryn dressed in warm clothing, suddenly determined to go for a horseback ride. She had enjoyed the security of her bedchamber long enough. All at once she longed for fresh air and the freedom of the countryside.

Thinking she might be gone most of the day, she stopped in the kitchen long enough to ask the cook for some bread and cheese, which she bound up in a linen napkin. When she arrived at the stable, a friendly stableboy helped her saddle the little mare she had ridden on the trip home. Shyly, the boy told her the horse's name was Kirsty and that her sure-footedness made her one of the best horses in the MacLinn stables.

"You're a real beauty, aren't you, Kirsty?" Cathryn said, patting the mare's soft nose. "We shall have to spend a lot of time together, getting to know one another."

The mare snorted, tossing her silky brown mane.

"Kirsty, you may be altogether too haughty," she said laughingly. She settled herself in the saddle and, as she rode the mare across the courtyard, she could already hear the faint creak of the portcullis being raised. As she passed the gatehouse, the men inside waved or nodded to her in a friendly fashion, and she smiled back. It seemed Revan had meant it when he'd told her he would no longer detain her inside Wolfcrag. Leaving this time was far easier than it had been that day she and Darroch had ridden out together.

She crossed the drawbridge and followed the narrow trail along the chasm, then turned Kirsty's head toward the north and west, hoping to find a path that would lead her to the sea.

The intermittent sunshine and warmer temperatures of the last two days had melted away much of the snow, leaving only patches here and there among the dark brown drifts of bracken and heather. Far in the distance, she could see a faint haze of snow-covered mountains, fading into the blue of the late morning sky.

As the little mare carried her along, Cathryn was suddenly filled with exhilaration. The freedom of being on her own with an entire day before her was pleasant, and she spurred the horse into a gallop. If only for this short time, she would cast off the feeling of gloom that had hung over her recently and enjoy herself.

It was obvious Kirsty knew the trail well, so Cathryn let her have her head, making no attempt to check her speed. Before too long, the trail curved upward along a grassy hillock, and there before them was the sea. A wide sand beach stretched out toward the water, ending in a line of smooth black stones upon which the waves crashed and foamed, sending spume high into the air. Reining the mare to a halt, Cathryn took in the scene before her, delighting in the feel of seaspray against her face.

Carefully, they picked their way across the damp sands, close to the water's edge, and then Cathryn rode slowly along the rock barrier. Scattered throughout the sand at their feet were small sea shells and ribbons of seaweed. Just off the shore, looking misty and forlorn, was a small rocky islet, with the remains of a crumbling tower visible. Cathryn wondered what the structure had been and to whom it had belonged. She sat and gazed at it for a long time, fascinated by the waves curling at its rugged base and the gulls weaving their way through the broken windows and turrets, crying hoarsely as they went.

Nearly a mile further along the beach, the land flattened out somewhat, and she could see a small settlement of rock cottages which she knew must belong to the MacLinn fisherfolk. The land made a broad curve and the ocean deepened into a natural harbor, where a stone quay had been built. A few small boats were anchored in the harbor, rising and falling with the restless waters, but she saw no large fishing boats and assumed the fleet was out.

As she rode closer to the cottages, she could see a few nets spread to dry on wooden racks or across stone fences. A child or two played outdoors and, as she passed, they waved shyly. Several women stepped to their doors to watch as she rode

291

by, and when she smiled and nodded, they all smiled back. One or two offered a friendly greeting in Gaelic. Cathryn regretted she was unable to stop and converse with them and, for the first time, considered the idea of trying to learn Gaelic. After all, she reasoned, she was now a displaced Lowlander and ideas that once would have seemed totally alien might now be most sensible.

Once past the fishing village, the coastline underwent a rapid change, becoming rocky and nearly impossible to traverse. Huge, misshapen granite boulders jutted skyward, and sometimes there were high cliffs with the ocean a heart-stopping distance below.

In one such spot, Cathryn saw a sheltered place and decided to stop for lunch. She tied Kirsty to a scrubby bush and walked through deep sand into the shelter of the boulders. Seating herself in the sand, with her back against a rock, she ate her bread and cheese while gazing out at the never-ending water, wondering what lay beyond. Lulled by the rhythmic motion of the waves and by the warm sun on her face, she soon fell asleep, nestled against the rock.

She must have slept for a long time, for when she awoke she felt stiff and sore, and there was a definite chill in the air. Brushing the clinging sand from her long skirts, she got to her feet and stretched, hoping to ease the tightness of cramped muscles.

A shadow fell across her and she whirled to see Revan MacLinn, astride his big black stallion, slowly riding across the sand toward her.

"I didn't mean to startle you," he said easily.

"You didn't," she lied. "I guess I must have fallen asleep watching the ocean."

She walked to Kirsty's side, untying the reins.

"Shall I ride with you back to Wolfcrag?"

"If you like." She mounted, conscious of his gaze. She wondered if he had followed her.

The two horses fell into stride with each other. Cathryn made her voice sound casual as she asked, "Did you think I wouldn't come back?"

"I didn't intend to force you to return, Catriona. I just

wanted to make certain you were safe. There are many hazards along the coast you know nothing of and my concern was only for your safety."

"I see. Thank you."

They rode in silence then, until Cathryn found the courage to ask, "Do you mean that, if I told you I meant to ride on past Wolfcrag now, and seek some other place of refuge, you would simply let me go?"

He threw her a mocking look, his quick smile flashing. "You are unable to believe I no longer think of you as my prisoner, aren't you?"

"Well, you must admit it is certainly a change of attitude from when I first came here."

"Much has changed since you first came here," he replied. "And, to answer your question, if you wish to ride off to some other place, I won't try to stop you. I would, of course, point out the foolishness of such an action, but that is all."

"I only wondered," she said quietly.

As they neared the fishing village again, Cathryn was aware of even more curious onlookers. Several children gathered round them as they passed among the stone cottages, and many of the women stepped to their doors to wave and smile again. At the end cottage, a tiny old woman came out, waving her walking stick and saying something in Gaelic that was plainly a demand for them to halt.

Cathryn thought the woman must surely be the oldest human being she had ever seen. Her face might have been carved from a dried apple it was so seamed and wrinkled; bright blue eyes twinkled under bushy gray brows, and wispy gray hair straggled out around the scarf she wore on her head. Below the skirts of her dark gray gown, Cathryn could see two shiny black boots, as small as a child's.

Revan grinned at the woman and called out something which caused her to throw back her head and laugh heartily, displaying a quite toothless smile.

"Who is she?" Cathryn asked, fascinated by the ancient soul.

"This is Granny MacLinn," Revan explained. "Quite the oldest member of our clan."

293

The old lady carefully scrutinized Cathryn's appearance before she stepped up to Kirsty's side and made a formal curtsy.

"How'd ye do, lady?" the old woman said, her voice a hoarse croak.

Cathryn cast a surprised look at Revan, whose face was amused. "She speaks English?"

"Aye, and Gaelic and French, so I'm told. Granny, this is Catriona."

"I ken, laddie. She be a fine-lookin' woman for the MacLinn." The old granny nodded her head in pleased approval. "Ye'll get many sons with this lass."

Cathryn's face flamed and she opened her mouth to protest, when Revan's voice cut in smoothly.

"Aye, could be."

Cathryn gave him an indignant look, which did not pass the notice of the woman. She cackled in delight and said brightly, "Of course, ye must tame the wee lassie first, m'boy. I dinna ken 'twill be easy, for she looks to be a fiery one."

She cast a roguish look up at the man on horseback and tapped his leg with a coquettish hand. "But that's the only kind worth the tamin', eh, lad?"

The two of them laughed together, much to Cathryn's discomfort. She was amazed that such an ancient old crone would treat Revan in such a flirtatious manner.

"Granny, my love, we must be on our way. 'Twas pleasant speaking to you."

Revan leaned down to lift the wrinkled hand to his lips, causing Granny MacLinn to beam with delight.

"Get on with ye, bonny man. Och! Were I a wee bit younger!" She favored them with another toothless smile as they rode away.

Cathryn's brief anger fled in the face of her surprise at Revan's gallantry. She looked sideways at him and said, "I think I am beginning to understand how you inspire such loyalty."

"And how is that?" He raised one brow, as though in some doubt he would enjoy hearing her reply.

"You were kind to that old woman, Revan. You stopped

to talk with her and made her feel she was quite important to you."

"Don't seem so surprised, my dear," he laughed. "After all, Granny is important to me. She's the midwife who delivered me, for one thing. For another, she knows more about medicines than anyone else except Adam. She keeps the fishermen healthy for the most part, which saves him considerable traveling. There isn't anything Granny can't do."

"She must be old," Cathryn said.

"Aye, no one knows for sure, and she won't admit to anything more than two score ten!"

Despite herself, Cathryn had to laugh. "Do you think I could come back to visit her some time?"

"Ah, interested in hearing more about all those fine sons?" he asked wickedly.

"Certainly not," she snapped. "Forget I asked."

She spurred Kirsty and rode on ahead, back straight and head in the air. Just as she became impressed with his polite manners, he had to say something to remind her how infuriating he really could be.

When they passed the little island with its picturesque castle ruins, she wanted to ask him about it, but her pride made her keep silent and ride on. As the trail wound down and away from the ocean, it became somewhat narrower, forcing Revan to stay behind, following her.

Back in the courtyard, he sprang down from his stallion and came to help her dismount.

"If you are still angry with me, I apologize," he said, lifting her down. "It seems I have a habit of saying the wrong thing."

"Indeed, you can be very irritating," she agreed. As he set her on her feet, his strong hands lingered at her waist.

"But, tell me the truth, Catriona. Weren't you just a wee bit interested in hearing about our future sons?"

"Oh, you really are insufferable!" She flung his hands away and stalked off across the yard, leaving him standing there looking after her, a broad smile on his lips.

Having had a taste of freedom, Cathryn found many ways to fill her time during the next two weeks. She rode every day, as long as the weather permitted. She began to know Kirsty very well, understanding her moods and whims. The two of them explored every path and trail around Wolfcrag, some days riding along the ocean and others, making their way through the rough and lonely glen.

Cathryn had become a familiar sight to the people in the fishing village, and they never failed to greet her with a certain dignified friendliness. Regrettably, it seemed the only one with whom she could communicate was Granny MacLinn, and though at first she hesitated, she soon grew to enjoy those times the old lady would hasten out of her cottage for a word or two. Even the fact that Cathryn often had to listen to the woman praising Revan in glowing terms was not unbearable. It only reinforced her notion that the young chieftain was greatly beloved among his clansmen.

Often as she moved about over the countryside, she caught glimpses of Revan. Once in a while she would see him at a distance, sitting motionless astride his horse, watching her. At first it irritated her, but since he never came forward or made any move to join her, she had to assume he was only concerned for her safety.

Sometimes, when it was too wet or cold to ride any distance, she would put on her warmest clothes and slip through the secret tunnel to the sheltered cove below the castle. She was a bit more used to the tunnel now and didn't mind the damp or the darkness so much. At one end of it, she knew, was a magnificent view of the ocean and, when she was thoroughly chilled, passing back through it would bring her again to the warmth and security of Wolfcrag. The only unease she felt now was when she passsed the spot where Revan had thrown her down onto the sand that day she had so angered him. She always swept by it, eyes averted, cheeks a little pinker, glad he was not there to see her.

Sometimes she walked the small curve of sandy beach, looking for unusual sea shells or bits of flotsam tossed up by the tide. At other times she would find a seat among the tumbled boulders and simply sit, looking out into the distance. At those times, she inevitably found herself thinking of home, wondering what her father was doing. Did he ever think about her or hope to see her again? Now and then she would allow herself the luxury of a daydream in which she returned to her village a second time, only to find her father a sad and humbled man — one who would throw himself at her feet, begging her forgiveness. Then, impatient with herself for such a hopeless fantasy, she would angrily shake out her skirts and pace furiously up and down on the sand for a time before returning to her room.

On those days when it was unusually nasty outdoors or when she found herself in a disagreeable mood, she would wander through the castle, looking into rooms she had not seen or staring at the faded MacLinn portraits. Often, as she passed through the echoing emptiness of the Great Hall, she would feel like some silent, unseen ghost, her feet gliding noiselessly over the stone floors.

She saw Meg often and, occasionally, would spend a morning with Margaret, sewing and talking quietly, or with Della, gossiping in front of the fire in her tidy cottage. But the greatest amount of time she spent alone, brooding and remembering. However, as time went on, she gradually felt herself beginning to chafe at this solitary existence. More and more she began to take notice of the noisy tide of life swirling all about her in the castle, and wondered what it would be like to immerse herself in it, rather than standing on the edge.

The time was approaching when she wouldn't feel so strongly about keeping herself apart, she knew. The pain in her heart was no less severe than a wound sustained in battle, and like that wound, someday a probing finger might prove it still tender, but somehow she would know it had started to heal.

Chapter Sixteen

One cold but sunny afternoon Cathryn had the idea of taking Meg riding with her. The child assured her she could ride and even had a spotted pony of her own, but that her father wouldn't allow her to ride alone, and no one seemed to have the time to go with her. Feeling chagrined that she hadn't thought of it sooner, Cathryn helped the little girl into warm clothes and off they went.

They found Revan and Owen in the stables, working at repairing some leather reins. Cathryn politely asked Revan's permission to take his daughter riding, and he just as politely gave it. As soon as the horses were saddled, the two of them rode off, chatting happily as they went through the castle gates.

Revan stood looking after them, a slight frown on his face. With a sigh, he turned back to his work.

"You know, Owen, that is the first time I have seen Cathryn so much as smile since we got back."

"Aye, I ken she had a spell of unhappiness to live through."

"I thought she would accept us a bit more after what happened," Revan commented, his lean hands busy with the splicing tool, "but she seems to have withdrawn even more."

" 'Tis natural, lad. She'll come 'round, don't you worry. 'Twas quite a blow to her pride, you know."

"Aye, to be sure. But day after day, I've watched her go off alone, never knowing if she'll come back or not. She rides out early and stays out all day. So much could happen to her! I've seen her sit and stare at the water for hours, never

298

moving. It nearly drives me mad, wondering what's going through her mind."

Owen flashed him a quick look. "Ye MacLinns are a jealous lot, by God! Can't the lass even have a few private thoughts?"

Revan flushed in anger, but before he could make a reply, Owen laid a big hand on his shoulder. "Dinna fash yerself, laddie. I was only teasing."

Revan managed a sheepish smile. "But you are right, Owen — I was jealous. Jealous of her memories, I suppose. Nothing to be proud of, I know."

Owen chuckled. "Women have a way of making you have feelings of which you sometimes canna be too proud. 'Tis the way of the world, son."

"Oh, do you know so much of women then, Owen?" Revan grinned.

"I know more than enough," Owen retorted. "Things are fine as long as a man tosses a wench in the hay, then leaves her for another. 'Tis when ye start tryin' to figure out what goes on in their minds that you're lost."

"I suspect you are right," Revan replied ruefully. "I never had so much trouble with a woman before. Sometimes I wonder why I had to kidnap such a stubborn one."

"It's just as well," Owen said dryly, "for no other type would satisfy ye. It takes a strong woman to make a mate for the MacLinn, and strong women are often stubborn and hard to handle."

"You impress me with your knowledge, Owen," Revan drawled, leaning back as if to get a better look at the big man facing him. "I didn't realize you were such an expert on the matter."

"Well, I'm no shaky-kneed virgin, if that's what you mean," the older man growled. "And I, at least, know how to keep a woman in my bed."

Revan rose to his feet, his face a deep red. "Damn it, MacIvor, you forget yourself!"

Owen's laugh rumbled. "Mayhap, but the truth of the matter is, someone needs to remind you of your objective, lad. You wanted the wench enough to risk everything to

bring her here. Now what do you intend to do about it?
Watching her from a distance won't win her over, ye know."

"To tell the truth, I don't know what else to do."

"Why don't you let me finish this and you catch up with
them? Talk to the girl, Revan, get to know her and let her get
to know you. Woo her gently, but firmly. Don't push her, but
don't take no for an answer."

Revan shook his dark head, laughing in spite of himself.
"You make it sound easy, man."

"On your way, lad, and good luck to ye."

Warrior's strong legs covered the ground swiftly and it
wasn't long before Revan caught up with Cathryn and Meg.
They had stopped on the beach across from the castle ruins
and appeared to be digging in the sand for something. As he
approached, they sat back on their heels and watched him.

"Hello, Father," Meg cried joyously. "Want to help us look
for shells?"

"Certainly. That is," here he gave Cathryn an inquiring
glance, "if I wouldn't be intruding."

"Of course not," she answered.

He tied the stallion beside the other horses and strode
across the deep sand, his boots sinking in with every step.

"If we can find enough of these little pinkish shells,
Cathryn has promised to help me string them for a neck-
lace," Meg explained to him. "Won't that be pretty?"

"Aye, 'twill be fit for a queen, Meg," Revan said seriously,
his eyes twinkling.

The three of them dug through the wet sand for a while,
Meg keeping up a steady stream of words. After a time, she
wandered further down the beach to look for the shells.
Revan and Cathryn were glad for the opportunity to abandon the search and settled themselves on the rounded
boulders to wait until the child tired of it, also.

"It is good of you to entertain Meg, Catriona," Revan said.
"It means a great deal to her that you will spend time with
her."

"I enjoy it," she replied. "As a matter of fact, I can't think why I have waited so long to bring her out with me. Are you sure you don't mind?"

"Nay, as long as you take no risks. We don't ordinarily have much to fear from strangers here, but you do have to beware of the rough terrain and the treacherous tides. Those are two things you must never take for granted. It is too easy to be caught off guard."

"Yes, I can see how that would be," she agreed. "I promise I will be careful with Meg."

He turned his golden eyes upon her. "I am concerned about your welfare, also."

"We will be as careful as we know how to be," Cathryn vowed. "And anyway, it is well into December now, so I feel certain the weather isn't always going to be this mild. When the heavy snows come, our trips abroad will no doubt be ended."

"Aye, in another few weeks there won't be much to do but sit indoors and wish for spring."

Revan leaned forward to gather a handful of sand, which he let slip slowly through his fingers to fly out in the wind.

"Of course, when spring does arrive, there is considerably more to do. When the weather is warm, we can venture out to visit friends who live in other parts of the Highlands. Sometimes we camp out in the hills for a night or two, which Meg has always loved doing. Then, there are picnics, and swimming, and sometimes we go out in the boats to fish or visit the seal islands."

"Have you ever gone out to that island?" she asked, pointing out the rocky isle crowned with the ruins.

"Certainly, many times."

"What was it used for?" Cathryn questioned.

"Why that's where the MacLinn chieftains always kept their captive brides," he said, his mouth lifting a little at one corner.

"If that were true, it would never have been allowed to fall into ruin," she said sharply, "for the MacLinns are still stealing brides!"

His laughter rang out, causing Meg to pause in her playing to look back at them. Assured all was well, she again

301

turned her attention to gathering shells.

Revan leaned closer to Cathryn and picked up one of her hands. She started, but did not pull away, and he lay the slim hand encased in its kidskin glove across his larger palm as though studying it.

"The little castle used to belong to a kinsman of my father's father, many years ago. They tell me it was once a beautiful home, but when its mistress fell ill and died, the old laird went insane with grief and, over the years, it all just went to ruin. The old man lived there alone, growing ever more disoriented, until one night he climbed to the top of the tower and threw himself down onto the jagged rocks below."

As he talked, he traced the stitching on the back of the glove with a calloused thumb.

"Poor old fellow," Cathryn murmured sympathetically.

"Now, of course, the villagers believe his ghost walks on moonlit nights. More than a few of them have reported seeing the old laird, his long white hair streaming out in the wind."

"It sounds horrible."

"There are such tales all across the breadth of Scotland," he reminded her. "I myself have seen no such ghost, though my brothers and I spent a lot of time playing on the island when we were younger."

"Would it be possible for me to go there sometime?" she asked.

"Aye, when the wind is a little less strong. I will take you there on a picnic next summer, shall I?"

The look he turned on her was so warm she suddenly felt shy and moved a little away from him, pulling her hand from his loose grip.

"That would be quite nice," she said. "I'm certain Meg would like that."

"I promise there will be many things to do here during the spring and summer. We will keep you very busy."

"If I am still here . . ."

After a long silence, Revan said, "Yes, of course — if you are still here."

Presently, Cathryn said, "There is something I would ask

you."

"Yes?"

"It's about Meg. Do you . . . would you object to my spending two or three hours each day teaching her?"

"Teaching her?"

"Yes," she replied. "I think I could help her learn to read and write, and perhaps the experience will allow me to discover whether or not I have the makings of a governess. After all, should I decide to leave Wolfcrag, I would have to have some livelihood."

"I cannot imagine you as a governess, Catriona, but if it pleases you, I have no objections. 'Twould be to Meg's advantage in any event."

"You would still come up to the nursery to read with her, wouldn't you?" Cathryn asked. "I would not want to be the cause of her losing that time with you."

"Aye, I would not care to forego it myself," he assured her. "Nevertheless, she would benefit from regular lessons, I've no doubt. I think it is a good idea."

"Then I shall begin immediately," she declared. "I thought I could look in the nursery cupboards for schoolbooks. We shouldn't need much at first."

"I do seem to recall there being some books there, and I have purchased a few more recent history books you may care to use."

"I thought perhaps history might be a subject you would prefer to teach yourself," Cathryn said primly.

He arched an eyebrow. "Why is that? At her young age, I shouldn't think she would need an overabundance of history just yet."

"Nor would I. But, if she should prove curious about the subject, I might find it difficult to know how you would have me teach her."

"What is it you are trying to say?"

"You surely recall I was not raised as you were and, therefore, I might give some historical event an interpretation you might not approve of."

"Are you insinuating I would have my child raised in ignorance to satisfy some belief of my own?" His voice had taken on a sharp edge.

"Just as an example," she said coolly, "what would I tell her about the battle at Culloden?"

"Tell her the truth," he said angrily.

"Whose truth? The one I was taught or the one you were raised to believe? Do you see the point I make?"

"No, I do not," he thundered. "It seems to me you are splitting hairs with me. Your request to become my daughter's teacher was so meek and respectful, and now, so quickly, you are deliberately trying to goad me into an argument. In God's name, Catriona, I don't understand you!"

"No, you don't, if you think I am trying to start a disagreement with you," she cried, leaping to her feet. "There is a purpose in what I said, and well you know it."

"Aye, and the purpose was to nettle me!"

"You . . . you egotistical oaf! Why should I waste my time trying to upset you?"

"I have asked myself the same question. Perhaps your life has been too quiet lately, and you seek to add a little spice to it by tormenting me."

"Don't flatter yourself!" Cathryn exclaimed, nearly choking on her ire. She whirled away from him and started toward her horse. "Meg! Come now, it is time we went home. The wind is getting quite chilly."

Reluctantly, Meg gathered up her handkerchief of sea shells and tucked them into the pocket of the dress she wore beneath her cloak. Revan watched as they remounted their horses, then he reached for Warrior's reins. As Cathryn rode close to him, she said, "I will begin teaching Meg, with your permission, but when you have decided the question of history, be so kind as to let me know."

With that she put her nose into the air and rode away, followed by Meg. With a short, heartfelt curse, Revan threw himself up onto the stallion's back and cantered after them.

Having arrived back at the stables, he tossed his reins to Owen, and favored the man with a baleful glare. "Next time, Owen," he said between clenched teeth, "keep your damned advice to yourself!"

The following evening Cathryn decided to join the others for the evening meal in the Great Hall. She had had enough of dining alone and, when Della told her she and the doctor would be present, Cathryn agreed to come down.

She dressed in the blue woolen gown, taking special care with her hair. She brushed it vigorously, then tied the cascade of curls high on the back of her head with a length of blue ribbon. She knew it was going to be difficult for her to face the large crowd that ordinarily gathered for the meal and she wanted to look presentable.

Della was kind enough to come up to her room for her, and the two of them went down, arm in arm. To her surprise, she was greeted in a friendly manner by everyone but Darroch. She felt relieved that no one seemed to take any undue notice of her. As the meal progressed, she began to relax and actually enjoy herself. She was seated next to Owen MacIvor this evening, and she was grateful for his solid no-nonsense presence. She didn't have to pretend around him and found it a delightful change to simply be herself.

Owen entertained her throughout the meal with tales of a recent fishing trip he had made with some of the men from the village. Having spent very little time on the water, he was unprepared for the sudden onslaught of an especially vicious attack of seasickness, and his plain-spoken descriptions of his dilemma caused her to laugh merrily.

She laid a hand on his thick arm and said, "Poor Owen! How terrible for you. You must be an inlander just like me!"

"Aye, lassie, and that's how I intend to stay from now on!" They laughed together again. Suddenly Cathryn raised her eyes and saw Revan sitting right across the table, glaring at them. Quickly, she removed her hand from Owen's arm, but the angry expression on Revan's face did not lighten.

After dinner was finished, Owen asked if she would care to have a game of chess with him. Surprised that the rugged outdoorsman knew the game, she accepted readily.

As he set up the board near the fire, he explained, "Revan and I often have a game or two at night, but to tell the truth, he's been somewhat irate with me lately and doesn't seem in the mood for games."

"So I've noticed," Cathryn said, looking to the far side of the room where Revan sat sprawled in a chair deep in the shadows. He was sipping whiskey with a glum expression on his handsome features. She turned back to Owen. "What is wrong with him?"

Owen grinned broadly. "I've always thought a surfeit of cold baths could make a man surly."

"Cold baths? What would he . . ." Suddenly, she realized what he was saying and thought it best to take refuge in pretended ignorance. She felt a deep blush starting, and busied herself with the first move of the game.

It didn't take long for Owen's superior skill to assert itself and, though she managed to fend him off for at least an hour, the match eventually ended in a checkmate. As they debated whether or not to set up the board for a second game, Della and Adam MacSween approached and announced their intention of teaching Cathryn to play a card game called "Robbers and Kings".

With Owen as her partner, Cathryn soon mastered the basic techniques of the game, and the foursome played on until nearly midnight. Cathryn found the game and their company very pleasing, and her green eyes sparkled with renewed life.

Watching from his self-imposed solitude, Revan practically ground his teeth in frustration. It seemed everyone could please the wench but him. She smiled and laughed with all of them, but whenever she chanced to look up and catch his eye, a sudden stillness would come over her features, and her smile would slowly fade. Finally, having reached the point he could no longer stand to witness her reaction to him, he left his chair and went upstairs to bed.

The following day Cathryn started her lessons with Meg, much to the child's delight. They searched the cupboards in the nursery and found several old schoolbooks that Cathryn thought would do nicely.

On the flyleaf of one of the primers she found the name "Revan MacLinn" scrawled in a childish hand and, beneath it, written in the same hand, was a short poem:

"If I were a bird,
I'd fly free on the moors.
But I'm just a lad,
Shut behind schoolroom doors."

Unbidden, the thought of Revan as a boy came into her mind, causing her to smile. She had no doubt he would have been as irrepressible a child as Meg. She could just imagine the unwilling scholar forced to sit indoors with his tutor, when his soul must have cried out to be free to run as he pleased. A momentary feeling of pity for that young boy rose up within her. Just as he would have achieved his freedom from the classroom, events had conspired to make him the chieftain of a troubled clan, bringing an early maturity. She shook her head to clear her thoughts — Revan the child was a very different prospect from Revan the man, and she warned herself not to forget it.

Her sessions with Meg quickly fell into a routine. They spent two hours working on the rudiments of reading and writing, then they shared lunch in the nursery and, after that, they studied from a variety of other books for perhaps another hour. Then, if the weather was nice enough, they would go for a ride or a walk. When it was too wintry to go out, they would sit in front of the fire to play games or sew.

Meg loved the afternoons when her grandmother would bring her stitchery and join them. It pleased her greatly that Cathryn's attempts at needlework were really no better than her own. They laughed a great deal, but rarely turned out any article that pleased Margaret MacLinn, who had to smile in spite of herself.

Once in a while Revan would slip quietly into the room to watch his daughter at her lessons, and though he never said anything, he always seemed well-pleased. He did not bring up the subject of history, nor did Cathryn. She felt somewhat confused about the matter. She did not think she had originally broached the subject in order to anger him, but after he accused her of doing just that, she wondered if there might be something to his theory. Unsure of her own motives, she kept silent rather than risk bringing it up a second time.

At any rate, her efforts to teach Meg had given a purpose to her life. She felt there was some small reason for her existence, and that feeling gave her a new self-esteem.

Late one afternoon when they had returned from horseback riding, Cathryn discovered she had lost one of her gloves and told Meg she was going back down to the stables to search for it there. The elegant kidskin gloves had been given to her by Margaret, and she didn't want her carelessness to result in the loss of one of them.

As she stepped into the dimness of the stable, she could hear the slight murmur of a voice and a strange noise like a soft whining. Alarmed, thinking someone might be lying injured in one of the stalls, she called out, "Who is there? Is someone hurt?"

A small face popped up over the railing of the end stall, and she was startled to recognize young Donald MacLinn, the freckle-faced stable boy.

"Is something wrong, Donald?" she asked.

"Nay, ma'm, 'tis just the little ones here."

"Little ones?" she questioned, crossing the hay-strewn floor to the back of the stable.

"Aye." His grubby hands swept aside a drift of straw to reveal a nest of fat puppies lying contentedly beside their mother.

"Oh, how precious!" Cathryn exclaimed, falling to her knees, heedless of her skirts. "Aren't they darling?"

"Would ye like to hold one?" Donald asked shyly, kneeling beside her. "I've just been talkin' to their ma, tellin' her as how it be almost time for her babes to be taken away."

"Taken away?" Cathryn asked fearfully. "Where are they to be taken?"

"Never fear, Mistress, they'll come to no harm. The MacLinn has spoken for this one for Miss Meg's Christmas present, and these other two are to go to her playmates,

Robbie and Ailsa. 'Tis a surprise, like, so promise ye won't tell."

Cathryn was so relieved to hear the puppies were not to be destroyed that she laughed aloud. "I promise, Donald. I won't say a word to anyone."

She lifted the puppy destined to become Meg's onto her lap. He was an exact replica of the hound King George, right down to his sorrowful brown eyes. She stroked his head with its miniature floppy ears, thinking how thrilled Meg was going to be on Christmas morning.

"How have you managed to keep these pups a secret from Meg?"

Donald smiled his infectious gap-toothed grin. "It hasn't been easy, I can tell ye that! She is in and out of the stable all the time, so me and the other lads hid them back here in the straw. 'Tis a good thing Christmas is coming, 'cause before too long they'll be big enough to wander away from their ma and play. Then she'd see them for sure."

Cathryn laid a hand on the boy's bony shoulder. "Donald, you've done a fine job with the puppies. Meg will be so pleased she won't know what to say. Later, I intend to tell her you deserve the full credit."

"Surely you will allow their mother to take some credit in the matter," said a voice behind them.

They got to their feet to face Revan MacLinn who had silently entered the stable and was now leaning against a wooden stall, his face looking quite foreboding in the half-light.

"Yes, of course," Cathryn stammered, aware she had angered the man, but uncertain as to why or how.

"What is it you want in the stable, Catriona?" he asked gruffly.

"I came to search for a glove I lost earlier," she answered.

"Oh, aye, I have it," Donald said. "I found it on the cobblestones."

He led them past the stalls to the front where he took the glove down from a shelf near the door.

Cathryn took it from him, saying, "Thank you so much, Donald. I was afraid I would not find it again."

He grinned cheerfully at her and, with a sudden feeling of affection for the young lad, she reached out a hand and ruffled his black hair. "Take care of the puppies now. If you don't mind, I would like to come back and see them sometime."

"Aye, any time, ma'm. Just don't tell Meg."

"I won't. Goodnight, Donald."

With a last puzzled look at Revan, she left the stable and hurried back toward the castle. Somehow she always seemed to find the fastest way to irritate and anger him, but this time she was really at a loss as to what she had done wrong.

Stepping from her bath, Cathryn wrapped herself in a towel and returned to her bedchamber to dress. In front of a crackling fire she got into her chemise and petticoats. Only this morning Margaret and Morag, the seamstress, had come to her room with the last of the new gowns they had been sewing for her. There were six more, each prettier than the last, and now it was difficult for her to choose which one to wear down to dinner this evening.

She finally decided on a cream-colored velvet with russet ribbons binding its long, puffed sleeves and edging the low neckline. She pulled it over her head in haste. She had ridden longer than usual this afternoon and now found herself short of time.

She caught her reflection in the cheval mirror which had been moved into her room and was dismayed. The gown was very becoming, but the neckline was even lower than she'd thought and she wondered if it wasn't a bit too daring. Perhaps she should change—but no, she really didn't have the time. It would just have to do.

She grabbed up the hairbrush and hurriedly brushed her hair, leaving it flowing down her back in a cloud of deeply burnished curls. She supposed it really wasn't proper to leave her hair unbound, but since she already felt like a naughty child, arriving late for dinner with no valid excuse, she might as well look like one.

She hastened down the stairs and slid into her place at the

table just as the first course was being served. Looking about her, she saw many familiar faces, but from their expressions, she realized her appearance was less like a child than she might have deduced. At the head of the table, Revan's look was frankly admiring, as was that of Doctor MacSween, just down from him. Della was gazing at her friend with a mixture of pride, envy and awe. At the opposite end of the table, Margaret beamed at the reaction the new gown was receiving. Clearly, the fashioning of Cathryn's wardrobe had been an absorbing project for her, and now she was prepared to enjoy the results.

From across the table, Darroch's expression was nasty as she took in the details of Cathryn's new dress. Her dark eyes narrowed in speculation as she wondered what the other woman might have done to earn such a reward.

Choosing to ignore the obvious hatred in Darroch's eyes, Cathryn turned her attention to the MacSweens.

"Are we going to play cards this evening?" she asked.

With an amused glance toward Revan, Della replied, "Nay, it seems our chieftain has called for dancing. It will be a nice change, don't you agree?"

Recalling the last dance she had attended, Cathryn felt embarrassed and made no answer. However, she promised herself she would severely restrict her intake of wine tonight.

When the meal was finished, the music began, and she was again captivated by the wild, gay sounds of the pipes droning out the dance tunes. Before too long, her toes were tapping, and she was clapping her hands in time to the music. The tables were pushed aside and the Great Hall was filled with dancers.

As she watched Adam MacSween lead his wife onto the dance floor, a warm hand was laid upon her arm and a deep voice was requesting the dance. Cathryn looked up into the smiling face of Ian MacLinn, her dance partner from that fateful evening weeks ago. She felt her face burn as she remembered her drunken behavior and, even as she got to her feet, she was trying to think of a polite way to refuse the man.

He seemed to read her thoughts because he quickly said,

"Come now, don't refuse me, milady. I seem to recall we were very good dancing partners once before."

"As you no doubt remember, I was rather inebriated that evening," Cathryn said stiffly.

"Nay, I do not remember that. I only recall being the envy of the entire hall because I had the most beautiful woman present as my partner."

"To tell you the truth, Ian, I am not even certain I can do the steps in a completely sober condition!"

He laughed warmly, and placing an arm about her waist, led her into the midst of the other dancers.

"Shall we see?"

"As you wish."

To her relief, the dance steps came easily to her and, once again, she felt herself being caught up in the music. As they whirled rapidly past the others on the floor, she had to fasten her eyes on Ian's face to keep from becoming quite dizzy. His merry blue eyes were filled with admiration for her, and she found it very flattering. It made her feel so much more like a lady than did the rapacious glances Revan MacLinn always turned upon her. Ian might be a few years younger than Revan, but she would be willing to wager the role of gentleman came more easily to him. He might never be worldly, but he possessed the courtly manners with which women liked to be wooed. Relaxing within the circle of his arms, their bodies at a respectable distance from each other, Cathryn truly began to enjoy herself and found she was smiling up at the young man in a way that might have been considered coquettish.

Lord knows I've had little enough opportunity for a bit of harmless flirtation since coming to this place, she thought. It would never do to smile at Revan in such a manner—I would find myself amongst the bedcovers at once! At least I can feel safe with Ian.

They shared two dances before she was claimed by Doctor MacSween, who was a vigorous dancer, flinging her here and there. It took all her concentration to match his steps and keep her slippered feet well out of reach of his heavy leather boots. As that dance ended she found Owen MacIvor beside her, hesitantly asking for the next dance.

"I can't promise I won't lame ye, lassie," he grumbled. "This dancing is a bit tricky for someone my size."

Breathlessly, Cathryn went into his arms, assuring him he would not harm her. Indeed, somewhat to her surprise, the large man proved himself to be an agile dancer, managing even the most intricate steps with ease. When he whirled her about, her feet nearly left the floor, and she felt quite fragile within his grasp. Once, as he lifted her and swung her about in time to a sprightly tune, she felt her feet fly out from under her and clutched at his broad shoulders, laughing helplessly. In that instant, the dancers beside them moved away and she found herself staring right into the angry amber eyes of the laird of Wolfcrag.

Revan was sitting in a chair, tipped back against the wall. His insolent grace and sarcastic expression sent a little chill down her spine. The fact that he chose to look at her in such a way was rather frightening. Somehow she had done something to offend or anger him, and she had the sinking feeling it would not be long before he disclosed just what that had been. She was not looking forward to any confrontation with the man.

Owen noticed her slight frown and followed her glance. "Take no notice of the man, lass," he said gently. " 'Tis a foul mood he is in, but it will pass before long. His tempers seldom run to any length."

Tearing her eyes away from Revan's, she murmured, "I hope something happens to make him regain a good mood. He positively terrifies me when he is like this."

Owen's big shaggy head was thrown back and his great roaring laugh echoed through the room. "Nay, I canna believe it! Ye who have faced the MacLinn with all the temerity of a raging lioness? Ye profess to be frightened of a wee scowl? I ken ye are just havin' a bit of sport with me."

"Owen, if only I were as brave as you seem to think I am!" she exclaimed. "I really am a most awful coward."

"Lass, I have fought beside men I would wish were as cowardly as ye!"

She inclined her head, smiling. "I shall take that as a

313

compliment, sir."

When the dance had ended, Ian was at her elbow once again, bringing her a glass of wine.

"Wine, Ian?" she asked in an amused tone. "I would have thought you might be afraid to offer me such a thing."

"I didn't think one glass would hurt," he chuckled. "It is a trifle warm in the hall, and I thought you might be thirsty from all the dancing."

"As a matter of fact, I am," she said, brushing loose wisps of hair off her warm forehead. "It would be rather nice to rest awhile and have something to drink. I'm glad you thought of it."

They strolled to the edge of the milling crowd, finding a spot within the deep window recess where they could stand. It was cooler there away from the fire, and Cathryn was grateful for the chance to simply watch the others moving in time to the riotous music.

"You Highlanders are an energetic lot," she stated. "I am not certain I could keep up with you, if it came to a test."

"I suppose you might say we are all rather athletically inclined," Ian agreed. "Right from the cradle we are taught to ride and hunt, to love sporting events and dancing, and to do battle when necessary. No doubt it makes us an active, fiercely competitive people."

She looked up at him, saying in a droll tone, "No doubt."

He laughed cheerfully. "Do you find us so difficult to deal with, Cathryn?"

"To tell you the truth of it, I finally think I am beginning to know you MacLinns a little. That isn't to say I completely agree with you on some matters," she said quickly, "but I do think I have come to a better understanding of you."

She studied his face — the broad brow, the fine eyes, the aquiline nose and gentle mouth. She had not noticed he was such a good-looking man, she realized. Was it because his mane of golden hair and fair complexion had been overshadowed by the darker, bolder image of his chieftain? She supposed it was to be expected that the head of the clan would be thrust forward in any social gathering, and men of lesser importance would be overlooked. However, she now found herself filled with pleasant surprise at the considerable amount of male beauty possessed by the man beside her.

"Tell me about yourself, Ian," Cathryn suggested, taking a sip of the wine.

"There isn't much to tell," he answered modestly. "My father is one of Revan's officers, and we live here within the walls of Wolfcrag. I, myself, have just recently returned from a university in Paris, and as yet, have no duties to undertake."

"Paris?" Cathryn exclaimed, impressed. "How is it a man from the far north of Scotland would be sent to a university in Paris?"

" 'Twas at our chief's request. The MacLinn is very anxious for the young men of our clan to have an effective education. It would not be especially wise to send us to either Edinburgh or London, so we are sent to the Continent. 'Tis the university Revan himself would have gone to had matters been different. 'Tis the school his brothers attended."

"How strange it is," she murmured, "that you Highlanders care so much for an education. All my life I have been taught you were no better than bloodthirsty savages, and now I am inclined to think you care more for cultural pursuits than we from the south."

"Not all clans are as anxious for their people to be educated as the MacLinns," he assured her. "Revan MacLinn just happens to feel it is the best way to rebuild our clan—to make it a power again."

"And do you agree?"

"Oh, certainly. When we go away to school, we return with new, modern ideas about farming and raising livestock. We learn more of politics and government. Some of our lads are studying medicine and surgery. All those things can benefit our people a great deal."

"What did you study, Ian?"

"I studied the law," he replied. "I am to be a solicitor."

Cathryn couldn't resist a slight giggle. "I should say that is something the MacLinns will find most useful. I do not think they have much knowledge of the law at the present time."

315

He laughed good-naturedly. " 'Tis not that they don't have knowledge of the law, 'tis just that they don't have the inclination to obey it."

His gaze moved over the crowd of people, and when he turned it to Cathryn once again, his eyes had grown more serious.

"All seems well for the time being, but Revan expects major changes in the next few years. He thinks our way of life is eventually going to come to an end, and I suspect he is correct. When that day comes, if there is anything left of us, we are going to be prepared."

Before she could ask the next question, a shadow fell across them and she looked up to see Revan.

"I thought perhaps I might claim a dance with you, Catriona," he said. Without waiting for her reply, he took the wineglass from her fingers and handed it to Ian. "Be so good as to hold this, will you?"

It irritated Cathryn that he was so high-handed, sweeping her away into a lively dance without her consent, leaving Ian standing there holding the wineglasses like a servant. She had no chance to voice her protest, however, for he swung her about violently, his hands clamped on her waist like iron bands. It was all she could do to follow his lead and not trip over her own feet.

At one point the music slowed somewhat, and as she moved close beside him to execute a difficult dance step, his voice sounded in her ear. "Are you having a pleasant evening, Catriona?"

She darted a quick look at him, again amazed at the hard glint of anger in his eyes.

"I was," she said pointedly, her chin going up.

"Until I came along to interrupt your intimate little tête-á-tête with my young kinsman?"

"Don't be ridiculous!" she snapped. "We were having a quite ordinary conversation, if you must know."

His mouth set stubbornly, but, as the music quickened again, he whirled her away from him and made no reply. His hands returned to her waist, nearly choking off her breath.

"You are hurting me," she hissed. He only looked straight

ahead, as if he really didn't care very much. When, at last, the music had ended, he took her arm and returned to Ian, none too gently. Then, with a curt nod, he turned on his heel and walked away, leaving her puzzled and angry.

"Is anything wrong, Cathryn?" Ian asked, a concerned look on his face.

"No, nothing is wrong," she assured him, though she wasn't so certain of it herself. "It seems your chieftain is in a rather sour mood tonight."

"Aye, I've heard talk of his bad temper recently. Mayhap he is worried about business affairs."

"Mayhap," she said in a noncommittal voice.

He bent a little closer to her. "Or mayhap it is affairs of another sort that have him so provoked."

She was uncomfortable meeting his eyes. "What do you mean?"

"You must know the castle is all agog trying to figure out the situation between the MacLinn and yourself. At first everyone believed you were his . . . pardon me for saying it, mistress . . ." At the fierceness of her look, he held up one hand, still holding the wineglass, and said, "Nay, don't be angry with me! I am only telling you what the gossips thought to be true."

Cathryn snatched away her glass and drained its contents. "What would they know of it?"

"After you went back to your village, and then returned with him, no one knew what to think. It does seem you are not his mistress, for, according to the servants, you occupy a private room."

Her silvery green eyes began to blaze, but before the angry words could reach her lips, he said, "You must forgive me for speaking to you of these matters. I know it is extremely rude and unseemly, but you see, it is important for me to learn your true status at Wolfcrag."

"Why should it make a difference?"

"If I thought you had no interest in the laird and he had no claim upon you, I would be quite tempted to plead my own case."

His eyes sparkled so warmly, and his manner was so

317

sincere she could not be angry with him. The fact she had to endure such bold references to her personal life was directly attributable to Revan MacLinn.

"We are letting this wonderful music go to waste," she said. "Shall we try another dance?"

After three more of the strenuous reels, Cathryn pleaded exhaustion and announced her intention of going up to her bedchamber. She sought out Della and Adam to say goodnight, then started up the stairway. She was surprised to find Ian waiting for her.

He took her elbow, saying, "I think I have had enough merrymaking for one night, also. Do you mind if I walk you to your room? After all, it's right on the way to my own."

"You have quarters on the third floor?"

"Aye. So you see, it will not inconvenience me at all to see you to your door."

She decided it would be churlish to refuse his offer and, anyway, she disliked walking the corridors alone at night because she feared another meeting with Darroch. Since the morning she moved into the new chamber, she had not been alone with the woman and that was how she preferred to leave it. Darroch made no secret of her animosity toward her and Cathryn was forced to admit to a rapidly growing sense of unease where Darroch was concerned.

There were only a few flaring torches in the hallway and the light was dim and shadowy. When they arrived at Cathryn's door, she pushed it open to reveal a room lit only by firelight.

"Would you mind waiting a moment until I can light a candle?" she asked.

"Not at all," Ian answered, stepping just inside the open door.

Cathryn busied herself with the lighting of a candle on her bedside table and another which she set on the chest of drawers beneath the portrait of the Stuart prince. She stepped back to face Ian.

"There, that makes the room a little cozier," she said. "I like it better here when it is not so dark."

"Do you fear the room is haunted?" he teased, smiling.

318

"No, I just don't care to walk into a darkened place. It's a fear that has been with me since childhood."

Ian hesitated, then, as if he'd made up his mind about something, asked, "Would you do me the honor of spending another evening with me, Cathryn? I should like very much to hear about your childhood and anything else you would care to tell me about yourself."

"Why, I would like that, too, Ian."

He stepped even closer, his hands closing around her upper arms. "I think you are a very lovely woman. I have truly enjoyed your company tonight."

She knew he was going to kiss her and for an instant, she considered stopping him. Being the gentleman he was, she knew instinctively that if she stepped away from him, he would not press the issue. Still, she suddenly wanted to know how it would feel to be kissed by someone other than Revan MacLinn. Her curiosity was so aroused that when he lowered his mouth to hers, she lifted her face without hesitation. His mouth was firm, not hard and demanding like Revan's, and his kiss was gentle, not designed to cause passion to flare. It was the kiss of a man wishing to pay her a compliment, not bend her to his lustful will.

"I hope the question of your relationship with Revan will soon be settled, so I can act accordingly," he murmured.

A ruthless hand gripped his shoulder, spinning him away from Cathryn, who gasped in shock at seeing Revan MacLinn appear out of the shadows.

"The question has been settled," Revan rapped out. "She is mine—no other man's. And you can act accordingly by getting yourself out of here and leaving us alone."

Ian was clearly distraught. It was evident by his bearing he thought he should physically defend Cathryn, but in his eyes could plainly be seen the knowledge that if he raised his hand against his chieftain, he would be an immediate exile.

Cathryn realized his dilemma and hurried to reassure him. "It would be best for you to go, Ian. I will be all right."

"She speaks the truth, Ian. This matter isn't worth severing all ties with your clan, and let me assure you, that is exactly what will happen if you take it one step further. I will

319

gladly talk this over with you another time, but for right now, you'd best just leave us alone."

Ian's disturbed glance met Cathryn's as he wavered in his decision.

"Please do as he says, Ian," she pleaded. "I don't want you alienated from your family on my behalf. This is all my fault, so, please—just go and let me explain things to Revan. Please!"

"All right," the younger man finally agreed. "I hope I have not caused you any unnecessary grief."

"You've done nothing of the kind," she said softly. "Goodnight, Ian."

She held her breath as, reluctantly, he walked away. Once he paused to look back at them, and she prayed silently he would go on, turn the corner and be gone.

When at last it appeared he had gone for good, Cathryn turned on Revan and cried, "What do you think you are doing?"

Viciously he kicked the door shut and came so close he towered over her.

"I might ask the same question," he bellowed.

"I do not have to account to you for my actions."

"That is where you are wrong, madam. Do you forget your presence in this household is only through my good graces? Therefore it would seem I have every right to call you to account for your actions."

"You have a twisted way of looking at things," she said angrily. "What is it I have done that has so angered you?"

He grabbed one arm in a painful grip. "Do you dare ask me such a question?"

She backed away from him, but he followed, retaining his tight hold on her arm.

"Yes, I dare ask it . . . because I cannot figure it out on my own," she exclaimed. "I know you have been angered with me for some days now, but I swear I don't know why."

"Christ! I walk in here and find you kissing another man, and you have the nerve to claim you don't know why I am angry with you?"

"You were angry with me long before this evening," she

retorted. "That can have nothing to do with Ian."

"You are not that stupid, Catriona," he stated, bringing his enraged face close to hers.

She pulled away with a rapid, twisting motion. "Yes! Yes, I am!" she shouted. "You yourself have called me stupid more than once, and if I am supposed to be able to read your mind to determine the reason for your wrath, then I must be stupid, for I cannot do it."

" 'Tis not difficult to figure out, my love," he said viciously. "But if you persist in your ignorance, I will be more than happy to spell it out for you."

"Do so," she flung at him defiantly.

He ran a distracted hand through his thick hair and abruptly turned away from her.

"When I brought you home with me that second time, I was filled with pity and rage. I would gladly have done murder on your behalf. I probably would have felt better if I could have murdered someone! But all I could do was sit back and watch you suffer."

He turned to face her, and she shrank away from the look in his topaz eyes.

"Every day you rode off alone, leaving me to wonder and worry. I was afraid you might run away again or throw yourself into the ocean, or do any number of other insane things. You didn't want my help or my company, so I promised myself I would keep away from you, let you heal on your own. There were times I wanted to offer my sympathy—times I wanted to put my arms around you and hold you, protect you. But no, I didn't allow myself to do those things. I wasn't going to force my attentions on you again. I planned to wait until you saw fit to turn to me."

He grabbed her arms and shook her angrily. "But, damn it, you didn't turn to me. No, you turned to nearly every other man in this castle, but not me."

"What are you talking about?" she stammered.

"You wouldn't come near me, but you could laugh and play games with Owen. You danced and flirted with Ian, hiding in a dark corner. Even Adam—you had time to flirt with Adam, and him a married man! Damn you, Catriona, you even had me jealous of a scrawny stable lad!"

His eyes burned with ire as they moved over her body. "And look at the way you are dressed—flaunting yourself for all to see!"

Cathryn gasped. "Are you insane?" she cried, stunned by his accusations. "Have you gone mad?"

"Aye, and you've driven me there," he sneered. "Do you know what it has been like, watching you, worrying about you—living so close to you but not allowed to . . . to even touch you? And then to see you throw yourself at any other man who happened along!"

"I did not!"

"How do you explain your conduct with Ian?"

"We were only dancing and talking," she defended.

"What about just now?" he reminded her.

"If you must know, I only kissed him because I was curious to see . . ." She broke off, horrified at the admission she had been about to make.

He laughed harshly. "Did you mean to see if his kisses could stir you the way mine do?"

"No, that's not it!"

"Aye, I can see it in your lying eyes, Catriona. And we both know the answer to that question. No one will ever stir you the way I can. Admit it."

"It's not so!" she cried.

"I can prove it easily enough." With that he drew her to him in a fierce embrace, his angry lips crushing down on hers. She struggled against him, but he merely tightened his grip until she could no longer move. She gasped for air as his searing kiss moved from her mouth along her cheekbone to a point just below her ear. She felt as if her flesh was burning each place he touched her—it was as if every kiss would leave a scar that would last forever.

Once again he claimed her mouth, forcing her lips to open and soften under his. It was a grinding, scorching kiss, almost insulting, and she was defenseless against it.

He released her mouth and leaned back to look into her face. She looked wide-eyed at the features so close to her, realizing they were rigid with a lustful rage. Her stunned mind took in the details of his face. His skin was fine-grained and tan, his darkly golden eyes hooded in passion and shadowed by slashing black brows. Within their depths she could see her own reflection and knew she looked terrified. The nostrils of his straight nose flared as he dragged in deep breaths and his arrogant mouth was set in a stubborn line. As her frightened eyes traced the contours of his lips, defined by the curling black beard, she felt a soft ache stir to life within herself. She kept her eyes on his hard mouth for a long moment and then Revan began kissing her again.

"I do stir you, don't I, lass?" he murmured against her lips.

Feebly, she shook her head. "No . . ."

Her whispered protest meant nothing, for in that moment, both of them knew the truth.

Now, as his mouth continued to move against hers, his hands started moving on her back, caressing her and holding her even closer against the full hard length of his body.

Unbelievably, she felt a melting warmth inside her that started at the knee and crept upward, rendering her limp and clinging within his arms. Furious with herself for the unexpected response to his passion, she fought for self-control, but there was no vestige of her pride left. Instead, she was only aware of a raging desire to be even closer to him, and she fitted her body into his as completely as she could. Her traitorous hands moved upward, across his muscular chest and over his wide shoulders, to entwine themselves in his thick black hair and press his sensuous mouth ever closer against hers.

"Catriona, I have wanted you so," he groaned. "These last weeks have been hell."

She opened her eyes to look into his, as if seeking an answer to some unspoken question.

"Nay, lass, I'll not take you by force—never again. Remember, I told you this time you would have to come to me." He moved his mouth against her silken hair, breathing in the warm fragrance of it. "I just thought you needed a reminder that you are mine, no matter how you'd like to deny it."

He traced the softly bruised contours of her lips with a

forefinger. "Do you still swear I do not stir you?" he asked in a low voice.

She looked down, her eyes fastening on the gold medallion he wore around his neck. He gave her a small shake.

"Tell me," he commanded in a hoarse whisper.

She disliked having to admit it, but knew it was the truth. "No, I cannot deny it."

She felt him draw a triumphant breath and then, in the next instant, he asked, "Now, will you promise to stay away from other men?"

Her back stiffened in anger, but he put his warm mouth to her ear. "Shh, lass. Don't be angry again. I only want you to know that if I can't have you, no one else will have the pleasure either."

His final kiss was a probing, searching one that awakened fires within her and left her clinging to him, unable to stand on her own. When he took his mouth away at last, he gently pushed her down onto the bed, then quickly turned and left the room.

When he had gone, she clung to the bedpost and felt herself shaken with helpless sobs. No matter how she wished things might be different, she knew she was angry and upset, not because he had so violated her with his kisses, but because he had not stayed to finish what he had begun.

Chapter Seventeen

For the first time in her life, Cathryn experienced a sleepless night of frustration, filled with unfulfilled longings to which she dared not give a name. In some way, she had begun to understand what it was Revan had gone through and perhaps feel a certain degree of sympathy.

Throughout the long night she huddled beneath the covers in the dark, determined not to light a candle to betray her restlessness to any chance observer. Her fevered mind was too busy with images of Revan for her to even think of being afraid in the darkness. Again and again she relived the scene that had taken place in the bedchamber that evening. The ferocity of her anger with the man for his arrogant disregard for Ian's feelings mingled with her unabashedly passionate response to his kisses. Her argument contending she was just reaching a stage in her life when natural appetites would assert themselves was weak. She most assuredly had not reacted to Ian's goodnight kiss in such a wanton manner. No, to her bitter and unrelenting shame, it was Revan MacLinn she had wanted, and the worst of it was, she had let him see her willingness.

She did not think he was the sort of man who would boast of his conquests to his comrades, but it rankled just to know every time he looked at her, he would be remembering the way she had clung to him, and the abandonment she had shown in returning his caresses. After this, any protest she made would be a sham and they would both know it.

Damn, damn, damn! she swore silently. How could I have allowed him to catch me so off guard?

When morning finally came, she flung herself out of bed and rapidly dressed in a plain serviceable brown wool dress. She needed to get away from her thoughts, and her first impulse was to run to Della and demand the other woman put her to work doing something useful. After all, she had been meaning to spend a day with Della anyway, and today was a perfect opportunity. She was not having lessons with Meg until later in the afternoon because it was Robbie's birthday, and all the castle children had been invited to luncheon followed by a birthday celebration.

Deciding not to bother with the heavy cloak, she threw a shawl about her shoulders, smiling a little at its tired, threadbare appearance. It was the shawl Darroch had given her to wear when she'd first come to Wolfcrag, and the only one of those shabby garments she still possessed. In the interim, though her wardrobe had been greatly enlarged and improved, no one had thought to replace the drab shawl. It didn't really matter to Cathryn, who still couldn't believe her good fortune in receiving all the other beautiful things. One faded shawl seemed of little importance.

When Cathryn arrived at the doctor's cottage, she found Della preparing to bake bread. Rolling up her sleeves and tying on a large white apron, Cathryn announced her intention of helping.

"I know a little about baking bread," she laughed, "but you will have to keep an eye on me. It has been a long time since Elspeth gave me lessons up at the old shieling hut."

"You will do just fine," Della assured her. "And I can certainly use the help."

Each week Della baked bread for her own cottage, as well as that for three other households. It delighted her to have someone to share the chore. She had immediately noticed Cathryn's distracted air and the shadows around her eyes, and sensed the activity would be good for her, also. Della did not know what the problem was, but she was certain it had something to do with Revan MacLinn.

"Did you enjoy yourself last evening?" she asked.

Cathryn shot her a quick look, but Della's absorption in her work convinced the younger woman the question was innocent, and she replied, "Yes, it was a nice dance."

"Ian MacLinn is such a fine young man," Della commented, vigorously stirring flour, raising a small cloud of white dust.

"Indeed, he seems to be. I was quite surprised to learn he has just returned from France."

"Aye, six of our young men are just back from the university. Now we must find enough to interest them in our life here or they will begin drifting away."

"Where do they go?"

"Oh, sometimes to towns in the Highlands, sometimes to Edinburgh or south to England. Actually, we have lost very few of our young people. I think it is because Revan is so young and they see him making a life for himself here. He seems to sense their problems and very likely has felt the same way himself. Mayhap they realize that, and it gives them some insight into the matter. At any rate, he still sends them away to learn, so they know he is willing to gamble on their return. Somehow that wins their loyalty." She shook her head, as if in wonder. "I suppose he has some inborn instinct for leading people. They tell us his father was much the same sort of man."

Della glanced up at Cathryn, who kept her hands busy and made no comment. It occurred to her that something odd was going on. Cathryn had not even made her usual deprecating remarks about Revan. Indeed, she seemed to be mulling over Della's statements. Did this indicate a softening in her attitude toward him?

After a few moments of silence, Della ventured another comment. "I couldn't help but notice you dancing with Ian most of the evening."

"He is a very good dancer," Cathryn said. "And an interesting conversationalist."

"Oh?"

Cathryn ignored Della's inquiring glance and suddenly,

looking as though she would rather not, asked an abrupt question. "Della, do you think I was flirting with Adam last night?"

Della's face registered shock and then mirth. She laughed merrily, bringing a mutinous look to the other's face.

"Let me guess!" Della giggled. "Revan said that, didn't he?"

"Why, yes, he did," Cathryn said stiffly.

"My dear, I have not been jealous of Adam for years! I do not believe you were flirting with him, but even if you had been, I suspect I would have said nothing and let him enjoy it. Short, balding men are very seldom the target of beautiful young girls' attention."

"All right, if you think I acted in a proper manner with Adam, what about Owen MacIvor? Do you think I was too forward with him?"

Della clapped one hand over her mouth to stifle peals of laughter, and when she finally took her hand away, her face was smudged with flour. Seeing it, Cathryn began to laugh and soon her face was similarly streaked with white.

"If Revan was upset because of your behavior with Adam and Owen, what on this earth did he say about you and Ian?" Della gasped. Then her smile faded and she said, "Oh, good heavens, did he make a scene when you went upstairs? I saw him following close behind."

Cathryn turned her bread dough onto the floured table and began kneading it. As she talked, the anger she had experienced the night before came flooding back, and she pummeled the dough with great feeling.

"Of course he followed us! Have you ever seen the man pass up an opportunity to create a scene? It was horrible."

"What happened?"

"Just as poor Ian gave me a goodnight kiss—a very proper goodnight kiss, let me assure you—Revan leaped out of the shadows and practically threw the man out of my room."

Della's brows shot up. "Out of your room?"

"Wait, don't jump to conclusions," Cathryn warned. "It was all quite innocent, believe me. We said goodnight at the door, but when I started to enter my room, it was so dark I asked Ian if he would wait until I could get a candle lighted. Of course, he obliged and then, when I had done that, he gave me a small kiss and that is when Revan attacked him."

"Was anyone hurt?"

"No, they didn't come to blows. I think Ian felt he should defend me, as any real gentleman would, but both Revan and I pleaded with him to just go away. I am afraid Revan made it perfectly clear he wouldn't allow any interference on Ian's part and, as you are all so fond of reminding me, he is the chieftain."

"Aye, and I am glad Ian kept that in mind."

"So am I. For a bit, I thought the whole thing could become very nasty."

"Oh, then Revan wasn't angry when Ian had gone?" Della asked.

Cathryn pounded the bread dough with her fists, again causing Della to smile.

"Revan wasn't angry with Ian — but, of course, he was angry with me! He is always angry with me. It's just that I am beginning to get accustomed to his hatefulness."

"Is that when Revan accused you of flirting with Adam and the others?"

"Not just flirting," Cathryn exclaimed wrathfully, "but throwing myself at them!"

"He can't have been serious. No doubt he was consumed by jealousy when you spent the entire evening with Ian. And then, if he interrupted an intimate moment . . ."

"I have never known anyone so . . . so sneaky! He creeps around spying on me, always picking the most inconvenient moment to burst out of hiding. Everywhere I go he follows me, I swear it. Each time I turn around I find the man underfoot!"

Della had to chuckle again. "Perhaps it does seem that way to you, Cathryn, but he still finds time for his other duties, so he can't be spying on you every minute."

"Why, just yesterday I had to go out to the stables to look for a lost glove, and suddenly, he appeared from nowhere. Then, last night during his tirade, he even accused me of trying to make him jealous of Donald, the stable boy!"

"Oh, no!" cried Della, doubling over with laughter. "Cathryn, you made that up!"

"I most certainly did not!"

"Young Donald?" Della cried. "Good Lord, the man must be daft!"

"Exactly what I told him," Cathryn said, attacking the bread dough with renewed vigor.

"Hold on, lass," Della said, wiping her eyes. "If you don't have a little mercy, that dough won't be fit for the oven. We'd best shape it into loaves."

Later, when the first of the loaves was nearly done baking, the delicious yeasty smell mingled with that of a meat stew bubbling over the fire, making Cathryn's mouth water hungrily. The little cottage was filled with good smells and the sound of laughter, for Della insisted on hearing all the details of Revan's lecture. Cathryn gladly related his words, but she made no mention of his actions and wisely, Della did not ask.

"And to think I always thought Revan was so sensible and level-headed," Della said, as she and Cathryn scrubbed down the wooden table. "It is somewhat shocking to learn he is just as jealous and unreasonable as any ordinary man."

"Might I remind you I have, on a number of occasions, tried to point out the man's failings?" Cathryn snapped.

Just at that moment the door to the cottage opened and Adam stamped in, followed by Revan MacLinn.

"Della, love, Revan has come to get the list of supplies I will be needing from Inverness. Do you remember where I put it?"

"Aye, 'tis there on the desk, along with a much shorter list of my own, if you don't mind, Revan."

"Nay, 'twill be a pleasure," Revan replied. Though his words were directed toward Della MacSween, his eyes were on Cathryn. He thought she made a lovely picture standing there, wrapped in the large apron, bronze curls tumbling down around a face made pink by the heat from the ovens. There was a smudge of flour on her nose and across one cheek. She had been beautiful last night, so vibrant and alive, but somehow, there was something infinitely more

330

appealing about her appearance this morning.

Cathryn couldn't quite meet his eyes, she was so uncomfortable about her actions the night before, so she failed to see his admiration. She was very much aware of her untidy state and her first thought was to escape.

"I . . . I think I should be going now, Della," she murmured to the other woman. "I hadn't realized it was so late."

"Nonsense," Della said calmly. "You have to stay for luncheon. We are going to sample a loaf of your bread." Without waiting for further protests, she then turned to Revan and said, "What about you? Would you care to eat with us? There is plenty of food for everyone."

"Then I accept with pleasure, Della. 'Tis kind of you to ask."

As the two men unwrapped their plaids and hung them on pegs beside the door, Della busied herself with setting the table. Cathryn handed her four crockery bowls from the sideboard, hissing, "How could you? I'll get my revenge, don't think I won't!"

Della smiled sweetly. "Surely you have heard of Highland hospitality, Cathryn? 'Twas just a casual invitation, nothing more."

Despite Cathryn's misgivings, the meal turned out to be very pleasant. Revan was planning a journey to Inverness and talk centered on that. Adam was sending an order for medical supplies he would need, and he spent a great deal of time explaining various items on the list. Cathryn soon forgot her self-consciousness in her interest in what they were saying. It seemed Adam and Della were formulating plans to set up a small hospital somewhere within the confines of Wolfcrag Castle. In spite of herself, she became ensnared in their enthusiasm and even found herself volunteering her services when the hospital was completed.

Though Revan addressed no words to her, several times she met his eyes and was surprised to find herself sharing smiles with him over something Della or her husband had said. All in all, it was as if the four of them had been friends for years, with a perfect understanding of each other's views and enthusiasms. It was the very first time she had considered Revan as a friend, and the idea was a novel one, especially after last night.

When the meal was done, Cathryn helped Della straighten the small cottage, then declared she had to go prepare for the afternoon's session with Meg in the classroom. Revan rose to his feet, saying he needed to get on with preparations for the trip and that he would escort Cathryn back to the castle.

"Goodbye, Della," Cathryn said in a low voice. "I want to thank you again for putting me to work. It was a relief to have something useful to do."

"I think the bread turned out rather well, considering," Della stated, her eyes mischievously alight.

At the door, Cathryn took down the old shawl, aware of Revan's close scrutiny of its shabbiness. Before she could throw it about her shoulders, he took it from her and deftly flung it into place, fastening it with the small cairngorm brooch she wore. When she waved a final farewell to the doctor and his wife, she knew they had not missed the intimate gesture and supposed they read considerably more into it than was necessary.

She crossed the courtyard beside Revan but they did not speak until they entered the Great Hall of the castle. As they started up the stairs, Revan turned to her and asked, "Would you like to make the trip to Inverness with us tomorrow, Catriona?"

Startled, she looked up at him.

"A small party of us usually goes there about this time of year to purchase the supplies we will need to see us through the heart of the winter. And, I must admit, it makes a very good opportunity to buy some things for Christmas. I always have a long list from Meg and my mother, and had planned on asking if there was anything I could purchase for you. But now that I've thought about it, perhaps you would like to go and do your own shopping. I'm told women enjoy that sort of thing."

Embarrassed, Cathryn looked away. "Yes, I do enjoy shopping, but . . . well, I really have to decline your invitation."

332

"Oh? And why is that? We have been on a recent journey together—surely you know you can trust me to behave in a most circumspect way."

Her green eyes flashed. "Yes, just as you did last evening."

His white teeth gleamed. "I admit I was not at my best then."

She held up a hand in protest. "No, I should not have mentioned it. And about the trip to Inverness, well, frankly, I do not have the money for shopping."

" 'Tis no problem, lass. I will gladly give you whatever money you need."

"Thank you, no. I am not interested in charity."

He sighed heavily as they paused in front of the door to the nursery classroom. "Will you ever get over being so damned stubborn?"

"Probably not." Her chin came up, but she could not resist a small smile.

"Very well, I have a proposition to make. You are spending several hours each day acting as Meg's governess. Does not a governess receive a salary?"

"If she is properly qualified," Cathryn said pointedly.

"In my opinion, you are properly qualified."

"In what way?" she questioned.

"Well, to my way of thinking, there should be no governesses who don't have hair the color of flame—hair that looks as if it would burn a man's hand to touch it." He lifted a strand of hair from her shoulder, gently rubbing it between two fingers. "And thistle-green eyes are another important requirement—and skin the color of ivory . . ."

"Revan! Please!" she laughed uncomfortably, pulling back slightly from his nearness. "You know precisely what I am talking about."

"Aye, I know. And you are still highly qualified, Catriona. You have the intelligence and ability and, more importantly, you actually seem to care about Meg. It's as if you take pleasure from teaching her. Surely those things are all the qualifications anyone would seek."

"I have no certificate to teach."

"It matters not. You are doing an excellent job, and I

333

insist on paying you fair wages."

She hesitated. "You would pay what an ordinary governess would receive under like circumstances?"

There was warmth in his voice as he said, "There are no circumstances quite like ours, lass, but aye, that is how I would pay you. No more and no less. Are we in agreement?"

"I think that would be a suitable arrangement," she replied. "I don't actually know of anything I need for myself, but I would like very much to buy some books for Meg and something special for Christmas for both Meg and Margaret. Yes, I think I would like to go to Inverness."

"We will be away two nights, so you will want to bring along some extra clothing. You will be pleased to know that when we go into the city, we spend the nights at an inn and not in a cave or some deserted croft!"

She smiled, happy at the thought of being in a city again. It had been quite some time since she had been allowed the freedom to wander along a busy street, stopping to browse through any shops that interested her. Tonight she would begin a long shopping list, but first she planned to calculate her wages. She suspected that, if she had left it to Revan, he would be far too generous, and she had no intention of taking money she hadn't earned.

"Oh dear," she said suddenly. "What would I do about Meg's lessons?"

"The child can have a holiday," he said. "In fact, if she is anything like her father, she will relish a little time without lessons."

"I will tell her today, then," Cathryn said, "and I shall not expect to find her brokenhearted over the prospect of two or three free days." She paused an instant. "Tell me, will there be other women on the journey?"

"One or two, mayhap. Most of them have children at home to care for, but I am certain you will not be the only female in our company. Does that make you feel safer?"

"Infinitely," she retorted, slipping under the arm he had rested on the door post and gently closing the classroom door behind her.

By the time they arrived at Inverness, Cathryn was in a state of excitement. She had not realized the journey would be so pleasant, nor had she expected to actually enjoy the hours spent on horseback. The terrain was not as rough and rugged as that around the castle, and they traveled at a much more leisurely pace than when they had made the trip to her father's house. They left the castle early the next morning and by nightfall had arrived in Inverness, an old city sprawled along the banks of the River Ness.

Cathryn had not been prepared for the size of the town, or for the number of people it contained. In her imagination, she had pictured it as a larger village than her own, and had not expected such a busy city. There was a line of shops along the river, their wares temptingly displayed in the front windows, which now reflected the evening sun. Revan told her they would have to visit the shops on the morrow since most of them had already closed their doors for the day.

Revan sent Owen and the rest of the party on to secure lodgings for the night, saying he and Cathryn would soon follow, but that there was something he wanted her to see. They rode up to Castlehill where the ruins of a massive old castle stood overlooking the broad river.

As they climbed to the top of one of the remaining towers, Revan explained that Prince Charles was responsible for the destruction of the castle. "It was blown up during his occupation of Inverness in '45," he said, "and has laid in ruins ever since."

From the top of the crumbling tower they had a wonderful view of the hills and mountains that ringed Inverness to the north, south and west. Away to the north and northwest were the incredibly dark blue waters of Beauly and Inverness Firths. Further north, Revan told her, was the new Fort George, built after the '45 Rising, and the main reason the MacLinns were careful to wear their leather breeches when they came to Inverness, leaving their tartan behind at Wolfcrag.

"The soldiers who come into town aren't exactly zealous defenders of the King's law," he said, "but it serves no purpose for us to flaunt our name and beliefs."

"What about the townspeople?" Cathryn asked, shivering in the whipping wind. "How do they feel about the Jacobites?"

"They had backed one earlier Stuart, you remember, so weren't anxious to bring further displeasure down upon themselves. Of course, even though they did not actively support Prince Charles, there was a fairly strong Jacobite stronghold here, so Charles was not without friends. However, for the sake of their town, there was little public support. Strangely enough, after the defeat of the Jacobites, the townspeople were treated just as savagely as if they had fostered the rebellion."

"Why was that?"

"Who knows?" Revan shrugged. "It does seem your good King George has a penchant for making examples of others, so mayhap that was his intention. At any rate, the English occupation of Inverness was brutal. Butcher Cumberland and his men ransacked homes and destroyed churches. They turned the school into an army commissary and made the town hall their headquarters. Prisoners were taken and sometimes shot, all at the whim of some officer or another. Inverness has been a long time recuperating. In some ways I'm not certain it has."

"Well, it seems a lovely city," Cathryn responded. "I am glad I came."

"I hope so. Offering to bring you here was my rather clumsy attempt at an apology for the other evening. I should not have reacted in such a way, and I will try not to let it happen again."

Hugging her cloak tightly about her, Cathryn turned her face up to look at the tall man beside her. An apology! Something she had learned not to expect from Revan MacLinn. She was still puzzling over it when his next words came.

"I would only ask that, if you find you cannot abide me, you will not choose anyone else from Wolfcrag. I swear, I could not stand by and see you belong to one of my own clansmen."

She opened her mouth to make an outraged reply, but he simply took her by the arms and turned her toward the west. "There," he said, "that is what I brought you up here to see."

A great crimson ball, the sun was just beginning to drop behind the hills, spreading a gentle golden-rose stain across the winter sky. Soft purple clouds massed above the sunset, forecasting harsher weather to come.

"It's beautiful," Cathryn said.

"Aye. The first time a person comes to Inverness, he should have the pleasure of watching a sunset from the castle turrets. It must be one of the finest sights on earth."

"Yes, I can almost believe it is," she agreed.

"But now we have to find the others. It is too cold to linger here any longer, and I, for one, am in the mood for a hot supper."

The inn was not new, but it was large and comfortable. It was set along a fork in the road that ran north of Inverness toward the firth.

After a hearty meal served in the big dining room downstairs, most of the MacLinns retired to their various rooms to get a good night's rest. The men were crowded into two large rooms, while the three women shared a small attic room. It contained a big bed and a cot set into an alcove under the eaves.

Cathryn was given the cot to herself and she got into it gratefully. The other women were friendly enough, but they spoke only Gaelic and were clearly in awe of her. At least she felt secure in their company and had no difficulty in falling asleep.

Once in the night she awakened to hear the sound of an icy rain falling, but she merely snuggled deeper into the warmth of the narrow bed and went right back to sleep.

The rain continued to fall throughout the morning hours, but even that did nothing to dampen the enthusiasm of people who had been too long away from a city. Everyone went their separate ways in order to attend to their own errands, and Cathryn found herself left with Owen and Revan, at Revan's suggestion. Nearly everyone in Inverness spoke Gaelic, he explained, and her shopping would be simplified if she stayed with them.

During the next few hours, she discovered yet another facet of Revan's personality. To her surprise, he was as much at ease selecting brightly-colored skeins of embroidery floss for his mother as he was handling farming tools or helping her choose suitable books for the classroom.

In a shop specializing in dry goods, while Revan consulted various lists and picked out bolts of cloth and spools of thread, she found a perfect Christmas gift for Meg. It was a beautiful doll with a delicate china face and hands. It had painted black hair and big blue-green eyes, and was dressed in a dress of white lace covered with an emerald green velvet cloak. Cathryn was certain the little girl would love to have this pretty addition to her doll collection. She also purchased some scraps of silk and velvet to make a wardrobe for the doll.

Next door was the apothecary's shop, and as Revan busied himself with the long list of supplies needed by Doctor MacSween, Cathryn browsed among the counters. She was pleased to find a selection of lovely crystal vials containing exotic French perfumes. She decided to buy one for Margaret's Christmas gift, and, on impulse, picked out a second one for Della. The sensible wife of a country doctor would never spend her husband's hard-earned money for such a luxury, but Cathryn was certain she would be well-pleased to receive it as a gift.

As she paid for the perfumes she realized this was the first time she had ever spent money to buy Christmas presents. In her own home, the holiday had never been celebrated to any great degree after her mother's death, and even when gifts were given, her father had insisted they be something she had made herself. It was a distinct pleasure to have her own money and be able to walk into a shop and choose whatever she desired. She smiled as she recalled Revan's look of protest when she had told him the amount of wages to which she thought she was entitled. He thought it was far too small a sum, but she persisted and had only taken what she felt she had earned. Now she was discovering the joy of spending the first money she had ever worked for and the feeling of being dependent on no one was truly gratifying.

In the tobacconist's establishment, Cathryn bought cigars for Adam MacSween and a leather pouch of tobacco for Owen's pipe. She couldn't resist two large boxes of chocolates imported from Belgium. One of these she would give to Margaret and the other to Granny MacLinn, for candy was a luxury not often enjoyed at the remote Wolfcrag.

As they left the tobacconist's, Revan laughed to see her arms so full of parcels.

" 'Tis just as well we brought the extra pack horses, Catriona," he said. "I fear you will have enough purchases to load one of them yourself."

Their final stop was in a tiny jewelry shop, whose dim interior revealed a profusion of glass cases filled with stones and jewelry. Revan announced his intention of finding a brooch for his mother's Christmas gift and, as he was making his selection, Cathryn wandered from case to case, fascinated by the beauty before her.

In one dark corner she discovered a display of antique gold jewelry and there, in the midst of stickpins, lockets and bracelets, she spied a beautiful gold pocket watch. It had an intricately fashioned gold chain, but what took her eye was the picture embossed on the ornate lid. It had a design of heather and thistles around the edge, and in the center were two adult wolves sitting side by side, surrounded by three playful cubs. The life-like detail of the animals intrigued her. She opened the case and was delighted to hear a deep, steady ticking. The clock had a lovely antique face with graceful gold hands. She caught her breath — it seemed a perfect gift for Revan.

She stole a quick look at the front of the shop where the men were still engaged in their search for a gift. She decided she could make her purchase without attracting their attention if she made haste. The watch was expensive and would consume nearly all the money she had left, but her shopping was finished, and she would have no further need of money until spring. Besides, she had bought things for everyone else so she should also have a gift for Revan, and it would be impossible to find anything more suitable.

She caught the proprietor's eye and hurriedly gave him the money for the watch, which he wrapped securely in a small brown parcel. She had just tucked it into the deep pocket of her cloak when Revan signaled he had made a decision, and the shopkeeper rushed away to assist him.

Leaving the shop, Cathryn breathed a huge sigh. It had been a wonderful day, and she was well-satisfied with her purchases.

The rain had finally stopped, but the trees still dripped and the surface of the river was wreathed in mist. Overhead the sky was dark and cloudy, but not threatening. It would seem the evening would be dry and cold.

The three of them arrived back at the inn at mid-afternoon, laden with their packages and supplies. Cathryn decided to take her purchases up to her room to sort and pack them for the trip back to Wolfcrag. Revan and Owen were going to the public room for a drink, so she told them she would see them at the evening meal.

She had just packed away the last of her things when a knock sounded at the door to the little attic room.

"Who is it?" she called.

"Owen," came the reply.

Startled, Cathryn crossed to the door and opened it to find the big man in the hallway, looking quite agitated.

"Is something wrong?" she asked quickly.

" 'Tis Revan," Owen told her. "He rode off in a temper just now . . ."

"What happened?"

"There were some soldiers in the public room having a drink," he explained. "One of them was making some remarks about Highlanders that Revan didn't like, and I had a devil of a time trying to calm the lad. He wanted to challenge the fool right then and there. Of course, he realized he couldn't do something so dangerous, so he had to swallow his pride and keep quiet. He took it as long as he could, then stomped out in a black mood. I thought I should go after him."

"Do you know where to look for him?" she questioned.

"Aye, I know where he'll go. I just thought I should follow to make certain he doesn't find himself in any trouble. I wondered if you might like to ride with me, if you are not too tired. You say you don't understand the lad, but if you come with me now, you may learn a bit about what drives him."

Cathryn's expression was puzzled, but she did not delay. "I'll just get my cloak," she said, causing a relieved grin to break across Owen's face.

As soon as their horses were saddled, they started off, following the narrow road that curved away from the inn to the northeast. They kept up a fast pace and had gone quite some distance before they caught sight of Revan. He was riding furiously, his black cape flying out behind him. As they followed, they saw him abandon the roadway and ride out across the moor before him. He slowed his horse now, and it was not long before they rode up behind him.

Revan did not acknowledge their presence in any way; he sat on his huge stallion like a statue and stared straight ahead. Cathryn studied his face, unable to determine his mood. She noticed a muscle working in his jaw, as if he kept his teeth clenched together.

She moved her gaze to Owen's face and whispered, "What is this place?"

"Culloden Moor," Revan said flatly, spurring his horse and riding slowly forward.

Cathryn felt a sudden chill which, as she quietly followed Owen's lead, grew into something stronger. It was an unexplained feeling that she had stumbled into a place that was evil — a place so filled with sorrow and gloom it seemed unearthly. Across the bleak stretch of flat moorland was a ragged mantle of fog and, as they rode into it, the long white fingers of mist curled around them and brushed their faces, sometimes blinding them momentarily. There were no trees, just a few low bushes whose thorny branches caught and held the mist.

The only structure visible on the entire moor was a small

tumble-down hut, thatched with heather. Its broken windows were like blind eyes and its door sagged open, looking like a gaping mouth in a silent cry.

Revan reined his horse to a halt and Cathryn stopped beside him, staying as close as possible.

"I come here every time I am in Inverness," he said suddenly, bitterly. "I never want to forget what this place stands for."

"Do you really think it necessary to torture yourself this way?" she asked in a low voice. "Surely it is time you learned to forget about Culloden."

Instead of the angry retort she had expected, he merely shook his head and said, "Nay, forgetting is not for any of us now. That will come with the next generations. Coming out here helps me remember just what it is I have to fight for. It gives meaning to the way we have chosen to live. It strengthens my resolve."

Against the clouded sky, his profile looked strong, pure and determined. To Cathryn, it seemed he embodied the true spirit of the Highlander in that moment. He was using his pain to bolster his determination to remain independent and, strangely enough, she had to admire him for it.

"Over there is where the Highlanders were positioned," he said, gesturing. "The rain and sleet were in their faces, and they were dead-tired from a night march. They had had little or nothing to eat—only small bits of bannock made from oathusks and the sweepings from a miller's floor. They took Communion before the battle and when their prince stepped out in front of them, they cheered and threw their bonnets into the air."

"Aye, they were gallant lads," came Owen's deep voice, close behind them.

"But there were only five thousand of them," Revan said. "Cumberland had nine thousand—all well-fed and well-trained. The English were there." Again, he pointed. "The two armies drew up within four hundred feet of each other."

"It was nearly two hours before the battle began, but once it did, they say the fighting lasted only forty minutes or so. The Highlanders attacked with their cannon, but they were no match for the bigger, newer guns of the Royalists. Cumberland's troops would have taken the day on the strength of their superior weapons alone, but that didn't satisfy them. Damn their eyes! They weren't content to merely shoot our men down. Nay, the blackguards stuffed their cannons with scraps of iron, rusty nails and lead balls that would rip a man to pieces. Our soldiers were mutilated by their grapeshot — left to die a horrible, agonized death. They allowed us no glory, Catriona."

Horrified, not only by his story, but by the flat, unemotional way he told it, she reached out to touch his arm. It might have been carved of stone, it was so hard and unyielding.

"The Highlanders rushed forward to die on the bayonets of the English army. They never had a chance — never a prayer of victory. The moor was strewn with bloodied corpses and the battle was over. Twelve hundred Highlanders died in the battle, and their bodies were buried in mass graves, over there near the burn."

Through the encroaching fog, Cathryn could see the misshapen earth where irregular mounds showed here and there among the heather. Revan urged his horse forward, and the other two followed. He paused to look down at the scattered burial mounds.

"I don't even know where my father and brothers are buried," he commented. "No doubt they were thrown into a pit with the other bodies around them, with no regard for rank or clan."

For the first time, he looked directly at Cathryn, and her heart lurched at the look in his eyes. She had never seen such pain and anguish on another human being's face. She felt like crying, but somehow, knew tears would not relieve the sorrow she was experiencing. Hers was not the sorrow of the person who had lost his family on this gloomy field of battle. Rather, hers was the sorrow of someone who sees another in need of solace and is helpless to give it. Revan had lived with the memories for a long time now, and she doubted if there was any way she could help eradicate them.

"Only fifty Royalist soldiers died," he went on. "Cumberland was well-pleased with the figure. Claimed the battle was little more than a skirmish. But, by God, they committed an endless number of atrocities that day."

His eyes narrowed and his mouth tightened. "They moved over the field stabbing the wounded and dying; they rode through the heath to shoot down or bayonet those who tried to escape. Several wounded men took refuge in an old barn and the bastards barred the doors and set fire to it, roasting them alive. 'Tis no wonder they call him Butcher Cumberland. He allowed no chivalry at Culloden."

Cathryn shivered, but the chill she felt was on the inside. It seemed as if she could hear the firing of muskets and cannon, the screams of the wounded and dying, and over it all, the eerie wail of the pipes, calling for retreat. A retreat that came too late.

Revan fell silent and the dripping of the heavy fog was the only sound to be heard. Finally Owen broke the somber mood by saying, " 'Tis time we went back to the inn, lad."

Revan nodded. "Aye."

With one last glance around him, he rode away, his dark figure almost immediately swallowed up by the swirling whiteness that hovered just above the ground. Cathryn and Owen followed.

"Is it always like this, Owen?" she asked.

"Aye, and now he'll go back to the inn and drink himself into a stupor, like as not. I've seen it happen time and again."

"Does he feel guilty because he is alive and his father and brothers died here?"

"That's part of it, to be sure. But more than that, it's an injustice he can't right and it rankles. He'll never be able to undo the wrongs done here on this field, and he doesn't like the feeling."

"It seems odd he would take it so personally," she said, "except, of course, for the fact that he lost his father and brothers."

"It cost him his life just as surely as it did the others, Cathryn . . . just as surely."

She pondered Owen's surprising statement all the way back to the warmth and comfort of the inn. What the big man said was actually quite true, in a sense. She had just never looked at it that way before.

She saw Revan toss his cloak onto a peg inside the front door and head straight for the public room. Owen flashed her a concerned look, then shrugged, knowing they would be wasting their time in trying to persuade Revan to do anything else.

Cathryn was so chilled after the ride through the thick mist that she went up to her room and changed into one of the other dresses she had brought with her. After brushing the dampness from her hair, she went down to the dining room for the evening meal.

As she entered the crowded room, she was startled to see Revan MacLinn rise from a chair near the fire and come to meet her.

"Ah, there you are, Catriona. I have been waiting, but I don't mind telling you I was about to give up. I am starved."

He took her arm ad steered her toward one of the smaller tables. As soon as they were seated, a buxom waitress brought them plates heaped with roast beef and vegetables and two tankards of mulled cider.

"I . . . uh, thought you were going to spend the evening in the public room drinking," she said, taking a sip of the spicy cider.

"I had a drink to drive the chill from my bones, but surely you must know I would prefer your company to that of anyone else?"

"No, I didn't know that," she laughed, glad to see his mood had changed so drastically.

"Well, mayhap you didn't know that, but I'll wager there is very little else you don't know about me by now."

"Oh?"

"You know my life's history, you know my life's occupation, and you are certainly well acquainted with all my moods and tempers. Quite a lot to know about one person, wouldn't you say?"

"I couldn't possibly know all there is to know about you," she protested. "I think you are a very complicated man, and I've no doubt you will manage to find other traits or talents

345

to confound me."

At the end of the meal, they took their refilled tankards and went to sit in front of the fire. Gradually, the other diners finished their suppers and drifted off to bed, leaving the two of them alone.

"I want to thank you for going out to Culloden Field with me," Revan said finally.

"Owen suggested it," she replied. "He thought it might help me to understand you a bit more."

"And did it?"

"I'm not certain, but, yes, I think it did. At least, I have a better idea of the enormity of your loss. Not just your father and brothers, but your entire way of life. Perhaps I am in more of a position to understand since my own journey home." She smiled ruefully.

"Aye, it can nearly destroy you when something you've always had, always relied upon, is taken away."

"Especially when you thought it so safe and secure."

"Mayhap it is a part of growing up, but 'tis a hard lesson." He stared into the tankard he held in his hand.

"Revan, would you tell me about your brothers now? I would like to hear about them."

"There isn't a lot to say, lass. I suppose they were ordinary men, even if they did seem like gods to me. Alexander was the older of the two — the one who would have succeeded my father as chieftain. He was serious, studious, artistic, full of ambition to better the world. He was five years older than me, and Christian was three years older. Christian was the one who should have been chieftain. I heard Alex say it many times. He was wild and brave and feared nothing! He could ride and fence and shoot like an expert by the time he was thirteen, and he was constantly poking fun at Alex because he liked books so well and cared nothing for sports. Of course, he was fiercely loyal to Alex and would never condone anyone else making fun of him. He bloodied many a lip over that very issue. It wasn't that Alex needed anyone to fight his battles for him — he was perfectly capable of fighting when he thought it necessary. It was just that, most of the time, he preferred to employ different methods."

Revan leaned back in his chair, propping a booted foot on the fender at the front of the fireplace. He smiled at Cathryn, but she suspected he didn't even see her, and the smile was for the memories he shared with his brothers.

"We ran wild on the moors most of the time," he continued, "and, of course, we were often in trouble for some mischievous prank or another. Christian would think them up, then bully me into going along with them; Alex got involved because he tried to keep a rein on us and see that we didn't get hurt or hurt someone else. Sometimes Chris would complain because he thought I was too young to be in on something, but Alex would stand up for me and see that I was included. He rescued me from many a difficulty, I can tell you. Can you imagine how I worshipped him?"

"Yes, I think I can," Cathryn said quietly.

"The three of us got into enough trouble for a dozen boys, but no matter what we did, our father just laughed heartily and made excuses for us. I fear my poor mother administered any discipline we received, and even then, if Alex couldn't reason her out of her anger, Christian would charm her out of it. Naturally, it was always left up to her to explain to others why we had seen fit to set fire to the roof of our tutor's thatched cottage or why we stole Granny MacLinn's underwear off her clothesline and flew it like a flag from the castle turrets."

"You must have had a wonderful childhood, Revan," she said wistfully. "I envy you that."

"I suppose it seems selfish to you that I can't be thankful for the time I had with my brothers instead of feeling so deprived because I don't have them now."

"No, I don't feel that way. I rather think you must feel like a man who has lost a limb—some vital and essential part of you is gone, and you know you will never be whole again."

"Aye, 'tis exactly how it feels. For a long time I didn't think I could possibly survive the loss, but little by little, I got used to the pain and though it made me angry with myself, I found I wanted to go on living. I miss my brothers and probably will until the end of my life. And I can never reconcile myself to the fact that they were sacrificed for a

347

symbolic gesture on the part of the English. I suppose that is the worst thing about Culloden—it was such a damned waste."

Cathryn nodded in agreement, for once not stirred to defend the English position.

"Things have changed for me lately," Revan said. "All at once I feel as if I can start being myself again—that I don't have to keep trying to make it up to everyone because Alex and Chris aren't here."

She leaned forward, impulsively laying a hand on his knee. "In the time I have been at Wolfcrag, Revan, I would swear that your people love and respect you for yourself, and not because you remind them of your brothers. You are the one who kept the MacLinns together, and you are the one who is trying so hard to build your clan into what it once was. Don't belittle yourself by thinking you are only carrying on in your brothers' absence."

"A very kind observation, Catriona," he said, pleasure showing in his deeply amber eyes. "I thank you for making it."

"And before we go upstairs, I have one other observation to make," she stated.

"That being?"

"Your brother Alex may have been an artist and a dreamer of serious dreams, and your brother Christian may have been a bold and daring rogue and a leader of men, but it seems quite evident to me that you are a combination of all those traits, Revan. Somehow you have found a way to blend all the characteristics you so admired in them into your own unique self. In that way you pay tribute to them, and I cannot help but think that perhaps the MacLinns have inherited the best chieftain after all."

He got to his feet and pulled her up from her chair. "You know, lass, my idea of bringing you with us to Inverness may have been the most intelligent one I have had in months. Your company certainly made shopping more pleasurable and, I cannot deny it has been a relief to talk to you about Culloden and my brothers. And now you have actually paid me a compliment! Dare I hope our relationship has taken a turn for the better?"

"God forbid that it take a turn for the worse!" she exclaimed in mock horror. His delighted laugh rang out, and the echo of it stayed with her, warming her until she fell asleep in the little cot set under the sloping eaves.

Chapter Eighteen

Wolfcrag Castle loomed up before them, its towers piercing the thick white wall of mist surrounding it. As she rode through the massive gates and into the echoing courtyard, Cathryn recalled the other times she had arrived at Wolfcrag after long and wearying journeys. She smiled to think how different her mood had been each time. That first night she had seen the castle in the gloomy twilight, she had been frightened and angry. The second time she rode past its gates, she had been too defeated and sick at heart to even be aware of her surroundings. Now, on her third return, she found herself in a strangely lighthearted mood, glad to be back within the secure walls she had come to think of as home.

There was no doubt but that her improved relationship with the castle's laird had a great deal to do with her contentment at being back at Wolfcrag. In the last two days she had come to sense the importance of their friendship. Had their acquaintance been allowed to begin on such a basis in the first place, matters might have been very different.

Of course, had Revan not taken matters into his own hands, their paths might never have crossed except casually, she realized. It came as something of a surprise to her to admit she no longer resented his reckless actions quite so much. Had he never disrupted the placid flow of her life, she might have grown old struggling to fit into the mold others required of her. She might never have learned the painful lesson of how shallow her father's emotions were where they concerned her. She might never have realized what a demanding and unbending husband Basil would have been. Most importantly, she might never have known the joy of discovering she could be responsible for herself. At first it had seemed Revan MacLinn only wanted her to exchange her role as dutiful daughter and wife for one of his choosing, but she was gradually accepting the fact that he had no interest in crushing her spirit or forcing her into a role she did not fit. Oddly enough, the more she learned about Revan, the more she learned about herself, and in some ways, she felt her life had only begun after she came to Wolfcrag.

The noise of the crowd waiting to greet them roused her from her thoughts and brought her back to the present. Their return from Inverness seemed an excuse for a festive occasion. Men, women and children all gathered around, anxiously awaiting the unloading of their particular supplies or packages, and the air of excitement and suspense that filled the courtyard made it seem like Christmas already.

A big meal had been prepared for them in the Great Hall and the hungry travelers dined on roast beef as they related tales of their adventures in the city. Cathryn enjoyed the noisy chatter and companionship, but it was not long before her eyelids began to droop and she felt overcome by drowsiness.

She excused herself after the meal and, with Elsa's help, carried her parcels up to her room where she stacked them on the chest of drawers, too tired to even unwrap them until morning.

In the faintly flaring light of the newly-made fire, she could see the portrait of Bonnie Prince Charlie, and it seemed his eyes rested on her with a new benevolence. Or maybe, she thought sleepily, it is just that I have looked at Culloden from his point of view now, and we are coming to a new understanding of each other.

With morning came a renewed desire to unwrap and

examine the things she had bought in the city. She removed the wrappings from the doll first and was once again delighted by its delicate beauty. She could barely stand to wait until Christmas to see Meg's face when she received it. She was smugly pleased with the cigars and tobacco, though she secretly thought them a bit foul-smelling. The boxes containing the Belgian chocolates were quite ornate, with beautifully executed paintings on the lids, and she smiled to think of Granny MacLinn's pleasure when she was presented with such an elegant gift.

Again, she was inordinately happy with the gold pocket watch for Revan. It might have been made for him. She only hoped it would not seem too intimate a gift. Well, she couldn't worry about that now, she thought, as she carefully replaced it in its velvet-lined box.

Lastly she unwrapped the two bottles containing the French perfume. She removed the stopper from one bottle and sniffed the heady aroma of the imported scent. Immediately she was assailed by such a wave of nausea her knees almost buckled. She quickly set the vial down, not wanting to spill it, and made her way back to the bed. She lay quietly until the roiling of her stomach ceased, then went into the dressing room to bathe her face with cold water. Obviously, the trip to Inverness had tired her more than she'd realized.

When she felt better, she rewrapped the gifts and hid them away in the bottom of the wardrobe. Not really feeling up to going downstairs to breakfast, she got back into the four poster bed and allowed herself to fall into a deep sleep that lasted until noon when Elsa knocked on her door to announce the midday meal.

In the afternoon, feeling much better, she and Meg resumed the child's classroom studies, then went for a leisurely walk around the castle grounds. The fog had not lifted, and now it seemed there was an increasing chill in the air. They could hear the restless crash of the ocean waves, but the air was so filled with the icy fog they couldn't see the water from the pathway. It had grown nearly dark by four in the afternoon, causing them to seek the light and warmth of the castle.

That evening at supper Cathryn looked up several times to find Revan's eyes upon her. She realized they had not had the chance to talk together since returning to Wolfcrag. She wondered what he was thinking when his amber eyes met hers, but something about the warmth in his expression made her almost certain of the message he wished to convey. She tried to keep her own gaze from drifting in his direction, but it was difficult to do. She was almost uncomfortably aware of the broad-shouldered man watching her through slightly narrowed, appraising eyes.

At the conclusion of the meal, the tables were pushed aside and two of the young MacLinn clansmen carried a thick mat into the room, tossing it down onto the floor. In an instant, two others jumped to their feet and, to Cathryn's amazement, proceeded to strip off their shirts and boots.

In a slow and methodical manner, the two faced each other and began to move about the mat, each stalking the other. Suddenly, a brawny arm snaked out, hooked around the opponent's neck, and the wrestling match began.

Cathryn's eyes grew wide — she had never seen the sport of wrestling before and was at a loss as to why grown men would suddenly get so passionately involved in what she thought of as child's play. All about her, the onlookers had immersed themselves in the sport and were calling out advice or support, cheering a move they particularly liked or jeering at something they considered unsportsmanlike.

Della MacSween slipped into the chair beside Cathryn, amused at the incredulous look on the younger woman's face.

"Haven't you ever seen wrestling before?" she asked, laughing. " 'Tis a favorite pastime here in the Highlands."

"These Highland men do like to play at being little boys, don't they?" Cathryn asked with asperity.

Della's eyebrows raised. "Don't let any of them hear you speak of wrestling as childish! Actually, it takes a great deal of strength and muscular coordination to excel at the sport."

Cathryn, unconvinced, turned her attention back to the

two men grappling on the mat. One of them clearly had the advantage now, and it was not long before he was proclaimed the victor by a wildly noisy crowd.

Having dispatched one opponent, the winner of the match was quickly given another; he proceeded to pin two more challengers to the mat before he himself was finally overcome, more by exhaustion than by his adversary's strength.

Stifling a yawn, Cathryn began to think longingly of her bed. Suddenly, Della nudged her, and she glanced up to see Revan get to his feet, pulling his shirt over his head. With renewed interest, she watched as he and the other wrestler moved around the mat, circling cautiously, bodies tensed. Quickly, contact was made and the pair went to their knees, their breath coming in harsh gasps as they struggled. Revan's opponent was a big man, but he moved slowly, deliberately. Revan's muscular grace and rapid reactions made him deadly. The chieftain's lithe strength was superior, and the match was quickly ended, amidst clamorous applause from the onlookers.

The next match started almost immediately, but Revan's strength did not waver. Cathryn found she was having a difficult time trying to appear nonchalant and not too interested in the man before her. She could not help but admire the image of maleness he presented. Her eyes were drawn to the straining muscles across his back, rippling smoothly beneath his tanned skin. His corded arms and shoulders gleamed with a sheen of sweat, drops of which glistened in the thick mat of curled hair that covered his chest. Clad only in tight leather breeches, he moved with a kind of graceful fluidity common to predatory animals whose survival depended on their mental alertness and physical superiority.

Revan deftly pinned his opponent, and Cathryn was embarrassed to hear herself join in the cheering and applause. She cast a look at Della which dared her to make a comment, and though the other woman smiled broadly, she wisely held her tongue.

Revan was victorious over the next three men who challenged him, but his final opponent was to prove too strong even for the superb physical attributes of the MacLinn chieftain.

Owen MacIvor seemed more massive than ever when half-naked, and Cathryn thought his arms looked like tree trunks. She held her breath as the huge man advanced on Revan, for she feared the outcome of the match might be tragic. After a moment, she realized Revan employed a certain cunning to avoid Owen's most effective holds and by the sheer force of his iron will and physical endurance, prolonged the match for longer than would first have seemed possible. Eventually, however, he had to bow to the superior strength of the bigger man. When he had been bested, he clapped Owen on the back, and the two of them shook hands the bonds of their friendship threatened in no way. Indeed, even the onlookers seemed pleased with the outcome and appeared not to think of Owen's victory as demeaning to their chieftain. In fact, it seemed to Cathryn that Revan received more congratulatory remarks for lasting so long against MacIvor than he had for defeating his earlier foes.

Later, as she was leaving the Hall to go upstairs to bed, Revan fell into step beside her.

"Did you enjoy the wrestling?" he asked, as they started up the stairs.

"I don't think I completely understand the sport," she answered, "but, yes, it was rather amusing."

"Rather amusing?" he groaned. "Good lord, I half kill myself trying to impress you, and you thought it was amusing! I don't think I'll ever understand women."

"And I don't think I will ever understand men," she retorted. They had arrived in the upper hallway and started toward her room. "What would induce them to engage in something as childish . . ."

"Shh." Revan stopped walking to lay one lean finger across her lips, silencing her. "No arguments, remember? I am sorry I started it."

Despite herself, she smiled. "I'm sorry, too. We have been managing to get along so well we really shouldn't spoil it now."

"I agree. I was just caught a bit off-guard because I have

never seen anything amusing about wrestling."

She laughed softly. "Perhaps it was a poor choice of words," she admitted. "I will confess I was actually quite impressed with your abilities."

"Someday, somehow, I swear I will get the best of MacIvor," he grinned. " 'Tis a shameful thing to go down in defeat every time I meet the man in a match."

"I don't see how anyone could ever overcome him," Cathryn said. "He is such a giant; it seems almost foolish to try."

"Aye, I'd hoped for a different opponent, but none was forthcoming, so Owen it had to be."

"Who had you hoped would challenge you?" she asked, pausing outside the door to her bedchamber.

"Oh, I had visions of grappling on the mat with an entirely different sort of partner," he said, his amber eyes laughing into hers. She quickly lowered her gaze, resting it on his bare chest, only inches from her face. "You wouldn't be interested in learning the rudiments of wrestling, would you?"

"I . . . I will let you know," she stammered, her mouth curving into a soft smile, in spite of her best efforts to keep it immobile.

His chuckle was deep and warm. "You know, we are making progress, Catriona. Here I have just made an indecent remark to you, and, instead of shoving me down the stairs as I had expected, you have answered me quite calmly and have even given me some hope you might take me up on my offer!"

"The only thing that prevents me from immediately accepting your challenge is that I would not care to take off my shirt in front of your assembled clansmen!"

Revan's black brows shot up and his white teeth gleamed through his beard. "My dear, I could arrange a match in the privacy of my chambers if that is all that worries you."

She smiled sweetly. "I will think on it and let you know."

He leaned forward to place a lingering kiss on her forehead. She closed her eyes, expecting to feel his lips move to her own. Instead, he said, "Aye, do let me know," and walked away, whistling a jaunty tune.

Cathryn opened her eyes and stared after him. Feeling foolish and more than a little frustrated, she let herself into the bedroom.

As she undressed, she relived the scene with Revan and came to the irritating conclusion he was trying to tease her, to goad her into begging for his sexual favors. Why else would he have indulged in such a display of his nearly nude body? Why else would he have addressed such provocative remarks to her? What other reason could he have had for placing that chaste kiss upon her brow when he must have been completely aware of her desire to feel his mouth on her own? No, not desire, she hurriedly corrected herself, but expectation. They had been alone in a dim and deserted hallway, and under normal circumstances she might have had every right to expect some untoward behavior on his part. Well, if he thought he could arouse, then frustrate her, he was mistaken. He would have to be shown she was impervious to his so-called charm.

She flounced into bed, pulling the covers up around her chin. He still had the ability to make her very angry, she realized, but he would just have to learn she was not as vulnerable as he seemed to think. After a time, despite herself, she began to envision the two of them engaged in a wrestling match, and when she fell asleep, there was a small, pleased smile on her face.

A winter storm settled over the Highlands late the next day, bringing with it an abundance of snow and ice. Cathryn shivered just hearing the wind as it moaned down the chimneys or tore at the windows. She spent most of the time huddled in her chair by the fire, stitching on the doll clothes for Meg's Christmas, or in the nursery with Meg herself, reading or helping with lessons. Her mood seemed to have deteriorated with the weather and suddenly, she felt tired, restless and somehow depleted.

She only saw Revan at mealtimes, and then he was usually preoccupied with talk of the repairs he and his men were planning for some of the older cottages around the court-yard. As soon as the weather cleared, he had told her, they were going to start some renovations.

Once in a while she suspected he might be paying less attention to the talk of repairs than he wanted her to think. She often sensed his gaze upon her, and though she had not actually caught him looking her way, some instinct warned her his behavior was only some plan on his part to nettle her. Perhaps he was deliberately avoiding her or allowing her only brief glimpses of himself as he went about his business in the castle in order to tease her, to make her realize she missed his company.

Occasionally she saw Ian MacLinn and though he was always polite, he very carefully kept his distance. She often wondered just what more Revan might have said to him and toyed with the idea of asking Ian, then decided it wasn't worth risking Revan's displeasure again. Now she knew she really had no serious interest in Ian, she didn't feel it would be right to take the chance of subjecting him to his chieftain's anger once more.

Thinking she might be able to put herself into a better frame of mind, she volunteered to help Della, agreeing to go with her to visit some of the elderly residents of Wolfcrag to make certain they were faring well in spite of the nasty weather. On the morning she was to have met the doctor's wife, she overslept and was awakened by knocking at her door.

"Cathryn! It's me, Della. Aren't you awake yet?"

"Oh, good heavens," Cathryn cried, sitting upright in bed. She threw back the covers and rushed to open the door and admit her friend. "I'm sorry I didn't wake up on time. I . . ."

Suddenly a tide of nausea engulfed her and, clamping one hand over her mouth, she fled into the dressing room.

In a few moments she returned, white and shaken, her green eyes looking huge in her stricken face. She met Della's sympathetic look and said miserably, "Della, what am I going to do? I've been sick every morning this week — I think I must be going to have a baby."

Della's smile was kindly. "Aye, I think so, too."

"But I don't want a baby!" she cried, wringing her hands in agitation. "I'm . . . not prepared to have a baby."

"You will have several months in which to get prepared," Della laughed. "You should be used to the idea by then."

Cathryn turned and walked to the windows at the far end of the room. In her long white nightgown she was a forlorn figure and, when she leaned her burning face against the cold glass and her slim shoulders began to shake with sobs, Della hurried to her and put an arm around her.

"Cathryn, listen to me! This is not the end of the world. Women have babies all the time."

"Not women married to a man who doesn't want her—a man who isn't even the father of the child." Her tears started afresh at the thought.

"The father of the child wants you," Della gently reminded her.

"Yes, but I am not free to marry him, so my baby will still be born a bastard."

Della shook her slightly. "Stop talking like that! If you go to Revan and explain the situation, he will make arrangements somehow. After all, Basil wanted to divorce you. If he does that, you will be free to marry Revan."

"I'm not sure I would want to," Cathryn cried. "It's just not fair! I haven't even made up my mind whether or not I want to stay at Wolfcrag . . . or whether I think I can work out some sort of relationship with Revan. Now everything is horribly complicated by this problem."

"Mayhap it will simplify instead of complicate," Della suggested. "Did you consider that possibility?"

Cathryn shook her head. "I don't see how it could simplify anything."

"I am not a complete fool, my dear," Della stated dryly. "I have seen the way you look at Revan these days. I think you have just about admitted to yourself you are in love with the man. If you could face the fact you care for him, it wouldn't be quite such a shock to you that you are having his child. The two things ofttimes go hand in hand, you know."

"I don't know why you would think I am in love with him," Cathryn said. "I have only recently begun to find I can get along with him, and that is a long way from love."

"You admire him, don't you?" Della questioned.

"I suppose so . . . in a way."

"What way?"

"Well, I do respect his treatment of his clansmen. I think he is genuinely fond of them, truly concerned about their welfare. He seems a good leader."

"All right, you respect him. Do you find him as maddening as you once did?"

"I'm not certain I know what you mean, but I will admit I can tolerate his presence now. I can even converse with him without sending him into a fury."

"You enjoy matching wits with him and you know it. Admit you find him intelligent and interesting."

"Yes, that is true enough."

"And he certainly proved to you he can be compassionate and sympathetic. You yourself told me he treated you most kindly after your confrontation with your father and Basil. Is that not correct?"

Cathryn nodded.

"He has shown himself to be a wonderful father to Meg, wouldn't you say?"

"I cannot fault him there," Cathryn murmured.

"And, finally, from the expression on your face the night you watched him wrestle, I would say you are physically attracted to him. My dear girl, what else do you want? You respect him, you find him intelligent and interesting, as well as kind and sympathetic, and you agree he is a good father. Of course, any woman in her right mind would acknowledge he is a magnificent physical specimen. What else could you possibly want or need?"

"Oh, I don't know! You are just trying to confuse me, Della."

"Nay, I'm trying to get you to stop being so damned stubborn and give in. It's perfectly true Revan didn't ask your permission to bring you here, and I am well aware you shared his bed without much enthusiasm. Now you find yourself in a situation from which there is no way out, but, lass, that is life. Things happen to you, and then you figure out a way to survive them. It isn't always possible to choose or plan."

"I have never been in a position to make any decisions for myself," Cathryn complained. "All my life I have been at the mercy of someone else's whims. Now, just when I am finding out I can have a say in my own life, I am suddenly confronted by this. Well, I don't want a baby, and I am not going to have a baby!"

"Cathryn, I should warn you — if I think you are serious about this and about to do something stupid, I will go to Revan and tell him about the babe. Otherwise, I won't mention it to anyone until you have made up your mind what you intend to do. Do you understand?"

"Your trouble is you can't decide if you are my friend or Revan's," Cathryn said angrily.

"Heaven help me, I have tried to be a friend to both of you. Sometimes it is a very wearying business, I assure you."

"Well, you can make it easy for yourself. Be Revan's friend and leave me alone. I promise I won't do anything foolish until I've given it a bit more thought."

"Very well. Now I have to get on with my errands. Mayhap you will feel more like helping me another time."

Cathryn began to feel ashamed of the tantrum she had thrown and by the next morning was knocking on her friend's door, an apologetic smile on her face.

"Cathryn? Won't you come in?"

"As usual, I am here to say I am sorry for my behavior yesterday. I know you are only trying to help, and it was unfair of me to be so selfish. You know as well as I do I couldn't bring myself to do anything to hurt this baby."

Della looked relieved. "I am certainly thankful to hear that. How do you feel this morning?"

"Rather queasy, I must admit. Does this stage last long?" she asked.

"Not usually, though, of course, it is different for every woman. Would you like to talk to Adam about it?"

"No, not yet. Let me get used to the idea first, and then I'll

361

decide what I am going to do with myself."

"Are you going to tell Revan?"

"I can't . . . not yet. As soon as I have sorted everything out, I promise I will tell him. Unless I am going to leave Wolfcrag—then I cannot let him know."

"You would deny Revan his own child?"

"Don't lecture me, please. I just don't know what to do and, if I ever find a way to straighten out this whole mess, I will tell you. In the meantime, let me go with you this morning to take my mind off my problems. I might be able to help you do something."

"Aye," said Della, taking down her woolen plaid, "you just might at that. I have to look in on Moira MacLinn and I am positive you will enjoy meeting her."

As soon as they arrived at Moira MacLinn's house, Cathryn understood why Della had wanted the two of them to meet. Moira was propped up in bed with her tiny newborn daughter in her arms.

"Cathryn, I'm going to bathe Moira and change her bed. While I'm doing that, why don't you manage the baby?"

Cathryn made a face at her. "You are a devious woman, Della MacSween," she laughed.

Taking the shawl-wrapped infant from its proud mother, she settled herself in an old rocking chair near the fire. The baby was sound asleep and did not stir as she began to rock it.

Cathryn marveled at the fragile beauty of the sleeping child. She had fine wispy red-gold hair that curled down over perfectly formed ears. Her eyelashes were smudges of gold against pink cheeks and her little chin had the faintest hint of a dimple.

Such a wee scrap of humanity, Cathryn thought, and yet, a living, breathing person. Her mother and father must feel a tremendous sense of responsibility and pride.

In that instant she was overwhelmed with a sudden tenderness for her own child and knew an unexpected feeling of fierce pride and possessiveness. Her own son or daughter! She made a silent vow she would never treat her own child as her father had treated her. Whether it was a boy or girl, whether she remained at Wolfcrag or left, she promised herself she would see to it that her child had something more than the bleak childhood she herself had known.

When the two women had finished their tasks at the cottage, they went back to Della's where they sat in front of a roaring fire and drank tea.

"You were very wise to take me there," Cathryn said after a while. "You knew it would make me feel differently about the baby, didn't you?"

"You are too decent a person to abandon someone or something entrusted to you, Cathryn, no matter how you might like to. The trouble was that you weren't able to think of your baby as real yet. Once you stopped to consider the person he will be, I knew you couldn't have any more thoughts of not having the baby."

Cathryn sighed. "Well, you are correct. It doesn't solve anything or make anything simpler, but it does make me realize I have to think of the child, too, and not just myself."

"Will you ever learn to trust Revan?" Della asked.

"It's not that I don't trust him," she protested. "I am just not certain I am ready to commit myself to him for the rest of my life."

"Nonsense!" snapped Della. "You committed yourself to Basil, didn't you?"

"Exactly," Cathryn answered, "and see where it got me. Surely you don't expect me to risk that again?"

"Someday, my girl, you are going to learn that Revan and Basil are in no way alike. For the sake of your child, I hope you learn it soon."

Later that afternoon Cathryn had another chance to reflect on Della's words of advice. She and Meg were in the nursery and, having finished the lessons for the day, were discussing Christmas when Revan came into the room.

"Father," cried Meg, a delighted smile on her face, "have you come to finish the story about Mary, Queen of Scots?"

"Aye, that I have," Revan MacLinn answered, reaching down an idle hand to fondle the dog's ears. "If you are done

363

with your lessons."

He directed an inquiring look at Cathryn, who assured him they were through for the day.

He stretched himself out in the big chair near the hearth, and Meg, the storybook in her hand, climbed onto his knee and quickly found the place where they had left the story of the ill-fated queen the last time they had read.

As she watched the two of them together, Cathryn knew this was the way it should be between a father and his child. Revan seemed to possess some paternal instinct that must not be automatically instilled in every man. Della was right — she would be a fool to deny her own child a father like this.

And yet, as she covertly studied the man, she knew in all honesty she would prefer not to tell him about the baby until she had made certain of his feelings for her. Somehow, if she were to remain at Wolfcrag with Revan, she would be happier knowing he wanted her for herself, and not out of duty to his unborn child.

She lay awake that night until nearly midnight, thinking over the situation and trying to make an intelligent decision. She finally came to the conclusion the only way to find out her true feelings for Revan MacLinn was to put herself into his hands and let events take their own course.

With a determined air, she got out of bed and put on the brown velvet robe she had borrowed so long ago. She would go to Revan now as he had once requested and though it meant swallowing her pride, she no longer had the time to be coy. She had to find out for herself what she really felt about the arrogant Highlander. Suddenly, a great deal depended upon that . . .

Taking a lighted candle, she opened the door of her bedchamber and quietly stepped out into the hallway. She had gone only a few steps before she heard the low murmur of voices. She came to a sudden halt, not wanting to rush around the corner and meet someone in the corridor who might spread word of her midnight wandering.

Cautiously peering around the corner, she caught sight of a half-dressed man standing in the doorway of Darroch's room. Darroch, dressed in a clinging silk robe, was speaking earnestly with him, her hand on his arm in a very possessive manner.

Cathryn's mouth felt dry. No other man in the castle was quite that tall or had that same lean physique; no other had such ebony black hair. The man leaving Darroch's bedroom in the middle of the night could be none other than Revan MacLinn.

Just then he turned slightly, putting a hand on Darroch's shoulder and saying something that brought a seductive smile to her face. It was Revan—there was no doubt.

Tears of rage filled her eyes and the hand holding the candle shook uncontrollably. It was an ironic joke of some kind that when she finally decided to humble her pride and creep into Revan's bedchamber at midnight, she would nearly stumble across him leaving a lovers' tryst with another woman.

Darroch had warned her she would find some way to get back into Revan's good graces, and it was quite obvious she had done so.

Cathryn turned abruptly and hurried back to her bedroom. The last thing she wanted was for them to discover her witnessing their tender scene.

She resisted the urge to slam the door and closed it quietly. She put the candle on the bedside table and crawled into bed without bothering to remove the heavy robe. She felt so cold that she was afraid she would never be warm again.

Face it, she told herself sternly. It has become quite obvious—Revan may be a wonderful father, but he will never be the sort of man to make a good husband.

Chapter Nineteen

Waking the next morning, Cathryn experienced a terrible feeling of depression. Miserably she realized her emotions were once again in a state of confusion. It seemed each time she made a decision about something, a new dilemma occurred, leaving her more uncertain than before.

Having finally allowed herself to admit she wanted Revan, it was a devastating blow to find he no longer wanted her. Or, at least, if he did, he was not yet ready to completely sever his past bonds with Darroch.

Now she felt she had no choice but to leave Wolfcrag, for she knew without doubt she would never be the sort of woman satisfied with whatever time and affection Revan could spare her; if she committed herself to him, she would not be willing to share him with any other woman.

During the next few days, she had occasion to thank the fates that she had learned the truth about Revan and Darroch before she made the humiliating mistake of appearing unannounced in his bedchamber. Each time she met his gaze she turned away, grateful he need never know how close she had come to surrender.

Still plagued by morning sickness, she rarely ventured belowstairs until midday. She was fearful someone would notice her illness and mention it to Revan. Now, more than ever, it seemed imperative she make up her mind about her future before he found out about the baby.

Several days before Christmas, Margaret and Meg came to see if she wished to help with the decorating. Some of the men had gone into the snowy woods to bring back baskets of greenery with which they could decorate the castle for the holidays, and Meg was insisting she come down to join in the fun.

Downstairs, she discovered several people engaged in making a garland of holly and cedar to hang above the huge front doors of the castle. Meg and her grandmother went into the Banqueting Hall to place holly and ivy down the length of the banqueting tables in preparation for the Christmas and Hogmanay, or New Year's, feasts to be held there, and Elsa was in the small Drawing Room adorning each of the family portraits with its own crown of cedar boughs.

Taking a basket of holly and ivy, Cathryn decided she would stay in the Great Hall and drape the mantel of the oversized fireplace with the greenery. Unable to reach the mantel, she found a bench which she placed near the hearth and, climbing onto it, began her task. In the rooms to either side of her she could hear happy, excited voices and laughter, and somehow it helped to lighten her mood. She had looked forward to celebrating with the MacLinns and vowed that even Revan's hurtful deceit was not going to spoil Christmas for her.

Just as she placed the last of the prickly holly on the mantel, she felt herself being lifted and swung high in the air by two powerful hands around her waist. The dizzying spin made her a little nauseous and when her feet were finally placed on the floor, she kept her eyes closed and clutched the forearms of the man who held her.

"Did I startle you?" asked Revan, concerned.

Struggling against the dizziness, she opened her eyes and stepped away from him. "Not at all," she answered coolly and turned to pick up the empty basket. Clutching it to her, she held it between them like a shield.

"Didn't you think how dangerous it might be for you to be standing on the bench like that?" he asked.

"Dangerous?"

"Aye, your long skirts were nearly brushing the flames. You should be more careful, Catriona."

"I'll try to remember that," she said in a clipped tone, stepping around him to leave the room.

He caught her arm. "Wait a moment. I think there is something we need to talk about," he said, his voice growing steely.

"What could we possibly have to talk about?"

"I should like to know just what has been wrong with you the last few days? Every time I approach you, you cut me down with one look from those frosty green eyes, then you rush out of the room, and I don't see you again for the rest of the day. I would like to know exactly what is troubling you."

"There is nothing troubling me that need concern you," she snapped.

"It concerns me when I see you looking at me as if you could gladly cut out my heart. I think you owe me an explanation, at least."

She whirled on him, her anger blazing.

"How dare you think I owe you anything! I refuse to stand here talking about something that . . . that . . ." She was horrified to feel tears springing to her eyes. Lowering her face so he would not see, she brushed past him and started out of the room.

"Cathryn, stop!" he commanded.

"No!"

He reached out a lean brown hand and caught a fistful of her long hair, bringing her to an abrupt halt.

"We are going to discuss this, whether you like it or not," he said grimly. He tugged at her hair, causing her to wince. Though she would have liked to have been stubborn, she began backing slowly toward him as he increased the pull on her hair.

"Let me go," she said faintly, hastily brushing the tears from her eyes.

"Not until you've told me what is wrong."

He led her to the long wooden table in the middle of the room and with one hard hand on her shoulder, pushed her down onto the bench along one side. Keeping his hold on her hair, he seated himself across the table on the other bench.

She kept her back to him, refusing to turn and face him. After a while, he loosened his grip on the long bronzed locks, but as soon as she felt the restraining hold released, she started to rise to her feet to flee the room. This time he took a larger strand of hair and wrapped it twice around one brawny wrist, which he placed firmly on the wooden planks of the table, securing her as his prisoner.

"Now, tell me what has happened," he ordered. "What have I done that has so angered you?"

Her chin went up, and she squared her shoulders. Even though they might have to sit there all day, she could not bear to shame herself by telling him the truth.

"I'm waiting, Catriona," he reminded her. "Surely you would rather get our chat over with and not have someone come into the room and see you like this."

"I am growing used to being humiliated at your hands," she said crossly.

"Oh, so I have done something to humiliate you, have I?" His voice was thoughtful. "I swear, I cannot imagine what it would be. As I promised, I have tried my best to behave like a gentleman when in your presence."

"You weren't aware you were in my presence," she retorted, "and you certainly were not acting like a gentleman!"

There was a long silence which he finally broke by saying, "I am sorry, lass, but I simply don't know what you are talking about. I think you had better tell me."

At that moment Della and Adam came into the room. They were talking and laughing, but stopped short when they saw the scene before them. Taking in the tearful, obstinate look on Cathryn's face and the determined one on Revan's, as well as the firm grip he had on her hair, they looked at each other uneasily and turned to leave the room.

"You might as well join us," Revan called after them. "Unless Cathryn decides to cease her childishness, we will be here all day. And all night, too, if that is what it takes," he added in a lower voice, meant for Cathryn's ears.

"We . . . we've got a few things to do in the Banqueting Hall," Adam said, his eyes moving from Revan to Cathryn, clearly unsure of the situation. 'We'll just go on through and not disturb you any longer."

Cathryn closed her eyes. "You are a beast!" she hissed at Revan when they had gone.

"So I have gathered," he said dryly. "Would you care to elaborate on that?"

"If you will let me up," she said.

"Forgive me if I don't trust you. Nay, madam, you will either tell me where you sit, or we will stay here all day."

"You overbearing brute," she muttered. "You ill-mannered . . ." A hard tug at her hair silenced her.

"I don't wish to hear you call me every insulting name you have ever heard. I just want to know why you have suddenly decided to hate me again."

"I do hate you!"

"I understand that. Now tell me why."

"Because you are a deceitful, conniving cad. You cannot be trusted!"

"Catriona, what in hell are you talking about?"

"I'm talking about you and Darroch," she stormed. "You lied to me about your relationship with her."

"I did? In what way, may I inquire?"

"You led me to believe she was merely the mother of your child and . . . and nothing more."

"That is true."

"There is no need for you to keep up your falsehoods," she told him. "I saw you coming out of her room at midnight."

There was another long silence, ended by a low chuckle. "And where were you?"

"In the corridor, just around the corner. It was very obvious the two of you had been . . ."

"Might I ask what you were doing in the hallway?"

Cathryn's mouth opened, then snapped shut. She could think of no valid explanation to give him for her presence in the corridor at that time of night.

"Catriona," he said softly, "could it be you were on your way to my bedchamber for some reason?"

She refused to answer, and her very refusal told him what he wanted to know.

Quickly, he released his hold on her hair and moved around the end of the table to pull her to her feet.

"Lass, there is an explanation, if you would care to hear it."

"You have no need to explain to me," she said stiffly.

"Oh, but I want to. Especially in light of the fact you may have been ready to give in to me at last."

She turned her face away, refusing to meet his amused eyes.

"The simple truth of the matter is this: Meg was awakened by a nightmare that night, and Darroch came to get me to calm her down. You do recall I was reading to her about Mary, Queen of Scots? Well, it seems the story may have been a bit too explicit, causing her to have a bad dream. Darroch has no patience with things like that and always prefers that I handle such situations."

"While your story may be true, it does not explain the seductive way in which Darroch was dressed . . . nor does it offer any excuse for your intimate conversation with her."

"Intimate?"

She flashed him a sullen look, saying, "You had your hand on her shoulder, and she was smiling at you as if . . . as if she had just. . ."

"Well, she hadn't," he grinned. "And I hadn't. Believe me, the thought never crossed my mind, Catriona. And as for Darroch's provocative nightclothes, she always did wear silly garb like that, as I recall."

"Oh!" The fury of her exclamation pleased him, and he laughed warmly.

"Your jealousy flatters me, love," he said.

"You are mistaken if you think I am jealous."

"Don't lie to me, lass!" He pulled her closer to him and put both arms around her. "You are lying about being jealous, aren't you?"

Suddenly weary of fighting her emotions, she let herself relax against him.

"And you were on your way to me, weren't you?"

She nodded, choosing not to look at him.

His arms tightened. "What a cruel twist of fate! Just as you decide to humble your pride and seek me out, you are confronted with the sight of me leaving my former mistress' bedchamber. Aye, I can imagine how it must have looked. If you had only trusted me, however, I could have made my explanations much sooner, saving you endless hours of doubt and anger."

"Yes, I suppose so," she whispered. "But I just couldn't bring myself to talk to you about it."

"Do you believe what I have told you?"

"Yes."

"Good. Now we can proceed with . . . well, with whatever you had in mind the night you were planning to pay me a visit in the wee hours."

"That was an impulsive action on my part," she said. "Who knows when that impulse will strike again?"

He laid his cheek against her hair. "Aye, who knows? I seem to have been waiting a long time. Just give me a little hope that I won't have to wait much longer."

"I . . . I just don't know."

"Well, I will be certain to leave my door unlocked at all times, just in case."

She smiled up at him, feeling happier than she had for days. A sudden thought crossed her mind and momentarily, her expression darkened.

"What is it, love?" he asked.

"It's nothing," she said quickly.

He bent a piercing stare at her serious face. "Won't you ever be willing to trust me?"

"I . . . well, all right," she acquiesced. "I was thinking of something Darroch said to me."

"A threat, no doubt?"

"Yes, a threat. She once told me that if I ever . . . became your mistress, she would take Meg away from the castle and you would never see her again."

"Knowing Darroch, I would guess it is an idle threat, but even if she really meant it, don't you think I could prevent it?"

"But how?"

"There is only one way she can leave Wolfcrag, so if my men are informed of her intentions, it would be a simple matter to refuse to open the gates for her unless she is alone."

"Then there is no danger?"

"I do not think so. Darroch is a spiteful woman, I admit, but she would hardly burden herself with the child. It was just a threat to frighten you and keep you out of my bed a while longer. I think Darroch is well aware it is only a matter to time until we are lovers, and she was just trying to delay the inevitable."

Cathryn was embarrassed by his calm assumption, but somehow, his words were also a cure for her injured pride. She had been mistaken—he did still want her and it didn't even distress her too much that now he knew she wanted him, too.

The day before Christmas Cathryn put the final touches on the doll clothes she was making for Meg, then folded and wrapped them in brown paper, hiding them with the other parcels in the bottom of her wardrobe. An air of excitement seemed to pervade the castle and ever more enticing aromas drifted upward from the kitchens. Cathryn awaited the holiday with all the enthusiasm of a child, for she had never been a part of such bustling activity.

In the afternoon Revan sought her out to go with him to the stables to look in on the puppies. They were lively and playful, now too curious to be confined in a small space. The stable boy assured them it was just as well tomorrow was Christmas, for it would soon be impossible to hide them from Meg's bright eyes.

As they left the stable and crossed the snow-dusted courtyard, Revan said, "There is a favor I would ask of you, Catriona."

"What is that?"

"My mother felt it her duty to point out the fact I am getting a wee bit shaggy-looking." He ruefully fingered his thick beard. "She seems to think I should make myself presentable for the holiday. I thought perhaps I might persuade you to help me trim my hair and beard this evening."

"But I know nothing about such things," she laughed.

" 'Tis not difficult. Elsa usually does it, but she has already left the castle to go down to her father's cottage in the fishing village. She wanted to spend Christmas with her family."

"What if I ruined you?" she asked.

" 'Twould be a fitting revenge, for you once thought I had ruined you, if I remember correctly."

"Must you always say such shameful things?" she asked, embarrassed.

"I apologize. Now, will you agree to come to my bedchamber this evening to help with my grooming?"

"Yes, but only on the condition you will promise to behave yourself and make no unseemly advances."

His amber eyes lighted warmly. "Far be it from me, lass, to annoy you with my unwanted attentions."

Cathryn felt a little apprehensive about being alone with Revan, but after all, he had vowed to behave in a trustworthy manner, so there was probably very little to fear.

As she went down the hallway toward his bedroom that evening, she almost felt a sense of disappointment. There had been times recently when she wished he had shown a little more of the old aggressiveness toward her; for some reason, it no longer seemed so repugnant.

Preoccupied with her thoughts, she knocked at his door and, thinking she heard him tell her to come in, was inside the room and closing the door before she looked up. Revan, completely naked, was just standing up to step out of the bathtub which was in front of the fireplace.

Cathryn's hand flew to her mouth in astonishment and her face turned a fiery scarlet. "Oh!' she cried.

Seeing the look on her face, Revan began to laugh. His own surprise faded as he witnessed her obvious distress.

Still laughing, he stepped on out of the bath and grabbed the towel flung over a nearby chair. Wrapping it around his waist, he said, "Didn't you hear me tell you to wait a moment?"

She shook her head violently. "I thought you told me to come in."

"We do seem to get off on the wrong foot every time, don't we?" he asked, a broad smile on his face.

Cathryn forced herself to face him and, in a second, smiled back. "I suppose it is my fault for wandering around day-dreaming."

"Oh? And what were you day-dreaming about?" he asked slyly.

She tossed her head. "Nothing of any great importance."

Despite herself, her eyes were drawn to his smoothly muscled chest, the tapering torso and strong thighs, which were further enhanced by the brevity of his costume. Her rapt appraisal of his masculinity ended abruptly as she caught sight of the amused and sardonic look in his golden eyes.

"Shall we get on with it?" he asked, arching one black brow wickedly.

"With the beard trimming, you mean?" she questioned, smiling uncertainly.

"Aye, with the beard trimming."

"Don't you think you should put on some clothes?"

"If you insist," he grinned.

"I do."

"Then, make yourself comfortable and I will be back in a few minutes." He disappeared into the dressing chamber. While he was gone, Cathryn looked about the room she had once shared with him. It seemed as if a great deal of time had passed since she had last been there.

When Revan returned, he was dressed in the usual leather breeches, which were only a little less revealing than the damp towel. Cathryn again suspected the man of deliberately displaying himself before her, but instead of angering her as it might once have done, it rather pleased her.

Revan placed a high stool in the center of the room and, seating himself upon it, handed her a pair of scissors and a comb. She listened as he instructed her on the proper way to trim a beard, then, cautiously she began to snip gently at the thick, curling hair. In a short while, having found it not as difficult as she feared, she lost her timidity and wielded the scissors with greater confidence.

Concentrating on the portion of his beard which framed his mouth, she moved a little closer to him, standing between his knees. She was so close she could see her own reflection in his eyes and the sheer intimacy of the moment made her heart beat erratically.

For the first time, shut away with him in the privacy of his bedroom, performing such a personal task as trimming his beard and hair, she could almost imagine being married to him. This seemed the sort of moment that would be shared by a husband and wife. She had never felt closer to Revan — nor more aware of his burning gaze on her face.

She forced herself to step back to take a look at her handiwork. Satisfied that the beard looked neater, she found a hand mirror in the dressing room and gave it to him so he could view her efforts.

" 'Tis much better," he said approvingly. "My mother will be most pleased."

"It wasn't as difficult as I thought it might be," she said. "Shall I try to cut your hair now?"

Again, he placed himself in her hands and, after another cautious beginning, she soon warmed to the task and had carefully trimmed his black hair in a short time.

He gave a deep chuckle. "You know, Darroch once told me that you and I were like Samson and Delilah, and that, one day, you would shear me like a Highland sheep."

"Oh?" She stood back, giving him a critical look, then stepped close again to snip away a stray curl near his ear. "What did she mean by that?"

"That you would be my downfall, I suppose. And you are, lass . . ." He turned his head and placed a swift kiss against the inside of her wrist. Startled, she moved back slightly and gave a squeal of surprise as his arms went around her, lifting her onto his lap.

"Revan!"

"Yes?"

His face was so close to hers she could feel his warm breath against her mouth. Her eyes closed and her traitorous lips grew soft, awaiting the touch of his. His breath hovered just at the corner of her mouth, then slowly slid away as he placed a light kiss on her cheek.

His deliberate attempt to frustrate her made her angry and her eyes flew open, fixing themselves on his with a smoldering look.

"Damn you, Revan MacLinn!" she said harshly, and her hands released the comb and scissors she held, letting them drop unheeded to the floor, while her fingers twisted themselves into his thick black hair, pulling his face to hers. Her mouth moved against his greedily, and after his initial surprise, his arms tightened and he responded with ardor. She kissed him until she had satisfied her frustrated hunger and common sense returned. Shamefaced, she pulled away, nestling against his chest so that she might hide her face from his penetrating gaze.

He rested his chin against the top of her head, holding her tightly. When his voice came, it was low and strained. "That was sweet, love."

He gave her a quick, hard squeeze. "I did not know you were so starved for kisses, lass, or I would have done something to remedy the situation."

She drew back to give him a glare. "I know you have been teasing and tempting me, Revan. I just got weary of your silly game."

He laughed softly. "Aye, lass, I understand. You tested me, then I tested you. Now I think we both know what we wanted to know, and there is nothing more to stand in the way of our loving each other."

Held securely in his strong arms, her face resting against his warm, bare chest, Cathryn gazed into the fire and reveled in the wonderful flood of happiness washing over her, sweeping away the doubts, fears and indecision that had plagued her. Without warning, the true depth of her feelings for Revan and her devout hope for a future with him had been made startlingly clear to her. She couldn't believe the relief of knowing her own mind at last — and it was so simple, why had it taken so long to realize what must have been in her heart all the time?

She raised her face to his again.

"Happy Christmas, Revan," she murmured. "It is going to be a good Christmas Day, isn't it?"

"Aye," he replied, his amber eyes growing dark. "That it 'tis."

Chapter Twenty

Christmas morning dawned cold and clear, and the residents of Wolfcrag were awake and stirring early. The sound of Christmas hymns being played on the pipes summoned everyone to an early morning service in the little chapel at the back side of the castle.

Cathryn rose at daylight and dressed in a simple black wool dress with a high neck and long sleeves. She knew the family would expect to see her in the chapel, and she was glad she felt well enough to join them.

Meg and Margaret came to take her to the worship service, and as the three of them walked down the broad stairs she saw Revan waiting for them at the bottom.

As she reached the last step, he came forward, smiling. "Good morning, Catriona," he said, and though he also greeted the others, his eyes remained on her.

"I have something for you," he said, holding out a flat parcel. She gave him a questioning look and he grinned. " 'Tis something you have needed for a long time."

She unwrapped the package to find a new shawl, made of the sheerest wool in the MacLinn tartan, fringed at the edges.

"Oh, Revan, it is beautiful," she cried, her green eyes shining. "And I do need it badly. My other one was so faded and threadbare I dared not wear it this morning."

"Here, let me help you." He took the shawl from her and, draping it gently around her shoulders, fastened it with a silver wolf's head brooch he took from his jacket pocket.

"You look very pretty, Cathryn," Meg announced, and her father nodded his pleased agreement. The plain black dress was a perfect foil for the bright red and black plaid.

Putting her small hands behind her back, Meg looked up at her father.

"Don't you have any gift for me, Father?"

His delighted laugh rang out, bringing an impudent grin to her heart-shaped face.

"Aye, I have several gifts for you, Meg, but I thought they should wait until after breakfast. After all, you have already had your Christmas stocking this morning, haven't you?"

"Oh, yes!" As they walked to the chapel, Meg kept up a stream of excited chatter describing the fruit and candy, the wooden puppet and the set of watercolor paints she had found in her stocking.

The chapel was small and rather plain. Its polished wood walls and benches were decorated with cedar and holly, and rows of thick candles flickered in the drafty dimness.

Due to the absence of a clergyman at Wolfcrag, the service was read by Doctor MacSween. His resonant voice reading from a Gaelic Bible left Cathryn spellbound and it didn't matter to her that she couldn't understand a single word of the service. She couldn't even join in the singing of the hymns, for they were also in Gaelic, but she was content to sit between Revan and Meg and enjoy the peaceful atmosphere. The simple odors of cedar boughs and burning candles would always invoke the memory of this moment.

When the service was over, the MacLinns gathered for a huge breakfast at the long tables in the Great Hall. As bowls of steaming porridge were being served, Revan leaned close to whisper in her ear.

"Remember your first breakfast at Wolfcrag, Catriona?"

Her chin came up quickly, but her eyes were sparkling. "Indeed I do. You did your best to make me hate you forever!"

"I trust I failed?"

"I'm afraid so, milord. Though there were moments . . ." She broke off laughing. Looking up, she caught Della MacSween's eye, and knew her friend was pleased to see her and Revan laughing together so amiably.

When the meal had ended, Revan announced the family and their friends would meet in the Drawing Room to exchange gifts. Immediately everyone scattered, hurrying to fetch their gifts for the others.

At the top of the stairs, Revan turned to Cathryn and said, "I have another gift or two for you, Catriona, but if you don't mind, I'd like to wait and give them to you later today when we are alone."

"All right," she agreed. "I will wait until then to give you my gift, also."

His white teeth gleamed behind the newly trimmed beard, and he leaned tantalizingly close to murmur, "I suspect you know what I've been hoping your gift is to be."

"I have no idea what you could possibly mean," she retorted, tossing her head. As he opened his mouth, she laid a quick hand against his chest. "And please! Don't bother to explain." A rosy blush on her cheeks, she hurried away down the hall, well aware that he stood watching her all the way, a bemused smile on his lean face.

Having gathered up all her parcels, she left her room again, to find Revan waiting patiently to escort her back downstairs. She was flattered by his attentiveness, and knew he also recognized the fact they had arrived at some sort of turning point the evening before. She felt a sudden, piercing thrill as she contemplated where their relationship might be after one more night.

Cathryn's Christmas gifts were a great success. She nearly cried as she watched Meg's astonished awe over the china doll. Hugging the toy to her, she climbed up onto Cathryn's lap and gave her a fervent kiss. "It is the most beautiful doll in the world," she cried. "I'm going to name her after you!"

Cathryn hugged her back, and then handed her a little woven-willow hamper filled with the elegant clothes she had sewn for the doll. This new gift sent Meg into further raptures of delight, causing everyone in the room to laugh.

Suddenly remembering her own gift for Cathryn, Meg jumped down and went to get the package. It was a small linen sampler which Meg had worked with her own hands.

Brightly colored threads reproduced a picture of Wolfcrag Castle, with the MacLinn crest in one corner. Across the top of the sampler, in slightly uneven letters, were the words: "This sampler was fashioned for Cathryn by her loyal friend Margaret Elizabeth MacLinn in the Year of Our Lord, 1756." Along the bottom edge of the needlework was the MacLinn motto: "Above all, faithfulness."

Cathryn hugged the sampler in its oaken frame close, her eyes shining with tears. She knew the effort that had gone into this gift and treasured it for all the long hours of labor and frustration she was certain it had cost the little girl.

"It's . . . it's really not very good," Meg said solemnly, her dark eyes on Cathryn's face.

"Oh, darling, it is perfect!" Cathryn assured her, gathering the child into her arms again. "It is the loveliest gift I have ever received, and I will keep it with me for the rest of my life, I promise!"

Meg smiled, delighted, and immediately produced a haphazardly wrapped package for her father.

Inside was a pair of kilt stockings, and when Revan held them up for all to see, it was quite obvious they had been knitted by his young daughter. One stocking was slightly longer than the other, and there was evidence of several dropped stitches.

"They are just a little lumpy," Meg apologized, but her father swept her up into his arms, kissing her and assuring her they were beautiful—by far the finest pair he owned.

Soon the room had erupted into a happy hubbub as gifts were handed back and forth. The MacSweens were very pleased with their presents from Cathryn, and they gifted her with a beautiful pair of cairngorm earrings with a bracelet to match. Owen MacIvor grinned sheepishly over his tobacco, and nearly blushed as he presented Cathryn with a new leather riding crop he had handtwisted himself.

"I thought you might need a new one, Cathryn," he said, "but don't be too hasty to use it. 'Tis no' the way to keep other women away from your man!"

His brown eyes twinkled, and she had to laugh, even though she still harbored a few guilt feelings over her treatment of Darroch.

Margaret MacLinn had sewn a lovely new dressing gown of soft cinnamon velvet for Cathryn, and with it was a pair of matching slippers. Revan's mother seemed very pleased with her French perfume and the elegant chocolates, as well as the jewelry Revan had chosen for her in Inverness.

Just as the last gift had been opened and displayed, Revan slipped out of the room and soon returned with a basket which he set down in front of Meg. Gingerly, she pulled aside the cloth with which it was covered, and instantly the puppy inside bounded out and led the child a merry chase around the room, through scattered pieces of wrapping paper.

When she had caught the animal and held his squirming body as tightly as she could, she announced she would name him "Prince Charlie" and the entire company showed their approval with a rousing cheer.

Luncheon was a very light meal as a feast had been planned for the evening; after eating, Meg was whisked away for a nap as she was to be allowed to stay up late for the festivities. While she slept, Revan and Cathryn decided to ride out to the fishing village to take Granny MacLinn her gifts and to wish the villagers a good holiday.

Wearing her cloak and bundled into the blanket of pelts, Cathryn was warm enough to thoroughly enjoy the ride along the coastal path to the little village. Sometimes the two of them rode in companionable silence, and other times, they shouted and raced, their breaths making lacy clouds of steam in the frosted air.

When they arrived at Granny MacLinn's cottage, she met them at the door and invited them inside. She was dressed in her best black dress with voluminous petticoats and a tartan shawl.

She flashed her toothless smile in appreciation for the chocolates which Cathryn had brought her, and for the large tin of tea which was a gift from Margaret MacLinn. Revan brought her tobacco for the little clay pipe she sometimes smoked, and that pleased her so much she danced a jig, lifting her petticoats daringly to show thin legs encased in

383

black stockings.

They sat around her table drinking hot tea and eating small spice cakes. As the afternoon drew on toward evening, the old lady's mood seemed to shift, and she became rather pensive. For a long moment she stared into her tea cup, and then she lifted somber eyes.

To Cathryn she said, "Ye have chosen to stay with this man, I ken. And ye have chosen well."

Cathryn felt rather than saw Revan's quick look at her. She was glad the old woman didn't wait for her to make any answer, as she would have felt embarrassment at discussing the matter in front of Revan.

"Ye know your man is likened to the wolf, don't ye?"

"Yes," Cathryn replied uncertainly.

"D'ye know anything about wolves, lass?"

Cathryn met Revan's amused eyes. "No, not really."

Granny MacLinn took a noisy sip of tea. "Ye see, the wolf has a puir reputation among humans. He is thought to be a cruel and dangerous animal. 'Tis not true, lass. Wolves keep to themselves and only kill when 'tis necessary, and then they kill the sick or lame. They're a boon to nature, sure enough. Aye, and they're a noble animal. They live for generations in the same den as their ancestors and do anything they can to protect their offspring." Here the old lady leaned forward and tapped Cathryn on the arm. "And ye'll like to be knowin' this, lassie — they always mate for life." The old lady winked broadly, nodding at Revan, whose laughing eyes fastened on Cathryn's face with unwavering intensity.

"But I think I should tell ye, Revan," Granny MacLinn continued, "lately I have had a darkenin' of the mind."

At Cathryn's puzzled expression, Revan murmured, "A premonition, love."

"Aye, a premonition," Granny nodded. "Ye know about Wolf Monat, don't ye?" she asked, bright eyes on Cathryn.

"No, I'm afraid not," she answered, trying not to smile. In truth, she found the strange old lady a bit frightening, as well as amusing.

" 'Tis the name the Saxons gave the month of January. In the old days, the whole month was set aside for the slayin' of

384

wolves because it was the season when the animals were starving and sometimes attacked humans. They were driven out of the forests by the bad weather and often wandered into the villages. 'Tis a dangerous time for the wolf . . ."

"But dangerous, also, for those they attack," put in Revan.

Her ancient face grew stern and she pointed one thin finger at Revan. "Mind you, Revan, you must take care! I feel it, you may be in mortal danger."

"Now, Granny," Revan said, taking her gnarled hand in his. "You know I always listen to you. I promise, I will be on my guard every minute!"

"See that ye are, lad. I see ye surrounded by fire, and I don't need to warn ye, fire is what the wolf fears most. Take care . . ."

"You have my oath, Granny. How could I allow myself to grow careless and risk being killed? Then I'd never be able to gaze upon your beauty again!"

"Och, away with ye, laddie! Would ye have the lady here wantin' to claw out me eyes?"

"Nay, I wouldn't. And she's a jealous one, I can tell you. Mayhap I had better hurry her away before she can do you any harm!"

"And before it grows any darker," the old woman agreed.

While Revan went out to the little byre beside the cottage to get the horses, Cathryn thanked Granny MacLinn for the tea and put on her cloak.

" 'Twas kind of ye to ride all the way out here to bring me the Christmas remembrances, lass. Give Margaret my best wishes, will ye?"

"Certainly, Granny. I'll be happy to."

The dark eyes behind the wrinkled lids studied her thoughtfully. "Ye love the lad, don't ye?"

Cathryn blushed, but couldn't help the smile she felt spreading across her face.

"Yes, I do—but you're the first person I've admitted it to. I've barely accepted it myself."

"Ye've chosen wisely, Cathryn, for he's a good man."

"I know."

"And when will the wee bairn be born?"

Cathryn gasped. "How did you know?"

"Ye have the look, lass." She smiled her toothless smile, her face crinkling. " 'Twould take a man to be blind enough to miss it. Ye havna told Revan, have ye?"

"Not yet."

" 'Tis best that ye don't—not just yet. The time will come when ye must tell him, but not yet, lass."

"When then?"

"Ye'll find the right time." The bright eyes moved over Cathryn's figure briefly. "The babe will be a lad, I ken. An heir for Wolfcrag, at last."

"Oh, I do hope so."

Just then Revan returned, a cold blast of air coming in the door with him.

"We'll be on our way now, Granny, but you can be certain we will be back one day soon to see you." Revan kissed the old woman's hand. "I hope you'll have more spice cakes."

"Away with ye," she cackled, "ye shameless knave!"

As they rode away, they turned to wave once more at the tiny black figure standing just inside the cottage door. Her reedy voice came to them through the gathering gloom of the winter afternoon.

"Haste ye back!"

Before she began to dress for the Christmas banquet, Cathryn decided to have a talk with Margaret. It was something she felt she owed to Revan's mother and somehow, today seemed the perfect time.

The older woman was sitting at a dressing table braiding her hair when Cathryn entered the room. She smiled warmly, delighted to see her.

"How did you find Granny MacLinn?" Margaret asked, coiling the long braid into a crown on top of her head.

"She seemed well," Cathryn replied," though she was a bit gloomy."

"Oh?"

"Yes, she'd had a premonition that Revan is in some sort of danger."

Margaret said, "Aye, Granny often has 'feelings' about things. Her own grandmother had the Sight, but poor Granny! Her premonitions are so vague she is often mistaken about what they mean. I learned long ago not to worry too much about them. Do you think Revan took her warning seriously?"

"I'm not sure. He didn't mention it again."

"Well, today is not the time for dire warnings and omens. I'll ask him about it in a day or so. If I know Revan, he only humored Granny and will soon forget all about it."

"But she seemed so certain," Cathryn said slowly, "that it seems to me we should at least keep her words in mind."

"I suppose that is true, dear. It won't hurt to let ourselves be forewarned, even if the warning comes to naught."

Cathryn moved a little closer to Margaret and said hesitantly, "There is something I want to speak to you about."

"What is it, Cathryn? Is something wrong?"

She smiled. "No, nothing is wrong. In fact, everything is starting to be much better."

"In what way?"

Cathryn looked down at her hands, rosy color creeping into her face.

"Do you recall the story you told me about your arrival here at Wolfcrag? About how you grew to love your husband?"

"Indeed I do."

"And, of course, you remember that I assured you I could never feel the same way about my own kidnapping?"

Margaret smiled. "Aye."

"I had to come and tell you I was mistaken. It seems time can bring a great many changes to one's life."

" 'Tis just as well we can't see the future, for we would never believe some of the things we'd see could ever be possible," Margaret said.

"I know. I never thought I would find myself actually . . . loving a Highland outlaw who took me away from the only life I had ever known. It seemed a kind of death to me to be shut away here in this lonely place without my friends and family. I truly thought I couldn't survive." She sat down beside Margaret. "Now I see my only hope of survival lay in leaving my old home. I was only a piece of goods with which to bargain — no one ever realized I was a person, myself least of all. And, Margaret, somehow — don't ask me to explain it — I have found my true friends and family here in this castle. No one has ever done as much for me as you and Della, and no one has ever needed me as Meg does."

"And Revan? What about him?"

"I think you know the answer to that," Cathryn said softly. "I think you have always known."

"Aye, at least, I hoped. That first night, seeing the two of you together, I felt it was meant to be. Despite all the obstacles."

"Some of the obstacles are still there," Cathryn stated.

"True enough, but am I correct in thinking the biggest obstacle is no longer a problem?"

"The biggest obstacle?"

"Do you love my son?"

"Yes, I do. You know I didn't want to fall in love with him — I tried to fight it every way I could, in fact. But I am not going to deny it any longer. I love him very much."

"Then there is nothing else standing between you that cannot be dealt with."

Cathryn considered this for a moment. "You are very wise, Margaret. If I had had your wisdom from the beginning, I might not have made so many silly mistakes."

"Things happen in the way they are meant to happen, child. There is a reason for everything. You can't worry about the past now — there is nothing to be gained by fretting over what is already done. You must think of the future."

"I want to stay at Wolfcrag, I have decided."

"Does Revan know?"

"I haven't told him in so many words," Cathryn answered, "but I think he knows anyway. Tonight, after the banquet, I intend to tell him how I feel."

Margaret laid her hand over Cathryn's. "It will be a gift he has waited for long and patiently."

"I know. He has been very kind to me."

"Does it worry you that you cannot legally marry Revan?"

"Not anymore. And who knows? Basil may have gone ahead with his plans for a divorce. I may be free sooner than we think. But it doesn't matter. If Revan will have me, I will live as his wife, for that is the way I feel."

"I am so happy, Cathryn. I can't help but think of you as the daughter I've always wanted. All these months I have forced myself to realize I mustn't get too close to you because you might choose to go away. Now I can forget those worries and truly open my heart. Meg has felt the same way, I know—you can't understand what this will mean to her when she finds out you aren't ever going to leave her. You're already a better mother to her than Darroch has ever been."

"I love her as much as I expect to love my own child," Cathryn said quietly.

As the significance of her words came to Margaret, her eyes began to shine with unshed tears. "Are you telling me you are going to have a child?"

"Yes," Cathryn replied, "in the summer. I . . . I haven't told Revan yet, but I thought you would like to know."

"I'm so happy for you!" The smile faded momentarily. "This isn't the reason you are staying?"

"No, I would not stay even for the child's sake if I did not love Revan. The fact that I am to have his child has only forced me to take a closer look at my feelings and to cease trying to lie to myself."

"Then you are happy about the babe?"

"I am beginning to be, I think. At first it seemed just one more problem. Now I am starting to feel rather pleased. And I think Revan will be happy about it."

"I'm certain of it," Margaret exclaimed. "Will you tell him tonight?"

"No, I don't think so. Granny MacLinn advised me to wait a while longer before telling him. Besides, I do think we should have as much time as possible to grow accustomed to each other before I inform him he is to be a father again. Granny says she is certain the baby will be a boy."

"Then there is no doubt," Margaret laughed, "for this has nothing to do with her spiritual powers. As a midwife, she has a very practiced eye. Of course, Revan would love a

389

daughter just as much."

"I know," she agreed. "Meg is proof of that. And, I daresay . . . there will be other children."

"I daresay!"

Margaret's face grew still, reflecting thoughts of her own youthful love. As Cathryn gazed at her, she realized it had been a long, long time since Margaret's eyes had had a dull and lifeless look.

"I want to give you something," Margaret was saying, as she crossed the room and opened a large wooden chest setting under the windows. She laid several carefully folded gowns aside before taking out the garments she sought.

Returning to Cathryn, she said, "I wore this on my own wedding night and thought perhaps you might like to have it."

The nightgown was a sheer white silk which had aged to the color of candlelight. The robe to cover it was made of delicate tatted lace, aged to the same subtle shade of ivory. They were so sheer Cathryn could hardly feel their weight in her hands. Faintly, they smelled of cedar from the chest in which they had been stored.

"They are so lovely, Margaret," Cathryn said. "Are you certain you want me to have them?"

"I have saved these things and my wedding gown for a daughter of my own. Now you are that daughter, and I want you to have them. It would please me more than I can say, Cathryn."

"Then I will wear them gladly. Thank you so much."

"And I will pray for the day when you will have need of my wedding gown."

The two women hugged each other warmly, unable to deny themselves a few joyful tears.

"I never thought I could ever be this happy," Cathryn said.

"Aye, I know — but then, I did try to warn you about these bonny Highland men, my dear!"

Returning to her room, Cathryn heard voices raised in anger as she passed Darroch's bedchamber.

Revan must have been standing just inside the door, for she clearly heard him say, "It will do you no good to threaten either Cathryn or myself, Darroch. I intend to see that your threats come to nothing, do you understand?"

Darroch's tearful reply was unintelligible, but again Cathryn heard Revan speak.

"Meg is my daughter more than she has ever been yours. You don't really want her, and I will never give her up, no matter what. As for Cathryn, she will be mistress of this castle and that is something you are powerless to change."

Cathryn waited to hear no more. She didn't want them to find her in the hallway and think she had been deliberately eavesdropping.

Inside her own room, she leaned against the door and hugged the bridal finery to her. Mistress of Wolfcrag, she thought—that is truly what I am going to be!

Chapter Twenty-one

At long last Cathryn had a reason to wear the beautiful green velvet evening gown she had been given so long ago. She vividly recalled the morning Elsa had brought the new gowns up to Revan's room. She had allowed herself an almost childish pleasure in the new clothes, but only to rid her mind of the harsh reality of the night before. Then she had thought she hated Revan for forcing himself upon her — now she questioned her earlier reluctance and timidity. Tonight, she promised herself, she was going to give Revan the night of love she had denied him before.

The gown bared her shoulders, allowing the candlelight to delicately shadow the hollows at the base of her neck. Its sleeves were short and puffed, and the waist fit tightly before flaring into a wide skirt, whose color shifted from silvery green to deepest emerald. She was wearing the cairngorm jewelry the MacSweens had given her, the greenish-brown color of the stones complimenting the dress.

She piled her hair high on her head, letting a few stray tendrils curl temptingly down her slender neck. In the bright coils of hair she tucked a sprig of mistletoe Revan had seen and cut down as they returned from the fishing village.

She and Meg were to meet Revan in the nursery before going down to dinner. When Cathryn arrived, she found the little girl happily dressing her new doll, the puppy asleep on the floor beside her, and the old hound standing guard.

Meg was wearing a crimson velvet gown with a wide white lace collar and a white satin sash. Her smoky black hair was held back on each side of her face by small bunches of tiny

392

red ribbons.

"You look beautiful, Meg!" Cathryn exclaimed.

"Oh, so do you! And look—here's Father. He's beautiful, too!"

Cathryn had to agree whole-heartedly.

Once more, Revan was dressed in the formal black velvet jacket and the kilt of MacLinn tartan. The startling white-ness of the lace at his throat and wrists made his skin look darkly warm by contrast. As he crossed the room toward them, she caught sight of his lean legs and thought her heart would burst with loving pride. Despite the immaculate perfection of the rest of his evening wear, Revan was wearing the less-than-perfect kilt stockings his daughter had made for him. Cathryn thought she could never love him more than she did at that moment.

Meg noticed the stockings right away, also, and a pleased smile swept over her face.

"Since you put the dirk in this stocking, Father, perhaps no one will notice it is shorter than the other!"

The three of them laughed heartily. Revan stooped to give Meg a kiss. "Should any man question my stockings, I shall challenge him to a duel, you may be sure."

He turned his laughing gaze on Cathryn, his golden eyes moving upwards to rest on the sprig of mistletoe in her hair.

"You do know the significance of the mistletoe?" he asked, one brow arching.

"It's an old Druidic custom, I believe," Cathryn answered primly.

"Aye, a custom that says a maiden standing beneath the mistletoe must forfeit a kiss to any man who requests it. Do you intend to comply?"

"I always observe old customs."

He placed a lingering kiss on her upturned mouth, then stepped back, frowning slightly.

"What about all those strutting rakes belowstairs?" he asked. "Must I expect to find you busily occupied dispensing kisses to them all evening?"

"You could challenge all of them to duels, too, Father," piped up Meg.

"Then I should find myself too busy to dine or dance!" he laughed.

"Perhaps I should simply remove the mistletoe," Cathryn smiled, one hand reaching upward.

Revan caught her hand. "Nay, lass, leave it. It looks quite festive. Besides, I have faith enough in my own fierce scowls—they should keep all but the most foolhardy men away."

He kissed her hand. "Just don't blame me if I should feel compelled to observe Druidic custom myself several times during the evening. Such a long-standing tradition must have great merit."

His smile was intimately warm, bringing a glow to her face.

"Now, may I escort the loveliest ladies in the castle down to our Christmas feast?" he asked politely, extending his arms to them.

The Banqueting Hall was a magnificent sight. Its polished wooden tables were centered with cedar boughs, holly and ivy, and each place was set with burnished pewter plates, red glass goblets and tartan napkins. Hundreds of bayberry candles, made especially for this night, lighted the room and sent out their subtle fragrance. The Yule log, which had been carried in the night before, still blazed on the hearth and would continue to do so until Twelfth Night, in the old tradition.

Though this feast was smaller than the one the MacLinns would host on New Year's, Hogmanay, there were still many guests present, most of them attired in the dramatic red and black tartan. Christmas, Revan told her, was more of a family affair, but invitations had been extended to all their friends and neighbors, as well as kinsmen, to join them at year's end.

The meal was a long and merry one, starting with cock-a-leekie soup and ending with a steamed Christmas pudding steeped in brandy. In between were courses of salmon, baked chicken, roast pork and venison. The red goblets were filled and re-filled with light wine and, after the dessert had been served, they were filled with wassail from a huge pewter punch bowl.

Raising his glass high, Revan got to his feet. "Let us toast to a happy Christmas and a prosperous New Year."

Voices were raised in approval of the toast and glasses were lifted. Cathryn drank a sip of the spicy wassail and said a silent prayer for the new year, already certain it would bring even more change to her life.

Down the table a clansman arose and boomed out, "We canna have our Christmas dinner without a toast to our dear king, Jamie Stuart."

A small silence fell over the crowd and suddenly, Cathryn realized they were all looking at her.

"Just pick up your glass, Catriona," Revan said in a low voice. "You need not drink."

Gathering her courage, she reached for the goblet again and rose to her feet. The silence became almost deafening.

She looked down the long table at the faces staring back at her. In her months at Wolfcrag she had come to know and like most of these people. If she planned to stay here among them, they had a right to know what was in her heart.

"Good people," she began, her voice a little shaky in her nervousness, "I am certain you will recall that I once made quite a scene at a banquet such as this when I refused to drink a toast to the Stuarts. Now I want to say I am sorry I was so rude. Since that time, I have come to understand much more about your history and why you believe as you do. I have visited the battlefield at Culloden and somehow, what I felt there has not left me since. It brought a realization of why you risk so much to defy the king—to do less would be to deny your heritage. I have come to believe you are justified in trying to keep your history and traditions alive. I am not certain I could ever become a Jacobite in practice, but please permit me to say to you that I do understand your cause and no longer condemn it." She took a deep breath. "And now, in the spirit of Christmas, let us toast the Stuarts, father and son."

"Hear! Hear!"

395

Candlelight sparkled on the red goblets as they were raised and emptied. Over the rim of her glass, Cathryn's eyes met the intense amber ones of Revan MacLinn and when she sank back into her chair, his hand closed over hers.

The pipers appeared and suddenly the strangely jubilant sounds of their instruments filled the hall, and the floor was rapidly cleared for dancing. Owen MacIvor stepped up to claim Meg for the first dance, leaving the two of them alone.

" 'Twas a fine speech, love," Revan said. "I can't believe it was you. I hadn't forgotten that first banquet!"

"I hope you will forget it now. The memory shames me terribly."

"You have made atonement, though none was asked."

"Thank you for allowing me to do so, without force."

"Catriona, I have learned my lesson where you are concerned. While force was . . . shall we say, rather delightful, I am beginning to think it might be far more favorable to let you do things in your own way, in your own time."

She only smiled, her look enigmatic.

"Come, love, shall we dance?"

As he whirled her out into the mainstream of dancers, she suddenly came face to face with Darroch, who was dancing with Adam MacSween. At the look of absolute hatred on her face, Cathryn felt chilled. Revan caught the look and said in her ear, "Don't let the woman worry you, lass. I had a talk with her this afternoon and assured her it would do no good for her to keep threatening you or to try to take Meg away from the castle. If she cannot abide by my rules, she will have to leave."

"She hates me so!" Cathryn shuddered. "Sometimes it's really frightening."

"You are safe enough with me, Catriona," he murmured. "Don't let her spoil your Christmas mood."

"No, I don't want that—I promise I won't think about her anymore."

"Good."

During the dancing, only two men were bold enough to claim a kiss because of the mistletoe she wore, but Revan took it with good grace. He could hardly challenge Doctor

396

MacSween to a duel and leave the castle without medical provision and, he laughed, only a fool would challenge the mighty sword arm of Owen MacIvor. Anyone else who approached Cathryn with a hopeful look on his face received the full force of Revan's angry black scowl and quickly moved on by, fading into the noisy crowd. Cathryn observed all this with a demure smile, secretly enjoying his jealous protection.

At one time, Della danced by and paused an instant to whisper, "My God, you look like the kitchen cat who swallowed the canary!" Then she smiled. "But I am glad you have come to your senses, at last!"

As the hour grew late, Meg began to get sleepy, stifling yawns behind her small hands. Revan danced a final reel with her, then he and Cathryn took her upstairs to bed.

Cathryn helped her into her nightgown, seeing no need to awaken the nurse who was asleep in the next room. They tucked her into bed, with her new doll and the puppy on either side of her. She gave them a last sleepy smile and snuggled deep into the covers, falling asleep quickly.

As they extinguished the candles in the room, Revan leaned close and whispered, "I want to give you your Christmas gifts before we go back down to the dance."

Softly closing the nursery door behind them, Cathryn looked into his face, her gaze unwavering.

"Let's not go back to the dance," she suggested.

Revan's lips curved into a delighted smile and deep in the back of his clear amber eyes a small flame began to burn.

"What do you have in mind, Catriona?"

"I thought we could exchange our gifts and . . . share a bottle of wine," she replied. "Will you come to my room?"

He put his hands on her shoulders and his voice grew husky.

"Lass, mayhap that is not a good idea. I . . . I may not be responsible for my actions if I am alone with you. Not tonight . . ."

She smiled slowly. "I will take full responsibility for whatever might happen."

She could sense his surprise and, by the tightening of his

grip on her shoulders, his pleasure at her words.

"Then I will gladly accept your invitation, love."

Revan went to his own bedchamber to get the Christmas gifts he had for her, and when he arrived at her room, he had taken off the velvet jacket and removed the lace jabot at the neck of his shirt. With his dark hair slightly mussed and the open collar of his shirt revealing his strong throat and furred chest, Cathryn thought he looked strikingly handsome. She caught the flash of his teeth through his beard and knew he was aware of her approving scrutiny, so she turned away and busied herself pouring the wine.

"Won't you sit down?" she asked politely, indicating the high-backed chair near the fire.

Revan dropped into the chair, stretching out his long legs and heaving a big sigh. "It's so peaceful here," he said, taking the wineglass from her.

They could just barely hear the sound of the pipes below, making them feel as if they were shut away in a world of their own. With the muffled sound of the wintry wind outside the windows and the hiss of the fire, a cozy, intimate atmosphere had been created, heightened by the softly glowing light of a half-dozen candles.

Cathryn sank down on the hearth rug, her full skirts billowing out around her. Reaching up for her wineglass, she said, "Shall we have one more toast?"

"Aye, let's toast to us," Revan agreed. He raised his glass and the light shone through the ruby red liquid.

"To us," Cathryn murmured, and they drank.

She replaced her glass on the little table and picked up Revan's gift, handing it to him with a smile.

He unwrapped the box and opened it. For a long moment his face was still, causing Cathryn's heart to sink.

"I'm sorry if you don't like it," she said hesitantly. "I . . . I couldn't think of anything else to buy you."

His lean fingers picked up the gold watch, laying aside the box and papers. "Nay, love, 'tis not that I don't like it. Quite the opposite, actually. You see, my father used to have a watch very much like this one and, just for a minute, I was simply taken back to the days of my youth. So many times I remember seeing him take out his watch and solemnly announce the time."

"I never thought about it bringing you such sad memories," she apologized.

"They're not sad memories, Catriona. In a way, it's as if you have given me back a little part of my father. There is no way I can thank you enough."

The sweet caressing look in his eyes as he raised them from the watch to her face was gratifying enough for Cathryn.

"I will always treasure it, love."

He snapped the lid shut and studied the embossed picture on the top.

"I thought it was appropriate for someone known as 'The Wolf'," she said shyly.

"Though I must point out, this particular fellow is somewhat luckier than I—he is surrounded by his mate and several offspring." He gave her a wicked look, then shook his head. "Oh well, someday . . . perhaps."

He gathered up three packages from the table and placed them in her lap.

"These are for you, Catriona."

The first proved to be a very lovely tortoise-shell comb and hand mirror, trimmed with delicate gold filigree.

"Oh, how pretty!" she exclaimed, smiling up at him.

In the second package was a pair of pearl earrings, the teardrop-shaped jewels glowing softly in their silver settings. Quickly she removed the cairngorm earrings and replaced them with the pearls. One of them tangled in her hair and Revan leaned down to give her assistance. As he freed the strand of hair from the earring, she gave him a fleeting kiss on the corner of his mouth.

"Thank you so much, Revan. Your gifts are truly wonderful, but you shouldn't have gotten me so many."

"It seemed everything I saw in Inverness reminded me of you. It gave Owen great amusement to watch me trying to purchase this or that without you noticing."

"You were successful, for I suspected nothing."

"This is something a bit more practical," he said, nodding at the last package. When unwrapped, it was revealed to be a slim, leather-bound book, written entirely in Gaelic.

"Gaelic?" she questioned.

"Aye. You once said you would like to learn the language, so I thought I could use this book to help you."

"Is it a grammar book?" she asked.

He grinned. "Actually, it's a book of Gaelic love poems," he said. "I thought it might be more interesting than an ordinary grammar book."

"No doubt, though I'm afraid it might take me a long time to master such a difficult language."

"I have plenty of time," he said quietly.

"Then, I shall do my best." She leafed through the book, looking at the strange foreign-looking words. "By next Christmas I hope to be able to understand a bit more of the worship service!"

"Next Christmas?"

"Yes, I couldn't even sing the hymns this morning."

"Catriona, are you saying you intend to remain at Wolfcrag?" Revan asked.

She met his eyes gravely. "Yes, that is what I am saying. That is, if you still want me."

"Still want you?" He reached down a hand and pulled her onto his lap, the new book slipping unnoticed to the floor. "How can you doubt it?"

Cradling her in his arms, he laid his cheek against hers. "You've no idea how afraid I've been that you would leave, lass."

He turned his head and kissed her, his mouth capturing hers with a passion that quickened her breathing and made her heart beat jerkily.

"I didn't know what I would do if you did try to go," he said against her hair. "I attempted to let you go once before and couldn't, but this time I had promised . . . given my oath . . . and I still wasn't sure I could do it. Thank you for not putting me to the test, lass."

"Thank you for opening my eyes," she whispered, as her

arms went around his neck and she kissed him warmly.

"I am sorry I was so stubborn, Revan. I can't think why I should have fought you so long."

"Ah, but you must admit, some of those fights were quite pleasant, love," he murmured. "And you had good enough reasons . . ."

"But we don't need to go into them again," she said softly. "All of that is in the past, and we are only concerned with right now."

He leaned back in the chair and gave her a solemn look. "Nay, we must be concerned about the future . . . our future."

"What do you mean?"

"I want you to understand my intentions completely, love. I want you to know beyond all doubt just how I feel about you."

"I think I do."

"Oh, I've said I desired you, or that I wanted you, but have I ever told you I loved you? Have I ever given you any indication that my feelings went beyond being captivated by the beauty of your face and your body? Nay, and that is one thing I want straight between us before we go any further."

She met his direct gaze questioningly. He put his large hands on either side of her face, cupping it gently.

"Catriona, I love you, lass. I loved you the first moment I saw you and, I swear by all that's holy, I will never stop loving you—not in this lifetime or the next."

His hard warm lips closed over hers in a sweet, yet searing kiss.

"I love you, too, Revan," she whispered. "So very much."

"I have waited an eternity to hear you say those words," he said.

"I know, and I'm sorry. It has taken me a long time to know my own mind."

"But now you are certain?"

"Oh, yes, completely."

"What about Basil?" he asked quietly.

She shrugged. "I have no feeling for Basil," she said slowly. "I think perhaps I defended him for so long because he was my father's choice for me and I thought that by scorning Basil, somehow I would be scorning my father. The day you took me home I learned a most painful lesson — my father deserved my scorn more than he deserved my obedience. No, Basil is no longer a consideration for me."

"And what about the problem of adultery?"

She lifted a hand to touch the lean cheek. "It is only an ugly word, that is all. I see now the reality lies in what we feel for each other and not what the rest of the world choose to call our love. I am like any other woman — I would prefer to be able to marry the man I love and live honorably with him. But since I cannot, I will not give up everything that makes me happy just for the sake of propriety. If that is wicked, I do not care."

He turned his face to kiss her fingers.

"Catriona, I must be dreaming."

"Why do you say that?"

"I have tried to be patient for so long — something I have never had to be in my lifetime. I didn't think I could go on much longer. I told myself that if you hadn't shown any indication of what was in your mind by Christmas, I would have to force the issue, even if it made you angry and you decided to leave. I had to know — I couldn't go on this way. You haven't given me much to hope for, Catriona, so when I came here to your room tonight, I was determined we would have it out once and for all. Now, suddenly, here you are saying all the things I have dreamed you would say. I keep thinking you are only teasing . . ."

"No, I mean every word I have said."

"You will not change your mind in a month or so?"

"No, I promise. It has taken me a long time to reach this decision, so I am not likely to reconsider so quickly."

"Then there is one more gift I would like to give you," he smiled, reaching into the small pocket sewn into his shirt. He picked up her left hand and placed a ring on the palm, closing her fingers over it. "I know you are not free to legally marry me, love — you may never be. But if we make a pledge between us, it will bind our hearts as surely as any civil ceremony could do."

402

"More surely," she agreed. "I stood in that kirk and gave my life to Basil, without any knowledge of what I was doing. I didn't know what it meant to commit myself to another human being. That is a thing I have learned here at Wolfcrag. Now I understand how it should be."

She opened her fingers and picked up the ring he had placed there. It was a circlet of tiny Scottish thistles fashioned of old gold.

"It is lovely, Revan."

"Just as you thought of me when you saw the watch with the wolves on it, so I thought of you when I saw this. I wasn't sure I would ever have an opportunity to present it to you, but I had to purchase it. You may recall that I have always thought you similar to our thistle?"

"Prickly was your word, I believe," she laughed.

" 'Twas not meant as an insult, love," he replied. "I only meant that you are not a prim and delicate flower to be found in some proper garden. Nay, you will flourish in some harsh and unexpected place, under great adversity, if necessary. And though you have startling beauty, you are not without your sting." He caressed her cheek with the back of one hand. "The thing I have always loved best about you, Catriona, is that, though you try your damnedest to be an elegant lady, there is just a wee bit of wildness in you that keeps slipping out."

"And you, Revan—no matter how wild you claim to be, there is just a wee bit of elegance that keeps slipping out! We should make an ideal pair."

"We will, lass, believe me."

He picked up the ring.

"Will you be my wife then, at least in spirit?"

"Yes, I will."

Taking her left hand, he gently slipped the ring onto her third finger, then kissed it.

"I give you my pledge, Catriona—I will stay beside you for the rest of my life, loving you, protecting you, trying in every way to make you happy."

"And I pledge myself to you also, Revan. I want to be with you always and I want to make you happy."

She looked down at her hand where the ring glowed softly in the light from the candles. It was not a stark reminder of reality, as Basil's shining gold ring had been. Instead, it seemed an old and familiar sight, comfortable . . . and comforting.

On bended knee, she reached up her arms to draw him closer and kissed him on the mouth.

"Somehow I truly feel more married at this moment than I did after a kirk ceremony with Basil. I don't think I will feel differently, even if the time comes when we can be legally wed."

"A piece of paper and a priest's blessing will not make me feel any more married either, lass. I have given my pledge and it is forever." He tightened his hold on her. "And you needn't think you will ever get away from me again, my love. I intend to see that you honor your vow to stay by my side."

"You have no need to worry, Revan. I am perfectly content to stay right here with you."

His smile deepened, as did the intent look in his topaz eyes.

"Do you suppose we could do something about this ridiculous separate bedrooms problem?" he asked.

"I suppose we could," Cathryn murmured in reply.

He started to rise from the chair, but she laughed and cried, "Not just yet, Revan! Be patient. Wouldn't you like another glass of wine?"

Before he could answer, she seized the decanter and filled his glass, handing it to him. He took it, clearly aware she was stalling for time. A tiny disappointed frown crossed his brow.

"I won't force you, Catriona. Please, trust me."

"Thank you, Revan." She looked down, demurely, secretly pleased he had misunderstood her motive in keeping him in the chair. "Why don't you remove your shoes and be comfortable?" she suggested.

She could tell by the new expression on his face that he didn't know how to interpret her mood at all. Obediently, he kicked off the leather brogues he wore and settled deeper into the chair.

Cathryn lifted the jeweled dagger from his stocking, removing it from its sheath so that the blade gleamed in the light.

His eyes on her face, Revan said in a low voice, "There was a time I wouldn't have dared sit so calmly while you knelt in front of me with a dagger in your hand."

She flashed her green eyes at him. "That is true enough. Of course, that was before I learned what a soft man you really are."

"Soft?" He arched one thick brow at her, obviously not well pleased with her assessment of his character.

"Yes! Would a cruel and vicious Highland outlaw wear a pair of mismatched kilt stockings just to keep from breaking a little girl's heart?"

He had to laugh, embarrassed. "Oh, that . . ."

"I'm inclined to think you are not the savage villain you would have me believe, Revan MacLinn," she teased.

"Shall I prove you wrong, my love?" he asked dangerously.

Instead of answering, she placed the dirk on the table and began to remove his stockings, causing him even further confusion.

"Cathryn?"

She laid one hand on his bare knee and, as she rose to her feet, let the fingers of her other hand trail up his leg. She pretended not to see the way he flinched or the way he clamped his jaws together, struggling for self-control.

"Will you excuse me for just a moment?" she asked sweetly. "There is something I want to show you."

Before he could answer, she swept out of the bedchamber and into the small dressing room. Revan sighed heavily and stared into the fire, his wine untasted.

A log shifted and settled on the grate, sending a shower of sparks up the chimney. Below, in the Banqueting Hall, the pipes droned on and an occasional shout of laughter could be heard.

Revan carefully set his glass on the table, next to the dangerous-looking dirk, and heaved himself out of the chair, crossing the room to throw open one of the tall leaded glass windows.

The night air was frosty but clear. A draft disturbed the thin layer of snow on the sill, tossing it up into his face and powdering the front of his black hair. He leaned forward to peer down into the darkened courtyard. No one was about— nothing stirred and the only sound was the faint roar of the ocean.

"Revan?" Cathryn's voice came from behind him. "I trust you are not contemplating throwing yourself from that window. 'Tis a long way down, I assure you."

He smiled as he heard the words he had once spoken to her. "Nay, I was just thinking . . ." He shut the window and secured the latch, turning to face her.

She smiled in pleasure as she saw his serious expression alter to one of delighted awe as he took in her appearance.

She stood before him wearing the gown and robe his mother had given her. The clinging silk of the gown bared her arms and shoulders, dipping low over the swell of her breasts and molding itself to her slim hips and legs. The robe of tatted lace both obscured his view and offered tantalizing glimpses of the lovely body beneath. It hung loosely about her, its long sleeves revealing the ivory flesh of her bare arms. She had brushed out her long bronze hair and now it swirled about her hips, glowing brightly in the candlelight.

He caught his breath.

"My God, Catriona, you are beautiful!"

She moved close to him and put her arms about his neck, drawing his dark head down to her own.

As she moved her lips against his firm mouth, she could feel his startled reaction, though she quickly felt his warm hands on her back.

"You look like a bride," he whispered, lips against her ear. "And, lass, my first inclination is to act like a bridegroom."

"Please do," she laughed, kissing him again. "I intended for this to be our wedding night, my love."

He drew back to study her face. "And all this time I thought you were trying to think of some method of politely sending me on my way. I thought you were still reluctant to share my bed."

"I must confess, Revan, your little games of late have done

406

much toward ridding me of reluctance. Now, it seems, I find myself rather . . . eager."

Grasping the sides of his shirt, she began pulling it over his head. As soon as he realized her intent, he aided in the removal of the garment.

"It has been a long time . . ." she whispered, moving her lips over the breadth of his chest in little nibbling kisses.

She could feel the astonished laughter rumble deep inside him. He put one hand under her chin and forced her to look up at him.

"Lass, I warn you, you are playing a dangerous game. If you persist in continuing this wanton display of affection, I won't be responsible for the consequences."

"Consequences?" she murmured, sea-green eyes full of interest.

"Keep goading me on and you may find yourself in that bed over there with a very ardent partner." He put his hands on her shoulders and gave her a little shake. "And, be assured, love, if such a thing happens, I will expect it to continue. If we share a bed now, it has to be for always — for every night the rest of our lives, not just now and then."

"Revan, I pledged myself to you. Did you think I was teasing?"

"Frankly, I don't know what to think of you, lass. I can't be certain what thoughts are lurking behind those beautiful green eyes."

"Then, let me tell you, milord," she whispered huskily. "You may consider me an impatient bride, one who is beginning to wonder when her husband will stop talking and take her to bed."

He pulled her against him roughly and kissed her with fervent passion. Her hands slid down the lean torso to the waistband of his kilt, where they slowly and deliberately unfastened the buckle of the garment, allowing it to drop to the floor at his feet.

"Catriona, you brazen minx," he said against her throat. "Can this be the same little Lowland lassie who once nearly swooned at the sight of my bare knees?"

He lifted her into his arms effortlessly, and she clung to

him, pressing close against his warm skin.

"Nay, it canna be," she replied laughingly. " 'Tis a Highland woman I am now—not a lass you can frighten with one
bold look."

He strode across the room to the curtained bed where he
set her feet on the floor, keeping one arm tight about her
waist. She swayed against him, and he crushed her mouth
with his own.

With his free hand, Revan pulled back the bedcovers,
tossing them to the foot of the big bed. Gently he began
removing her robe, kissing each shoulder as he bared it. His
amber eyes darkened and glowed as he moved them over her
slim body clad only in the revealing nightgown. He cupped
one breast with a large hand, then slowly moved his fingers
downward to her hip, enjoying the silky sensuousness of the
fabric.

He gripped her small waist with both hands and lifted her
into the bed, pressing her back against the plump pillows.
Bending over her, he kissed her eyelids, her ears, her neck.
The loving warmth of his mouth stirred a fiery tenderness
within her, nearly making her frantic in her indecision—she
didn't know whether to cover the strong column of his neck
with feathery kisses or whether to claw at his back in her
urgent need for him to claim her body as his own.

His arrogant mouth on her bared breasts brought a moan
to her lips, and her body seemed to respond as if it had only
been waiting for this moment. Revan gave a short triumphant laugh, but even that did not lessen her pleasure at
surrendering to him.

Realizing her growing impatience, Revan deliberately
slowed the pace. His lips continued their assault on hers, but
softly and with a calculated slowness designed to increase her
desire. His hands moved over her body, stirring her to
frenzy, arousing and teasing her.

As she gave herself up to his lovemaking she felt she was
being consumed by flames, devoured by a passion so intense
it robbed her of reason or propriety. She knew she was no
longer wearing the silk gown, but her sweetly tormented
mind could not remember what had happened to it. The

fierce heat generated by their entwined bodies could have sent it up in flames for all she knew — or cared.

She pressed herself tightly to Revan and urged him to come closer, as close as he could.

"Don't make me beg, Revan," she cried, her hair flying out over the pillows as she turned her head from side to side.

His lean face was mocking as it hovered over her.

"Ah, lass, you don't know how wonderful it feels for me to hear you begging, instead of the other way around! Let me enjoy it just this once."

"All right, you fiend! I'm begging — please, Revan, please love me. Please!"

His laugh was throaty and warm as he gathered her body close within his embrace.

"I love you, Catriona . . . so much."

He lowered himself over her and, with a cry of joy, she wrapped her arms tightly around him and their bodies moved together rhythmically. Her hair twisted around them, binding them together like shining copper bands. The passion between them became an almost tangible thing, filling them and elevating them to new heights of pleasure. They were driven nearly to the edge of sanity before the intensity of their desire exploded into a maelstrom of feelings and emotions, leaving them breathless and spent, clinging to each other like the survivors of some catastrophic shipwreck.

Revan buried his face in her hair, murmuring in Gaelic, and she snuggled against him, stroking his shoulder and back. She knew she would never feel closer to any human being than she now felt to Revan. In that moment she had become, once and for always, mistress of Wolfcrag.

Chapter Twenty-two

The next morning Cathryn was awakened by warm kisses on her throat. She opened sleepy eyes to see the laughing amber ones of Revan MacLinn hovering just above her. His slow smile made her blush as memories of the night they had just spent together came rushing back to her.

"Good morning, love," he said, pulling her into his arms. "Did you sleep well?"

The wicked audacity of his question only increased her embarrassment, and she turned her face away, her chin rising haughtily. He gave a low laugh and followed her lips with his.

Instantly stirred by his ardent mouth, she allowed her own to soften beneath his kiss, and soon her arms crept about his neck, holding him close.

His breath warm against her neck, he whispered, "I have always known that my teasing could make the thistle grow prickly, but now, my love, at last I have succeeded in learning how to make you lose your sting and become a harmless little blossom."

"Oh!" She tried to push away from him. "Will you never stop shaming me?" she cried. But there was a hint of laughter deep within her silvery eyes, and the hands she had placed against his chest were now moving along the muscled ridges of his shoulders, gently massaging.

"I love you, Catriona," he murmured, burying his face in her fragrant hair. "Thank you for a most glorious, though exhausting, wedding night."

"Must it end so soon?" she whispered, snuggling close to him. It pleased her to hear his deep laugh and to see the small flames leap up in his eyes.

At that moment a loud knock sounded at the door and Cathryn groaned.

"Damn!" Revan said fiercely. "Who could that be?"

"It must be one of the serving girls with breakfast," Cathryn said, tossing aside the covers and sliding out of bed. "I'll get my robe."

Under his amused and admiring gaze, she dashed across the room to the wardrobe. Flinging open the door, she pulled out her new velvet dressing gown and slipped into it, tying the sash quickly. Reaching into the wooden chest, she pulled out the borrowed brown robe she had worn so long. As she approached the bed and tossed it to him, the impatient knocking sounded again.

"I'm coming," she called. "Who is it?"

She pulled open the door prepared to dismiss the serving girl she thought to find waiting there, but the words died on her lips.

Darroch pushed her way into the room, her face a mask of fury.

"You conniving bitch!" she said in a low and deadly voice. "You ran to Revan the first chance you got, didn't you?"

"No, I . . ."

"You told him I would leave with Meg if you didn't stay away from him. Don't bother to deny it. You have finally succeeded in turning him against me." The normally low voice was strident and sharply edged with hysteria. "But of course, that is what you have wanted all along."

"That's not true," Cathryn exclaimed.

"Oh, but it is. You tried to ruin my beauty in order to drive him from my bed. You have used any and every means to lure him into yours—now you have even attempted to steal my child from me. If only you knew how very much I despise you!"

The insane hatred blazing out of the dark eyes told Cathryn just how precarious the situation had become.

"Darroch, please listen to me," she said, determined to

411

reason with the angered woman. "I never meant to hurt you . . ."

"You lying Lowland slut! No, I won't listen to you anymore. I don't want to hear anything you have to say. I warned you what would happen if you ran to Revan, and now . . ."

Suddenly, her eyes fell upon the crumpled kilt of MacLinn tartan lying on the floor. Realization dawned as her dark gaze moved across the room toward the bed, coming to rest upon the nightgown and robe so carelessly discarded the night before.

A shrill cry of disbelief ripped from her throat as she raised stricken eyes to meet the furious gaze of Revan MacLinn, just pulling the velvet robe over his naked body.

Cathryn turned away from the pain in Darroch's face, holding cold hands toward the sluggish fire, hoping to warm them.

Darroch, attracted by Cathryn's sudden motion, turned toward her and in the same instant, saw the unsheathed dirk lying on the table before her. In one swift and desperate movement, she seized the dagger and plunged it into Cathryn's unprotected back.

As she fell, Cathryn heard Revan's anguished cry, but waves of pain and darkness closed over her, shutting out everything else.

Revan ran across the room, giving Darroch a shove that sent her sprawling into the corner, the bloody dirk clattering against the hearthstone as she dropped it. He knelt by Cathryn, lifting her gently into his arms.

Bellowing for help, he carried the limp form to the bed where he carefully placed her against the pillows and began easing the robe from her shoulders.

The wound was a jagged tear high on the left shoulder. Seeing the ivory perfection of her skin marred by the injury caused Revan to clench his teeth in helpless fury.

Looking much like an enraged bull, Owen MacIvor burst into the room, sword in hand. He was followed by several other men.

"What is it, lad?" he panted. "What is wrong?"

412

"Darroch has stabbed Cathryn," Revan replied tersely. "Someone get the doctor. Owen, get Darroch out of this room but keep a guard on her until I am finished here."

"Aye, Revan."

His orders were quickly obeyed, but his full attention was on the injured woman before him. Her eyelids fluttered and her breathing was shallow, causing numbing ripples of fear to course up and down his spine.

"Catriona," he whispered, chafing her hands. "Can you hear me, love? Please don't leave me now."

The color had drained from her face, leaving him to dread the worst. He had never felt such fear, but then, he considered, never before had he so much to lose.

Adam MacSween came into the room, swiftly crossing the floor and motioning Revan aside. He made a rapid examination of Cathryn, then turned to the distraught man beside him.

"Pull yourself together, lad. She'll be all right. 'Tis a nasty shoulder wound, but the knife struck bone before it could do any real harm. Her life is not in any danger."

Revan sank down on the edge of the bed, face in his hands.

"Thank God, Adam. I . . . I thought I had finally won Catriona over just to have her taken away from me. I don't think I could have survived that."

The doctor placed a firm hand on Revan's shoulder. "Once I have bandaged the wound, she will be up and about in no time, I promise. She'll suffer a little pain, but the injury should heal quickly."

He bent to pick up the bridal robe and nightgown, entangled with his feet, and tossed them to the younger man. With a twinkle in his eye, he said, "But for the next few days, she may need to keep these *on!*"

One black brow went up. "Do you mean she is to stay in bed?"

Adam laughed. "No, I mean that any undue physical exertion may cause her pain."

"Oh. Well, you may be certain I will keep that in mind."

Revan had called a council in the Great Hall for later in the day and now he stood, surrounded by his kinsmen, preparing to decide Darroch's fate. The defiant woman stood before them, head held high, not in the least repentant. As she had boldly stated, her only regret lay in the fact she had failed to kill Cathryn.

Cathryn herself sat watching the proceedings, with Meg gathered close beside her. The injured shoulder felt stiff and painful beneath the bulky bandage, but her apprehension over the scene before her diminished any discomfort it caused. It would please her to have Darroch's evil influence removed from Wolfcrag, but she was worried about the method Revan would choose. He would have to act carefully, making a wise decision, or the situation could bring disaster down upon his own head. She knew his earlier raging anger had finally quieted once he was certain she was out of danger, but she was still anxious. Darroch could easily goad him into another display of wrath, she realized.

She looked down at the little girl beside her. Other than an unusually serious face, there was no indication of her emotions. Revan had spent a long time with her in the nursery, explaining the circumstances. When he came out, he said, briefly, "She understands."

Cathryn wasn't really certain a child of that age could completely understand why her mother was being sent away, but perhaps a great deal of Meg's stoicism stemmed from years of being ignored and neglected by Darroch.

Revan paced back and forth in front of the fireplace, his lean features creased in a thoughtful frown. Cathryn's loving eyes followed him, but once more, he seemed the stern chieftain, the unyielding and ruthless man who could fill her with unease. He was so different from the laughing, sensually gentle man of the night before.

Dressed in black leather, he was again the Highland outlaw, dispensing his own kind of justice.

"What do you propose to do with the wench?" Owen asked finally.

Revan stopped pacing and ran a distracted hand through

414

his hair.

"I want her out of Wolfcrag."

" 'Twould be simplest to kill her," came a suggestion from a clansman whose light blue eyes chilled Cathryn.

"I don't kill women," Revan said shortly.

"Where will you send her?" another asked.

"I will banish her from this castle, and she may go where she pleases," Revan replied.

"Lad, you can't do that," insisted Owen. "If you let her go, she'll have the law down on you before you know what has happened."

"Mayhap . . ."

"Can we take that chance?" Adam MacSween's voice was quiet, but the others halted their own comments to hear his. "Is there any way you could get her out of the country?"

"Why not toss her into the dungeon and forget her?" came another voice from the back of the crowd.

"I say we kill the bitch. She is a troublemaker . . ."

Revan held up his hand for silence, and the babble of voices ceased.

"I repeat, I will not be responsible for killing a woman. I will send her out with a small escort — they can take her to the far side of Scotland before they release her."

Darroch's voice cut across his. "It doesn't matter where you send me or how long it takes me to get back. I swear, I will come back with enough government troops to pull this castle down around you."

Owen laid a big hand on Revan's shoulder. "She speaks the truth, lad. She won't rest until she destroys you one way or another. You can't afford to let her go."

"I don't want her here . . . even if she is behind bars. I can't take the chance of her hurting Cathryn or Meg, you know that."

Owen's voice was low, but Cathryn still heard his words. "But can you take the chance of her hurting all of us? It could happen, Revan, and you know it."

"Aye, I know." Revan turned away, dropping into a nearby chair. He heaved a weary sigh. "There has to be a way . . ."

"I . . . I have an idea, my lord."

Revan raised his head to see the gatekeeper, MacQueen, standing before him.

"Yes?"

"Give her to me," the man went on. "For my wife. I could take her away from Wolfcrag and promise you she'll cause no more trouble."

"No!" screamed Darroch. "I'd never marry a low-born wretch like you!"

Revan looked from one to the other of them, straightening in his chair, obviously interested. "Go on, MacQueen."

"Give me the money, my lord, and I can take her anywhere you say — to France or Spain, even further. I can see she never returns to bother you or your lady."

"Why would you do this?" Revan asked.

"The woman owes me," MacQueen finally replied. "We made a bargain once, and I found out she never intended to keep her end of it. I'd like to collect on that debt. Besides, I need a wife, and she suits me."

Darroch drew herself up and spat in the stocky man's unshaven face. With a muttered curse, he drew back a brawny arm and struck her across the face. She flew at him in enraged fury, but Revan motioned to two of his men who quickly subdued her.

"What do you think of this idea, Owen?" Revan asked.

The big man grinned. " 'Tis not exactly a love match, but it might work. It would depend on MacQueen's ability to tame the she-devil."

"I'd enjoy the task, you may be certain," MacQueen growled unpleasantly. "I'd keep her by my side day and night, until we're safely out of the country. She'd not bother you again."

Revan looked thoughtfully at the man, considering. "Are you strong enough to control her, I wonder?"

"Aye, I'd be strong enough," MacQueen said. "I'll keep her in chains if I have to."

"All right, men, I want you to tell me what you think of this idea. 'Tis not the best plan, but I won't deny it is tempting."

One by one, each of the MacLinn clansmen gave Revan

416

is opinion of turning Darroch over to MacQueen. Most of them agreed it would be an expedient plan, except for two or three who thought she should be silenced once and for all.

Revan leaned back in his chair, staring into the shadowed recesses of the ceiling. No matter what the others thought, his was the final decision, and they waited quietly to hear what he would have to say.

Cathryn thought the scene was chilling, and she gave thanks she was not the one on trial. Darroch remained silent, but her eyes moved from face to face as if to memorize the features of those who had decided her fate. She looked at Revan longest, her gaze venomous. She then turned her accusing eyes on Cathryn who, with her heart in her throat, refused to be daunted and returned the stare as coolly as she could. Meg looked from one to the other, aware of the deadly animosity, then snuggled closer to Cathryn.

Finally Revan spoke. Rising to his feet, he announced, "I have made a final decision in the matter. Owen, you and six others will escort Darroch and MacQueen to the nearest village. There you are to see that they are married. Pick one man to continue on with MacQueen to Aberdeen and see the two of them safely on board ship for Europe. With two men to guard her, surely she can cause no further mischief."

Darroch shrieked in anger, but Revan didn't even look in her direction.

"MacQueen, I'll have money for you. Can you be ready to leave in two hours' time?"

The other man nodded, pleased with the chief's decision.

"Good. I'll give you each a horse as well as a pack horse. Once you get to Europe, you may go as far as you please. Just don't come back here or let Darroch return. If you do, I will let my men kill you both. Is that understood?"

"Aye. Completely."

"Darroch," Revan said, facing the dark-haired woman for the first time. "You will be locked in your room so you can prepare your belongings for the journey. Before you leave, I will allow you ten minutes with Meg so you may tell her goodbye."

"You can't do this to me, Revan MacLinn!" she burst out.

"I won't marry that man! I won't leave Wolfcrag!"

Revan merely motioned for the men to take her away, but as they half-dragged her from the room, she pointed an accusing finger at Cathryn.

"You! You're to blame for all of this. I hope to God you will pay for what you have done to me!"

When the screaming woman had been taken from the room, Cathryn allowed herself to breathe again, feeling both fear and relief.

As she went to stand beside Revan, Meg still clutching her hand, she heard him say, "I hope we're doing the right thing, Owen."

"Aye, lad, so do I."

Cathryn and Meg stood at the nursery windows watching the small procession as it wound its way through the gates of Wolfcrag and out into the long glen. Owen MacIvor was in the lead, followed by MacQueen, Darroch, and six of the MacLinn men.

Darroch's hands were bound in front of her, and she kept her back ramrod straight, not giving in to the desolation Cathryn knew she must be feeling. Remembering quite clearly what it felt like to be cast out of her home, she couldn't repress a feeling of sympathy for the woman though she realized Darroch would despise her even more for it, if she knew.

Meg had emerged from her final farewell with her mother looking faintly puzzled, and not saddened, as Cathryn had feared.

"Mother told me I should not let you take her place, Cathryn," the child said. "She said you were evil and would try to hurt me. I told her she was wrong, that you were a nice lady . . . and she slapped me!"

"She is only upset because she has to leave you and her home," Cathryn said gently. "She will be sorry for slapping you when she gets over being so angry."

"It isn't right for her to say things that aren't true, is it?" Meg asked, her eyes wide with concern. "She says you have

ewitched Father and you will try to ruin him. That isn't so,
is it?"

"No, it isn't so, Meg. I love your father and you know I
love you. I wouldn't do anything to hurt either of you. You
can trust me, I swear."

"My mother tried to hurt you, didn't she?"

"She was desperately unhappy, Meg. I don't think she
really knew what she was doing."

Meg considered this for a time. "Do you think I will ever
see her again?"

"I don't know, dear, but perhaps . . . someday."

"I don't think she wanted to see me again," Meg stated.
"She wouldn't have slapped me if she was sorry to be leaving
me, would she?"

Cathryn had no answer for the child, so she knelt awk-
wardly, wincing in pain as she moved her shoulder. She put
her arms around the child and held her close.

She felt a gentle hand on her hair and looked up to see
Revan. He carefully drew her up to her feet, then lifted Meg
into his arms. Together, the three of them stood at the
window and watched the riders until they had faded away
into the misty afternoon.

Later that night, shut away in the quiet haven of their
bedchamber, Revan sat in the chair near the fire with
Cathryn leaning against his knee. She was clad in the silk
nightgown, which allowed her freedom for the bandaged
shoulder. Revan was idly pulling the tortoise-shell comb
through her long tresses, watching the firelight play over the
burnished strands.

"Does your shoulder pain you, love?" he asked.

"No, not much."

"I thought the witch had killed you," he muttered. "There I
was, in the same room, and thought I had let her kill you!"

Clumsily, she turned to face him. "Shh, Revan, it was not
your fault. Anyway, Darroch is out of our lives forever, and I
hope we won't have to think about her again."

"Aye, that would be nice. Now she will be MacQueen's

problem."

"I hope he has better luck dealing with her than we have had."

"Come, put them out of your mind. It's late—let's go to bed, shall we?"

With his help, she got to her feet and crossed the room to the bed. Pulling aside the covers, she eased her body into it, turning on her right side to protect the other shoulder. Careful not to jar the bed, Revan climbed in beside her and slipped an arm around her, pulling her close.

Her face against his chest, she began kissing him, letting her lips move upward along his throat to his mouth. He returned the kiss fiercely, then pulled away with a groan.

"We'd best go to sleep, lass."

"To sleep?" she laughed. "Is the honeymoon over so soon?"

"There will be no honeymoon tonight, my love. Doctor's orders."

She raised one shapely brow. "And just what does the doctor have to do with it?"

"He . . . he hinted it would be too painful for you if we attempted to . . . to . . . why are you laughing?"

"How would he know anything about it?" she smiled. "Might I ask what he suggested we do?"

"He suggested we do nothing! Now, just lie there and go to sleep."

"How can I go to sleep when you are so near, Revan? How can I possibly resist you?"

"I seem to recall several nights when I was forced to sleep beside you and resist your charms. If I could do it, so can you."

"But you know I am not as strong as you, my love," she whispered, returning her mouth to his, tracing the outline of his firm lips with her tongue.

"God damn it, Catriona," he gasped. "Stop that!"

Her hand caressed his chest, sliding along his lean ribs to his hip. He shuddered beneath her touch and quickly took her hand in one of his own to still its insistent search.

"Revan, please . . ." she murmured, nibbling at his ear. "You don't intend to make me beg every night, do you?"

420

"Nay, lass, but this is only for your own good."

"Let me be the judge of what is good for me," she pleaded.

"Oh, Catriona, what am I going to do with you?" he groaned.

She smiled sweetly. "Let me tell you," she said, and began whispering in his ear. His deep laugh rang out, and he lay back on the pillows, defeated.

"Have it your own way then, but don't say I didn't warn you!"

He lifted her onto his chest and held her firmly.

"Are you sure, lass?"

She stretched out against the hard, muscled length of the man beneath her.

"Yes, I'm sure," she said. "As sure as I've ever been about anything. Tonight we need a diversion, and I can't think of a more pleasant one."

"Nor can I, love," he said against her hair. "Nor can I."

The days between Christmas and Hogmanay passed quickly, with the mood at the castle considerably lighter since Owen and his men had returned to announce Darroch was legally married to MacQueen and on her way across Scotland to the port city of Aberdeen.

Preparations for the huge feast to be served the last night of the year went on under the supervision of Margaret and Cathryn. Spare rooms had to be cleaned and bedding aired in readiness for overnight guests. Fresh holly and ivy were strewn throughout the castle, the old being preserved for burning on Twelfth Night, according to tradition.

In the kitchen menus were discussed, and bottles of wine brought up from the cellars to be on hand for the Hogmanay dinner. Margaret opened a score of tins to check the Scotch Buns, or Hogmanay cakes, which had been baked a month earlier. These flaky crusts stuffed with raisins, currants and spices were stored in airtight containers until the holiday. As the tins were opened, then re-sealed, the kitchen was filled with a delicious spicy aroma.

Cathryn enjoyed her first experience in being mistress of

the castle, but she was grateful Margaret was there to assist her. Though she had learned much from old Elspeth in the shieling hut, it seemed there was much more she would have to know before she could manage Wolfcrag on her own.

She felt fortunate the servants appeared to respect and even like her. They obeyed her orders readily, and she encountered no resentment. Margaret had taught her enough Gaelic commands to enable her to communicate with everyone and, because she was willing to do this, the Highlanders accepted her authority, no longer thinking of her as a stranger.

Meg had seemed overly solemn for a few days after Darroch's departure, but she soon regained her normally happy disposition. Cathryn still gave her lessons each day, and the continuation of the regular routine seemed to help stabilize the little girl, giving her a feeling of security. After all, Cathryn reasoned, Darroch had not been that much a part of her life anyway.

The most important change in Cathryn's life was her relationship with Revan MacLinn. Having allowed herself to accept and even return his love, she felt she could never bear to be parted from him again. She marveled over this feeling a great deal of the time. Sometimes, in the middle of a household task, she would lose herself in thoughts of her early days at Wolfcrag. At the time it had seemed so important she not give in to the Highlander, but in truth, looking back, she could no longer determine just when it had been that she had decided she didn't really hate him. Her treacherous emotions had betrayed her somehow and, little by little, he had won her over.

Sometimes it rankled that she should be so besotted with the man, but it seemed there was little she could do about it. One glance from his caressing golden eyes or one touch of his hard, tanned hands, and she had no will of her own. In truth, she was unable to imagine how she had arrived at this state of being. If some instinct had warned her that, if she ever surrendered herself to this outlaw, she would be his slave for the rest of her life, she had failed to listen. And now the time was past when she might have helped herself. She

hought of the past week, of the times she had awakened in a
room filled with winter's chill, snuggled warm against his
broad back—or the times they had lain awake whispering
and laughing half the night, and knew she must admit she
was a most willing slave.

Cathryn's wound had started healing nicely and gave her
very little pain. Late in the afternoon before the Hogmanay
feast, Doctor MacSween came to her bedchamber to exam-
ne her shoulder and change the dressing. Revan accompa-
nied him and, as they entered the room, Adam was saying,
"The courtyard is swarming with guests, Revan. I swear, I
don't know where they all came from, or how you intend to
feed them all."

"Aye, the weather held so all the invited will no doubt be
in attendance. Hogmanay makes a nice break in the long
winter months."

"I saw old man MacRae and his sons belowstairs. It has
been an age since they ventured out so far."

Adam greeted Cathryn and asked her to sit on the edge of
the bed so he could look at the shoulder.

While Adam cut away the bandage, Revan hovered nearby, anxious to get a look at the knife wound. Cathryn had
assured him she felt fine, that she rarely suffered any pain
from it, but he would not rest until he had seen for himself.

"How does it look?" he asked anxiously.

Adam smiled broadly. "It's healing very nicely, very nicely
indeed."

Revan stepped closer and was relieved to see a small, clean
wound. There was no swelling or festering at the edges.

"Cathryn, I'm amazed at the condition of this injury. It is
healing much faster than I'd expected," Doctor MacSween
said, preparing a new bandage for it. "I think a much
smaller dressing will do. I'm certain that will please you.
Twill be much easier to conceal beneath an evening gown."

"Yes, that will be nice." Cathryn looked up to catch
Revan's gaze, and casually stated, a devilish gleam in her
green eyes, "I expect Revan deserves the credit for the wound
healing so quickly."

"Hmmm?" muttered the doctor, busy with his strips of

423

gauze. "Why is that?"

"Why, he insisted that vigorous . . . exercise was the best thing for an injury of this sort. He saw to it that I engaged in just such exercise immediately."

Adam MacSween paused in his work to look up, a half amused, half-angry look on his face.

"Aye, I'll just wager he did!"

Revan's face reddened and he gave Cathryn a threatening look. "Doc, the lass is . . ."

"Whatever your method of treatment, lad, it doesn't seem to have hurt the girl."

"But, I . . ."

"I'd advise, in fact, that you keep it up. Someday, when have a bit more time, I'd like to hear more about this . . vigorous exercise of yours." He shut the leather bag he carried, gave Cathryn a broad wink, and left the room chuckling.

"See you at dinner," he called out as he went down the hall

Slamming the door shut, Revan turned on Cathryn and gripped her waist in his hands.

"You little vixen!" he cried. "Will you never learn respect for your chieftain? You'll pay for this!"

"For what?" she asked innocently.

"For lying to Adam like that. We both know you were the one who pursued me!"

He pulled her closer and captured her mouth in a bold and stirring kiss.

"Is this how you plan to exact your payment?"

"Can you think of a better way?"

"No," she whispered laughingly, "but there's no time now I'm afraid my punishment will have to wait."

His face was stern as he claimed one more kiss. "Just don't think I will forget about it," he warned, his topaz eyes glowing.

Her mouth against his, she murmured, "Nay, don't think I'll let you forget!"

The Great Hall and Banqueting Hall were filled to

overflowing with guests. It was a boisterous crowd, with conversations being carried on in shouts. Vast amounts of food had been consumed, and the servants were kept busy running back and forth to the cellars, bringing up more wine.

Cathryn thought the toasts would go on forever, and she carefully concealed a yawn behind one slim hand. There were simply too many people for the banquet to have been of manageable proportions. She much preferred the smaller group present for the Christmas dinner. She hoped Revan would be in favor of greatly reducing the guest list for next year's Hogmanay feast and, from the look on his face as his eyes met hers, she somehow felt he would.

The most pleasant part of the evening was when the harpists entertained them with a few ballads before the dancing began. Recognizing the strains of the Jacobite tune she had admired at her first banquet at Wolfcrag, she turned to Revan and said, "They say this song always brings tears to the eyes of Bonnie Prince Charlie."

His mouth lifted in a smile. "Aye, so they say."

"It is haunting, isn't it? Will you teach me the words someday?"

"Best let Meg do that, love. I sing like . . . like a howling wolf."

She giggled. "How very appropriate! But, aren't you proud of me, wanting to learn a Jacobite air?"

"Indeed I am. It would seem I will make a Jacobite of you yet."

"Sir, you seem very sure of yourself where I am concerned," she said, her chin raising.

"And why wouldn't I be, madam?" he answered in a low voice. "You throw yourself at me day and night. It would seem I have only to ask and you comply."

"Oh?" The candlelight made little stars in her sea-green eyes and cast a soft glow about her bronzed hair.

"Can you deny it, love?"

"If you are saying I will do anything you say, then yes, I deny it!" She tried to look stern, but the corners of her soft mouth insisted on turning up.

425

"Shall we wager?" he challenged.

"Yes, let's do," she agreed. "What shall the wager be?"

He looked thoughtful for a long moment, his intense gaze warm on her face.

"I'll wager that I can make you obey my slightest command within thirty minutes after we retire to our bedchamber. If not, I promise to take you on a trip to Edinburgh next spring."

"And if you are the victor?"

"Ah, if I am the victor, I ask only that you be my slave for one short week, staying at my side and obeying my every order." He leaned closer and murmured, "I would expect absolute obedience in everything. *Everything.*"

"You will never win this bet, my dear sir," she said haughtily. "Therefore, I need not concern myself with your conditions."

"As you wish. Do we have a wager or not?"

"Let me understand this. All I have to do is resist your manly charms for thirty minutes, and I win the wager?"

"Aye, that is all."

"I have had much practice in disobeying you, Revan. This should be quite simple for me. I fear your rashness will cost you a trip to Edinburgh."

"That, love, remains to be seen."

"Yes, it does. The wager is on."

He leaned back in his chair, a satisfied look on his face. "I am going to enjoy proving to you how weak-willed you are where I am concerned."

"You really are an arrogant, conceited brute, Revan!"

"I believe you have mentioned that before," he laughed.

Terrible confusion reigned in the hall as the dining tables were pushed aside to allow room for dancing. As the pipers took their place in the Pipers' Gallery and began the noisy business of preparing their instruments to play, Revan leaned close and said, "Shall we slip away, Catriona? I have no great desire to dance. With all these people crushed into one room, it will seem more like a stampede."

"Yes, let's go somewhere quieter," she agreed.

Just as she approached the staircase to the upper floor,

Revan swooped her up and gently tossed her over his shoulder.

"What do you think you are doing?" she cried.

"We once left a dance like this, don't you remember?"

"How could I forget?" she wailed.

" 'Twas a most pleasant night," he recalled. "I just got the urge to repeat it all."

It strained her sore shoulder to pound on his back and since no one in the clamorous crowd below seemed to have noticed their unusual departure, she gave in and let him carry her to the bedchamber. At the door he set her down and drew out his new watch.

"Shall we begin the wager, Catriona?" he asked with a gleam in his eye.

"Whenever you say."

She pushed past him and entered the room. A small fire burned on the hearth, giving the room a cozy, welcoming air. Revan came up behind her and wrapped his arms around her waist, kissing her neck.

"Turn around and kiss me, love," he said softly.

She turned in his arms and lifted her hands to his shoulders. Leaning close to him, she smiled. "Did you really think you would win the bet so easily, Revan MacLinn?"

She twisted away and moved to the fireplace. Relentlessly, he followed. He took her hand and began to kiss it, letting his mouth move up her bare arm to her throat. He drew her carefully into his embrace and covered her lips with his. The kiss was deep and searching, causing her to clutch his arms to keep from falling. Inside, a flame began to burn, threatening her reason. After a moment, she pulled away from him and loosened her hold on his jacket sleeves.

"Kiss me again, love," he suggested, moving his mouth closer. She kept her eyes on his lips, but resisted temptation.

"No," she responded. "I . . . I don't care to . . . kiss you anymore."

He moved his mouth downward, along her cheek and jawline, down the length of her throat and to the hollow between her breasts. His lean hands stroked the velvet fabric where it covered her breasts, moving down to her narrow

427

waist. He pulled her closer.

"Kiss me, Catriona. You know you want to."

She pushed him away and moved across the room.

He drew out the watch again and checked the time. "There is still ample time left, love. I'll put the watch here so you can see the minutes slowly ticking away."

He put the watch on the little table near the bed. He himself began removing his jacket, his eyes never leaving hers. The silver buttons gleamed as he tossed the coat into a chair. Next he kicked off his shoes and knelt to remove his stockings. Cathryn watched as he undid the lace jabot at his collar, opening the shirt to reveal his hairy chest.

"Come here, lass," he said in an inviting tone.

She laughed harshly. "Never! This is only a silly wager, but I intend to win it."

"Why not give in now? Is it so important to win?"

" 'Tis the principle of the thing! I dislike knowing you think you have only to snap your fingers and I will come running," she exclaimed, aware she had been thinking the same thing all week.

An idea occurred to her as she watched him turn away to pull off his shirt. Sidling toward the desk, she opened the top drawer and drew out a key.

Quickly she crossed the room, throwing open the door. Revan turned in surprise, clad only in his kilt.

"Oh, no, you don't, lass," he shouted. "You cannot leave this room!"

"But now, if I stay, you will deem it obedience to your command," she said, "so you leave me no choice. I have to go."

"Catriona!" He followed her into the hallway. "I'm not trying to trick you. I am only saying you must stay inside the bedchamber until the thirty minutes is up."

"If you tell me not to go back inside the bedroom, I will," she said. "But I will not be tricked into obeying you."

He rolled his eyes heavenward. "You are right. This was a silly wager. I must be daft these days, playing games like a lovesick boy! All right, Catriona," he said wearily, "don't go back into your bedroom."

She darted back inside the door immediately, slamming it and thrusting the key into the lock in one swift motion. When he realized what had happened, Revan cursed loudly.

"Damn it, Cathryn, open this door!"

"I can't, Revan, for I intend to win this wager!"

"You can't leave me out here, half-dressed. Open this door!" His voice thundered and for a moment, she wondered if he was really getting angry.

She leaned against the door and heaved a sigh of relief. Had she remained in this room under his influence any longer, she was certain she would have succumbed. Wager or not, pride or not, she would have thrown caution to the winds and let herself enjoy his kisses.

"Do you hear me? Open this damned door before I kick it down!"

She stifled a laugh, but he heard it and roared with rage.

"I see nothing amusing about this! You are not playing fair and well you know it."

"Time is running out, Revan," she reminded him.

He didn't answer and his silence intrigued her more than his shouts had. She wondered if he still stood outside the door.

Suddenly, she could imagine him standing in the hallway, arms crossed across his chest, legs strong and bare below the swinging kilt. She thought of the golden fires she could ignite within the depths of his eyes—of his sensuous mouth that could be sweetly gentle or masterfully firm—of the thick dark hair in which she loved to entwine her fingers, guiding his mouth upon her own. In a moment of weakness, she leaned against the door and remembered his strong arms around her, his wicked hands moving against her skin.

Taking a deep breath, she whirled and unlocked the door. He was still there and, as he sprang into the room, she went into his arms.

"Revan, I'm sorry I cheated. I forfeit the wager."

"Love," he whispered laughingly against her lips, "you need only have waited a few more minutes, and you would have won."

"I know, but I just couldn't do it. I find I am unable to

429

deny you anything. To deny you is to deny myself, my love. And as for being your slave, I already am. One week more or less will make no difference."

He rested his face against her hair. "Had you no desire to see Edinburgh?"

"Yes, a little. But, in truth, I would rather be with you."

He smiled down into her face, then lifted her into his arms. "It doesn't matter, love. I intend to travel to Edinburgh next spring anyway, and wherever I go, I always take my slaves."

A noise just outside the door awakened Cathryn. She sat up, reaching out a hand for Revan, only to discover he was no longer in the bed beside her. She pulled the covers up around her chin and peered into the shadows of the room, searching for him.

Slowly, the door opened and a tall figure carrying a tray on which stood a lighted candle came into the bedchamber.

"Revan?" she asked, uncertainly.

"Aye," came his familiar voice. "Happy New Year to you, lass."

She gave a small relieved laugh. "What are you doing?"

"Have you never heard of the fine old Scottish custom of first-footing?"

"Of course I've heard of it," she replied. "Is it past midnight?"

"Just past. I wanted to be the first person to walk through your doorway in the new year. A dark-haired man bringing whiskey and oatcakes signifies the best fortune of all, they say."

"And you got up in the middle of the night just for this?"

"Aye, I couldn't leave it to chance, could I? If I had, no doubt we would have been favored with an early morning visit from MacIvor, and you know that redheads bring bad luck."

"I never thought you to be so superstitious, Revan," she commented, a twinkle in her eyes.

He placed the candle on the bedside table and, shrugging

out of the robe he wore, got back beneath the covers with her, carefully balancing the tray he carried. It contained a decanter of whiskey, two small glasses and a plate of oatcakes.

"All Gaels are superstitious, Catriona. 'Tis in the blood and can't be helped!"

"I see," she said, her expression warming as she studied his handsome face. "Then I shall indulge your whims at all times."

"You see? My first stroke of good luck." He leaned forward to place a soft kiss on her lips. "Now, shall we have a dram?"

He poured out two measures of the whiskey and handed a glass to her.

Lifting his own glass, he murmured, "To *auld lang syne,* my love."

Cathryn touched the rim of her glass to his and said, "And to all the good times to come."

They sipped the fiery whiskey slowly. Cathryn's eyes, emerald in the dim light, met his.

"What are you thinking, Revan?"

"Of the first time we drank Highland whiskey together. Do you remember?"

"How could I forget! You offered me your flask and I expected water. I nearly choked!" She picked up an oatcake and began to nibble it, striving to hide her discomfiture. It still embarrassed her to recall her arrival at Wolfcrag as a captive, clad only in her nightgown.

"You were so fierce and angry, pacing back and forth in front of that campfire, providing Owen and myself with such a lovely view."

"Will you never let me forget that awful night?" she cried. "I was frightened and cold and . . ."

"Stubborn," he put in. "Don't neglect to add that. You soon got over being frightened and cold, but I've begun to doubt you'll ever entirely give up being stubborn."

"Perhaps it is in my blood, just as you claim superstition is in yours," she said, tossing her head.

White teeth gleamed behind the dark beard and his amber eyes were appraising. "Mayhap. And if that is so, I cannot

431

fault you, for your blood is responsible for several other traits I greatly enjoy."

"Oh?"

He set aside his glass of whiskey and, taking Cathryn's from her, put it beside his on the table.

Placing warm hands on her shoulders, he murmured, "Aye, your blood is full of passion . . . and fire . . ."

He pressed against her, bringing his bold mouth down on hers in a kiss laced with the heady taste of Highland whiskey.

When she pulled away, she laughed. "Revan, you've crushed the oatcake! Now the bed will be full of crumbs."

His lips grazed her ear. "I don't mind if you don't."

Her laugh caught in her throat as she raised wide green eyes to his.

"Blow out the candle, my love," she whispered.

Chapter Twenty-Three

Most of the Hogmanay guests were already gone by mid-morning when Revan and Cathryn arose. Looking down into the courtyard from the bedroom windows, Cathryn watched the huge gates close behind one of the last groups to depart.

"Let's not invite so many guests next year, Revan," she suggested. "I think the smaller banquet we gave at Christmas was much nicer, don't you?"

He came up behind her and put his arms around her waist. "Aye, you're right. But, no matter how many guests we have at Wolfcrag for New Year's, I think you and I should always celebrate just as we did last night."

She gave a gentle laugh. "I agree. It was a perfectly lovely evening."

He lifted the heavy fall of bronze hair to place a kiss at the nape of her neck, giving a deep sigh.

"I had better go to my own chamber to dress, love."

"Yes, and I should go downstairs. I am certain there is much to be done this morning."

"Later, when we have the time, I think we should move your things back to my room, don't you?"

She turned in his arms and swept the room with a warm glance. "Yes, if you wish, though I have been happy here in this room. I have even become quite tolerant of Bonnie Prince Charlie."

"We could stay here, if you prefer," he said.

"No, your room is larger, and you are more accustomed to

it. Besides, I . . . I have other plans for this room, Revan."

"Plans?"

"Yes, you see . . ."

At that moment they heard the ring of booted feet running in the corridor, followed by a mighty pounding on the door.

Revan strode across the room to open it.

"Owen? What the hell is going on?"

"Something's amiss at the fishing village, Revan. We can see smoke."

Another man wearing MacLinn tartan burst into the room behind Owen, panting for breath.

"The MacRae and his sons just rode back to tell us the village is being attacked. They heard gunfire."

"Oh, no!" cried Cathryn. "What is happening?"

"Owen, alert the rest of the men," ordered Revan. "Rouse everyone in the castle and get the women and children into the Great Hall, just in case there is trouble later. Cathryn, come with me."

As he dressed, Revan told Cathryn what he expected her to do in his absence.

"I don't know what is going on or how long we will be away, Catriona, but your main concern must be your own safety and that of Meg and my mother. Stay with them until I come back. All the women and children will be gathered inside the castle, and it will be up to you to see to their needs, should we be gone any length of time. The most difficult part will be to calm their fears, I'm afraid."

He pulled on his boots and grabbed up a woolen plaid.

"I'm not certain I can deal with my own fears, Revan," she whispered, ashamed to show her cowardice but compelled to say what she felt.

He placed his warm hands over hers. "You are a Highland woman now, lass." His admiring gaze moved over her face. "Nay, in your heart I think you have always been a Highland woman. You are braver and stronger than you know. Don't let your love for me weaken you now."

"I would die if anything should happen to you, Revan. How can I be brave knowing that?"

"You will be, love. You don't have it in you to be a

434

coward. And nothing is going to happen to me, I promise."

Her throat tight with fear, she leaned against him.

"I must go, Catriona. I will give orders the gates are only to be opened upon our return. Everyone inside the castle should be safe, but take no chances."

"I understand," she said, moving away from him and hugging herself against the sudden chill she felt. "What do you think is happening in the village?"

"I have no idea," Revan said grimly, "but I intend to find out."

She followed him down the stairs into the Great Hall, where general confusion reigned. The front doors were ajar, spilling cold air into the room. From outside came the sounds of horses stamping impatiently, the clink of bits and creak of leather, and the hollow sound of boots on the cobblestones.

Inside the hall men were rushing to and fro, taking weapons down from the walls or sliding deadly-looking swords into the sheaths strapped at their sides. They were preparing for a possible battle, and an atmosphere of repressed excitement permeated the room. It was as if the very stones of the castle stirred in response to the ancient call to arms.

Damn these Highlanders, Cathryn raged silently, miserably. They welcome danger.

Her eyes moved over the room, seeing other women milling about, their children in tow, searching out their men for reassurance. It was a disquieting scene and one she had not previously witnessed at Wolfcrag.

Revan strode into the mass of people, immediately commanding their attention. He was dressed in black with the bold MacLinn plaid thrown across one wide shoulder. Standing head and shoulders above most of the men in the room, he was a target for all eyes. He gave concise orders to his clansmen, and they began an orderly exit from the castle. With a softening of his expression, he then assured the women they would soon return with news of the neighboring village.

When he finished speaking, his amber eyes sought

435

Cathryn, and he rapidly crossed the floor to where she stood, enveloping her in a last fierce embrace.

"I'll be back soon, lass," he murmured.

"Revan, please be careful," she pleaded.

"I will." His kiss was sudden and hard. "I love you, Catriona."

Then he was gone, the plaid billowing out behind him as he moved from the room.

Cathryn turned away, dismayed by the fear that gripped her. Somehow she knew something was terribly wrong and Revan was in grave danger. A knot formed in the pit of her stomach, twisting tighter. At this moment she hated the role she had to play. How much better it would be to ride out into the thick of battle than to stay behind, waiting patiently to see if everything she loved in life was to be snatched away from her.

She started up the stairway, needing time to compose herself. Perhaps if she returned to her room to dress, the mundane activity would ease her mind.

In her bedchamber, she hurried to the windows in time to catch a last glimpse of Revan, riding at the head of his men, leading them through the huge gates of Wolfcrag and onto the drawbridge. In spite of her dread, her heart lifted at the sight of the gallant red and black of the MacLinn tartan, brilliant against the gray of the winter day. As the last man rode through, the ponderous gates were closed and secured.

Instead of feeling safer, Cathryn suddenly felt trapped. Weakened by an overwhelming sense of helplessness and tormented by vague fears for Revan, she pressed her shaking hands together. Unexpectedly, nausea choked her and for the first time in nearly a week, her morning sickness returned.

The nausea served to remind her of her duties and responsibilities. She dressed quickly, putting on a plain black wool dress and throwing her old shawl around her shoulders. She must find Margaret and Meg and see they were safely settled with the others in the hall below.

Revan's mother and daughter were in the nursery, stand

ing by the long windows where they, too, had watched the departure.

"What is happening?" Margaret asked, her face ashen.

"It seems someone has attacked the fishing village," Cathryn informed her quietly. "Revan and his men have gone to see what is wrong."

"I can think of no reason for anyone to attack the village," Margaret said in surprise.

"Nor can I." She turned to Meg and said, "Why don't you find a shawl to wear and get your puppy so we can go downstairs? Robbie and Ailsa will be there."

When the child had moved out of earshot, Cathryn turned back to Margaret. "I fear it's a trick—I'm so worried about Revan."

"He will surely have considered that possibility, my dear. He has had to deal with much treachery in his lifetime."

"I hate having to wait and wonder," she complained. Suddenly she realized Margaret had been through this before, with devastatingly tragic results. She laid a hand on the older woman's arm. "I'm sorry," she apologized. "I won't whine anymore. I am going to try to be . . . brave. I'm not sure I can do it, but I am going to try."

Margaret smiled softly. "Revan would be very proud of you, my dear."

When they had returned to the Great Hall, Cathryn set about organizing the people left under her care. Taking the children into the Banqueting Hall, she set them to playing games under the supervision of some of the older girls. She sent a group of women into the kitchen to carry out supplies for the midday meal. They would all dine together, she declared, thinking it might serve to keep their minds off the possibilities of what might be occurring in the little fishing village.

Having made the elderly people comfortable near the fire, Cathryn started toward the kitchen to see about making a quantity of tea. Suddenly Della MacSween burst into the hall amid a blast of frigid air.

"Cathryn! Help me bar this door!"

"What's wrong?"

Della didn't speak until the door was latched and bolted. Then, breathlessly, she said, "They've opened the gates! Troops are coming in!"

"Who opened the gates?" Cathryn asked.

"I don't know who they are, but they're not MacLinns. Our men . . ." She swallowed hard, forcing herself to go on. "I saw their bodies, Cathryn. The men Revan left guarding the gates have all been slain."

"Do you mean to say the castle has been invaded?" Cathryn asked, shocked.

Della bobbed her head up and down. "Government troops . . ."

"It doesn't matter who they are," Cathryn said calmly. "What can we do to protect ourselves?"

"We have no choice," one woman wailed. "We must stay here and pray our men will get back in time to save us."

"No!" Della shouted. "They'll batter down this door. It will never hold."

"My God, what should we do?" someone exclaimed. "We'll all be killed."

"Hush that kind of talk!" Cathryn snapped. Looking about her, she spied a wooden bench and, climbing onto it, waved her arms above her head. "Silence! Listen to me, everyone!"

The nervous babble of voices died. "Wolfcrag is being invaded . . ." Cries of horrified disbelief drowned her voice momentarily, but again she shouted for silence and gradually, the din quieted enough for her to be heard. "If we stay here, the invaders will batter down the door. There is only one place we can go. We will have to hide in the secret tunnel leading down to the beach, and pray that whoever is invading the castle knows nothing of it. Margaret, you open the tunnel and start getting the children into it. Caution them to remain as quiet as they can so we will not give away our hiding place. Hurry now! The rest of us will follow, carrying what food we can. Move as quickly and quietly as possible."

Thinking it another game, the children clambered into the

tunnel eagerly, Margaret trying to discourage their excited chattering. Just as the first of the women started into the tunnel, a crashing blow fell upon the doors in the Great Hall. Cathryn and Della exchanged frightened looks, urging the others to move faster.

Two more earth-shaking blows fell before they were all crowded into the dark, damp passageway. Della and Cathryn ducked inside, but as her hand moved to press the mechanism to close the door, Cathryn had a sudden thought. She couldn't leave Wolfcrag without the Jacobite relics of which the MacLinns were so proud.

"Della, I've got to get something important," she exclaimed, stepping back into the Banqueting Hall. "Close the tunnel and keep the women quiet."

"Are you insane?" Della cried. "You don't have time."

"I'll be careful. I . . . I just can't go without this. If they should break through before I get back, I'll hide somewhere upstairs — in the tower or on the roof. Don't worry!"

Cathryn didn't wait to hear Della's next words. As she dashed through the Great Hall she heard the unmistakable splintering of wood and knew it wouldn't be much longer before the enemy broke through. She flew up the stairs and down the hall to her room. Taking a basket from the bottom of the clothespress, she began packing the relics into it, at a loss as to why she would so foolishly risk her life for things she once held in contempt.

Through her open door she could hear a shuddering crash as the heavy wooden doors below gave way at last. She wouldn't be able to get back to the tunnel now — she would have to seek a hiding place in the upper part of the castle.

Rifling through the wooden chest near the door, she found her embroidery where she had thrown it a few days earlier. She put it in the basket, carefully concealing what lay beneath. She tossed in some skeins of thread, then placed the basket by the chair near the fire. She hoped it would appear to be nothing more interesting than a lady's sewing. Certainly they would never expect her to leave anything of value in plain sight.

Her best hope of remaining undiscovered lay in getting to

439

the next floor, she decided. If she went right to the top of the castle and hid in some seldom-used chamber, perhaps they would tire of the search before they reached her.

She stepped to the high windows and lifted a corner of the drape to look down into the courtyard. It was half-full of men and horses. As she watched, several of the men began tossing lighted torches onto the straw roofs of the stables and cottages lying at the foot of the castle. Fury stabbed through her as she saw the flames leap high, destroying the homes of people she cared about. Two men were driving the animals from the stables, she saw with relief, and fervently hoped no one had been hiding in any of the burning cottages.

Her eyes were drawn to a figure in the center of the melee. Still astride a nervously prancing horse, he was dressed in a MacLinn plaid and, as she stared, he slid from the horse and started toward the front entrance to the castle. The wind gusted around him, whipping the plaid from his head, revealing blowing strands of smoky black hair.

Cathryn gasped. Darroch! How was it possible?

She whirled away from the window, one thought foremost in her mind. Darroch knew about the tunnel and when the soldiers were unable to find anyone in the castle, she would know immediately where they were hidden. Cathryn had to distract her, get her away from the main part of Wolfcrag.

She raced down the corridor, past Revan's room and onto the stairs leading into the Great Hall.

When Darroch walked through the entrance, Cathryn's voice whipped out, "Darroch! May God damn you for the evil witch you are!"

Just for an instant, Darroch's lithe form was rigid, then her head lifted as she searched the dim shadows at the top of the stairs for Cathryn. When she saw her, she started up the steps, menace glinting in her eyes.

"Did you think never to see me again, Cathryn?"

"I had hoped," Cathryn answered. "Are you proud of what you have brought down upon Wolfcrag?" She gestured to the room below where booted men were ripping at the drapes and hacking the furniture with battleaxes and broadswords.

Darroch ignored her gesture, keeping her icy eyes fastened

n Cathryn's face. "I warned you," she said calmly. "I tried to tell Revan what would happen if he forced me to marry that scum."

"Where is MacQueen?" questioned Cathryn, letting Darroch come closer and closer.

"Do you think he could treat me as he pleased and still live?"

"He's . . . dead?"

"Aye, he's dead, and so is the man Revan sent with him. They were fools to think they could best me."

"How did he die?" Cathryn asked quietly.

As Darroch approached her, she stepped slowly away, luring the woman toward Revan's bedchamber. She had to get her behind a closed door and think of some way to detain her.

"I stabbed him while he slept," Darroch stated in a flat, unemotional voice. "He thought he had subdued me so on our wedding night that I would be afraid to resist him. He was a stupid pig! On our second night away from Wolfcrag, we stopped at a small inn and, while he swilled ale, I was fortunate enough to make the acquaintance of some gentlemen. One of them was kind enough to slip me a knife and later, when MacQueen had drunk himself to sleep, I killed him." Her lips twisted in a taut smile. "I had no qualms about slaying him, if that is what you are wondering. I pretended it was you, and this time I made sure it was more than just a wound."

"And the other man?"

"He heard MacQueen cry out, I'm afraid, and came into the room behind me. I simply whirled about and slipped the knife into his heart. Then I went to find the men who had helped me."

Her smile widened as she reached the top of the stairs. "Dear Cathryn, you will never guess just who those men were."

"No, I could not," Cathryn said, her mind frantically grappling with the problem of what to do with Darroch. She had no weapon and couldn't be sure whether or not Darroch carried one.

441

"Look there behind me and see," Darroch invited. Sh[e] stepped aside and Cathryn's heart missed a beat as she sa[w] her father and Basil Calderwood standing at the foot of th[e] stairs. One hand flew to her mouth to stifle a scream. [A] nightmare had closed around her, crippling her ability f[or] rational thought.

"Hello, dear wife," said Basil sarcastically. "Have you n[o] welcome for me?"

"How . . . how did you get here?"

He slipped off his long black gloves as he started up th[e] stairs toward her.

"Your outlaw grew careless in his lust for you, dea[r] Cathryn. My men followed you from the village with ver[y] little trouble. They lost the trail just a few miles from her[e] when your little party seemed to disappear into thin ai[r] leading them to believe there was some hidden entrance [to] the glen. They had succeeded in narrowing our searc[h] considerably, so your father and I rode north to find you — [it] was only a matter of time."

"All this time you have been searching the area for th[e] castle?"

"Yes, and we have found these Highlanders to be [a] damned tight-mouthed bunch. That is, until we met up wit[h] this lovely lady. She had no scruples when it came to tellin[g] us everything we wanted to know. Can you believe th[e] strange coincidence that led us to that small country inn o[n] the very night she spent there, desperately seeking someon[e] who would listen to her tale of woe?"

"No . . ."

" 'Twas no coincidence, dear wife. We have been staying i[n] the villages near here, and it just so happened we wer[e] watching when the lady was escorted into town by me[n] wearing plaids of a tartan very like the one your outlaw wor[e] the night he rescued you. After the reluctant bride was se[nt] on her way with her new husband, we simply followed an[d] arranged to meet up with her. As luck would have it, ou[r] timing was excellent. Had we made her acquaintance befor[e] her wedding night with the brute, I doubt if she would hav[e] been quite so willing to betray her clan . . ."

442

"Then, you gave her the weapon with which to slay her husband?" Cathryn gasped.

"Naturally. In exchange for her freedom, she promised us valuable information about Revan MacLinn."

Cathryn groaned inwardly. It was true then. Basil knew Revan's name—no doubt there was nothing Darroch had failed to tell him.

"What is it you want, Basil?" she asked in a chilled voice.

"It's really very simple. I want the Highlander destroyed."

"And you, Father, what did you come for?" For the first time Cathryn turned her gaze on her father. He had difficulty meeting her eyes.

"I'll take you back home, if you want to go," he muttered.

"I don't," she said flatly. "This is my home now."

"What do you think will be left of this place when these men have finished with it?" Basil asked, his voice amused.

"We can re-build it," Cathryn said defiantly.

"And who is we?" Darroch laughed.

"Revan and myself," she answered, throwing back her head.

"Oh, my dear, you just don't understand," drawled Basil. "Your lover won't be coming back to you. Why, at this very moment he is probably lying dead somewhere along the road."

"No! That isn't true . . . I don't believe you!"

"When we enlisted the help of the government troops, Cathryn, their first requirement was the death of Revan MacLinn and the destruction of his stronghold. With Darroch's help, they devised a nearly foolproof plan to dispose of him."

Cathryn whirled on Darroch. "You told them about the fishing village? It was a trap?"

"Clever, wouldn't you say? I knew Revan would dash right off to aid his people. Once Revan was lured outside Wolfcrag, it was a simple thing to surround him with soldiers."

Cathryn longed to claw the smug look off Darroch's face. Her throat filled with such hatred she was barely able to get out her next words.

"How were you able to get inside Wolfcrag?"

"It could never have been done without the help of someone familiar with the routine," Basil smiled. His small black eyes swung toward Darroch.

"It was an easy matter to slip five or six men in with the guests arriving for Hogmanay," Darroch explained. "There were so many passing through the gates these last two days, a few extra weren't even noticed. I told them where to hide out until this morning. Then, when Revan and his men had ridden away, all they had to do was overpower the guards on the gates and open the castle to us."

"Treachery of the worst kind," Cathryn spat out. "Oh, Darroch, how could you? Look what you have caused!"

"Don't blame me, you whoring slut," Darroch snarled. "You are the one who brought disaster to Wolfcrag. You are the one who destroyed Revan."

"You're lying!" Cathryn shouted.

"No, you know it's true. From the first moment you came here things were different. You bewitched Revan with your harlot's ways, making him grow careless. You're the one who really killed him."

"He's not dead," Cathryn cried, covering her ears with her hands. "I know he's not dead."

"Let me assure you, Cathryn," Basil said smoothly, "if Revan isn't dead, he soon will be. Whether he is shot today or hanged tomorrow, 'tis all the same. He is a doomed man."

"I refuse to believe it," she said stubbornly.

"Believe what you like," he replied, "but know this—my revenge against the man has been very, very sweet. I have enjoyed seeing his home destroyed, and I will enjoy seeing his broken body when they bring it in. That only leaves one more thing for me to savor—my revenge upon you."

"What do you mean?"

"I have decided to take you back with me as my wife."

"I won't go," she said angrily. "You can't make me."

Darroch shoved in between Basil and Cathryn, her eyes dangerous. "What is this, Calderwood? She belongs to me, remember? You vowed to let me kill her if I led you to Revan MacLinn."

444

"I've changed my mind," he said coldly.

"You can't do that! I'm going to kill her . . ."

"I'm beginning to tire of your harping, woman," Basil snapped. "Get out of my way. She is my wife, and I intend to claim a husband's rights before I take her with me."

"Now wait a minute, Calderwood." Cathryn's father spoke suddenly, clearly not pleased with the turn of events. "You said Cathryn could go with me. I can't let you go back on your word."

"I'll do what I please, old man, and you can't stop me. And for your information, I fully intended to let this bitch kill her. But after seeing her again, I can't see any reason why she shouldn't act the part of the loving wife for a while. We can travel abroad for a time—you may be certain I won't take her back to our village. When I tire of her . . . charms, shall I say? . . . she can come to you or go wherever she pleases."

"I'll not have it," thundered Hugh Campbell. "You've seen the outlaw ruined—there's no need to harm Cathryn."

"Quite a change of heart for you, Campbell," Basil sneered. "Since when has it been wrong for a husband to bed his own wife?"

"I will never go with you, Basil," Cathryn spoke up. "No matter what."

"You've nothing to say about it," he responded in clipped tones. "Just stay out of this."

"I won't. It's my fate we're talking about. I have a right to say what I will or will not . . ."

He struck her viciously with the back of one hand, causing her to reel against the closed door behind her. As her father leaped forward to defend her, Basil drew a pistol from inside his cape and pointed it directly at the man.

"Stay back, Campbell, unless you want to die."

A sharp metallic click told Cathryn Basil's threat was not idle.

"Stay back, Father," she warned. Forcing herself to face Basil's cold eyes, she went on. "I cannot believe Basil will still want me as his wife when I tell him I am to have Revan MacLinn's child."

445

Her chin went up and she met his wrathful look defiantl

"You are to have the outlaw's babe?" Basil asked, his voic
low, deadly.

At her nod, Darroch pushed forward, a shrill cry eruptin
from her throat.

"No! I'll kill you first!"

Reaching beneath the bright woolen plaid she wore, sh
withdrew a short, sharp dagger. "This time I won't make an
mistakes."

Before she could lunge at Cathryn, Basil turned on he
and gave her a hard push. "I told you to get out of my way
he shouted.

Fighting to regain her balance, Darroch stepped backwar
onto the stairs, her feet tangling in the long plaid. Her arm
flailed the air and a high scream ripped through the castle a
she realized she was falling backward. Cathryn cried ou
then covered her ears against the horrible sound of Darroch
body thudding against each step as it hurtled downward
ending in an awkward sprawl on the hallway floor.

The screams had attracted the soldiers ransacking th
bottom floor of the castle and now they gathered around th
lifeless body. They did not seem especially upset by Dar
roch's violent death and soon lost interest as they swarme
up the staircase to the upper floors.

"We can't find anyone in the castle," one of them said t
Basil. "They have to be hiding somewhere—we'll kee
looking until we find them."

Cathryn couldn't bear to watch the vandals as the
chopped and hacked their way through Wolfcrag. Sh
thought of the nursery and all the lovely books and toys—o
the tapestries in Margaret's room—the beautiful dark pan
elling in the room where she had slept. She wished she ha
the means of killing each one of the looters herself. Sh
clenched her hands at her sides and fought down a rising tid
of nausea.

"What's wrong, my dear? Does it pain you so much to se
your lover's home ruined?"

"Wanton destruction is always painful," she said shortly
"There was no need for this."

Basil waved a careless hand. "It doesn't matter now. What does matter is whether or not you are telling the truth about having MacLinn's baby."

"Of course I'm telling the truth! I'm proud of it, why should I lie?"

He leveled the gun at her. "Perhaps you should have lied, Cathryn. Perhaps it would have saved your life and that of your damned brat. Of course I can't allow my wife to bear another man's bastard . . . I must kill you."

"Wait, Basil," she pleaded. "Please listen to reason . . ."

A cold smile flickered across his thin face.

"I'm sorry, my dear, it's simply too late."

He steadied the hand holding the gun, his intent plainly visible in his cold eyes. Instinctively, Cathryn crossed her arms to protect her baby, her body turning to ice.

"No!" Hugh Campbell flung himself at Basil, knocking the thinner man off balance. Grappling for the pistol, Campbell slammed his stocky body against the other man and they fell. A sudden shot rang down the stone corridor in shocking echoes.

For an instant, neither man moved, then, slowly, Basil Calderwood got to his feet and stood looking at the body on the floor before him. Hugh Campbell was dying, a hole torn in his chest.

"Oh, my God!" Cathryn cried out. "Father!"

She threw herself down beside him, clutching his hand in hers. There was an almost imperceptible tightening of the hand and the brief shadow of a smile on his lips as though he sought to reassure her in the seconds it took him to die.

Cathryn looked up at the tall, thin man standing over her, her eyes full of loathing. "You've killed him."

"He should have stayed out of what didn't concern him," Basil said coldly.

"And let you kill me?" she asked incredulously.

"He was a fool to risk his life. It only means that both of you will die."

"Don't you realize you have already killed two people? What has happened to you—have you lost your mind? Do you intend to go on and on murdering?"

447

He grasped her arm in a claw-like grip, yanking her to her feet. "If it is necessary, Cathryn. Make no mistake — you will die today and your lover's brat with you. But first, I think I will find out just what I missed by having you stolen from our marriage bed."

He pushed open the door to Revan's bedchamber and thrust her inside. She tried to twist away, but he dealt her a stinging blow to the face. She fell to her knees, dizzy and nauseated.

"Get up, you slut. Let me see what you have learned from all these months in the outlaw's bed!" Basil tossed aside the pistol and unfastened his black cape, letting it drop to the floor.

"Never!" she hissed.

He wound one hand in her long hair and snapped her head backward. "Get up, I said."

Tears stinging her eyes, she slowly got to her feet. He released his hold on her hair to spin her around and shove her toward the bed.

Revan's bed, her mind shouted. She'd never lie with this fiend in Revan's bed. Let him kill her first!

"I hate you, Basil," she snarled. "I despise you because you could never be half the man Revan MacLinn is. After being with him, what makes you think I would let you touch me? I'd rather die!"

"Shut up!" he screamed, his features contorted with insane fury. "I will show you I am as good a man as the Highlander."

Hysterical laughter welled up within her throat. "Impossible."

He pushed her down on the bed and she screamed as he began to tear at her clothes. "You dare deny me what you offer freely to any other?"

She struggled against him, her breath coming in ragged gasps.

"You make me sick," she cried. "After Revan, I can't stand the sight of you!"

"Quiet, you adulterous whore. You'd do best to please me — perhaps I will let you live a while longer."

"You may as well kill me now," she muttered. "If Revan is

dead, I don't want to live anyway."

"I'm not ready to slay you yet, dear wife," he cackled. "Not yet . . ."

She turned her head away, gagging as his wet lips closed over her own, sliding along her neck to her breasts, bared by the torn gown.

Just then, an unearthly war cry rang through the room causing Basil to jerk away from her, his eyes full of terror. He turned to see a maddened red-haired giant crashing through the doorway, brandishing a sword. As Basil leaped forward, reaching for the pistol, a look of horrified surprise came over his face as he felt himself impaled. For a moment he seemed to hang on the slender blade, then slowly crumpled to the floor and lay in a widening pool of scarlet blood.

"Owen!" cried Cathryn.

The big man gathered her into his arms, letting her weep against his massive chest. The same huge hands that had just savagely murdered his enemy now stroked her hair tenderly, calming her.

She pulled away from him, suddenly remembering. "There are men all through the castle. It isn't safe."

"I ken, lassie," he replied. "But we have returned in full force now, and it should be a simple thing to rout the bastards. Where are the women and children?"

She smiled wearily. "They're hiding in the secret tunnel. They must be frozen by now, poor things."

He chuckled. "They may be cold, but they're alive. 'Tis the important thing."

"Owen, is Revan here?" she asked anxiously.

The look in his eyes cut right through her heart. He shook his shaggy head.

"Oh, God, please don't tell me he is dead!"

"I . . . I don't know, lass. I don't think so, but I canna be certain."

She clutched his arm. "Tell me what happened," she insisted.

"As soon as we got to the village, we knew the attack was just a trick to lure Revan out of the castle. He decided to draw the main body of the troops away from the village by acting as a decoy." He cocked one thick sandy eyebrow at her. " 'Tis a trick of the wolf, ye know. The male will act as a decoy to lead the enemy away from his lair."

Cathryn's mouth was dry. "Do you mean Revan . . . sacrificed himself to save the others?"

"Nay, lass, that was not his plan — to sacrifice himself. He thought merely to draw them away while we emptied the village. He knew they would follow him. After all, he is the one they really wanted. But he knows this country like no one else, and one man riding alone can cover far more ground than many riding together. He will no doubt lead them on a merry chase through the hills and glens, get them hopelessly lost and confused, then give them the slip. He'll be back at Wolfcrag before you know it."

"Did he know the castle was under attack?" she asked.

"Nay, he had ridden away and knew nothing of it. Those of us who stayed behind made short work of the few troops left to fight us, and we were evacuating the village when we saw the smoke and knew something was wrong."

"Where are the people from the village to go?"

"The men are loading the fishing boats with food and provisions," he answered. "The women and children are on their way here to wait with the rest of us."

"To wait?"

"Aye. We'll have to leave Wolfcrag now. Those bastards destroyed the main gates and jammed the portcullis. We have no way of keeping the enemy out. Our location has been discovered . . ." He shrugged. "We have no choice but to leave."

"Where will we go, Owen?"

"Revan said we'd have to sail into the western isles and find a place there to hide out for a while. He realized that if they knew about the fishing village, they knew the location of Wolfcrag. He gave orders for us to ready the fishing boats and sail them into the cove behind the castle. We will transport the entire clan to the islands and . . . start all over again."

"Will we have to wait long for Revan?"

"He said to leave without him if he wasn't back here within

450

two days' time."

"If he isn't here by then, will it mean . . . something has happened to him?"

"Aye, most likely. But he'll be here, lass, he'll be here."

"I hope so," she said in a tired voice, "because I won't leave without him."

Within an hour, the soldiers had been driven from the castle. The MacLinn men, driven by fear for their wives and children and rage at the sight of what had been done to their homes, fought like they were possessed by demons. Frustrated by the lack of a significant battle at the fishing village because the main body of soldiers had ridden in pursuit of their chieftain, they swept through Wolfcrag like a tide of fury, driving out the attackers with little mercy.

Now, suddenly, there was much to be done and no one to take charge but Owen. His first action was to release the women and children from their hiding place, bringing them back inside the castle to warm themselves and to start preparations for their exodus. He designated people to search the kitchen and cellars for food supplies, and others to comb the bedchambers for warm clothing or salvageable items to take with them.

Guards were set to watch for a return of the troops; they could no longer close the gates or portcullis, or even raise the drawbridge, because the machinery had been smashed beyond repair. Owen instructed the guards to set fire to the wooden bridge the minute they saw any strangers approaching the castle. With no way to cross the chasm that lay along the front edge of Wolfcrag, entry would be denied. They agreed to delay the burning until necessary, in the event Revan might return.

The bodies of those killed in the skirmish were carried to the chasm and hurled over the edge. There was no time for burial for it would take hours and valuable manpower to hack through the frozen earth.

Owen himself dragged Basil Calderwood's gaunt body out of the castle, feeling a savage satisfaction in the act. With a booted foot, he rolled the body over the edge and experienced no remorse. Somehow he felt he had evened the score between himself and the Campbells and repaid Revan a debt long owed.

He took Della MacSween up to Cathryn, dismayed by her pallor and the way her eyes seemed to stare without seeing anything. When he had asked if she would like her father given a special burial, she had merely shaken her head and said, "No, Owen, it isn't important. He won't care now and you haven't the time." She looked up at him, tears sliding down her face. "He tried to save my life, did you know that?"

The big man laid a gentle hand on her shoulder. "No doubt he regretted what happened before, lass. Mayhap he only came with Basil to protect you and make up for the wrong he'd done."

"I'd like to think so," she agreed softly.

"Cathryn," Della said, "why don't you come with me now? You need to wash yourself and change clothes."

Cathryn nodded wearily, passing a trembling hand over her face.

"I just can't believe all that has happened today . . . such destruction and hatred."

"Don't think of it now, lass," Della soothed her. "You need to rest, for the baby's sake."

Owen's shaggy eyebrows moved upward in surprise, but he said nothing.

"Yes, my poor baby," she laughed hollowly. "How will all this horror and violence affect him?"

"Don't worry over it, Cathryn. The bairn is the child of the MacLinn — centuries of violence are already in his blood. 'Twill only make him a strong, bold child." Della put an arm around her friend, leading her to the door of the bedchamber.

"I hope you are right," Cathryn murmured. She turned back to Owen. "Margaret and Meg? Are they all right?"

"Aye, they're fine. Worried about you, though. I will go down and tell them you are well."

"Have the people from the fishing village arrived yet?"

"Aye, they're here. Some came on horseback, some on

452

oot. They're cold and weary, but at least they are safe."

"Was anyone in the village hurt?" Cathryn asked.

"Three of the men were killed," he said hesitantly.

"What else, Owen?" The reluctance of his tone frightened her.

"Granny MacLinn . . ."

"Granny?" Cathryn's voice rose on a sharp note. "What happened?"

"The whoresons set fire to her cottage," he ground out between clenched teeth. "She was standing there in the midst of the flames cursing them like a witch when one of the soldiers cut her down. Revan saw it but he couldn't get there in time to save her. She . . . she saw him coming and called out his name . . . but, it was too late. I think Revan must have gone mad just then. That's one English soldier who'll never see the light of day again."

"How horrible! Oh, poor Granny," Cathryn said brokenly. "She told us she'd had a premonition of danger for Revan. She saw him surrounded by flames. Poor thing, the danger was for her."

She turned away and walked through the door. In the hallway she caught the acrid smell of smoke drifting down from the floors above and looked questioningly at Owen.

He nodded his head sorrowfully. "Aye," he stated, "they've burned all the rooms upstairs. The bastards nearly destroyed everything."

Cathryn clenched her fists. "How I hate them!" she exclaimed. "For Revan's sake, how I hate them all!"

In her own bedchamber everything was a shambles. The lovely Stuart tartan draperies and bedspread had been cut to ribbons, the mattress shredded, leaving a dusting of feathers covering the debris. The portrait of Bonnie Prince Charlie had been ripped apart and the panelling hacked and scarred. Most of the contents of the wardrobe had been slashed or thrown on the fire, but Cathryn found three gowns that were relatively unharmed. She unearthed the basket from beneath the overturned chair and was relieved to see its contents had been undisturbed.

In the dressing chamber she found an unbroken pitcher containing a little cold water. She used this to bathe her face and arms after removing her ruined clothing. Feeling somewhat refreshed, she donned one of the gowns she had discovered—a dark green wool that matched her somber mood—and folded the others to take with her.

Searching through the ruins of her room she came upon the tortoise-shell comb and the volume of Gaelic poems. There was no trace of anything else. Clutching the book to her chest, she was stricken with a tremendous longing for Revan. Where was he? she wondered. Was he safe? Did he think of her?

Seeing Cathryn's overwrought state, Della insisted she lie down and rest. Since the only remaining bed in Wolfcrag was the one in Revan's chamber, that is where Della led her. Cathryn placed the basket nearby where she could see it, but kept the book with her.

"Della, do you think Revan is all right?"

"Aye, he's fine. No doubt he'll be back before you wake again."

Cathryn sighed heavily. "I hope so. I . . . couldn't go on without him."

"I know," Della said, patting her hand.

"And I think he is going to need me, too. He's going to be so hurt when he sees what they've done to his home."

"Yes, he'll need you," Della agreed. "Now try to go to sleep so you will feel better when he gets here."

"If . . . if something has happened to Revan, I'll never forgive myself for letting him go without telling him about the baby," she whispered.

"Mayhap it was better that he didn't know—it would have been just one more thing to worry him. This way, you can tell him when he returns, and it may ease his mind."

"I hope you are right, Della."

Wearily, her eyes closed and she drifted into an uneasy sleep.

By the next afternoon the last of the supplies had been loaded onto the fleet of fishing ships anchored in the deep water beyond the cove, and the process of ferrying the clan members out in smaller boats had begun.

Revan had not yet returned, and Owen MacIvor was struggling to hide his concern. Cathryn and Margaret both refused to leave the castle until he came and Owen prayed he would not have to force them to go. It was too dangerous to wait much longer, and he would like to take advantage of tonight's tide. His worried eyes scanned the distance, but there was no sign of the clan chieftain.

Cathryn, wrapped in a plaid she had found in Revan's room, alternately braved the icy winds to pace the battlements or wandered listlessly through the ruined rooms of the castle.

Now, once again, she slowly climbed the narrow staircase spiraling up through the tower to the castle turrets. She could tell by the furtive glances Owen had been sending her way that he was becoming anxious to depart, but feared her reaction. In truth, she knew Owen would not abandon hope as far as Revan was concerned until the last possible moment. She had seen him watching the horizon, also, but now that he was responsible for the entire clan, he would be forced to act in their behalf, taking fewer chances than he might otherwise have done.

She stepped out onto the windswept walkway, pulling the plaid close about her but letting her long hair whip in the wintry gale. The clean cold air was pleasant after the smoke-filled castle.

She looked to the sea and was reassured by the sight of the sturdy fishing vessels that were going to carry them to safety. The little cove was filled with activity, the beach littered with people. By nightfall she knew Wolfcrag would lie silent and empty . . . .

Revan, where are you? her thoughts cried. She suddenly remembered the time, months ago, when he had brought her up to the top of the castle to show her the views from the turrets. They had stood together beneath the shelter of his plaid, his firm hand guarding her hair from the cruel fingers of the wind. She shut her eyes tightly, conjuring up the moment again. She still recalled her fear of him, her anger at his daring in kidnapping her. Yet, even then, her senses were alarmingly aware of him, and perhaps she had already begun to love him just a little.

She opened her eyes slowly, praying she would not have to make do with memories for the rest of her life. There was too much she had to say to Revan, too much they should share. He had to come back . . . .

She had spent so many hours staring hopefully into the distance that when the lone figure of a horseman did appear, she hardly dared believe it was reality. The rider, crouched low in the saddle and riding furiously, was wearing a MacLinn tartan.

Cathryn's breath caught in her throat. It was Revan—it had to be!

She stood where she was, waiting. The fringed end of her plaid snapped and whipped about her slender body, and her hair was a furious banner of bronze silk. If it were Revan, she wanted him to know she had never given up—that she was waiting patiently as any good Highland wife would do.

The rider was close enough now she could see his face lifted to look up at her. Winter sunshine glinted off hair as black as ebony, and she knew if she were close enough to see them, his eyes would be warm amber.

The horse's hoofs clattered across the wooden drawbridge, and the man passed through the ruined gateway of Wolfcrag. Cathryn darted across the width of the walkway to look down into the courtyard. Men came running to greet their chieftain, but all the time he was answering their questions and dismounting from his stallion, his eyes were raised to hers. When he strode toward the castle, she pulled open the tower door and flew down the spiraling steps as fast as she could.

She paused at the top of the stairs above the Great Hall and saw Revan below, standing just inside the entrance. He had not known the castle had been attacked and had returned completely unprepared for the sight of his home in ruin.

Slowly she continued down the stairs and crossed the stone

floor to stand at his side. He reached out one gloved hand and she took it in both of hers.

"Are you well, lass?" he asked, his eyes ending their sweeping survey of the hall and coming to rest on her face.

"Yes, I'm fine. So is Meg and your mother." She swallowed deeply. "Revan, I wish there was some way I could soften your first look at Wolfcrag . . ."

He put out an arm and drew her hard against his chest.

"It helps just to have you here, Catriona." He brushed her mouth with a kiss, then laid his cheek against her hair. "Come, walk with me, and tell me what happened."

Behind them, she could hear Owen giving Donald, the stable lad, instructions to ride Warrior back toward the fishing village to a place along the beach where the animals would be ferried out to the larger boats. Then, in a bitter tone, he ordered the burning of the drawbridge.

As they moved from room to room, viewing the obscene mutilation of his beloved home, Cathryn told him all she knew of Darroch's treachery and how her plan had been supported by the unexpected appearance of Basil Calderwood.

When they stood in the doorway of the Jacobite bedchamber, and she saw the weariness in his stance, the bleakness in his eyes, she could hold back the tears no longer.

"I'm so sorry, Revan," she sobbed. "I feel so guilty—this is all my fault."

"Why should you feel guilty?" he asked, astonishment plain in his voice.

"Had Basil not come after me—or had Darroch not hated me so much . . ." she began.

He gripped her shoulders and gave her a gentle shake. "Catriona, for God's sake, when will we ever get beyond the place where we must lay the blame for everything that happens at either your door or mine? This is not your fault—lass, I brought you here. If you want to blame someone, blame me. But no one can be blamed for the sickness that festered in the minds of Basil and Darroch. If

457

this had not happened, Basil would have found some other way to make you suffer, and I've no doubt Darroch would have caused me some other sort of misery."

"But for Wolfcrag to be torn apart . . . for your entire family to have to make a new home in a strange place . . . it's just not fair!"

"It may not be fair, but it's something that happens in Scotland." His defeated gaze moved over the room. "Maybe we were fools to think we could go on living like this," he said in a flat tone. "Maybe we should have given up long ago."

"No! You were right to keep your beliefs, Revan, and you can't give them up now. Besides, you don't know any other way of life."

"Mayhap it is time we learned another way," he shrugged. She stood before him, green eyes blazing.

"I can't believe this is the MacLinn talking," she cried. "Your people have packed up all they have left in this world and are down there on that beach preparing to sail off to some place they've never seen before and start their lives all over. What do you suppose they would think if they could hear you talk of giving up?" She put her hands on her hips, tossing her head. "I didn't know you were a coward, Revan!"

He towered over her, his golden eyes piercing.

"I'm not a coward," he stated quietly. "But I am responsible for a great many people."

"Those people are going with you because they want to," she said. "Because they trust and respect you."

"And what about you, Catriona? Why are you going with me?"

"Because I love you and I made a vow to stay by your side. I am not afraid of the unknown, even if you are."

"Once you said you treasured your freedom too much to share the life of an outlaw," he reminded her, fiercely scowling.

Her chin came up. "As you very well know, I once said a great many things that made no sense!" She reached out and took his hands. "Oh, Revan, don't you know I would follow you wherever you have to go—live any kind of life we have to live? The only real happiness I have ever had in my life ha

458

been since I came to Wolfcrag. Now I see we can have that happiness no matter where we live, as long as we are all together. As for the law, after yesterday, I know it isn't always right."

His amber eyes began to twinkle.

"So you think I am afraid?"

"Well . . . it sounded as if you were."

"Nay, I was just tired," he said, drawing her into his arms. "Suddenly, I feel very refreshed, ready to embark on our next adventure. Somehow, Catriona, I have a feeling all of my life with you is going to be one adventure after another."

As they walked down the stairs into the Great Hall, Cathryn said, "But someday, Revan, when we have grown weary of adventure, do you suppose we could return to Wolfcrag and re-build it? Someday when the government is not so interested in what you are doing?"

He cast a doubtful glance around the hall. "I'm not certain it would be possible to re-build, love."

"Of course it would! The stones are still standing, aren't they? All we have to do is reconstruct the inside. I know it would be possible."

He smiled down at her. "You continually amaze me, Catriona."

Della MacSween was waiting for them and, at Revan's words, she began to laugh. "You could never be any more amazed than I was when, just as we were about to escape the invading troops, Cathryn dashed back out of the tunnel and informed me she was going after something!" She shook her head. "I couldn't believe it — and all I could think of was how furious you were going to be with me for letting her go, Revan!"

He grinned wryly. "Nay, I am well aware of how independent Cathryn can be. No doubt I would have realized there was little you could do to make her behave herself. But," he asked, turning to Cathryn, "what on earth was important enough to make you risk your life?"

Della held out the basket. "Whatever it was, it's in here. Cathryn has barely let this out of her sight all day."

Cathryn took the basket, saying, "See for yourself, Revan."

459

Placing the basket on the floor, they knelt beside it. The first thing he held up was Bonnie Prince Charlie's dagger.

"And there is the little chest containing the gold cross belonging to the prince," said Cathryn proudly. "Those relics were too precious and too valuable to be left for the looters. See, here is the sketch of the prince your brother drew — I knew you would want to save that." She motioned to Revan's daughter who was standing nearby with Margaret. "Look, Meg, didn't I tell you I would keep your Christmas gift with me forever?"

She held up the framed sampler Meg had given her, causing the small heart-shaped face to glow with happy pride.

"What is this?" Revan asked, reaching into the basket. "Why have you put your new shawl in here? I thought you didn't care for it — you never wore it. Why would you risk your life saving something like this?"

His confusion was evident in the expression on his lean face.

She studied him with silvery-green eyes that had suddenly started to soften and glow.

"I never wore the shawl because I was saving it, Revan."

"Saving it? For what?"

"To wrap your child in when he is born. I thought it would be most appropriate for the son of the MacLinn . . ."

The look in his golden eyes was like a warm caress.

"Catriona, love, are you trying to tell me . . . you are . . ."

She nodded smugly. "Yes, that is exactly what I am trying to tell you. Our child will be born this summer. Now do you see why I had to risk saving these things? I did not want the son of the MacLinn to grow up without his rightful inheritance."

He pulled her to her feet and wrapped her in a fierce embrace. "My God, lass, all you have been through! Are you certain you are all right?"

"I knew I was going to be fine the moment I saw you riding back to the castle," she laughed. "Until then, I really didn't know for certain."

"Well, now I can understand your determination to go on

460

love. The prospect of an heir does change things. You are right, we will have to return to Wolfcrag and make it habitable again. But first things first . . ."

He bent his dark head to hers and slowly, lovingly kissed her soft mouth.

Her arms went around his neck, and she pressed herself to him. "If you don't mind," she whispered, "I thought we might name the child Alexander Christian—for your brothers."

" 'Above all, faithfulness'—'tis a good motto for you, lass."

"And why not?" she challenged with a smile. "After all, I am a MacLinn!"

They stood for a long moment, oblivious to the onlookers, oblivious to the ruin and devastation around them.

The moment was broken by Owen MacIvor's quiet voice. "The last boat is ready, Revan. We've got to go."

Silently, the small group said their farewells to the home they had loved, remembering it as it had been and not as it was now. In their minds it still rang with the haunting strains of a Jacobite ballad or the harshly beautiful droning of the pipes. Dancers still whirled, voices laughed, and glasses were raised to toast the rightful king.

Cathryn sat in the little boat, close within the secure circle of Revan's arms, looking back toward Wolfcrag. She had seen it for the first time in the gloaming, and now she was leaving it the same way. But it was no longer frightening or unwelcoming. Indeed, as it crouched along the shore, nearly indistinguishable from the huge gray boulders that formed its base, it seemed ancient and indestructible. She knew it would always be there—waiting for their return.

<u>FREE</u> Preview Each Month and $ave

Zebra has made arrangements for you to preview 4 brand new HEARTFIRE novels each month...FREE for 10 days. You'll get them as soon as they are published. If you are not delighted with any of them, just return them with no questions asked. But if you decide these are everything we said they are, you'll pay just $3.25 each— a total of $13.00 (a $15.00 value). **That's a $2.00 saving each month off the regular price.** Plus there is NO shipping or handling charge. These are delivered right to your door absolutely free! There is no obligation and there is no minimum number of books to buy.

TO GET YOUR FIRST MONTH'S PREVIEW... Mail the Coupon Below!

Mail to:

HEARTFIRE Home Subscription Service, Inc.
120 Brighton Road
P.O. Box 5214
Clifton, NJ 07015-5214

YES! I want to subscribe to Zebra's HEARTFIRE Home Subscription Service. Please send me my first month's books to preview free for ten days. I understand that if I am not pleased I may return them and owe nothing, but if I keep them I will pay just $3.25 each; a total of $13.00. That is a savings of $2.00 each month off the cover price. There are no shipping, handling or other hidden charges and there is no minimum number of books I must buy. I can cancel this subscription at any time with no questions asked.

NAME

ADDRESS   APT. NO.

CITY   STATE   ZIP

SIGNATURE   (if under 18, parent or guardian must sign)   2053
Terms and prices are subject to change.